T0356467

ALSO BY BREANNE RANDALL

The Unfortunate Side Effects of Heartbreak and Magic

SPELLS, STRINGS, *and* FORGOTTEN THINGS

SPELLS, STRINGS,

and

FORGOTTEN THINGS

A Novel

BREANNE RANDALL

Dell
New York

Published in the United States by Dell, an imprint of Random House, a division of Penguin Random House LLC, New York.

DELL and the D colophon are registered trademarks of Penguin Random House LLC.
RANDOM HOUSE BOOK CLUB and colophon are trademarks of Penguin Random House LLC.

LIBRARY OF CONGRESS CATALOGING-IN-PUBLICATION DATA
Names: Randall, Breanne, author.
Title: Spells, strings, and forgotten things : a novel / Breanne Randall.
Description: New York : Dell, 2025.
Identifiers: LCCN 2024042478 (print) | LCCN 2024042479 (ebook) |
ISBN 9780593875001 (trade paperback ; acid-free paper) |
ISBN 9780593875018 (ebook)
Subjects: LCGFT: Romance fiction. | Fantasy fiction. | Witch fiction. |
Novels.
Classification: LCC PS3618.A6243 S64 2025 (print) |
LCC PS3618.A6243 (ebook) | DDC 813/.6--dc23/eng/20240925
LC record available at https://lccn.loc.gov/2024042478
LC ebook record available at https://lccn.loc.gov/2024042479

Printed in the United States of America on acid-free paper

randomhousebooks.com
randomhousebookclub.com

1st Printing

Book design by Virginia Norey
Moon and stars art: Kate Macate/stock.adobe.com

For Sydney, my little peach, and Raquel, my little orange—
this one's for you because I wouldn't have been able to do it
without your love and support.

Spells, Strings,
and Forgotten Things

PROLOGUE

ON A SUMMER DAY RIPE WITH DREAMS AND MIS-chief, a trail of whispers trickled like honey into Calliope Petridi's ear. She had just turned ten years old. Her older sisters, Thalia and Eurydice, were tending the garden outside the manor, and for one wild moment, Calliope allowed herself to believe that, perhaps, their mother had finally returned to them.

Following the whispers through the halls, Calliope approached a door that she had never seen before. The rusted handle was shaped into ivy that matched the pattern on the wall. Despite the heat of the day, it was cool to Calliope's eager touch and turned with a sigh. As the door creaked open into darkness, the whispers grew louder.

She checked over her shoulder for Thalia, who had a knack for always knowing when Calliope was about to get into trouble, or Eurydice, whose gentle censure would have been even harder to bear. Yet the hall remained silent and hot save for the cool breeze that blew from the doorway. She danced down the precarious stairs, her feet so light with excitement they might as well have sprouted wings.

The air was musty, but magic was there, too, soft as stepping barefoot into fresh earth, crisp as biting into an apple. Her skin tickled the same way it had when her mother would whisper spells in Greek. Calliope's honey-wheat hair, the same as all the sisters', swayed about her shoulders with the magic in the air until she sneezed, sparks of light flying out of her mouth.

She turned on the light, and an amber glow lit the basement, if it could be called that. It looked more like a mausoleum of secrets better left kept, lined with shelves of apothecary bottles and tinctures and old books. She followed the trail of whispers to a heavy leather-bound tome. It wasn't hidden or wrapped in ancient cloth or locked behind a series of riddles, like in the books Calliope loved to read. It was waiting. Asking to be found.

Calliope remembered her mother's warnings. Earlier that spring, one clear morning, she had left. The ground had shifted beneath the sisters' feet, a crevice dividing their lives into *before* and *after*.

Penelope had ushered her daughters into the kitchen, her eyes brighter and clearer than they had been in months. Embers glowed in the grate, no warmth to be found.

"Listen," she said, clutching their hands and pulling them in close. "You are the sole guardians of the Dark Oak now. You must stay away from it at all costs or the curse will—" She paused, her eyes misting over.

"The curse will what, Mother?" Thalia asked, focused as always.

"Mama?" Calliope said, her voice thick with worry.

On her lucid days, Penelope had told them that the price

of their magic was memories, and she forbade Calliope and her sisters from practicing it.

Now Penelope's eyes cleared once more, and the old warnings spun out of her mouth like spiderwebs. The girls had heard them before, but the news of an unknown aspect of the curse ensnared them with fear.

"Where magic gathers, there will be those who seek to claim it. Protect your bond at all costs. It's the only thing that can save you. *Never* trust a Shadowcrafter, do you understand?"

"Yes, Mother," Thalia said. Calliope could see her oldest sister was trying to hold back tears and felt her own spill over. "But what about the curse?"

"The curse?" Penelope asked, releasing the girls' hands. Her voice now held a dreamy quality. "What curse?"

Outside in the driveway, a horn honked.

"I'll be back," she promised, but her words were weightless, and they floated away on the wind like a memory she'd already sacrificed.

The sisters watched at the window as their mother climbed into the cab, watched until she rounded a bend and disappeared. They hadn't heard from her since, and though they'd looked in every crack and crevice, there were no answers to be found.

But here, now, within Calliope's grasp, was a font of knowledge. Power leaked from the book like light dripping from the sun. She knew, somehow, that the book had belonged to her mother.

When she reached out a steady finger to trace down the well-worn leather, eager to decipher the markings etched there, the book woke up.

And, for the first time, so did Calliope.

Welcome, my child, the grimoire wrote, the ink splashing across an empty page. *Are you ready to begin?*

Calliope didn't hesitate.

"Yes," she whispered fervently. And the thrill of a new-found power soothed the devastation of her mother's disappearance, at least for a little while.

CHAPTER 1

Fifteen years later

CALLIOPE RAN BAREFOOT THROUGH THE FIELD, shadows unfurling around her like a sinister promise. Any moment, her skin would burn, and her bones would turn to ash. The shadows whispered things that made Calliope's blood sing with terror. She ran fast and faster still. The Altar was just there, and she knew if she could reach it, she'd be safe on that hallowed ground. But a tendril of shadow swept out, wrapping around her wrist. The pain was a song of death and ice, and a scream tore from her throat as she was pulled into the night—

CALLIOPE JOLTED AWAKE. Her heart beat so hard and fast she thought it might shatter like glass. The sheets were a tangled mess that smelled of sweat and fear and forgotten things.

Only a dream, she told herself over and over. But when she rubbed her wrist, she hissed in pain. In the soft dawn light filtering through her high windows, she could see her skin was burned where the dream shadow had touched her. The mark was raised and blistered in places, but instead of feeling hot, it was cold to the touch.

Calliope scrambled out of bed and riffled through her drawers, tossing things haphazardly onto the floor until she found a tin of calendula cream. She would tell her sisters about the nightmares, she would, but not today. Not on the anniversary of their mother's leaving. Too many ghosts were already chasing them; she didn't want to add another. And so, she sacrificed a small memory—Marigold brushing her hair behind her ear during their first date—and chanted a spell in Greek that closed the open wound and soothed the irritated skin. The scar that remained was pink and tender and shaped like a snake. She pulled her sleeve down over it.

The grimoire's pages rustled like an invitation from where it sat on her desk. As she approached, it flipped to a blank page, and Calliope recorded the date before jotting down her dream in a hasty scrawl. Sighing, she stared at the words, willing Grim to help her make sense of them, but for now, the book was silent.

Grim was more than a book. Over the years it had become a friend and confidant, something to turn to when the weight of loneliness became too much, pages to scribble her thoughts in. She'd spend hours poring over chapter upon chapter of spells and potions and recipes. At times it felt like her only connection to her mother. With another sigh, she closed the grimoire and patted its cover lovingly.

By the time she reached the kitchen, her sisters were already awake. The wind whistled through the old stone, and even through the closed windows, Calliope could hear the

birds chirping their songs to welcome spring. Herbs and flowers were strung from the ceiling in various stages of drying,
tangles of garlic hung from nails, and heavy cast-iron pots
were stacked neatly below the old wood table that served as
a kitchen island. It was a witch's kitchen, and Calliope was
more at home here than anywhere else in the world.

Thalia held her hands over the teakettle on the stove, her
pretty, delicate features pulled into a well-worn frown. Eurydice hugged her from behind. Eurydice was so much shorter
that her head rested between Thalia's shoulder blades.

"I think you'd be cold on a beach in summertime," Eurydice said with a laugh, and it was such a sweet sound it
made Calliope's teeth nearly ache to hear it.

Thalia groaned and tried to bend her fingers. "It's this
house. The stone seeps all the warmth away, even in the
spring."

"Let me see," Calliope said, holding out her hands. Thalia
paused for only a moment before slipping her fingers into
Calliope's palms. Calliope closed her eyes and offered up
the memory of her favorite childhood hiding spot—nestled
among the branches of an old oak tree—then channeled every
warm thing she could think of: summer afternoons, river
rocks baked by the sun, apple pie straight out of the oven,
and a freshly poured cup of tea that was so hot it burned
your tongue. "Na eísai zestós," she whispered. And Thalia's
icy hands thawed. Thalia flexed her fingers and gave the type
of sigh you release after slipping into a hot bath after a long
winter day.

"You shouldn't have done that," Thalia said with a frown.
"But thank you."

"Don't you ever miss it?" Calliope asked quietly. "Doing
magic?"

"It's not worth the price," Thalia answered without hesitation. "Let's get ready for work."

Thalia had turned eighteen years old the year their mother vanished. And the moment her mother left, Thalia, with two younger sisters to care for, vowed to follow their mother's forbiddance of magic. To this day, she never let a drop of magic pass her fingertips, swearing to guard her memories like the treasures she knew them to be. Magic had made their mother weak, Thalia always said. By the end, there had been so many patches in their mother's memory that a dozen spools of the finest thread couldn't stitch it back together. For Petridi magic was cursed to be only as strong as the memory they sacrificed to fuel it. It was a curse they knew little else about.

Over the years, the sisters had had too many arguments to count about finding their mother. Calliope had spent more than half her life searching for answers, and neither Eurydice nor Thalia had been able to dissuade her. She'd pored over the grimoire, offered up memories, brewed potions, and cast spells, and no matter what she tried or how many memories she sacrificed, always, she came up empty. As if their mother had been swallowed by an impenetrable void.

Still, perhaps this would be the year. The year that something changed. *For the better,* Calliope thought, glancing down at her wrist.

The sisters settled into their routine in a comfortable silence, moving around one another in a long-practiced dance. Calliope handed Dissy the tea cannister before she reached for it. Thalia slid a travel mug beneath the spout just as Dissy picked up the kettle to pour. At the front door, Thalia looped the long end of Calliope's rainbow wool scarf over her shoulder, a simple thing filled with a motherly touch. Calliope was reminded that her eldest sister had been taking care of them since she was barely old enough to care for herself. When she was younger, Calliope would have rolled her eyes. Even now it grated, just a little. But the feeling was overshadowed by love, as so many small irritations were.

All the while, three cats trailed after them, winding through their feet and rubbing against their legs. Fen—short for Fengári, the Greek word for *moon*—was the oldest, a lanky barn cat that had adopted them two years ago by showing up at their front door one day. And after she had a litter of kittens under their porch last summer, Calliope and Dissy each kept one. Astro, with her fluffy gray-and-white coat, belonged to Calliope, and Solis, the smallest of the litter, had climbed into Dissy's heart and never left. And though Thalia demanded that under no circumstances would those cats be allowed in the house, they always found their way in. Dissy would swear up and down that she wasn't the one who left the window open and little saucers of milk in the kitchen, but Calliope didn't believe her. Meanwhile, despite her protestations, Thalia could be found most evenings with a book in her hands and Fen curled up in her lap.

As the fresh spring air kissed Calliope's cheeks, a family of deer grazed nearby. They tipped their heads lazily as the women passed, their large glassy eyes mysterious but friendly.

"You're feeding them again," Thalia accused Dissy.

"They were hungry!"

"It's spring, Dissy." Thalia sighed, though now there was a hint of laughter to her words. "There's literally green everywhere."

"Okay, fine." Dissy shrugged. "I like to look at them while I drink my tea."

On the mile-long trek into town, the sun warmed their backs as they walked with their arms linked and footsteps in sync. Calliope welcomed the kiss of heat on her skin from the fresh spring morning.

But Calliope knew that behind them trailed the ghost of their mother's presence. Though they didn't talk about such things, it colored the lens through which each sister saw the world.

When the sisters rounded the corner to Main Street, the roads were too narrow for the memory of their mother to sneak through. The little shops and friendly townsfolk and looming clock tower always running a few minutes ahead filled a fraction of the hole left by their mother's absence. Spring banners printed with bright orange poppies hung from streetlamps, and the smell of freshly baked croissants wafted from Whisk and Spoon bakery. They passed the Botanic Dreams plant shop, where Dissy sometimes brought roses from her renowned garden to be sold; she magically grew a dozen different varieties that smelled stronger and bloomed brighter than any you could find elsewhere. As they passed the diner, they waved to Mr. and Mrs. Nakamura, the elderly retired couple who could be found there most mornings, sharing a crossword puzzle and a plate of pancakes. Everywhere Calliope looked, she was met with a kaleidoscope of colors that heralded spring. Birds sang with wild abandon, and a street musician strummed her guitar on the corner, softly crooning a Joni Mitchell song.

The front door to Tea and Tome was red as a ruby-throated hummingbird and enchanted with luck, thanks to a spell Calliope had gotten from Grim. The door swung open of its own accord as the sisters neared; they never needed a key. The little shop of tea and books was the sisters' labor of love and, usually, the only thing they actually agreed on. When they walked through that luck-laden door, Calliope sighed in relief as the earthy scent of old books enveloped her and the invisible weights on her shoulders lifted, the ghosts and hurts of the morning sloughing away like so much dead skin.

Soon, the air would be alive with the gentle hum of whispered conversations and the rustle of pages turning. Shelves lined with books stretched to the ceiling, ivy cascading down their sides. Soft lighting illuminated cozy reading nooks, and teacups potted with succulents adorned each wooden table.

The heart of the shop was the tea bar, where an array of tea blends and their mystical properties were written neatly on a chalkboard. Each concoction was meticulously crafted to ignite the senses and evoke feelings of comfort and enchantment. A mix of loose-leaf teas, herbs, and botanicals filled each glass jar, their vibrant colors enticing visitors to explore the flavors and magic within. Whether they needed courage or hope, a dash of desire or a drop of respite, customers would find it there.

On the bar next to a vase of sunflowers sat a stack of one of their bestsellers. The *Tea and Tome Recipe Book* had been Dissy's idea, and the sisters had worked, for once, in harmony until the pages were filled with their favorite recipes, the symbolism they called forth, and hand-drawn illustrations of the dishes.

Thalia settled behind the checkout counter and Dissy behind the tea bar where she was neatly arranging the scones she'd baked that morning, while Calliope flitted about the store, watering plants, straightening pillows, and dusting bookshelves. She'd always envied her sisters' ability to be still. Thalia, in particular, had perfected the art. But Calliope was always moving, needing her hands busy and her mind busier.

She snuck a glance at Thalia, her back straight, delicate neck angled down as she went over receipts. It might have been her imagination, but Calliope thought her shoulders looked more tense than usual, the groove between her furrowed brows deeper. And she wondered if Thalia, too, was thinking of their mother's disappearance. Was she remembering those soft days when they were younger, when fighting over the last piece of baklava was their biggest worry? Or was she playing their mother's warnings over in her head the way Calliope was?

As the morning bloomed, customers began to trickle in, the entry bell tinkling, and the shop buzzed with the chatter of locals and tourists alike, seeking respite and a taste of the magical brews on this perfect California spring day. Regulars gravitated toward their favorite corners, holding worn copies of beloved books like cherished treasures.

During a quiet hour in the early afternoon, the red front door opened, but the bell didn't chime. Calliope looked up from where she'd been restocking a shelf. For it was said that whoever opened a witch bell–adorned door without causing the bell to ring would be an important person in the lives of those who hung the bell in the first place. The last and only other time it had happened, Rosalind, one of their dearest friends, had entered their lives.

Now, though, it was Sean Zhao who entered, ruggedly beautiful in navy-blue pants, boots, and a T-shirt emblazoned with the logo for the Gold Springs Fire Station. He looked around the shop, his dark eyes seeming lost.

"Sean?" Calliope approached him, feeling her sisters' eyes on her.

"Calliope, right?" he asked, his full lips stretching into a smile. "Danny introduced us a while back. They're friends with my buddy Joe? Anyway, I remembered Danny saying you owned a bookstore, and I just got off my shift but it's my sister's birthday and I'm meeting her at my parents' house for dinner. If I show up without a gift, I'm toast." His words tumbled out with a boyish kind of charm.

"You've come to the right place," Calliope said with a laugh. "What kind of books does your sister read?"

"She likes biographies about women in history," Sean said.

There was a flurry of movement behind them, and Calliope saw Dissy out of the corner of her eye as she fetched a book from the nonfiction section.

"We, um, we just got this book of essays about women who changed the course of World War Two," Dissy said quietly, holding the book out to Sean but not meeting his eyes. "It only came out two days ago, so I don't think she'll have it yet."

"Oh," he said, his dark eyebrows shooting up like she was some kind of magical book fairy. Which, to be fair, she was. "Thank you, that's actually perfect." His eyes turned thoughtful as he studied Dissy. "You're Eurydice, right?" he asked. "We were in the same grade in high school, I think, but you ran with the smart kids," he added with a self-deprecating laugh. "So, our paths didn't cross much."

Dissy looked anywhere but at him and, instead of answering, barreled on. "And we also have, um, a tote bag of women who changed the world." She walked to the register and came back to hand him the tote bag decorated with illustrations of female suffragettes, scientists, secret agents, and politicians. Her cheeks were splotched with red. Without another word, she disappeared behind the tea counter and busied herself with rearranging cannisters and wiping down the already spotless tabletop.

Sean shook his head as though to clear it and then looked at the items in his hands. "I guess I'm ready to check out. I couldn't have picked these out if I spent two hours looking."

"We'll gift wrap them for you," Thalia said with a smile from behind the register.

While Sean chatted idly with Thalia, Calliope looked at her shy, quiet other sister. "What was that about?" Calliope asked Dissy under her breath.

"What do you mean?" she whispered, not meeting her sister's eye. "I just wanted him gone quickly."

Sean left with a merry wave and another chorus of gratitude, and when he opened the door, again, the witch bell stayed silent.

"Weird," Thalia said as she stared at the red door.

"Do you know him?" Calliope asked.

"No, not really," Dissy said quietly but firmly. "There's already so much going on. I don't think we need anyone new in our lives right now."

"When the witch bell stays silent, it doesn't really matter what we want," Calliope said. "Look at Roz. If Sean's meant to be in our lives in some way, it'll happen whether we want it to or not."

"Perhaps," Dissy answered, organizing the teacups so all the handles were facing right.

✳

THE HOURS WORE on, and Calliope had almost forgotten about the shadow dream, even their mother's absence. But near closing time, as she was on a ladder shelving a stack of books at the back of the shop, she felt a whisper of cold brush her skin. Books cascaded out of her arms and clattered to the floor as she whipped around, only to find the shop nearly empty. Her eyes went wide, her heart beating fast, her whole body immobile as the whisper came again.

Sisters, it hissed. And Calliope shivered. *Three,* it said, though it sounded farther away this time. Calliope's hands were numb, her feet leaden, as though the words were a spell that rendered her frozen.

"Opie?" Dissy asked. "What is it? What's wrong?"

"You didn't hear that?" she demanded.

"You're scaring me, Opie. What did you hear?"

"A whisper," she said. Grabbing Dissy's wrist, she dragged her over to the register where Thalia was going over a list of inventory. "Did you hear anything?" Calliope asked. Thalia glanced back and forth between Calliope and Dissy.

"No," she said. "What's going on?"

"You're telling me neither of you heard that whisper? It was calling us. It felt . . ." Calliope shuddered. "Dangerous."

"You're tired," Thalia said, her lips flattening to a thin line. "You haven't been sleeping well. And now you're dropping stacks of books and hearing things." For all that being a witch entailed, Thalia was reluctant to ascribe meaning to things she couldn't see with her own eyes or hear with her own ears.

The memory of the shadow dream she'd had that morning flared in her mind. Maybe now was the time to tell them. "This wasn't sleep deprivation," she said, taking a deep breath. "I *heard* it. I had a dream this morning, too. Look." Calliope held up the burn on her wrist, and Thalia's eyes flicked over it dismissively. "And you know that Grim says—"

"No, no," Thalia snapped, her eyes darting to the customers who were still browsing the romance section. "We are not bringing that book into this. Not here."

"Would you just listen—"

"I said *no*. Not now."

"Sisters," Dissy said, laying a hand on Calliope's arm. "Let's not argue. Calliope, I'm sure you heard something. But perhaps it was just the breeze? I did prop open the door earlier. And are you sure you didn't just burn yourself when we were baking?"

"This wasn't the wind!" Calliope snarled. "And I would've noticed a burn in the kitchen." Her sisters merely stared at her. "Very well," she said, squaring her shoulders and clenching her jaw to keep from saying anything she'd regret. "I'm going for a walk. You can close up without me."

As she walked out, Thalia's ire seared her like a hot brand, a worse pain than the burn on her wrist. It had taken years of shouting matches and slammed doors, but she'd finally learned that when her sister got that look on her face, there was little she could do to make her listen. But the timing of that whisper seemed too fateful to be a coincidence.

The sun was nearly set, turning the sky into a cascade of flaming colors. Calliope inhaled the crisp spring air and smelled a sharp, spicy amber cutting through the scent of fresh earth and new blooms. The hair on the back of her neck prickled as the feeling of being watched swept over her, as soft as a caress. But when her eyes scanned the streets, she saw nothing unusual. Shaking off the feeling, she set off in search of Roz, ignoring the unease coiling in her chest.

CHAPTER 2

STEPPING THROUGH THE DOOR OF ROZ'S PALM-istry and tarot shop felt a little like walking into a dream. The sweet smell of incense filled the air, and soft nature sounds played on a loop. Dressed in a flowing ankle-length skirt and peasant blouse, her long moonlight-silver hair hanging straight down her back, Rosalind stood at a long shelf that held all manner of tarot decks, crystals, and candles. This was the woman who had checked in on the Petridi sisters after their mother had left. Thalia had been eighteen and assumed legal guardianship of her sisters, but Rosalind was the one who cooked holiday dinners, made sure every girl was celebrated on her birthday, and answered questions they were too embarrassed to ask one another. She'd woven her-self into the fabric of their lives and created a beautiful tapes-try of love and kindness that the girls never forgot.

Rosalind was the only other practitioner of magic in town, but she wasn't a witch in the way the sisters were. Instead of access to Lightcraft or Shadowcraft, she had the Sight, and she spoke in signs and symbolism, tea leaves and tarot, palm-istry and dreams. Now Roz pulled down Calliope's favorite moon witch tarot deck and turned to her, eyes crinkling as she smiled, the lines on her face deep from years of laughter.

"Did you know I was coming?" Calliope demanded, her eyes narrowing.

"Yes," Roz said. "But not because of the Sight. I saw you marching down the street with war in your eyes and thought you might be seeking some clarity." She waved the deck in the air like a white flag, and Calliope flopped into one of the chairs around a large wooden table. Her foot *tap-tap-tapped* against the leg of the table, a stark contrast to the way Roz slid gracefully into her own chair and began shuffling the cards with long, practiced fingers.

"Darling," Roz said, her head quirked to the side as she calmly studied Calliope's drawn features. It was a single word, but a statement and question and invitation all in one.

"Our mother left fifteen years ago today," Calliope said quietly, as though if she spoke any louder it might give the words more weight.

"Ah, yes," Roz said. "They're barbed, those memories of the past, you know." She tsked. "If you try to take them out, they tear you to ribbons. Better to leave them in. Come to terms with them. Find out how they shape you and learn to live with it."

"Easier said than done," Calliope muttered.

"If it was easy, we wouldn't need therapy, darling," Roz said. "Now, what do you want to know?"

"What do I need to hear right now?" Calliope asked. It was always a go-to when she couldn't quite figure out what to focus on. She always had too many questions, and this, it seemed, would steer her in the right direction.

"Very well," Roz said, laying the cards in front of her in a single pile. "I have your permission to read your cards?"

"You do." Consent was how Roz began every reading.

"Infuse your energy into the deck, please," Roz said with a nod toward the cards. Calliope closed her eyes and willed her energy to the surface, directing it to the tarot deck, searching for the connection there. "A three-card spread, I think," Roz said decisively. "Please cut the deck, darling. You know the drill. Three separate piles using your left hand only."

Calliope hovered her left hand over the deck and separated the cards into three piles. Roz drew the cards and slowly turned them over, one by one.

The Nine of Swords. *Anxiety, fear, worry. Emotional distress.*

The Moon. *Illusion, uncertainty, hidden truths. Things may not be as they seem.*

Calliope swallowed hard and absentmindedly rubbed the burn on her wrist. With a shiver, she remembered the viscous shadows chasing her, the sound of that bodiless whisper raising the hairs on her arms. Roz looked up at her, the corners of her mouth creasing in worry, and pulled the last card.

The Tower. *Sudden change, upheaval, disruption. Your whole life is about to be upended.*

Calliope sagged back in her seat. Her foot stopped tapping. The burn on her arm thrummed heavily. The Tower she could handle. But the Tower pulled after the Moon? In relation to the Nine of Swords?

The truth came crashing down. The dream, the whispers, and now the reading. Her mother had warned them of many things. Always reinforce the enchantments around the Dark Oak from the safety of the Altar at midnight on each solstice and equinox. Stay away from Shadowcrafters. And when three bad omens occur in a row, run. Because it could only mean one thing . . .

The Dark Oak was awakening.

"Calliope, what's going on?" Roz asked.

"I need to talk to my sisters," Calliope breathed, pulling her jacket tight.

Roz called her name as Calliope left her shop. Her sisters needed to know. Roz's readings meant more than anyone else's. Her readings were so accurate that the sisters often wondered just how she came by her talent. They'd asked once, when they were younger, but Roz didn't have an answer to their question. Not a proper one, at any rate. She had no family in Gold Springs, and her memories of her past were hazy. She'd simply woken up one day and discovered her dormant talent. She'd offered her services at festivals and fairs until word of mouth brought clients to her door. Again, she didn't know where her apartment had come from. But it was in her name, fully paid for. She could have gone mad with wondering. Instead, she grabbed on to her new life and molded it to her will. And that tenacity was something the girls latched on to like a life raft.

The dark clouds above mirrored Calliope's mood on the walk home, the wind at her back. Her sisters would have to believe her now. These were no mere coincidences. They'd be home soon from closing the shop, and she needed to speak with Grim first. Grim, who'd taught her so much of what she knew about magic. Who'd given her recipes for period cramps and broken hearts and sweet dreams.

Thalia tolerated the grimoire but still refused to use magic. Dissy had let her fear stop her from digging too deep, casting spells very rarely. And both sisters grew further and further away from their magic. But Calliope had pored over the pages, the words growing roots inside of her. She'd memorized whole sections, practiced her spell work, and offered up memories like candy. Because perhaps, if she got good enough, her mother would come back. And when she got older and realized that no matter how great she became, her mother wasn't returning, it was too late. The magic was alive inside of her, and Grim had been the one to foster it.

Though Grim's pages shifted and whole chapters disappeared for months or even years at a time, there was one warning that always remained on page seventy-six. Grim would periodically flip open to it, the letters trembling like leaves in the wind.

Should the Dark Oak begin to stir, three signs will present themselves. First, your dreams will chase you with razor-sharp claws. Run quickly. Second, the wind will whisper words only you can hear. Listen closely. Third, the cards will foretell a change. Read carefully. A shift in the magical balance is forthcoming.

Calliope shivered against the wind as the familiar words settled into her skin and Lethe Manor came into view. Her hope was a fragile thing. Hope that she was wrong, that she was reading too much into things.

The house was empty and cold when she entered and bounded up the stairs to her room. No sooner had she thrown open her door than Grim flew up and slammed into her chest. The grimoire had always been able to sense when things weren't right, and just the sight of the book brought a small measure of comfort.

"I'm okay," she assured it, patting its binding. Grim flew back and fluttered its pages as if to say it didn't believe her. She told the book about her dream, the whispers in the shop, and Roz's tarot reading. The book settled on her desk and opened, its familiar script flowing across a blank page.

Have you told your sisters?

"Not yet." She shook her head. "They should be home soon."

They are not as in tune with their magic as you are. They may not be able to sense the omens the same way you can.

"I'm right then?" Calliope's voice rose with panic. "The Dark Oak is awakening?"

She heard the front door open, the sound of her sisters' voices floating up the stairs.

I can't be sure, Grim wrote. *It seems that may be the case. But, Opie, you must tell your sisters. You must not do anything foolish.*

"What do we *do*?" she asked, panic clawing at her throat. She wanted to hear that she was being silly. That everything would be fine.

You take the next step, it wrote. *Come.* And she followed Grim as the book flew out of the room and into the kitchen, where Dissy and Thalia were beginning to prepare dinner. The smell of crocuses and wet earth drifted in from the open window. For some reason, the tranquility made Calliope want to scream.

Her words came out in a rush when she told her sisters about her tarot reading.

"Grim, show us page seventy-six, please," Calliope said, keeping her voice as calm as possible all while her blood trembled and her fingers shook. The grimoire flipped its pages until it settled open on the right section. "See?" she said. "Here."

Dissy and Thalia bent over Grim to read the passage.

"Wait," Thalia said, straightening in her chair, "you're telling me you think these things are omens? That the Dark Oak is awakening?"

"Yes," Calliope said emphatically, breathing a sigh of relief that her sister was finally understanding. But then Thalia laughed.

"Opie, the Dark Oak has been dormant for hundreds of years. Why on the goddess's green earth would it be waking up now?"

"I don't know! But something is shifting. You can't tell me you don't feel it. Dissy?"

"I'm sorry," Eurydice said quietly, not looking at Calliope. "I haven't felt anything."

"But—" Calliope stuttered. "But you believe me, don't you?"

"I believe you've felt something. A shift with the changing of the seasons, perhaps? The coming full moon?" Dissy asked. Calliope's heart turned brown at the edges and shriveled in her chest.

"If the Dark Oak is awakening, it means the enchantments are threatened. Someone or something is trying to break them! Maybe if we went to the Dark Oak, we could check the spells. Strengthen them somehow. They clearly need more than what I've been doing on every equinox."

"Absolutely not," Thalia said, aghast. "I forbid it, Calliope. It's far too dangerous, I mean it. None of us will step foot there, least of all you." Her words were a black hole of anger, threatening anyone who came near with total oblivion.

"Fine," Calliope spat. "Then if we could just find a Lightcraft coven, we could ask them—"

Thalia silenced her with a look. "The nearest coven is a two-hour drive away, and it's too risky," she said sharply. "You know that. *No one* can know about the Dark Oak who doesn't already. Even Lightcraft witches can be lured to darkness with that much power. There's a reason Mother told us to stay away from it."

"Yes, but Grim says we also need to protect it! Why won't you believe me?" Calliope asked, her voice breaking. She couldn't bear to be in their presence a moment longer. Dissy called after her as she left, but she refused to let them see her tears. Grim flapped its pages in the air behind her and flew into her room just before her door slammed shut.

It wasn't the first time Calliope had begged her sister to join the nearest Lightcraft coven. Or at the very least, expand their circle so that it included more Lightcraft witches. But Thalia trusted no one, and so they marched on alone. Or at least, Thalia thought they did. But years ago, Calliope had directly defied her sister's wishes and made the two-hour drive to Aurèlia by herself. She'd sacrificed a memory to fuel a locator spell, which led her to a little yellow house with a white picket fence. There, she'd met a witch in her mid-fifties named Alice who welcomed her with instant coffee, powdered creamer, and stale sugar cookies. As the High Priestess, Alice led the coven, and her home was open to any witches in need.

When Alice had asked her if she was there to join the coven, Calliope told her about Thalia's reservations, careful to avoid mentioning the Dark Oak. Alice had nodded understandingly, saying, "Magic is like love. Once it breaks your heart, well, it's hard to come back from that." She'd patted Calliope's hand and promised to send a bird with any news of import and to stay in touch. And now, with a mother who'd abandoned them, no coven for support, and a sister who refused to listen, she was alone. Just like always.

Clothes were strewn about her room, hanging over the back of her chair and piled in corners. The high windows with their mottled glass were framed by black velvet curtains and let in the fragmented light of dusk. Her room had always reflected the chaos in her head, and she liked it that way. It wasn't dirty—cleaning spells took care of that—but it *was* messy, just like her. It smelled faintly of lavender and chamomile from the flowers she dried and tied around each post on her bed.

Like the rest of the house, the room had the faded elegance of a bygone era. When she was little, Calliope would sit at her window in an old-fashioned nightgown and stare at the stars, wishing on every single one while pretending she was Wendy from *Peter Pan*. After all, she'd spent her childhood feeling like the overlooked sidekick. Abandoned by her own mother and left mostly to her own devices, she longed to be the hero of her own story. To be able to take back the power that was forever slipping through her fingers. And wishing on the stars always seemed like its own kind of magic. They shimmered in the night, just waiting to ignite the sky and fall toward earth, bringing with them all the possibilities of a dream.

But now the stars were hidden behind a cloud bank, and wishes seemed very far away.

She turned to Grim, who had settled on the brass book stand. Next to it stood a large plaster bust of Athena, the plume of her Corinthian helmet standing tall and proud. Calliope ran her fingers over the cool plaster, wishing for a little of the goddess's wisdom. The flickering candlelight cast dancing shadows across the room, illuminating Grim as it opened to a blank page. It was an invitation to talk.

"Please, *tell* them," she begged, swiping at the traitorous tears that streamed down her cheeks.

Thalia and Eurydice think of me only as a book. They've never given me the same credence you have. No matter what I tell them, they must come to their own conclusions.

She knew it was right. When she'd found Grim all those years ago, it had set her on a separate path from her sisters. Thalia had already sworn off magic, and Eurydice was too frightened to try. Calliope had learned almost exclusively from Grim, along with a healthy dash of trial and error and a sprinkling of recklessness.

"I'm going to the Piano Rouge," she said instead of pleading her cause further. The dark bar in downtown Gold Springs had live music, and her best friend, Danny, had texted her earlier that they would be there tonight. And, best of all, it was ripe for forming strong memories to sacrifice.

Dusting glitter over her collarbones and adding winged liner to her eyes, she resolutely ignored the way Grim followed her, trying to grab her attention as it flipped to various pages. One, a spell for finding calm in the chaos; another, a potion for stopping reckless acts. She added a stack of silver bracelets that had been blessed in moon water and a crystal ring on every finger and refused to look at the book.

Pushing Grim out of the way, she opened her sock drawer. Socks were her unseen armor. They all lay jumbled together, none of them in pairs, and she riffled through them haphazardly, choosing one black sock patterned in tiny broomsticks and a blue one with white doves.

She stood in front of her closet and hesitated for a moment before finally pulling out a tight ankle-length black dress, woven with shimmering silver threads. When she danced in it, her limbs looked like a latticework of stars. She slipped it on and tried to ignore the memories that came with the feel of its soft fabric against her skin.

Once, when she'd worn it, Marigold had said that her curves were the secrets between shadows, and she wanted to spend the rest of her life plumbing those secrets with her tongue. Calliope's stomach fluttered with the memory until she flicked it away. Instead, she pulled on a pair of black leather boots, then frowned down at them. They were missing something tonight.

Without thinking, she sacrificed the memory of Marigold's words to fuel a simple spell that changed the leather of her boots to red and added silver studs all over them. She stared at herself in the mirror, trying to remember why she'd been sad when she'd chosen this dress. It was something about the shimmering silver . . . She shook her head. If she'd sacrificed it, she clearly didn't need it.

What she did need was her best friend. She needed loud music thrumming in her ears, drowning out her sisters' disbelieving voices, filling up the silence. She needed liquor burning down her throat and a pair of hands around her waist and a beat she could feel in her bones. Most of all, she needed fuel for another spell. And for that, bigger memories needed to be made. Because she would *make* her sisters believe. She hadn't spent her life sacrificing memories, performing spells four times a year from the safety of the Altar to strengthen the enchantments around the Dark Oak.

She was the only one who knew of Grim's warnings about what would happen if those generations of protections wore thin. She was the only one who'd lain awake at night when they were younger, imagining the pervasive evil that would seek the power of the Dark Oak if those enchantments were dismantled. Even now she could hear her mother's voice echoing like a long-forgotten dream. *Where magic gathers, there will be those who seek to claim it.* They'd been told to protect their string at all costs and to keep it hidden. Particularly from Shadowcraft practitioners who would stop at nothing to get the power they thought they deserved.

The old stories of the Great Rift had been passed down from generation to generation. When the earth was new and civilization was young, magic was widespread and there was only the Craft, with no delineation between Light and Shadow. It was a time when witches worked together. But those days were now barely a memory. The Great Rift had torn the witches in two. All that remained was a perpetual war between Light and Shadow, fueled by centuries of accusations and hatred. And while the Petridi sisters had never learned what, exactly, the curse of the Dark Oak entailed, they knew they had to do all within their power to keep it contained. They'd followed their mother's instructions and never told a single soul. Even Danny and Roz didn't know everything.

So, Calliope would do whatever it took to find out who or what was threatening them. Even if it meant making memories just to sacrifice them. Even if it meant defying her sisters' wishes and journeying to the Dark Oak in the Forgotten Forest. And perhaps, there, she would finally find some answers.

CHAPTER 3

"I HATE THE WAY YOUR SKIN GLOWS," DANNY shouted to Calliope over the din of music. Their short, curly hair was slicked back, showing their androgynous features to luminous effect. "I wish you were hideous."

The lights were strobing, the techno was far too loud, and the smell of spilled alcohol and sweat pervaded the air. Calliope loved every second of it.

"What are you talking about?" Calliope laughed and drained her third drink in what seemed as many minutes. "I'm a beast. And you're a deity among humans."

"You were named after one of the nine Muses, you idiot. If anyone is a deity, it's you." Danny signaled the bartender for a refill, their multitude of piercings glinting against their brown skin in the dim light. They truly were a sight to behold. The bartender didn't see them, so they leaned on the counter, trying to flag them down, and then quickly peeled their arm off the bar.

"Oh god, it's sticky," they said in a panic, which only made Calliope laugh harder.

"Did you know I absolutely love you?" Calliope demanded, staring at her best friend with wonder.

"Here we go," Danny said over the music, rolling their eyes. "You're such a sentimental drunk."

"I mean it," Calliope yelled back, swaying toward them. "You keep my secrets. You don't judge me. You should have seen Thalia's face." Calliope frowned. "Did I tell you they don't believe me?"

"Only six or twelve times," Danny said, looking to the bartender who'd finally ambled over with an aggrieved face that said *do you see what I have to put up with?*

"I wanted to shake her." Calliope licked the salt from the rim of the margarita that had finally been delivered. "I wanted to just scream at her until she believed me. Because if she did, Dissy would, too. Sometimes I hate how much power we give Thalia. Does that make me a bad person after everything she's done for us?"

"Yes," Danny answered without hesitating.

"Shut up." Calliope laughed, shoving Danny in the shoulder.

"Joke, joke. Sisters are sisters, bro. They drive you to do stupid stuff. But Thalia—" Here Danny paused, their eyes turning distant before snapping back to Calliope. "She's probably just trying to protect you from yourself."

"Are you . . . are you *sticking up for my sister*?" Calliope demanded, her mouth hanging open. Danny rolled their eyes but didn't answer.

Calliope pushed her empty drink toward the bartender, a six-foot-two Black man who had eyes darker than a starless night. *If only he weren't behind the bar,* Calliope thought.

"Look, I know you and your sisters are . . ." Danny lowered their voice, eyes darting around. "*Different.*"

"Witches," Calliope said, straight-faced. "It's not a bad word, Danny. You can say it out loud. No one would believe you, anyway."

"Well, *I* believe you. I've seen what you can do. And that's what I'm saying, you have different kinds of problems than most people, and—"

"I can't hear you," Calliope lied, shouting over the music. "I'm going to dance!"

"You can't just dance away all your problems," Danny said, voice rising again in frustration.

Calliope grinned at them with a challenge in her eye as she slid off the stool. "Watch me."

The DJ put a new track on, the music a driving beat. The dance floor was a sea of bodies, writhing and glistening and *living*. Calliope hungered for it. She slithered through the crowd to the very center and could feel Danny behind her. It wasn't that Danny didn't know what she was. They knew about the Petridis. Knew that they were true witches. They'd met at a class Calliope had been teaching on making charm bags. Though many of the participants called themselves witches, they'd never seen true magic. Others simply practiced the spirituality that came with the rituals, crystals, and herbs. When Calliope had asked Danny what their charm bag represented, they'd said, "It's to ward off the negative energy from my uncle. He thinks my being a nonbinary bisexual is the greatest sin on earth. So, it's either this"—they'd held up the charm bag—"or murder him in his sleep." That was three years ago, and their friendship had only grown since then. Now they were perfectly in tune with each other.

Calliope swallowed the music into her very being. Let it fuel her and direct her limbs, her body rolling with every beat as her eyes scanned the floor looking for the right dance partner. Her eyes zeroed in on a woman with glowing skin and long blond hair, and she was about to beg her for a dance when a familiar caress ghosted over her. Her stomach somersaulted. Not the pleasant dip from a roller coaster where you had a safety harness, but like she'd just jumped off a cliff into a cold, yawning darkness. A presence moved through the club, simmering with danger and power, like the shadows were pressing in on her. Magic. And if she had to guess, Shadowcraft magic.

A Shadowcrafter? Here?

Impossible. Calliope had gone her whole life in Gold Springs without ever coming across a Shadowcrafter. Why would today be different?

She kept dancing, but the alcohol was dimming her awareness, and it was harder than it should have been to detect where the presence might be.

Then she saw a tall figure moving through the shadows on the club's periphery. His back was to her, his broad shoulders taking up too much space. As though he sensed her eyes on him, he turned just a fraction. She caught the profile of his face—hard jawline, dark hair falling around his ears, stubble painting his cheeks, plush lips pulled into a slight smile.

Her breath caught, and she tried to ignore the sizzle of attraction heating her blood. But before she could approach, a pair of slender hands snaked around her waist, pulling her back against a soft body.

"Is this okay?" a melodic voice asked in her ear.

She turned her head to find the blonde with glowing skin staring up at her, and when she looked back to find the tall figure in the crowd, he'd vanished entirely, along with the dark, magical presence she'd felt just moments ago. She shook herself. She wasn't here to find more problems; she was here to forget the ones she already had. She leaned back into the woman and began to move her body against hers.

"More than okay," Calliope answered with a smile, and she did *not* mind the way her soft hands settled against her curves. "I'm Calliope," she added.

"Emily," the woman said, "I saw you staring." Her full lips stretched into a grin.

"Hard not to, looking like that." Calliope laughed, her eyes raking down Emily's short yellow sheath dress.

She looked around to find Danny dancing with someone nearby. She and Danny had a rule that they didn't dance alone, and their buddy emergency system meant they were always watching each other's backs.

"I feel a bad decision coming on," Danny mouthed, glancing at Emily.

Bad decisions are the only thing I'm good at, she thought, turning and pressing herself against Emily, delighting in the feel of her thigh between hers. Her head dropped back as they swayed until, with Emily's hands against her waist, she drew her in closer. She pressed her nose against her neck and inhaled the scent of her soap and sweat and citrus perfume mixing with the tang of spilled beer and humid air from so many bodies on the floor.

The music thrummed through her, lighting her up, and she tilted her head, offering her lips as a sacrifice on the altar of a good time. Emily didn't hesitate and kissed her hard and deep, her tongue sweeping in and claiming hers. It wasn't perfect, but it was what she needed, and she gave herself to it wholly. When Emily tilted her head, deepening the kiss, Marigold's face flitted into Calliope's mind, but she pushed it away. She would forget this, anyway. And so, she reveled in the whiskey on Emily's tongue and the way her sinuous body moved against hers. By the time the song was over, they were both breathing heavily. Emily's cornflower blue eyes had turned the color of a stormy sky, and there was an invitation there. But Calliope had gotten what she needed: the fuel for another memory. She smiled at Emily before she turned to head off the dance floor, but the woman caught her hand to stop her.

"I don't normally do things like this," Emily confessed, nearly shouting as the next song began playing. "Should I . . . Can I call you?"

Calliope laughed, and then immediately regretted it when she saw the hurt in Emily's eyes. "This was great," she said, kissing her on the cheek. "But trust me, no, you don't want this." And she was right. It was better for her to be ruthless, to cut any ideas of romantic feeling away with a hot knife. Because in the end, she would break Emily's heart just like she'd broken Marigold's. The guilt ate at her stomach like acid as she left Emily staring after her while the sparkling threads on her dress winked like shooting stars in the dark.

"Was it everything you hoped it would be?" Danny demanded when Calliope met them back at the bar.

"Whiskey on the rocks," Calliope said, slapping her hand on the counter before turning to her best friend. "Nothing happened." She shrugged with a smile, but it felt dry and chafed against her teeth. In a passing moment, the music that had fueled her before was now too loud, the dress that made her feel like a goddess too itchy, and her head was pounding. But she threw the whiskey back and pulled Danny into a goodbye hug.

"Don't do anything stupid," Danny warned, pulling her in tight.

"Metaxý Skýllas kai Cháryvdis," Calliope said.

Danny frowned. "English, please."

"Between Scylla and Charybdis. You know, sea monsters, one on either side so that the strait's impassable. It's like being between a rock and a hard place, but far more poetic. That's me."

"Which means?"

"Which means I'll *have* to do something stupid in order to get out."

CHAPTER 4

BY THE TIME HER CAB REACHED LETHE MANOR, half the alcohol she'd consumed had burned off. A by-product of the magic coursing through her veins. It took a great deal of effort and fortitude to get and stay drunk as a witch. She stared at the manor house looming against the midnight sky, a sprawling estate of such resplendence that shone like a tantalizing piece of fairy fruit, despite its ramshackle state. Her childhood home, a bastion of memories and magic and nightmares. She could go in now. Peel off her dress made of starlight and slip into her bed. Wake up the following morning and do it all again. Face her sisters' skepticism and ignore this feeling that fractured her heart into a thousand tiny shards, each one screaming that something was wrong. The dreams, the whispers, the tarot reading, and now the shadow presence following her. Something was coming.

Instead, she went to the place she saw in her dream that morning. A place she hadn't visited in months. The Altar of Fate.

The Altar sat nestled in the clearing behind Lethe Manor.

Just past the crumbling stone ruins of the old horse stable but before the weeping willow that had been known to shed emerald tears. The path to the Altar was a familiar one, yet it seemed different tonight, imbued with an air of foreboding, and her senses heightened in the shadows. Despite the late hour, a yellow-rumped warbler whistled his slow, soft trill. *I'm here,* it said. *You're not alone.*

The spring equinox was two weeks away, and already, the ground was overrun with new growth, the green glowing ethereally in the moonlight. Calliope pushed through brambles and tripped over jutting rocks until she reached the ancient stones. She had been sacrificing pieces of herself for so long that holes had begun to form in the very fabric of her being. And now she would give another piece of herself. Another memory. Many nights, she couldn't sleep, plagued by thoughts of who she might be when the constellation of her memories winked out and only a few scattered stars of recollection were left. And at that thought, she was reminded of her mother. Her ghost really was everywhere today.

Calliope's heart lurched unpleasantly as, without invitation, she remembered the way the light in her mother's eyes would fade so suddenly. Even all these years later, the anger clawed its way up her throat, threatening to exit with a scream. Why had magic stolen so many of her mother's memories? Why had she left and never come back? The mark on her arm throbbed, and the memory of her dream filtered through her thoughts. She wanted to sacrifice it, that memory, the terror and fear of it. But it felt like a puzzle piece she couldn't quite let go of yet, until she knew where it fit.

The tall grass swayed in welcome as she approached the Altar, and the night around her stilled. To look at the Altar, one wouldn't see much. A circle of stones engraved with ancient marks, grass growing around the edges. But to a well-trained eye, a witch's eye, one would see the pulsing in the fabric of reality. A subtle hum, an ancient call, soft as the sound of wings sluicing through air.

She removed her shoes before stepping onto the Altar, for this was hallowed ground. All around her, the wild depths of the forest swelled in anticipation.

The presence of a Shadowcrafter at the club could not be a coincidence, but she knew her sisters wouldn't believe her about that, either. She needed a guide to the Dark Oak, needed to inspect the binding enchantments herself. She'd never been to the Dark Oak before, had always woven the reinforcement spells at the Altar, and she couldn't discern the path herself. And that's what this spell would give her. A trail of breadcrumbs to follow.

She thought about sacrificing the memory that plagued her so often. Her mother disappearing down the driveway. But the pain was what grounded her. Reminded her that there were some things magic could never fix.

Instead, she thought of Emily. She held the memory of her face in her mind, the way her body had moved against hers, and as the spell took hold, Emily's features dimmed, and Calliope's heart turned cold as the encounter fled as if it'd never been. Memories were a delicate currency, and sacrificing them for magic came with its own set of consequences. But in her quest for answers, she was willing to pay the price.

As the memory dissipated, she spoke the spell.

Whispers of the past concealed,
In shadows deep and truths revealed.
With words of power, the veil shall part,
Unmasking secrets of the heart.

She should have said it in Greek, for spells were always more powerful when spoken in the language of your ancestors. But in her tipsy state, she couldn't remember all the words. What mattered the most was her intention and having a well of magic to draw from. And for the Petridis, that came from memories.

As the memory vanished and the magic took hold, a light appeared. It was gentle and pulsing and ethereal, emanating warmth. She reached toward it, but it darted away. She stepped forward, and again, the light jumped like a will-o'-the-wisp. Despite it all—her sisters' mistrust, her fear of what she'd find if the enchantments were broken, the call of the Dark Oak, her mother's warnings—she laughed. And at the sound, the light jumped farther, beckoning her forward. She'd asked for a guide, and she'd gotten one. She just hadn't expected it to have golden retriever energy.

Even with the pale light guiding her, the dark of the Forgotten Forest was suffocating, its slipperiness eellike, the very air pulsing with something that tasted coppery and stale. She'd never been this deep into the forest before, had never violated her mother's and Thalia's warnings to stay away from the Dark Oak and the forest. The sounds were more muted, the canopy of trees so dense the sky was no longer visible.

She tripped over roots and rocks and, once, a deer skull, her boot crushing through the bones with an echoing crack. The closer she got to the Dark Oak, the more signs of life faded. Birdsong died away; the air tasted stale and humid. Even the leaves and dirt looked leached of color, as though infected by whatever magic was contained within the Dark Oak.

Her heartbeat quickened. She'd spent her whole adult life protecting the Dark Oak, from the safety of the Altar of Fate.

Now that ancient tree called to her. She could feel it in her blood, in her bones, in the way the whispers beckoned. And the farther she went, the clearer the words became.

> *Through each enchantment's whispered lore*
> *Three sisters guard, forevermore*
> *But when darkness comes, a curse is spoken*
> *And all is lost if their bond is broken*
> *The air ablaze with demon's calls*
> *At last, at last, the Dark Oak falls*
> *With magic woven, strings so fine*
> *Shadow and Light shall never align.*

The whispered words swelled in the dark until Calliope was queasy, the weight of them settling in her stomach and mind. She would analyze them later with Grim.

The light she followed pulsed brighter and the hum of energy along her skin grew stronger just as she broke through to a clearing. This was nothing like the Altar. There, the sky was her ceiling, and the meadow was vast and welcoming, dotted with wildflowers and the warmth of old memories. Here, the power was a bottomless well that vibrated until the air itself distorted, like a heat mirage.

And there, in the middle of the glade, towered an oak tree that took her breath away. It was ancient and sweeping, a dark and twisted thing. The limbs were ashen as if petrified by time, branches twisting out like arms, twigs crooked like beckoning fingers, leaves made of smoke. The bark on the massive trunk swirled in the center, forming a gaping hole that felt sentient, like it might be watching her every move. The oak swayed and creaked despite the lack of wind. In fact, the air was denser here, humid and still.

She stood at the tree line, unsure if she wanted to step into the clearing where the gnarled roots snaked over the ground. When she looked closely, she swore she saw those roots slithering.

And yet, the light that had led her there continued forward until it rested at the base of the Dark Oak. Once there, it didn't wink out instantly. Instead, the light settled onto the bark, and then, slowly, it seeped in as though the tree hungered for it. And when her guide was gone, the silence grew thicker still.

Calliope reached out a hand, the air viscous against her fingers, and it was as though generations of secrets caressed her skin. She closed her eyes. Focusing her intention and power, she forced her shoulders to relax, her heart to slow, all while ignoring the prickling along the back of her neck. The magic of the Dark Oak was heavy and pungent, but there was something else here, too. An unnamable darkness that was strangely familiar. Still, she focused on the task at hand. She needed to see the enchantments, ensure that everything was as it should be. She wanted nothing more than to prove her sisters right, that there was nothing wrong, but she heard her mother's warnings in the back of her mind like an infinite echo.

Her hand moved through the air, feeling, searching, until, yes, just there—she plucked an invisible thread.

The surge that tore through her body was so powerful it blew her back onto the forest floor, knocking the air out of her. She gasped for breath and then her eyes went wide. The thread she'd plucked was now visible and shimmered with the same ethereal light her guide had. The glow sped along that thread, illuminating others, until the clearing was lit with a web of light, chasing away the shadows. It radiated around the Dark Oak, the light of Petridi magic fighting against the darkness that pulsed there.

Calliope pushed herself to her feet, ignoring the dirt on her knees and palms.

The sight before her brought tears to her eyes. The threads of ancient magic that generations of Petridi women had woven and protected hummed with a beauty so pure it was breathtaking. On shaking legs, she stepped into the clearing, and the glow of those gold and silver threads washed over her. She traced one string and then another without touching them, marveling at the beauty, the power, the magic. The threads crisscrossed, all leading to the Dark Oak, wrapping around its trunk and up its branches, threading through the root system. And as the threads brightened at her nearness, the Dark Oak . . . shuddered. The void in its trunk seemed to radiate anger, the twigs curling like the fingers of a clenched fist.

If a random bystander were to walk near the clearing, they wouldn't see the threads, wouldn't feel the hum, but they would sense the ancient power of the place. They wouldn't see the leaves of shadow and roots that moved like pythons. Calliope had cast too many veiling spells that would compel them to walk on. Each enchantment obscured the Dark Oak's very existence.

As she followed another thread that brought her close to the ends of the roots, she stilled, her eyes snagging on a point in the line where the light dulled and flickered like a dying star. It looked frayed, as though something had tried to slice through it, and her heart twisted in her chest. Something or someone had done this.

"Okay," she breathed. "That's probably not good." Could

she fix it? Heal it? Cast another protection spell that would strengthen the line? She thought of her sisters, knew they would disapprove. That they would screech in horror if they even knew she was here. But if they could see this, the tear in the enchantment, they would have to believe her. She contemplated leaving right then and dragging them back, but what would happen to the enchantment if it was left alone? Would it deteriorate further? Would the perpetrator come back and slice through more of the enchantment? She knew there was already a Shadowcrafter somewhere in town.

Her mother's warnings echoed in her ears. *Stay away from the Dark Oak at all costs.* And then, something about a curse. But none of that helped her now. She was *here,* and the omens she'd seen in town meant the Dark Oak might be awakening, and surely that meant there was some leeway with those warnings.

"Right," she said. And even her voice sounded different here. Clearer and purer in the light of so much Petridi magic. "Let's see what happens, shall we?"

She reached out a hand and steadied herself, her finger poised to test the string, to see what she could glean from the story of its break and how she might fix it.

"Please don't knock me down again," she said, her voice barely above a whisper.

But when she touched the torn enchantment, two things happened simultaneously.

The air was knocked once again from her lungs as she flew back, and the Dark Oak's branches shook violently until shadow leaves rained down.

The strings of light began to dim as the Dark Oak's trunk trembled violently, and an unnatural wind picked up.

And then, a thick black fog began to seep from the crack in the enchantment, curled in wisps that stained the air. It smelled of death and rot.

Calliope screamed and scrambled to her feet.

The fog screamed back, an unholy sound that rattled her skull. And she knew, without understanding how, that if that fog touched her, it would consume her, just like in her dream. She told herself to run, but she couldn't move, could barely breathe. Somewhere in a dark recess of her mind, she wondered if this was the end. There was no flash of life before her eyes. No thoughts of dreams not realized or a last cry for help. Only the ceaseless advance of that viscous black fog, so dark it leached what little light was left from the forest around it.

She called forth her magic, hands outstretched, ready to sacrifice any memory to send the hellish fog back where it belonged.

But she wasn't fast enough. Tendrils of the mist licked at her feet like flames of black ice.

She opened her mouth to cast a spell, but the words wouldn't come. A wisp began to coil around her ankle, and she screamed at the searing pain.

She reached out, trying to find the thread that connected her to her sisters to pull from their magic, but they were too far away. Her mother had always said that their bond was what would protect them, save them, but she hadn't listened. She was alone.

The air turned pungent and burnt against her tongue, and she gagged. The hum around her grew quieter, and she tried to let go of the spell, but it clung to her, and she realized this was it. She could feel the flow of life ebbing from her no matter how hard she tried to hold on. Before long there was no more hum, just a persistent roar that crashed like ocean waves.

And then, through the smell of rot and ash and regret, there was another scent. It was apples and spice and power. A kind of magic that tasted foreign and dark, nearly melding with the magic that leaked from the Dark Oak. But it was a thread, and that was all she needed.

With a deep, shuddering breath, she called out to that power. It slammed into her with the force of a gale. It made her bones luminous and stretched her skin taut. She was burning from the inside out, a supernova inside her chest, and it terrified her. But with that new power raging inside her, amplifying her own magic, she sacrificed a memory. She brought Thalia to her mind's eye. Thalia, draping her scarf around her shoulders every morning, the loving caress, the gentle way she tucked the loose ends away. She used it to cast a spell to contain the Dark Oak fog that threatened to consume her. The threads of those ancient Petridi enchantments all around her pulsed bright and brighter still, and as the incantation echoed through the dark night, Calliope's vision blurred, her body trembling from the sudden strain. The air pulsed, thick with energy.

She uttered the incantation again, panting through the struggle of holding on to her magic, of focusing the spell. She pulled from the nature around her. The sweet smell of damp earth, the strength of the towering pine trees in the Forgotten Forest, the power of the ancient rocks beneath her feet. The energy simmering in her from that new, terrifying bond. And as the fog threatened to engulf her, a surge of strength welled from within her. She projected the spell out, pushing back against the fog. As she gasped for breath, her heart pounding, her vision turned black around the edges, and pinpricks of stars danced in and out of focus. She fell to the ground even as the fog began to seep back into the crack it had come from. She'd contained it for the time being, but she knew it wasn't a permanent fix.

The earth was cold beneath her now, her body laid out as an offering to the gods of arrogance and foolishness. The string inside her pulled tight and tighter still until the ground trembled with thunder. In her haze, she distantly heard a voice as she floated in the ether between lands. It was the last thing she remembered before the black swallowed her like a whale swallows a minnow, easily and with no consequence at all.

CHAPTER 5

WHEN CALLIOPE WOKE, HER VERY BONES CRIED out in anguish. As her eyes flickered open, she saw the first rays of dawn, the golden light painting the sky like a dream. She was no longer in the middle of the Forgotten Forest. She wondered, briefly, if she was dead.

Gingerly, she pushed to her knees, and stone bit into her skin. *Alive.* She was at the Altar. Though she couldn't feel the string connected to her sisters, when she reached within, she felt it connected to . . . someone. A presence. And when she acknowledged it, she felt her magic wake up. That fresh, crisp apple taste coated her tongue like a lover's kiss, and the connection hummed along her skin like a caress.

A cold breeze blew from the Forgotten Forest, and goose-bumps sprouted on her skin. The Altar of Fate's stone was bruising her knees where she knelt, but the pain was a wel-come reminder of the life she'd nearly forfeited.

Calliope could feel herself unravel in that moment of quiet. It was the sharp slice of fear, the bitter tang of regret, and, underneath it all, a dull pounding of anger that slithered through her blood. Anger at herself for attempting to fix the enchantment alone, for nearly failing; at her sisters for not being there with her. At her mother for abandoning them.

She held out her hands, closed her eyes, tilted her head back toward the dark morning sky where the stars were beginning to fade, and tried to surrender the rage that simmered in her blood. The clouds hung low as if waiting for the moon to carry them home. Gradually, calm returned to her. The whole world was fragile and soft, and Calliope wanted to sink into the peace of the dawn etching itself across her skin. Birds chirped in the distance, and somewhere, an owl hooted. A gentle breeze caressed her hair. She drew air deep into her lungs and thought of all the things she'd almost missed out on. She imagined her favorite cozy chair at Tea and Tome. The rush of customers during the holidays. Dancing with Danny and laughing with their friends at absolutely nothing. And the smaller things, too. Those moments she all too often sacrificed for a small piece of magic. The sound of cicadas in summer. The way a bowl of soup warmed her throat on a cold day and settled in her stomach like a reminder that everything was going to be okay. The anticipation of a fresh batch of cookies baking in the oven and how, every single time, she turned into a kid waiting for them to finish. The way she always got socks for Christmas because everyone knew she loved them.

Tears stung her eyes, and, in that moment, she hated her magic for all the other memories she'd lost.

She took another deep breath. Remembered the searing pain on her ankle that now somehow seemed to be the one place on her body that *didn't* ache.

She smelled rain coming. But there was something else. Ash and burned oak, charred pine.

And then, the air shifted.

Her eyes opened.

She caught a presence at the edge of her vision and startled to see a figure leaning casually against an outcropping of rock. Even from a distance, she could feel the threat of him, ominous as storm clouds and just as dark.

"She's awake," he said. His voice was indolent but laced with power that tasted bitter as aconite.

"Who are you?" Her own voice was hoarse and weak.

The stranger turned to look at her, and her breath caught in her chest. His eyes were bright as a whetted blade, and there was an extravagant kind of anger in the downturn of his mouth. As though he had plenty to spare and would not be miserly with it.

The Shadowcrafter.

"What are you doing here?" she tried again, loathing the fear that filled her.

Still, he didn't answer but looked toward the sky, his arms crossed against his chest. Though she felt shaky, Calliope rose from the Altar and strode toward him.

The taste of tart apple juice filled her mouth. The golden hum grew stronger.

"You," she choked out. "This magic is yours?"

He eyed her distastefully, looking down from his towering height. He was a beast of a man, she realized. Broad and unyielding, with thick dark hair and darker eyes that seemed nearly luminescent. His harsh beauty unsettled her. Worked its way under her skin until she couldn't stop staring at the strong line of his jaw and his plush, frowning lips.

Leisurely, he moved his muscled arms until his hands were clapping in a slow and deliberate movement. Her eyes snapped to his, her anger flaring, and she reached inside herself for a spell that would knock the arrogance off the sculpted planes of his face. But she was shocked into silence. For as she pulled on the frayed string of her magic, she found the end was connected to . . . him.

"My name is Lucien Deniz," he said, bending in a mocking bow. "And we're now bound to each other, thanks to that little trick you pulled."

Calliope's mouth dropped open. She had heard of Lucien. News traveled even among witchkind, though Thalia tried to forestall it, and his name was whispered along currents of wind like a freshly sharpened knife, drawing blood wherever it was uttered. Alice, the High Priestess of the Lightcraft coven in Aurelia, had sent a sparrow some years ago telling of a heist in Egypt that left a village nearly decimated from earthquakes. He'd been at the helm of it. She'd heard the Denizes were some of the most dangerous and powerful Shadowcrafters in the world. And that Lucien in particular was heartless, without mercy, drawing on Shadowcraft magic until it ate at his soul. And this was the man she'd bonded herself to?

Desperation clawed at her as the string connecting them glowed bright. She detested him on principle. Feared him as a rule. Here before her was the living embodiment of her mother's warnings. Another result of the Great Rift, the Shadowcrafters' war against Lightcraft.

"And before you try anything . . ." He paused as if turning words over in his mind like stones for a slingshot, searching for the sharpest one. "I only mean to help you," he finished. But it was the way he said it, with a glint in his eye, his voice a melody coated with venom. And the more he spoke, the more Calliope noticed his accent. There was the soft, subtle lilt of French and something else she couldn't quite place. Danger seeped out of every harsh line of him.

His presence, his magic, seemed to awaken something in her, a memory on the tip of her tongue, but she couldn't place it.

"I don't believe you," she said. "I know who you are. *What* you are." There was no mistaking the disgust in her voice.

"Watch your words, little muse," he said, inspecting his fingernails flippantly. "Though I'm bound to you, I will tear you down where you stand." Here he looked up, eyes locking on hers with such anger it sent a shiver down her spine. And this time, she believed him. His magic pulsed around him, a throbbing that she felt in her body.

A memory flashed through her mind. Thumping music, a drink in her hand, and Danny at the Piano Rouge. She'd sensed his magic there, the scent of dark power and spiced apples, and even before that, when she had stepped out of Tea and Tome. "You've been following me," Calliope choked out. "Why? What do you want?"

She was again met with silence.

"Fine." She turned her back on him and marched resolutely toward Lethe Manor. But the sound of his heavy boots squelching over wet grass caught up to her. He grabbed her forearm and pulled her to a stop, his hand hot on her skin as electricity crackled up her spine. She whirled around to face him, breathing hard.

"If I hadn't been, you'd be dead by now," he growled.

"If I'd have known what you were, I would have preferred that end." She wrenched her arm free, turning back toward Lethe Manor.

"We are not done here," he said, following her still.

"Like hell we aren't," Calliope answered without slowing her stride.

"Why were you alone in that forest?" he asked, anger coloring his words. "It was foolish and reckless."

"As if I'd tell you." She laughed darkly. "Though I clearly see why you're here. You've heard tales of the Dark Oak and seek its power. Good luck breaking through the generations of spells keeping you from it." Her bravado was an act. This was the very thing her mother had warned about—Shadowcrafters seeking the Dark Oak. After all their years protecting it, the Dark Oak was a secret no longer, and the thought sent tendrils of terror snaking through her blood until her hands trembled and her heart raced. And if she'd truly bound him to herself, she'd led him right to it and given him a head start.

Goddess. She had bound herself to one of the most dangerous Shadowcrafters in the world.

She was shaking. Her magic was tainted with Shadowcraft now. Would her sisters be able to sense it? *My sisters,* she thought in horror. They had tried to tell her, tried to warn her, but she hadn't listened. And now . . .

She reached out with her magic, feeling for the string that always connected them. She was approaching the house now; she should be able to feel it. And she could, but something was . . . broken. Muddied by this strange new bond with the man following her.

"You bound yourself to me," he said in a low voice as though reading her mind. "That's why it was so easy for me to heal your ankle while you slept. You're welcome, by the way."

"I didn't ask for that. Didn't ask for your help! I release you," she huffed, stopping short when he stepped in front of her.

"It's not that simple." He crossed his arms.

"Sure it is," she snapped. "Presumably you know as much about the Great Rift as I do. Our magic is incompatible. We break the bond right here. Right now."

She fumbled for her magic, but when she tried to sever the connection, the string pushed back so forcefully that she lost her footing. Lucien's hands darted out to steady her, then he dropped his hands immediately.

"I'll find a way," she told him resolutely. "Now move."

He didn't.

Calliope let out a muffled scream and flew at him, shoving him hard in the chest. She bounced off the solid wall of muscle, and he didn't so much as budge. Instead, to her surprise, he let out a laugh.

"You're nothing but a street cat, little muse. You'd claw the one who saved you? Fine. Find a way to break the binding and I'd be glad to be rid of you."

She was breathing hard by the time he finished speaking, wanting nothing more than to scratch his eyes out.

"I don't know how this works yet. But I'm going home. I'll deal with you later."

And when she turned away, he didn't follow. His words nipped at her heels, and she tripped over rocks and brambles in her haste to reach home. The echo of his mirthless laughter trailed her like a ghost.

She stomped through the grass to Lethe Manor, the grounds eerily silent. Morning had arrived, but it was so misty it still looked like night. She passed the herb garden, inhaling the rosemary and mint, then the flower garden with its delicate scent of jasmine and roses, which leaned toward her, as though her secrets were the fertilizer that would make them grow.

All the while, her stomach churned with despair. A frayed enchantment and a bond with a Shadowcraft practitioner.

What had she done?

Chapter 6

She entered the cold house, tiptoeing through the dark, silent halls filled with statues and paintings from their summers in Greece. She didn't want to wake her sisters, couldn't face them just yet.

She was tired, and her knees and feet were still wet, her hands covered in dirt. Her starlight dress was ruined. Dread settled in her stomach and across her shoulders like a mantle. For someone who thrived on action, even if it was wrong, the inability to *do* anything to fix the problem she'd created was suffocating. The enchantments were weakening, and she was bound to a Shadowcrafter. If it weren't so terrifying, she might laugh.

Her room was freezing, but she was bathed in sweat. Quickly, she discarded her dress and boots and left them where they fell on the floor, then stepped into the bathroom for a shower.

The scalding water poured over her head, mixing with her tears, which came hot and fast. Thalia and Eurydice would never have let this happen. Growing up, Thalia had always been the fixer. When their mother's forgetting got worse, it was Thalia who had saved the house from falling into disrepair. At thirteen, she cleaned with gloves and Lysol, never magic. Eurydice had always been the peacekeeper, never asking questions and always smoothing over fights. But Calliope had always been too inquisitive, too reckless. Why did their mother forget to pick them up at school? Why did she disappear for days at a time, and where did she go? Because even when their mother had been physically present, she wasn't always completely *there.* But when Calliope asked these questions, no satisfying answers ever came. At times, Penelope Petridi seemed to forget she even had any children.

But when she remembered, oh, it was a marvelous thing. In winter, she would wake them at midnight with whispers and promises, and they would bake baklava, their fingers sticky with honey and the air smelling of cinnamon as they danced while the oven heated. In spring, she would braid their hair with narcissus, the smell so sickly sweet it made the girls' heads spin, and they'd lie back in the grass, laughing and pointing out shapes in the clouds. In summer, they traveled to their ancestral home in Greece. The tiny island of Milos was a haven of magic all its own. Craggy cliffs and pebble beaches gave way to moonlike craters formed from volcanic rock where Penelope chased them like she was afraid to let them go. Come autumn, they would return home and walk arm in arm through town, and she would pull them close.

"Where magic gathers, there will be those who seek to claim it," she'd say. "You must protect your string and stay away from the Dark Oak at all costs." Penelope's warnings were oft repeated and came fast as rain from a storm-laden sky, like time was running out. *Tell no one about the enchantments or magic. Stay away from Shadowcrafters. If the Great Rift taught us anything, it's that Lightcraft and Shadowcraft cannot co-exist.* She'd never said more about the curse other than that they had to sacrifice a memory in order to practice magic, and the sisters didn't know much else about it.

Now it seemed her mother's warnings were finally coming to pass. Because of Calliope.

Once she finally felt clean, she sacrificed a memory of Astro curling up in her lap to dry herself instantly, then pulled on a purple knee-length sweatshirt with black witch hats printed all over it and BAD WITCH emblazoned across the chest in orange.

She sat on her four-poster bed, sinking into the soft mattress and pulling up the emerald-green velvet duvet. Astro chirruped and jumped up beside her. Calliope tangled her fingers in her gray fluff and the cat began to purr loudly, pressing her cold nose into Calliope's arm. Despite the fatigue, her eyes refused to close. What the hell was she going to do? There was nothing that she'd be able to say to her sisters that would justify the consequences of her actions. She played the whole night out over and over until she threw herself onto her pillow and screamed into it. *I just wanted to help,* she thought savagely.

Energy crackled, and Calliope sensed a presence in her room. The hairs raised on the back of her neck.

She bolted upright, heart beating fast, and saw a looming figure leaning against the window, silhouetted by the morning light and framed by the rolling mist on the lawn beyond.

Lucien looked entirely bored: arms crossed, his head tilted back, staring at the ceiling.

"This is going to get old," he said on a sigh.

"How did you get in here?" Calliope screeched.

"You have no wards. Anyone could get in here." His hair

was in disarray, like he'd repeatedly run his hand through it after Calliope had left him only a bit ago. His white button-down shirt was wrinkled, the sleeves rolled up to reveal a series of tattoos that snaked around his forearms.

"I haven't needed wards until now," Calliope practically growled, her heart hammering. "Get out."

"This isn't Victorian England, and I don't plan on ravishing you," he said, eyeing the way she clutched at the sheet. "Even if you are"—his gaze lingered on her chest—"a 'bad witch.'"

"Get. Out," she said, seething, pulling the covers up to her neck, which sent Astro scurrying away with an affronted yowl. Color splotched high on her cheeks. She hadn't decided what to tell her sisters yet, and if they sensed his magic in the house before she came up with an explanation . . . She shuddered at the thought.

"You called me here," he said, annoyance seeping into his tone now. "Trust me, I'd much prefer to be anywhere else."

"I did *not* call you here," she argued, but even as she said it, she thought of her scream into the pillow and the silent plea that she'd just wanted to help. Had he heard the cry but mistaken it for her asking for help? Lucien responded only with an arched eyebrow. "Okay, if I did, it was an accident. Purely coincidental. So, you can just, you know, *go*." Once he was gone, maybe she'd be able to focus on a plan instead of the way he had gotten under her skin like a burr, irritating and prickly.

Still, he didn't budge. Calliope let out a muffled groan and launched her pillow at him. With a lackadaisical wave of his hand, the pillow switched its trajectory mid-flight and landed with a soft thump on the floor.

"Do you enjoy sleeping in an ice palace?" With another lazy wave, a fire crackled merrily in the grate as though it had been lit for hours. Again, she smelled fresh-cut apple, an undernote of honey. It would seem that, unlike her, it cost him nothing to cast such small spells.

"No one is forcing you to be here. I've told you to leave twice."

He sighed. "Undesirous as it may be, the bond makes me privy to the fact that you *do* need me. I can help you."

"I have no desire to hear anything you say," Calliope said. Her eyes darted to his mouth, begrudgingly noticing his perfectly full lips.

"Be that as it may," he said coldly, sitting in the armchair by the fire and crossing his ankle over his knee. "We're stuck together."

"Why were you in the Forgotten Forest?" Calliope asked, giving voice to the question that had been nagging at the back of her mind. She'd accused him of trying to track down the Dark Oak, but how could he even know about it? Its very existence was a closely kept secret.

"Why were *you*?" he countered. Calliope laughed, and it came out cold. She didn't trust him. Refused to tell him about the weakening enchantments, which Calliope guessed was being caused by the Dark Oak beginning to awaken. Telling a Shadowcrafter that the Dark Oak enchantments might be vulnerable was too risky, even if she was bound to him. At least until she knew more.

"This is my home," she said. "I don't have to tell you anything. Now answer my question."

He stared at the fire, and Calliope thought he would refuse, but then he said, "I'm here on family business."

"So you decided to take a walk at night?" she demanded archly. "In the middle of the woods?"

"I felt like a stroll," he said, narrowing his eyes.

"And it had nothing to do with the powerful tree that's guarded with enchantments?"

"I had no idea that tree was even there," he said, and the pressure in Calliope's chest eased a little at the obvious truth in his words. "But power calls to power," he said. "And I happen to be very fucking powerful. And if you must know, I was nowhere near that forest when I felt the power flare. I followed the pull and then someone tapped into my magic— thank you for that, by the way—and when I finally found you, I had two choices. Pull my magic back and let you die or allow you to borrow from my well of power. I may be a heart-less bastard, but the choice seemed obvious."

"Oh," Calliope said, hating that there seemed to be a note of truth to his words, of logic. "Oh, well, then." The words *thank* and *you* were on the tip of her tongue, but then he continued.

"Of course, if I knew you had planned on *binding* yourself to me, I would have taken longer to consider."

"It wasn't purposeful," she muttered.

"And I presume you'll have a very good reason for why *you* were in the middle of the forest at night, almost getting consumed by ancient magic? Perhaps you laid a trap for me. Waiting until I was close enough that you could steal my power since you weren't strong enough to do it on your own."

"I—what—how could you?" Calliope spluttered. "I don't owe you any explanations."

"Then it only follows that I owe you none, either," he said.

"Fine," Calliope said. "Fine." She threw the covers back and stomped over to her dresser, silently cursing the cold stone floor on her bare feet. "Thank you for being absolutely no help at all." She tore through her clothes and threw several shirts onto the floor. "So glad that I almost died trying to help and got *your* broody ass in return for it." She finally found the velour sweatshirt she was looking for, which had a cauldron outlined in rhinestones, and turned around to find Lucien staring at her with a look of unfettered disgust on his face. "What?"

"Are you going to pick those up?" he asked, nodding to the discarded clothes on the floor.

"A broody ass *and* OCD? What a delightful combo." She glanced down at the clothes lying in a heap and then back at him before pulling the drawer back open. "You know," she said, pulling out the contents and dropping them on the floor one by one. "I don't think I will." His nostrils flared as the clothes piled up. "I'll just leave them there, let them marinate. Gather a little dust. And then shove them back in the drawer in a couple weeks." He narrowed his eyes but still didn't speak.

"What?" Calliope continued, relishing the small act of control when everything else in her life was spiraling. "Going to beg me to let you iron them? Fold them? Maybe throw in some color coding?" She huffed a laugh.

"Trust me, little muse," he growled. His tone was clipped, his accent more pronounced as he glared at her. "There is only one kind of begging I submit to, and you will never be on the receiving end of it."

Calliope felt a flash of heat—*unwelcome*—and before she could splutter a response, he pushed open the window.

"Do not call to me again," he said, "unless you've found a way to break the bond." And with that, he pulled himself up onto the ledge and stepped off.

Despite herself, Calliope rushed to the window, where she saw Lucien strolling through the mist, completely at ease. And though she longed to grab one of the crystals off her desk and aim for his head, she turned on her heel and got dressed, all while wondering what, exactly, she was going to tell her sisters.

CHAPTER 7

THIS WAS NOT IN HIS PLANS. *SHE* WAS NOT IN HIS plans. The task was always going to be difficult, but this added a layer of complication he detested. His trepidation turned to ire. Her ignorance irked him, the audacity to attempt such a spell without knowing the consequences. It was untenable. *Why* had she done it? His nostrils flared in anger as his fingers itched to go back to her icy room, to grab her shoulders and shake her.

He'd been following her for days, and the more he saw, the more worry gnawed at him. Calliope Petridi. She was reckless, and that invited risk. The image of her on the dance floor was seared into his mind. The way her starlight dress had winked in the darkness, clinging to her curves. The confusing flash of desire that had burned through him like a living thing. He'd squashed it quickly.

How dare she, a cursed Lightcraft witch, bind *him*. He was a Shadowcrafter. And when she'd drawn from his well of magic, he had felt her emotions. The hot fear that burned like whiskey down his throat when she fought back those shadows. Her determination, shining like a beacon in the dark and making his chest ache in a way that was entirely unwelcome. Her indignation when she found out he was a Shadowcrafter. He'd been testing the waters by telling her his full name. But it was clear she knew only of his reputation and nothing of the history between their two families. Otherwise, she would have vaporized him on the spot. And though before he would have scoffed at that idea, the fact that she'd been able to sense his presence and draw from his power meant she was not to be underestimated, even if she *was* cursed. This bond was not in his plans, but perhaps he could use it to his advantage. There was too much at stake not to.

Summoning his magic, he gave a flick of his hand and vanished, appearing an instant later at the house he was renting on the opposite side of town. Sarai and Malik would be waiting for him there, he knew, while the others would be at headquarters, a small clearing far in the Forgotten Forest where the coven had magicked a small house. Close enough that Lucien could keep an eye on them but warded so well that no one, witch or human, would ever sense it.

"What happened?" Sarai demanded the moment he appeared. Her voice was shaky, as though she'd been holding her breath. "Where were you? You were supposed to be back over an hour ago!" The white hijab she wore covered her hair completely but exposed part of her slender neck and contrasted against her brown skin. Her dark eyes burned with worry, which, Lucien thought, was her natural state. As always, she was impeccably dressed in a simple but chic abaya that reached her ankles and reminded him of their first meeting under the hot Egyptian sun. Staring at her now, he remembered just how much power was hidden in that short frame of hers.

Lucien threw himself into an armchair, growing more furious by the second from his unexpected encounter with one Calliope Petridi.

"That bad?" Malik asked when Lucien didn't answer. Malik, Lucien's second-in-command of their small coven, paced in front of the fire with a frown on his face. His long legs ate up the space in only a few strides. Everything about him was angular, from his sharp high cheekbones and square jaw to his long nose. Even his beard was shaved into a short goatee with lines so precise they looked measured. His deep-set eyes, usually alive with mirth, were now dancing with danger. Malik was roughly the same age as Lucien and the only real friend he'd had growing up, though it began as circumstance rather than choice.

Where Lucien was brusque and taciturn by nature, Malik traded on his charm and pleasantness, which belied a powerful bent toward Shadowcraft.

Memories flashed in Lucien's mind of two boys sneaking around the château in the French countryside, unraveling their magic by night and exploring the grounds by day. Lucien shook off the memories like a bad habit when Sarai cut into his thoughts.

"You disappeared," Sarai said, her slight Arabic accent soft and lilting. "Whatever it is, it's derailing our plans, isn't it? I knew this was going to happen. I should never have come. We're going to be found out." She dropped her head into her hands with a groan.

"We're more powerful than the Lightcrafters could ever hope to be," Lucien said finally. He recounted the events and watched as Sarai's face fell further and a gleam burned in Malik's eyes. "This is exactly what I'd planned, it's just not *how* I'd planned it." A dull ache was beginning to grow behind his temples as a light spring rain started to beat against the windows. He hadn't slept, and the sun was fully risen now, but he knew it would be impossible to find rest. He could feel the bond to Calliope, an ember of warmth in his cold soul that he longed to extinguish. When he closed his eyes, she was imprinted on his lids. The way her blond hair haloed her head, wild and half alive. The pink flush of anger kissing her cheeks. How even though she had been scared, she had stood tall and proud and fearsome.

"You wanted to get close to them," Sarai said, breaking into his thoughts like a thief. "Trick them into undoing the enchantments. Not *bind* yourself to one of them. She's the one you've been watching, yes? You said she's wild and unpredictable. This could go very wrong indeed." Sarai frowned, worrying her lower lip between her teeth.

"I know this was the plan all along, I'm just curious how, exactly, she bound herself to you?" Malik asked, eyes sparkling with mirth now. "A little Lightcraft witch alone in the middle of the forest?" He adjusted the collar of his navy blue suit jacket, his dark skin backlit by the glow of the fire as he tried and failed to hide his grin.

Lucien scowled at his second-in-command, the Summoner of the coven, the one who kept tabs on everyone and ensured that everyone was where they were supposed to be.

"I let her," Lucien answered tiredly. "She would have died otherwise, and we need the sisters alive. I had planned on waiting to reveal myself until I knew more, but she was reckless. And now . . ."

"Now that plan is fast-tracked," Malik said, his voice far

too cheerful and positive. "So, gain her trust. Keep her busy trying to find ways to break the bond. Those witches have had the Dark Oak for far too long, so long they've grown complacent. It shouldn't be hard." He shrugged with indifference.

"I don't know," Sarai said, looking back and forth between Lucien and Malik. "This seems too risky."

"You think taking a walk outside is too risky, Rai." Malik laughed good-naturedly, tapping the end of her nose. "It makes you very endearing but a somewhat ineffective Shadowcrafter."

"Sarai has more power in her little finger than most Shadowcrafters have in their whole body, Malik. She simply chooses when to wield it. Now, leave her alone."

"Yes, boss." Malik grinned, knowing Lucien hated the moniker. If Lucien had been in any other mood, he might have laughed.

But Lucien's words were true. He had come across Sarai years ago when his father had sent him to a cursed dig site in Egypt to recover a dark, powerful artifact: an ancient canopic jar that was able to store vast amounts of magic. But Sarai had gotten there first and already begun to unravel the spells that guarded it. She was young, at least a decade younger than him. And he was so impressed by her magic that he didn't even try to undermine her, knowing he'd probably lose. His father could go to hell for all he cared. He was tired of running his errands at that point, anyway. But when the enchantments broke, they unleashed Apep, a fifty-foot-long snake that brought with it earthquakes and thunderstorms. He couldn't leave then, and as they fought and vanquished that great serpent together, they formed a connection.

Afterward, over cups of hibiscus tea, Lucien learned that

Sarai and her mother had left Egypt and immigrated to the United Arab Emirates when she was a girl. They commiserated over having each foot in a different country and never feeling like they truly belonged to either. And through it all, he was silently in awe of the natural power that emanated from her. Lucien should have known, for his father, Ahmed, had always had a talent for finding the most powerful Shadowcrafters to do his bidding and join his cause.

When he got back home, he lied to his father and told him the artifact was already gone by the time he got there. He'd kept in touch with Sarai over the years, and she was the first person he contacted when his plan for the Dark Oak formulated. Her talent was why he'd named her Cursebreaker of the coven.

Lucien had handpicked these witches, chosen for the hunger for power that drove them. And they each had a role to play. The coven hierarchy was simple, but still, Lucien would have dispensed with roles entirely if Malik hadn't convinced him they were necessary to establish authority. It was something that came more naturally to Malik than it did to Lucien. He'd often wondered what had happened in Malik's past before he came to the family château, and how he maintained such a genial disposition after being orphaned so young. But Malik never spoke of his parents or his past, and the only reason Lucien knew anything about them at all was from eavesdropping at his father's office door with a stealth spell when Ahmed first brought Malik home. He remembered listening to his father's questions, eyes wide at the patience in his voice that he'd never heard before. But no matter how much Ahmed pried and cajoled, Malik would only say that his ancestors hailed from Bamako, the capital of Mali, and migrated to Tangier, which is where he'd been born and raised for the first decade of his life. Malik spoke English perfectly, had picked up French like a native, and could still converse easily in Arabic. And more than that, his propensity for Shadowcraft meant his past was of no consequence to Ahmed.

But to this day, Lucien didn't know how Malik had ended up in Paris, orphaned and alone, and he had grown to respect their friendship too much to seek answers where none were willingly given. He and Malik had accepted each other when they were boys, and their bond, though fraught with family tension over the years, was one of the only constants in Lucien's life.

Lucien was drawn back to the present when the front door flew open with a resounding bang, and Feng bounded into the room, Luna following him. She wore an aggrieved look on her face that said *this is too much energy to deal with,* and Lucien couldn't quite blame her.

"Hey, boss," Feng said, throwing himself into an armchair, legs splayed out and head thrown back like he'd melted the second he sat. "Back from patrol. Took some notes. Looking good." His words were clipped as always, short and to the point. No fillers. Lucien liked that about the kid. Feng, known in the coven as the Guardian, couldn't be older than nineteen. But he had a knack for optimism and a skill with protection spells, both of which Lucien sorely lacked. Malik had found Feng in San Francisco of all places, where he sold his services for an exorbitant fee, to the utter anxiety of his doting mother.

Luna sat primly in the chair opposite, glasses slipping down her nose. She was in her thirties and known in the coven as the Scholar. She worked closely with Feng to structure the bigger rituals. Her nuanced understanding of the major arcana of Shadowcraft meant she was able to identify the weak points of a spell. Helpful for building rituals, or, in this case, unraveling them. Lucien had heard tell of her skill through his network and followed the trail to Oxford, where she taught graduate-level courses on mysticism. He thought he'd have to convince her, but she'd listened to his plan carefully while grading papers, and by the time he'd finished, she had already decided to join him. "Stay here and teach these twats about magic they don't believe in," she'd said in her thick Yorkshire accent, "or get back at the Lightcrafter wazzocks that tried to wipe my family out. Shadowcraft is in my blood, right? They think we're all evil. We're not, but I don't mind giving them a taste of their own medicine. And when we're done, I can study the limitations of our magic without the threat of turning into a soul-sucking monster."

Like Lightcraft, Shadowcraft was inherited. And whichever you were born into, you did not stray. The Great Rift had made sure of that. The prejudice was too deeply ingrained.

"Ey up," Luna said now, wearily nodding to Lucien. "We're making progress."

Lucien looked around. The Guardian, the Scholar, the Summoner, and the Cursebreaker. And then there were the five second-degree initiates who were back at headquarters. The sole purpose of their presence was the ability for the others to draw on their power when necessary. He knew them well enough that he trusted that they all sought the same thing. Power. And when all was said and done, when Lucien had the power of the Dark Oak in his hands, running through his veins, he would share it with them in exchange for their services.

"Tell us the plan for the girl," Malik said.

Lucien's jaw tightened as he thought of Calliope's defiant

expression when she first learned he was a Shadowcrafter. How she'd tried to send him away, dismissing his help as unnecessary. He wasn't sure what infuriated him more, her arrogance or her complete disregard for her own safety. If she didn't have such an obvious abhorrence toward Shadow-craft, she'd be well suited to it.

"She wanted nothing to do with me," he said, his voice growing hoarse from the lack of sleep. "I'll go on with my original plan. Gain her confidence." He rubbed his temples, closing his eyes at the dull ache there. He should have already planted the seeds of trust, made a better first impression, but her immediate ire toward him had gotten under his skin.

He longed for two fingers of whiskey and to be back in Turkey where he belonged, instead of halfway across the world on what seemed like a fool's errand. He'd spent half his life in the bustling city of Istanbul, running the legitimate side of his father's shipping business, and the other half tending to his sister at their family estate in the French countryside. But each time he returned to the château, it felt less and less like home. Perhaps he'd inherited more of his father's genes than he cared to admit, but Turkish rolled off his tongue easier than French. He reveled in the inherent kindness of the Turk-ish culture, the way you were welcomed wherever you went, an offer of tea only a breath away. It was a place where men greeted one another with a kiss to the cheek and the strong clap of a hand on the shoulder.

At this point though, either Turkey or France would be welcome, but his desires had been of no consequence for quite some time. As if to drive that point home, his second-in-command spoke again.

"You did say you'd do whatever it took," Malik said, his ex-pression turning dark again when he looked at Lucien. "And we all know why you're doing this. You want this fast-tracked more than the rest of us. Though, of course, there is an easier way. If you just told your father—"

"No," Lucien growled, his fingers curling into a fist. "You know what would happen if he found out. He will be told nothing. Don't bring him up again."

"He'll find out eventually," Malik said, walking the knife's edge of Lucien's anger. "He always does."

"I took precautions," Lucien said tightly. "In fact, I took great pains to ensure he wouldn't follow us here." He frowned as his father's face appeared in his mind's eye. He would sooner go to hell and bargain with the devil than ask his father for anything. There was Shadowcraft, and there was evil. His father just happened to be both.

"Very well," Malik said, holding his hands up in surrender. "You're in charge."

"Are you sure about this, Lucien?" Sarai raised an eyebrow, her doubt still apparent. "Trusting this witch seems like a dangerous game."

"This is not about trust. It's about getting what we want from her, and her sisters."

"I have a bad feeling about this," Sarai said. "Lightcraft users believe—"

"Their beliefs are inconsequential," Lucien answered sharply. "Her magic is nothing compared to the power we wield. And we will prove it. Now leave; I don't want you to wake Eléa."

For his plan to work, he needed Calliope to trust him. But where he'd been expecting a meek and grateful girl who would beg for his help with the waning enchantments, he instead got a headstrong, stubborn witch who looked prepared to claw his eyes out.

He hadn't meant to let her get to him. Hadn't meant to rise to her bait. But something about her provoked him. And there was too much at stake here to let that wretched little muse derail his plans. He would try again. Extend the olive branch and gain her trust, so long as she didn't find out the truth behind why he was in Gold Springs. Whether Calliope would accept his help and be willing to trust him remained uncertain, and that uncertainty gnawed at Lucien like an itch he couldn't scratch. The pain in his temples radiated out as the light spring rain turned into something heavier and more sinister.

The game has begun, Lucien thought.

CHAPTER 8

CALLIOPE STAYED IN HER ROOM, PACING BACK and forth as rain started pattering the roof. Perhaps she didn't have to tell her sisters about the bond with Lucien, she thought. If she figured out how to break it before they suspected anything, they need be none the wiser.

Her heart nearly flew into her throat when there was a soft tapping at her door. She wasn't ready to face them yet. But when the tap came again, she realized it was Grim. She hated keeping secrets, and it was particularly hard hiding anything from the book. But she let it in, and it flew to the brass stand and opened to a blank page.

What happened? The letters splashed across the page like an accusation.

"I don't know what you mean," Calliope answered, forcing her voice not to wobble. Grim's pages ruffled, almost as though it were smelling Calliope. And indeed, the next words confirmed it.

Something about you is different.

"Way to compliment a girl." Calliope laughed, though

it was too high-pitched to sound real. And if a book could frown, that's exactly what Grim was doing, the pages fluttering in a sigh that said it knew it wasn't going to get anything more out of her.

You need to see your sisters, it wrote, somewhat ominously. *They're in the kitchen. They did not hear you come home.*

Squaring her shoulders and taking a deep breath, she marched downstairs, Grim trailing behind her. Old marble statues that needed dusting lined the walls, their ancient carved faces shining with wisdom. Gilt frames housed oil paintings of various ancestors and the isle of Milos.

Entering the kitchen, Calliope was expecting a battle. What she didn't expect was to see Thalia and Dissy hunched over mugs of tea, looking miserable, with dark circles beneath their eyes.

"Did someone die?" Calliope asked at the doorway. Both sisters looked up simultaneously and then jumped to their feet. They rushed toward Calliope, crushing her in a group hug that stole her breath. Grim flapped excitedly around their heads.

"What did I miss?" Calliope asked, confused.

"Where *were* you?" Thalia demanded. "We were worried sick, Opie."

"I'm so glad you're okay," Dissy said, wiping her eyes.

"I—" Did they somehow know? Did their string of fate alert them in some way to what she'd done? Her stomach sank. "I can explain," she said. "I was out with Danny, and—"

"We know you were," Thalia interrupted. "We called them. But they said you'd left to come home."

"And then the fire sprang up out of nowhere," Dissy said. "We smelled the smoke and—"

"Fire?" Calliope breathed. "Where?" She thought of the

ash and burned oak and charred pine she'd smelled at the Altar. She had assumed it was the effects of Lucien's magic.

"At the edge of the Forgotten Forest," Dissy said. "Thalia smelled the smoke first and we followed it. We were so worried, Opie."

"Worried that you'd done something foolish," Thalia said. "You didn't, though, did you?"

"Of course she didn't. She wouldn't," Dissy said, though her voice trailed up at the end so it sounded more like a question.

"What started the fire?" Calliope asked quietly. Guilt turned her heart into a bird that beat against the bars of her rib cage. She swallowed hard, wondering if those flames had stemmed from her attempt at healing those broken threads. Magic out of hand. What other disasters had she brought?

"Nobody knows," Dissy answered. "We called the fire department and tried to control the flames until they got there. But Ava Ramirez, the fire captain, said it might take a few days to ascertain what started it. She said she'll have Sean keep us posted. He's the assistant chief at the station." Her cheeks bloomed with color, and Calliope filed that information away to examine later. "Anyway, Sean said it was strange in this weather, with the earth so wet from spring. So, Thalia and I thought that you might be right. That something *is* happening with the Dark Oak."

"You believe me?" Calliope whispered, regret blooming along the edges of her vision. It was what she'd longed for, what she'd been trying to prove. If only she'd waited, none of this would have happened.

"Where were you last night?" Thalia asked instead of answering. Her eyes narrowed as she catalogued Calliope's shifting eyes, the way she bit the inside of her cheek. "After you left Danny, where did you go?"

"I—" Calliope couldn't find the words. "I . . ."

"Spit it out, sister," Thalia said, and already, her chest was heaving, nostrils flared, lips pursed in a thin line.

"Thalia," Dissy chided gently, but Thalia held up a hand.

"No, I want to hear this from Calliope." Thalia was still, her face hardening like she was carved from the finest marble.

"I went to the Dark Oak," Calliope whispered.

Thalia glared at Calliope. Anger curled from her, as pungent as smoke. Calliope, like her sisters, loved their kitchen and wanted to have this conversation anywhere else. For negative emotions let loose in the kitchen typically seeped their way into the things created there.

"Explain yourself," Thalia demanded.

"I had to do something!" Calliope wrung her hands together. "You didn't believe me, and I—well, I went to the Dark Oak, and I was right. The enchantments are frayed, weakened. So, I—I had to do something. I tried to, you know . . . fix it."

Dissy moaned and covered her face with her hands. Calliope waited for Thalia to shout or shake her or storm off or threaten her. But her sister only stared. Her fathomless blue eyes were the color of a storm-tossed sea.

"I didn't mean to," Calliope said. The prolonged silence made her voice louder than she intended.

"You didn't mean to," Dissy echoed her younger sister; sweat dotted her brow despite the cold of the kitchen.

Thalia moved to the hearth, over which hung a sizable cauldron. Calliope couldn't count the number of times she'd found Thalia there, an apron tied around her waist and a wooden spoon in her hand as she stirred yet another batch of mnimi soup. The sage and rosemary in the vegetable soup were their own kind of magic and worked as the mildest form of antidote to hastily sacrificed memories. And that was only on rare occasions. It never brought back full memories, only glimpses. Now Thalia clenched the ladle as if imagining it were Calliope's throat.

"She didn't mean to?" Thalia finally said and laughed. "She didn't mean to what? Completely disregard us? March into the heart of the Forgotten Forest and try to fix something that isn't even broken? *You're* the one who started that fire, Calliope. With whatever reckless spell you did."

"No, Grim agrees with me, and I—" Calliope said, but Thalia barreled on.

"I forbade you from going to the Dark Oak. *Mother* forbade us all from going—"

And that's when Calliope snapped.

"Yes, but Mother isn't here, is she?" Calliope hissed. "She left us. Abandoned us. She told us not to go to the Dark Oak, but we also need to guard it. I was just trying to do what I thought was best."

"No," Thalia said, her words slithering into Calliope's heart and turning it cold. "Your wild streak has gotten worse ever since she left. You're reckless and self-destructive, and you haven't grown up at all. I expected this in your teens, but now? By the goddess, you're almost twenty-five years old." She looked away as if she couldn't bear the sight of Calliope's face.

"And you sound like you're ancient. And act like it, too. If it weren't for me, who would protect this town from the Dark Oak? Did you forget about that part of our legacy, or is it just another part of yourself you choose to ignore? I went to the Dark Oak because I had no other choice!" Calliope was pacing back and forth now, her eyes wild but with a hint of pleading. If she could just get Thalia to *see*, maybe she would understand.

"The wards and protections are still in place from over two centuries of Petridi women who—"

"Sisters," Calliope interrupted. "Not just women. *Sisters.* Three of them. Always three. But it's not this time, is it? It's just me," she said, and her voice broke then. "If you'd just listen to me—"

"Listen to you? All I do is listen to you! You never stop talking, Calliope. Never stop spewing your feelings all over the place. It's always about you, so stop acting like this is about the town." Thalia's tone was scathing, and her slender frame trembled in anger.

"Can't we just—" Eurydice started softly, blue-gray eyes luminous with unshed tears.

"No," Calliope and Thalia shouted simultaneously.

"Not this time," Thalia said, her voice quieter now. "The town is fine. This is about Calliope wanting to ruin her life because Marigold broke her heart. It's the equivalent of drinking yourself into a stupor, but it's worse because you—"

"Don't you dare bring Marigold into this," Calliope interrupted, her voice venomously calm. "Grim said—"

"Grim is a *book,*" Thalia snarled. "You think some darkness is threatening us? This town? It's *you.*"

The moment the words were out of her mouth, her eyes went wide, and Calliope took a step back.

"You don't have to believe me," Calliope said quietly, "but it'd be nice if you trusted me for once. We may not know what happens if those enchantments break, but I, for one, don't want to find out. I'll stop it with or without your help."

It was only after she'd stormed out of the kitchen that Calliope realized she hadn't even mentioned Lucien to them.

CHAPTER 9

CALLIOPE FLEW TO HER BEDROOM AND SLAMMED the door as a storm began to rage in earnest. Fat, heavy raindrops hit the windows, and a flash of purple lightning lit up the azure sky. Astro, who had been sleeping on her bed, lifted her head imperiously, eyes tracking Calliope's movements as though questioning why she was there.

A moment later, there was a soft tapping on the door. She opened it to find Grim hovering at eye level, spine down, the pages flipping sadly back and forth.

"She didn't mean it," Calliope said in a quiet voice as soon as the door was closed.

Grim flew to the brass book stand on her vintage rolltop desk. It was timeworn but elegant and stood between the high windows. Half-burned candles were strewn about next to piles of crystals and incense, but the book never seemed to mind the mess. As she looked up at the dark morning sky, her thumb traced the carvings in the wooden window frame. There were intricate runes for sweet sleep and charms for silence she'd etched there as a teenager, so Thalia wouldn't hear her sneaking out.

She shoved away from the window, away from the swirling sky that mirrored her despair. Grim flipped to a blank page and began to fill it with text.

She's worried about you. And she's right. You shouldn't have attempted the spell on your own.

"And who was going to help me? Thalia doesn't use her magic anymore, as you're well aware, and Eurydice won't sacrifice any memory bigger than her morning coffee. It's only you and me." She lit the candles on her desk so that Grim was bathed in a warm light.

Grim's slanted writing began to fill up the page again. *You sacrificed needlessly. You know that your magic isn't supposed to be used like that, Opie. Your most powerful magic stems from the string of fate that connects you.*

She winced at the nickname, hating the way it fed into her guilt.

"I already heard it from Thalia. I don't need it from you, too." Calliope rubbed the heels of her palms against her eyes until red spots bloomed behind her eyelids.

What did you do yesterday?

"Right, yeah." She sat down hard in her desk chair and began to rake her fingers through her hair. "I get it, okay? I'm reckless. Is that so terrible?" She looked back at her four-poster bed and contemplated throwing herself onto it. The draperies, a light pistachio green to complement the emerald-green velvet duvet, swayed slightly even though there was no breeze.

Only if you're doing it because you don't want to remember, it wrote.

"You're the one who taught me, pígaine kai kópse to laimó sou. Remember?"

I often regret imparting my wisdom to you.

"Yeah, well." She laughed despite herself. "I agree: do everything you must about a situation, but do it now."

Grim didn't write anything for a minute, and Calliope began to shift uncomfortably. If the book were a person, she imagined their eyes would be narrowed about now.

You're keeping something from me, it wrote finally.

Calliope swallowed hard.

"Thalia freaked out not even knowing the worst of it," she said, and the truth spilled from her mouth. How she'd tried to fix the break in the enchantment and ended up binding herself to Lucien Deniz. "A Shadowcrafter," she said, her head falling into her hands. "And what was he doing there? Nothing good. I don't trust him. Can you tell me how to break the bond between us?"

I do not know how to break a bond such as this. I only know of the bond between Petridi sisters, the string of fate that connects you.

Calliope frowned. When she was younger, she'd loved the idea that she was tied to her sisters. Had begged Grim to tell her why they were connected in such a way when no other witches were. But it had no answers for her. Calliope had thought their string of fate made them special. Now, though, it seemed like more of a burden than anything else. Especially when she had this bond with Lucien to contend with.

Bonds are like curses, Grim continued. *They grow roots over time. I don't know how to fix it, but Opie, you must be careful. If you attempt to sever the bond . . . you don't know what the consequences will be.*

"It doesn't make sense. There was a whisper that chased me in the Forgotten Forest." She repeated the words to Grim and frowned over the last two lines. "'With magic woven, strings so fine, Shadow and Light shall never align,'" she repeated. "But we *did* align. I broke that rule by somehow binding us together."

Perhaps this is just the first piece of the puzzle, Grim wrote.

"Puzzle or no, I'll figure out how to break this bond one way or another, and damn the consequences," Calliope said, seething. And the sooner the better.

Grim had fluttered its pages to show its displeasure when there was another knock at her door.

"Go away," she said without thinking, feeling like she was a teenager again and Thalia was there to reprimand her about sneaking out.

"It's me," came Dissy's soft reply.

"Fine, come in then."

Dissy entered with a mug of tea in her hands.

"Serenity brew," she said, handing the cup to Calliope. She didn't frown at the mess as Thalia would have done. Instead, she sat cross-legged on the ground by the pile of clothes and began to fold. Calliope closed her eyes and inhaled the steam from her mug. Chamomile, lavender, and lemon balm with a hint of rose and honey. She drank, letting the warmth seep into her hands.

"There's something you're not telling us," Dissy said softly, her eyes trained on the shirt she was folding to within an inch of its life. "You don't have to tell me, not yet. I don't blame you after the way we didn't listen. I'm sorry, Opie. Sorry that we didn't believe you."

"But now you do?" Calliope asked, hope making her voice bright and sharp as an arrow.

"That fire last night," Dissy said, holding up different pairs of socks and trying to find matching ones. "I've never felt anything like it. This isn't an excuse, but I'm not attuned to our magic the way you are. And Thalia is even less connected. She used her magic for the first time last night, trying to fight those flames. And I think she feels like she betrayed herself, betrayed the promise she made to herself after Mother left. And she hates herself for it because she's so scared of becoming like her. But it's easier to take it out on you than it is to look too closely at the why. Anyway, I think that lack of connection is why it took me longer to feel what you were feeling. That dark presence seeping in. But yes, I do believe you."

Calliope exhaled a breath that made her lungs burn. These were the words she had longed to hear, but the guilt of her secret bond with Lucien ate at her. Thalia and Dissy were so out of tune with their magic, she didn't know when, if ever, they'd realize their string of fate was compromised. If she could figure out how to break the bond with Lucien, perhaps they'd be none the wiser that it had begun to fray in the first place. Still, she pushed the thoughts away, not wanting to disturb this tenuous peace.

"Thank you," Calliope said simply.

"Have I mentioned how much I hate that you don't have any matching socks?" Dissy asked, and Calliope laughed weakly.

"What do we do now, if Thalia still doesn't believe?" Calliope asked. "How do we fix the enchantments?"

Eurydice pursed her lips as she folded a pair of sparkly leggings.

"If the Dark Oak is awakening, there's no way she'll be able to not use her magic. I think she's afraid to accept that. She's angry with you not just for going to the Dark Oak, but because it put you in danger. And fear makes fools of us all.

For now, though, we go to work. And maybe, Opie, perhaps, you could try to give her some grace."

After Dissy left the room, Grim following her, Calliope warred with guilt and anger, wishing Thalia could see she was only trying to help. She thought of Dissy's sweet nature, the way she could always defuse her sisters' anger. Dissy was gentle, yes, but it was led by a steely resolve that commanded respect from both Thalia and Calliope. Full of love, but also logic. And maybe, if Calliope could take Dissy's lead, Thalia would forgive her. If she forgave her, perhaps she'd be more willing to listen. It went against Calliope's nature, but at this point, she was willing to try anything if it meant protecting the Dark Oak and their beloved town.

She reached inside herself, feeling for the connection to her sisters, and her heart stuttered when it felt even thinner than it had that morning. But there, amid the light and power, pulsed the thread of Lucien's magic, mixed with hers. She pushed back against it, imagined a pair of shears cutting that dark thread that bound them, but the shears bounced off. If she could just . . . She gave one last push, but when the shears made contact, her body crumpled, and she cried out in agony. The pain vanished as soon as she left the bond alone.

Her curtains swished, and Lucien appeared. Calliope stifled a scream.

"Next time you do that, I'm going to lob the nearest ceramic at your head," she said, pushing to her feet, her heart beating too fast. If he'd appeared only a minute earlier, Dissy would have seen him. At Lucien's appearance, Astro jumped off the bed and trotted toward him. She sniffed his legs and then, the absolute traitor that she was, began to rub her head against his shins and weave through his legs. Calliope could hear her purring from across the room.

"At least one of you can tolerate me," Lucien said, bending down to run a large hand across Astro's fur. The cat arched her back, her tail swishing happily back and forth. "You, on the other hand . . ." He straightened. "I cannot think with the incessant chaos that you're sending down our bond," he said darkly, crossing his arms over his chest. Calliope tried not to focus on the muscles flexing in his forearms or the freshly spiced scent emanating from him. She trained her eyes on his face instead, silently begging her cheeks not to blush. He looked fresh from a shower, hair neatly combed, the tips of it curling up, and his shirt perfectly pressed with the sleeves rolled up. He wore a gold ring set with onyx on his index finger, a signet ring on his ring finger, and a simple band on his pinky. A gold chain hung around his neck with a small druzy pendant. Everything about him was elegant yet dangerous, from his clean-shaven face showcasing his sharp cheekbones to the way he carried himself so effortlessly that it made her heart catch in her chest. Everything about him called to her in a way that sent her stomach spiraling and warmth gathering between her thighs. His otherworldly beauty went against every image Calliope had of Shadowcrafters. Though, admittedly, she'd never actually met one.

Calliope matched his crossed-arm stance. "The sooner we get rid of this bond, the better. Have you come up with any ideas yet?"

Lucien regarded her carefully.

"You've not yet told your sisters about me," he noted instead of answering. "It's causing turmoil among you. This is why you've been talking in circles in your head, no?"

"You can hear my thoughts?" Calliope demanded, horror-stricken.

"I can feel the nature of your thoughts. Your mood. You could feel mine as well if you weren't so consumed with your own problems. Or perhaps if your magic were stronger." He shrugged nonchalantly. The man was infuriating.

"You," she said, stalking toward him. "My mother warned us away from Shadowcrafters, and now I know why, Lucien Deniz."

"Because she knew you'd recklessly bind yourself to one when your Lightcraft wasn't strong enough to do the job?" he challenged, arching a single thick brow. Up close, his brown eyes seemed even darker. He stared down at her, his pupils dilated.

"She said you're all arrogant." She poked him in the chest. "Dangerous." She poked him again. "And untrustworthy." She went to poke him one last time, but he caught her wrist before she could.

"She failed to mention quick and powerful," he said with a wicked grin. His grip on her was loose but threatened to pull tighter if she moved away, and she silently hoped he didn't feel her pulse fluttering in her wrist. "It sounds like your mother had one bad run-in with a Shadowcrafter and tainted her daughters' view toward the rest of them because of it. We're not all the same, you know."

Calliope stared at him and hated that she was wondering if he was right. But those warnings ran deep. And she remembered her mother's earnest eyes when she spoke. She wouldn't have said it unless she believed it with every ounce of her being.

His eyes dropped to where he gripped her wrist, and when

they caught on the burn mark there, they darkened, his lips pursing, but he said nothing.

"You didn't know my mother," she said, wrenching her arm away from his grip, breathing hard. Harder than the situation warranted. Her wrist throbbed where he'd touched her. The same spot where the shadow had burned her in her dream.

"Sounds like I wouldn't want to," he said. "If she was that prejudiced against something she didn't know anything about."

"Get out," Calliope said, vehemence coating her words like poison.

"I know," he answered, voice calm and level. "You've made your position clear, little muse. I'll simply be waiting for you to ask for help. In the meantime, perhaps try not to attempt any other spells beyond your power. We don't want any more forest fires, do we?"

He stared at her for a beat, his eyes burrowing into hers. He was seeing too much of her. Counting the bricks in the walls she'd built around her heart. She shivered, and then he was gone.

She shook it off, rolled her shoulders, but the sensation of his touch still lingered. She refused to let his accusation get to her.

Her phone pinged with a message.

ARE YOU OKAY? Danny had messaged with a dozen fire emojis.

Fine, Calliope messaged back. *Only suffering from the heat of Thalia's indignation.*

I nearly had a heart attack when I stopped by Whisk and Spoon and all everyone was talking about was the fire by Lethe.

Let me guess, you got the almond croissant? Calliope typed. *You know you're going to turn into an almond one of these days.*

If only I could be so lucky. And stop trying to dodge. I expect a call later.

Aye aye, Captain Almond.

Danny sent back a middle finger emoji followed by a dozen croissants.

Calliope smiled and opened her thread with Roz and fired off a quick text asking to meet her at Tea and Tome.

I'll be there with bells on, Roz texted back.

Taking a last deep breath and draining the dregs of the Serenity tea, Calliope squared her shoulders and went back down to the kitchen.

Eurydice greeted her as she entered the kitchen, her voice like a gentle breeze. "We decided that the best way to move forward is to start the morning over. Right, Thalia?"

Thalia studiously looked anywhere but at Calliope and begrudgingly nodded.

"Okay," Calliope said, drawing the word out. "Good morning, then."

"Good." Dissy nodded, pleased. "Now, I thought some scones might lift our spirits. Baked them for Tea and Tome, but we should probably sample them." She smiled, and Calliope, ever grateful for her sister's peacekeeping ways, took one off the tray.

"No, thank you," Thalia responded coldly. "We'd better get going if we want to open on time. If, that is, Calliope doesn't plan on setting any more forests on fire."

"Thalia," Dissy chided gently.

"It's okay." Calliope stopped her with a hand on her arm. "I know I was reckless and stupid. I didn't know what I did at the Dark Oak would start that fire. But I could have burned down Lethe Manor—hell, the whole town. I should have waited. I'm sorry."

Thalia pursed her lips, finally staring at Calliope. She didn't speak, didn't offer forgiveness, but she gave a curt nod. And that, Calliope knew, was as much as she was going to get for now.

"Good job," Dissy whispered, knocking her shoulder gently into Calliope's.

"Just trying to be more like you, dear sister." Calliope sighed, watching Thalia's retreating back as she left the kitchen. "But you make it look easy."

"You don't need to be like me," Dissy said. "You need to be you."

"Perhaps easier said than done. Sometimes it feels like I don't know who that person is. Or at least, who I want her to be."

"Keep looking," Dissy said with a soft smile. "You'll find her, I promise."

CHAPTER 10

IN UNEASY SILENCE, THE THREE SISTERS MADE their way through the picturesque streets of Gold Springs's historic Old Town. The storm had passed, and the air was warmer today, the last frost of winter having finally relinquished its spindly grip. Spring painted its pastel brushstrokes over the charming buildings and cobblestone pathways. Snowdrops and narcissus could be seen sprouting up in the flower beds, waving their green fronds in a cheery hello. Usama Muhammad and his daughter, Tamir, were unloading a set of battered antique chairs from the bed of his rusty old pickup truck and taking them into their store, Timeless Treasures. Usama and Tamir scoured estate sales far and wide looking for pieces to restore, and the sisters had gotten most of their furniture for Tea and Tome from them. Tamir smiled at the sisters and gave them a small wave.

"Those are going to be a pair of beauties when you're done with them," Dissy called out as they walked by. "Need any help?"

"Oh no, no," Usama said, wiping his brow with his shirt-sleeve. He was in his mid-forties with strong arms, broad shoulders, and a kind smile. "Thank you for the offer, but you ladies have your own work to get to, I'm sure. Tamir and I can handle this."

"Stop by Tea and Tome later," Dissy said. "I'll make you a restorative brew, so your muscles aren't sore tomorrow!"

"Dissy," Calliope hissed, hooking her arm through her sister's and yanking her close. "If she wanted to stop by, she would. We haven't really spoken since Marigold left. It's already awkward enough." Tamir had been close friends with Marigold, and one of the downsides of the breakup was that Calliope had lost Tamir, too. Neither of them quite knew how to continue on without her. Marigold had moved to Portland but still came back to visit Tamir, and Calliope wondered if Tamir had seen her recently.

"It's only awkward if you let it be," Dissy chided gently. "If you want to be friends, be friends."

"What's the point?" Calliope asked, though she said it so quietly that Dissy didn't hear her. But then the sound of footsteps hitting pavement had her turning to find Tamir running up to her.

"Can I talk to you for a sec?" she asked.

Calliope's heart bottomed out, and she told Dissy she'd meet her up ahead. Dissy looked reluctant to leave, but Thalia pulled her away.

"So," Tamir said, taking a deep breath. "I just thought you should know that Marigold is coming back for a visit. She left some things in our storage unit and is driving out to pick them up."

"Ah," Calliope said, nodding like this was normal, everyday news. "Yes, excellent. Thanks. For that." She began braiding her hair, needing something to do with her hands, and Tamir kindly averted her eyes from Calliope's trembling fingers. "I mean, we're adults, after all. If we happen to run into each other, which you know is kind of probable here, then we can be friendly."

"Okay, well, yeah. I just wanted you to know, so, I guess I'll see you later then." Tamir turned to walk away, but Calliope grabbed her arm.

"Hey," she said. "Thanks. For letting me know. And I . . . I'm sorry we don't, you know . . . I'm sorry things fell apart after she left. That I fell apart."

Tamir shrugged. "Adult friendships are hard. And weird. There's so much politics to navigate even when you don't want to take sides. But for what it's worth, I miss having you as a friend." And then she turned back to the store and was gone.

Calliope had spent two years loving Marigold, but that love wasn't enough. She still couldn't tell her the truth of who she was or why she couldn't remember things like their anniversary or what they'd had for dinner the night before. But even now, Calliope's heart beat fast as bird wings. She saw Marigold in her mind. Pixie-short hair always dyed a different color. Her pert, upturned nose and high cheekbones. Blue eyes that sparkled and brightly painted lips that could quote every line from every Reese Witherspoon movie ever created. Jewel-toned dresses and magazine-worthy makeup. She was always perfectly put together, and she certainly didn't believe in mismatched socks. They were opposites in every way, but hadn't they complemented each other? Or was Marigold just another project in a long line of Calliope's efforts to fill the hole in her heart left by her mother? Calliope didn't blame Marigold for leaving her. She knew she couldn't give enough of herself to their relationship because she'd already sacrificed too much, but it didn't take away the sting of loneliness.

By the time she caught up with Thalia and Dissy, her hands were clammy and her mind was sticky with the few memories of Marigold she hadn't already sacrificed.

In the central square, the gazebo shone with a fresh coat of white paint. The fountain sparkled in the sun as children played tag around its basin, their laughter glimmering like jewels. Families sat outside Whisk and Spoon sipping iced coffees and lemonade, mothers made their way to Danny's yoga studio with mats tucked beneath their arms, and visitors took photos of every charming storefront and patch of flowers. Spring here was more than a season. It was rebirth. But it was hard for Calliope to drink in the beauty of it all. The news of Marigold's return weighed heavily on her and was compounded by the secret she was keeping from her sisters.

But once inside the walls of Tea and Tome, with the smell of tea and books enveloping her, Calliope thought, *Maybe, just maybe, we'll be okay after all.*

As she got to work, Calliope watched her sisters—Thalia smiling at a customer, Dissy laughing her cotton-candy laugh—and hope unfurled even as it was followed by talon-sharp guilt that she still hadn't told them about Lucien. *Later,* she thought. When she had a firm grip on how to break their bond and restore the string of fate. Even now, as she felt for that connection to her sisters, she could tell it was growing thinner.

Now customers began to trickle in, and the shop buzzed with the chatter of locals and tourists alike, seeking respite and a taste of the magical brews. Several of the regulars asked about the fire last night. Gold Springs wasn't a town where something like a small forest fire could go unmentioned.

Divya Hayes, in particular, was difficult to appease. She stormed into the shop with a purpose for ranting and wouldn't be denied. "I tell you, these wildfires get worse every year," she grumbled. "Smoke so thick you could chew on it. And it's not even summer yet! I have half a mind to leave California and never come back. Maybe I'll go to Florida. John would love that," she said in reference to her husband, who said one word for every fifty of Divya's. "Then again, they have hurricanes to deal with."

"Plus, we'd miss you too much if you left," Dissy said. "And then you wouldn't be able to try my new tea blend. I added chai masala like you recommended."

"Oh, you know just how to get to me. Be a dear and pour me a cup," Divya said, her wrinkles stretching as she smiled.

Calliope smiled at Dissy, who winked at her as she turned to the teakettle.

Calliope continued to steal glances at Thalia as she helped customers choose books or served tea in delicate patterned cups with mismatched saucers. And all the while, she thought, *How, how, how? How do I break this bond with Lucien?*

The bell over the door chimed, and Calliope knew who it was before she even looked up. The hard knot in her chest unfurled just a little at seeing Rosalind sweep into the shop.

"You said you'd be here with bells on. Where are they?" Calliope demanded with a smile.

"Darling, I am nothing if not a woman of my word," Roz said, pulling up her long skirt and showing her ankle, where a silver anklet adorned with tiny bells jingled merrily. Calliope laughed. "Now, tell me what's going on."

"Let me get you something to drink first," Dissy said as Rosalind approached the counter and Calliope joined her.

Rosalind leaned in, almost conspiratorially. "Perhaps a cup of Serendipity Spice might help me uncover the truth behind last night's fire. Didn't you once tell me it's supposed to reveal secrets hidden in the flames?" She winked at Dissy, whose eyes twinkled.

There was something about Roz that brought a spirit of merriment wherever she went. Soon, fragrant steam rose from the teacup, a harmonious dance of cinnamon, cloves, and a hint of cardamom.

As the sisters gathered around Rosalind, the air danced with a sense of anticipation. The shop seemed to hold its breath, its walls absorbing the secrets that were whispered through the air.

Calliope leaned closer, unable to keep quiet a moment longer. "Rosalind, what did you sense about last night?"

Rosalind took a sip of the steaming tea, savoring it before she answered.

"Oh, my dear, the flames have their secrets, but they also have a way of revealing hidden truths. That fire was not a happenstance born from your wayward magic." She ran a loving hand down Calliope's hair. "I'm not sure exactly what this all means, but it's obvious you three are at the center of it."

The sisters fell silent, and Roz looked among them with her eyebrows raised.

"You girls aren't usually this quiet," she said. "What aren't you telling me?"

Thalia's expression hardened as Dissy's turned to concern. But Calliope cleared her throat and haltingly whispered a brief history of the Dark Oak and what little they knew about it. Rosalind listened intently, eyes wide, her full lips pulled into a frown.

"I've felt a darkness trying to get in," Calliope finished finally. "Grim agreed, and—" She paused when Dissy laid a calming hand on her arm.

Rosalind placed her teacup gently on the table, her gaze fixed upon the Petridi sisters.

"Those flames were but a prelude to something much larger, my dears. The town's magic is shifting, and it seeks solace in your hands. Embrace your destiny, for the threads of fate are woven within you."

"Oh, really?" Thalia retorted, a touch of defensiveness in her voice. "The town's magic seeking solace in our hands? The Petridis' enchantments have been protecting this town for generations. They've held strong all this time, and I have no doubt they'll endure unless Calliope continues on this path."

"And if you're wrong?" Calliope demanded.

"I'm not," Thalia answered, her lips pursing.

Calliope let out a moan of frustration. "If those enchantments break, hell will be *unleashed*," Calliope said, her voice dripping with anger as she locked eyes with Thalia. And then, taking a deep breath, she finally told them about the voice she'd heard in the Forgotten Forest as she went to the Dark Oak, now that it seemed possible they might believe her. She recited the verses easily. They'd been seared into her brain.

Through each enchantment's whispered lore
Three sisters guard, forevermore
But when darkness comes, a curse is spoken
And all is lost if their bond is broken
The air ablaze with demon's calls

At last, at last, the Dark Oak falls
With magic woven, strings so fine
Shadow and Light shall never align.

Dissy's eyes were wide as Calliope spoke, but Thalia's face remained stony and impassive. Roz, meanwhile, looked worried.

"And?" Thalia asked, raising her eyebrows and pursing her lips.

"*And?*" Calliope echoed in disbelief, her voice rising higher than she meant it to in her anger because, again, they were back to this.

"Whose bond will be broken? Ours?" Dissy asked, and Calliope's stomach dropped. She realized now that the words could reference the bond with her sisters or the one between her and Lucien, which they still didn't know about. But those verses had been spoken *before* she'd bonded with Lucien, which pointed to the former.

"I don't know," Calliope answered tightly. "None of it makes sense, but if the words are to be believed and the Dark Oak falls . . . who knows what would be unleashed?" She shuddered. "We have to do everything in our power to stop it."

"That's just it, though: How do you know this disembodied voice *can* be trusted?" Thalia whispered fiercely. "Maybe it was planted to make you think—"

"Think *what?*" Calliope cried. "No one else knows about the Dark Oak!" *Except Lucien,* a quiet voice echoed in her head.

"Keep your voice down," Thalia grumbled, glancing at the patrons in the store. "They may accept our shop, but they won't accept actual witches." And it was true. The town was unaware of real magic in its midst, and certainly unaware of the Dark Oak and the enchantments. And they were safer that way.

"Thalia is right," Roz said. "If there's one thing I've learned, it's that while people may come to me to see their past and their future, they still want to believe that they're in control of their present. They'll do anything to explain away the supernatural. Silly, of course. There's only so much we can actually control. But they wouldn't take kindly to, shall we say, the way you look after Gold Springs."

"They wouldn't believe it even if the evidence was right in front of their face," Thalia agreed. Calliope bit back the urge to point out the irony of the statement.

"If people come to you for the future, can't you see the *town's* future?" Calliope asked Roz.

"I'm afraid not. No tea leaves or palms to read for a bunch of buildings and land, my sweet. But I did readings for each of you, and they all said the same thing. Change is coming, and your strength lies in approaching it together."

Calliope closed her eyes and clenched her fists so hard she almost drew blood. The pain felt good. Grounded her. But it wasn't enough to detract from the fact that the enchantments were weakening, and that she'd accidentally bound herself to a Shadowcrafter.

"It's time to start asking more questions," Roz said now, her voice firm but kind. "You've enforced those enchantments for years without knowing what they contain. Long ago you told me your mother mentioned a curse. Speak with Grim, search the library at Lethe Manor. Find out everything you can. Information will be your best weapon here."

Thalia crossed her arms. "We already did that when our mother left."

"Maybe this time something new will reveal itself to you," Roz said.

"I wish we could talk to her," Calliope said, pursing her lips to stop them from quivering.

"Only the future knows the past." Rosalind gave them a sad smile. "Now, my dear girls," she said, sipping the last of her tea. "Speaking of the future, I see a vanilla scone in mine and a walk down to the river."

Roz bid them farewell, and the conversation hung heavily in the air, a tense silence settling among the sisters that Calliope itched to fill with idle chatter. But now Thalia was refusing to look at her, and Dissy was lost in her own thoughts. Calliope would lose it if she stayed still for another minute.

"I'll be back," Calliope called to her sisters, wrapping a burnt-umber knit scarf around her neck.

As she walked, Calliope saw familiar faces everywhere. The townspeople smiled as she passed, and Mrs. Jenkins stopped her outside her plant shop, Botanic Dreams, to tell her the begonias Eurydice ordered had finally come in. Across the street, Mr. Thompson tipped his hat from where he sat in his old rocking chair. She waved and kept walking, knowing he'd rope her into one of his long-winded fishing stories if she so much as slowed down.

The townspeople of Gold Springs had become an extended family to her after her mother left, and their welfare and happiness held almost too much significance. She took pride in the town's traditions, from the town meetings and holiday festivals to the way everyone seemed to know your business even when you didn't want them to.

And already, preparations were under way for her favorite night of the year. The Moonlight Masquerade, less than two weeks away, was a night to celebrate Ostara, the spring equinox. For even though Gold Springs didn't know about magic, they still loved to celebrate pagan holidays. And Ostara was a time to honor the spring's warmth and the awakening of the earth. As the moon rose high in the night sky, townsfolk would gather in the central square, dressed in elaborate costumes adorned with flowers and masks obscuring their features. Twinkling fairy lights would decorate trees and bushes, and a large bonfire crackled in the center, casting warmth and dancing shadows upon the revelers. There would be booths for Potion Tasting, which were elaborate cocktails, and Fairy Cakes, which were just baked treats from Whisk and Spoon bakery. She'd loved that festival since she was a little girl.

But her excitement was overshadowed by her argument with Thalia. Stubbornness was a Petridi trait, and while it usually seemed like a superpower, it also happened to be their downfall. But more than that, she still hadn't told them about Lucien, and the lie formed a pit in her stomach that made her queasy.

She watched Mr. Johnson on the tall ladder, attempting to hang a HAPPY SPRING! sign. He leaned out too far, and her heart leapt into her throat. As though in slow motion, the ladder began to scrape sideways against the building. No one was paying attention to him; no one saw the look of terror on his face as his arms windmilled and he began to fall.

Without thinking, Calliope sacrificed the first memory that came to mind—her fight with Thalia, the frustration, the fear, the anger—and sent a spell on the wind to right the ladder. Mr. Johnson looked around wildly before slowly climbing down.

"Did you see that?" he said to his wife once he was safe on solid ground.

"See what?" she asked.

"Never mind," he said, shaking his head in disbelief. "You wouldn't believe me if I told you."

Calliope smiled to herself and kept walking. Her steps were lighter, freer. She still remembered what she and Thalia had been arguing about, but the bitterness was gone. The frustration was replaced with a sense of hope.

She would confront the looming darkness, even if *she* was the darkness that threatened to tear it all apart. As she soaked in the vibrant colors of spring, she reaffirmed her commitment to preserving those enchantments, come what may.

But as she stood on the sidewalk with her freshly sacrificed memory, her thoughts grew hazy. What had she just been doing? She couldn't quite remember . . . Something was calling her. A distant whisper. The world around her faded, and there was a tug in the center of her chest. Her willpower slipped away, and her limbs moved of their own accord as she followed the voice that was calling her, still unable to discern what it was saying.

She stumbled over the curb, and the last thing she heard was the blare of a car horn before everything went black.

CHAPTER 11

"CALLIOPE," A VOICE CALLED TO HER, BUT IT sounded far away. "Calliope!" They called her name again, more frantic this time. It was a familiar voice that made her think of gin and tonics, midnight laughter, and comfort. "If you don't snap out of it right now, I'm going to see if slapping you does the trick. I've already called your sisters."

That, more than anything else, brought reality crashing down. Calliope's vision slid into focus, and she saw Danny staring at her with a worried look in their dark eyes.

"Damn, woman," Danny said, exhaling a long breath. "Are you trying to give me a heart attack?"

"I . . . what happened?" Calliope asked, dazed.

"What happened? What happened is I saw you out here on the sidewalk and you almost walked into the street. I ran out to knock some sense into you, but before I could, someone seemed to materialize out of thin freaking air and did the job for me. Grabbed you and pulled you back. And by the time I reached you, he'd vanished again. It was like you were in some kind of trance."

"I don't . . . I don't even remember walking here." Fear bit hard and cold into Calliope's heart. The faded scar on her wrist from the shadow dream pulsed in pain. And no matter how hard she tried to trace the events that led her here, she couldn't find the thread. Was this what her mother had felt like? *Why* couldn't she remember? Though she knew who'd pulled her back. Lucien. He'd saved her. Again.

"Come inside," Danny demanded, dragging her by the arm into the yoga studio. "And you're going to tell me everything on pain of death, you understand?"

And Calliope did. Slowly at first, and then all in a rush until the words were an exorcism that left her trembling. Danny knew the Petridis were witches, of course, but their eyes grew wide at Calliope's mention of the Dark Oak. Of the enchantments that Petridi women had enforced over generations. Of the Great Rift and the delineation between Lightcraft and Shadowcraft. By the time she was done, Calliope was finally able to draw a deep breath, and her shoulders loosened.

"You have to tell your sisters about the Shadowcrafter," Danny said at once, shoving a water bottle into Calliope's hands and practically forcing her to drink. "I mean it, Calliope. This isn't shit to mess around with! Rip the Band-Aid off and speak your truth or it will come back to bite you in the ass. Once they have the information, it's up to them what they do with it."

"I will, I will," Calliope mumbled. "Everything is just already so strained that I'm afraid if I tell them—"

"Tell who what?" Thalia demanded, striding through the yoga studio door wearing a frown, her honey-wheat hair blowing in the breeze. Dissy followed her with Grim tucked beneath her arm.

"Danny said something was wrong with you," Dissy said, rushing to Calliope and brushing a strand of hair back from her face. She rested the back of her hand against her sister's forehead as though checking for a fever.

"I'm fine," Calliope lied.

"You don't look fine," Dissy said softly. "You're pale as a sheet and your pupils are blown."

Calliope glanced at Danny, who gave her a look that said *go on*. Danny was the type of person who believed things were best gotten over with quickly.

Finally, Calliope filled them in on the full details of the dream and the burn on her wrist. "And, well, that's not all," Calliope continued, willing her hands to stop trembling. "When I went to the Dark Oak, I actually . . . met someone there." And she launched into the tale of the shadows that tried to attack her, how she'd tried to call on their string of fate to fight it, but they were too far away. And so, when she sensed that other magic, so powerful and raw, she drew from it, and in so doing simultaneously saved herself and forged an unwelcome bond with the person it belonged to.

"And who is this person?" Thalia asked, her voice deceptively calm. "What were they doing near the Dark Oak, Calliope? They must be a powerful practitioner, and now you've *bound* yourself to them?"

"I'm going to break it," Calliope said quickly. "Of course I am, I just have to figure out . . . how to do it first. And the thing is—" She paused, her eyes sliding to Danny, who gave her an encouraging nod. "His name is Lucien Deniz, and he's . . . a Shadowcrafter." She closed her eyes once the words were spoken. And even as she did, she could feel that bond with him pulsing. Taste its raw power. There was something almost tantalizing about it. When neither of her sisters spoke, she opened her eyes. Dissy's mouth hung open, her own eyes wide with concern. But Thalia's were narrowed, and she looked at her sister as though she were finally seeing her for the first time.

Grim flew out from under Dissy's arm and began to fly around the yoga studio, but no one paid the book any heed.

"Nothing you say could possibly make me feel worse than I already do, Thalia," Calliope said, dropping her head into her hands. "I was just trying to do the right thing. I didn't mean to—"

"Didn't mean to what? Put us all in jeopardy? Bind yourself to the very thing we've been warned against our entire lives? You lied to us." Her words cut to the marrow, and Calliope realized she was wrong. Her sister *could* make her feel worse. "You went against my wishes," she continued. "And you've reaped the consequences. Maybe now you'll finally learn your lesson." Thalia was breathing hard, and despite Calliope's guilt, anger rose unbidden to the surface.

"If you had believed me in the first place, I wouldn't have gone to the Dark Oak alone!" Calliope cried, shoving to her feet. Grim knocked insistently against her shoulder, but she shoved it away and focused on Thalia. "I *told* you something was coming. Those enchantments are the only thing keeping us safe, keeping this town safe from the jackals that would kill us all just to get a taste of that power. Shadowcraft covens, even Lightcraft witches. They'll all come seeking, Thalia. And what then? What happens if that kind of power is unleashed?"

"Are you hearing yourself?" Thalia laughed coldly. "*You* are the one who bound yourself to a Shadowcrafter. You're the one who started that fire. Who forced my hand and made me use my magic. I know there's darkness coming.

But what if you're the one who brought it on with all your meddling?"

"Listen," Danny said. "I hate to butt in on what's so obviously a moment of sisterly love and bonding, but that's my best friend you're talking about. Yeah, okay, she's a little reckless sometimes. But she's also terrified of you— No, Calliope, shut up," Danny said when Calliope opened her mouth to protest. "She's so obsessed with meeting your impossible standards, and you can't even see part of the reason she did this was to try to prove herself to you." Danny pushed their sleeves up, facing Thalia. "So why don't you lose the righteous attitude for a hot second and listen to your fucking sister?"

Thalia stared at Danny, her cheeks splotched with red. She started to speak but couldn't seem to find the words. The two were facing off, daring each other to see who would give in first. And then, Dissy giggled. All eyes swiveled to her.

"I'm sorry," she said breathlessly, wiping tears of mirth from her eyes as she tried to regain her composure. "But Danny's right. I wouldn't have said it quite that way, of course, but it is hard sometimes to live up to your expectations, Thalia." Her voice grew quieter, all traces of laughter gone. "And you're so perfect all the time that when we mess up, we're afraid you're going to judge us." As she spoke, Grim nudged her hand, but Dissy was staring at the floor.

"I am *not* perfect, and I don't judge you when you screw up!" Thalia said angrily. "The only problem I see here is that Calliope's bound herself in some idiotic move that—" She caught herself, realizing she was giving credence to the very thing Dissy had just accused her of. "That is to say, I mean— *What is it, Grim?*" she demanded as the book rapped its spine on the low table.

"If I had to wager a guess, I'd say that book has something to tell you," Danny said drily.

"Remind me why you're here again? Intruding on family matters?" Thalia demanded.

"Um, because you're in my studio," Danny said, entirely deadpan. "I called you here. Or did your memory curse make you forget?"

Thalia frowned. "What I don't *remember* is you being this much of a smart-mouth."

"Been thinking about my mouth, Thalia?" Danny asked, arching their eyebrow.

"I have not been doing any such thing," Thalia remarked, splotches of red appearing on her fair cheeks. Calliope would have laughed at the shocked expression on Thalia's face if it weren't for everything else. "Now, can we please get back to the matter at— Oh, for the love of the goddess, say what you need to say, Grim!" The book, which had been circling Thalia's head, began to knock into her forcefully.

Finally getting their attention, Grim hovered in place and fluttered open, and Calliope and the group converged in a small circle to read the book's slanted writing.

You must stop this fighting, it wrote. Thalia huffed, and Calliope rolled her eyes, but Grim continued. *It is driving a wedge between you, and it's more important now than ever that you remain united.*

"Why?" Calliope asked, feeling the need to hold her breath as more of Grim's words spilled across the page.

When three Petridi sisters are born, for it is always three, they are connected by a string of fate.

"We *know*," Thalia said starkly. "Mother gave us enough warnings about it."

"Maybe you should let the thing finish before interrupting," Danny said. Their tone was blithe, but their dark eyes were shining as they glared at Thalia. Calliope tore her eyes from Grim and stared between her sister and her best friend. Thalia wasn't used to being challenged, and Danny had spent the last decade building up their confidence. Even in the years since Calliope had first met them, they'd been on a journey of healing. Danny had always been firmly rooted in who they were, but the years of therapy and self-love had taught them to stand up for themself and the ones they loved. Calliope was honored to be on the receiving end of that love, but it was mildly terrifying to see someone finally standing up to Thalia on her behalf.

Thalia glared right back at Danny, but when Danny didn't look away or back down, Thalia shifted uncomfortably.

"Fine," she said brusquely. "Sorry. Please, go on, Grim."

This string fuels your magic and strengthens the protections around the Dark Oak, it wrote. *I don't know why, for it is not this way with any other witches. But I've always believed it has something to do with the curse that binds you to the Dark Oak. And if your string is broken or tainted in any way . . . your magic weakens. And so, too, do the protections over the Dark Oak. And the longer the string remains broken, the more your magic drains, the more you'll forget.*

"Oh, by the goddess." Calliope leaned back, eyes shutting tight. It felt like she couldn't get enough air. "I'd just done magic before everything went hazy and I almost walked into traffic. That must be why. Thalia was right. I *am* the darkness you warned about. This is all my fault. If I'd just left it alone—" She broke off with a muffled cry.

"If what you say is true," Thalia said calmly, "your bond with this Shadowcrafter is putting us all in jeopardy whether we like it or not. So, it seems we have no choice."

"No . . . choice?" Calliope asked. "No choice but to what? You're being ominous, sister. I'm sorry, okay? I'm sorry I brought this all on us—" But she broke off when Thalia pulled her into a tight hug, shocking Calliope so much that her arms hung stiff by her sides for a moment before she returned it.

"Danny is right," Thalia said, pulling back.

"They are?" Calliope asked.

"I am?" Danny echoed.

"I should have listened to you," Thalia said firmly. "We need to start researching how to break this bond and preserve our string, so we can fight whatever's coming. And in the meantime, we're going to meet this Shadowcrafter so we know what we're up against. This bond is inextricably tied to his magic. If we have any hope of severing it, we need to know more."

Calliope groaned. "We can figure this out by ourselves. I want nothing to do with Shadowcraft or him. He's surly and rude and obviously looks down on us. The little witches of Gold Springs with their faulty memory magic."

"Did he say any of that?" Dissy questioned with a raised eyebrow.

"He didn't have to," Calliope said, frowning as she remembered his arrogance, the downturn of that plush mouth.

"Maybe he's not as terrible as he seems," Dissy said.

"Dissy," Calliope said sharply. "Don't get me wrong, I love your sunshine and optimism, but he's a *Shadowcrafter*."

"A Shadowcrafter that's bound to you," Thalia said. "We don't have to trust him, but we do need to meet him." She used her oldest sister voice, and that, as far as she was concerned, was that.

"Shadow daddy dinner date," Danny said, wiggling their

eyebrows. Calliope made a sound of disgust in the back of her throat.

"And we should tell Roz, too," Dissy said. "She might be able to help."

"Tomorrow," Thalia said. "I'll text Roz so she can be there."

"Shouldn't we do it tonight?" Calliope asked. "There's too much at stake to risk waiting."

"The enchantments have held for this long, they'll hold for another day," Thalia answered briskly. "Tomorrow we're hosting the book club at Tea and Tome, and then we'll have a meeting at home before he arrives to organize our thoughts and questions. Calliope, you make sure Lucien is there for dinner."

"Do we have to feed him? It feels too . . . *civilized*," Calliope complained. "Can't we just tie him up and demand he tell us everything he knows?"

"I rather think tying him up might defeat the whole purpose of getting him to work with us willingly," Thalia said archly.

"Yes," Calliope said. "But think how much fun it would be."

CHAPTER 12

THE FOLLOWING EVENING, THALIA AND EURYDICE lounged on the squashy leather couch in the front room of Lethe Manor, and Calliope sat with her legs crossed in the brocade chair by the fireplace. The thick green curtains were pulled back, the soft light of dusk filtering through the immense windows. A low mist was creeping over the grounds, typical for spring in California when the weather couldn't quite decide if it wanted to move on from winter. Grim rested on the low table between them, opened to a blank page. Beside it were three steaming cups of Witch's Wisdom tea. The earthy scents of rosemary, peppermint, and lemon balm filled the air, and Calliope dropped a heaping dollop of local orange blossom honey into hers and stirred.

"Our goal here is to break the bond so we can keep hold of our magic and protect the Dark Oak," Thalia said, taking charge as always. Fen was on her lap, eyes closed as Thalia ran an idle hand down her fur.

"But once the bond is broken, how do we *do* that?" Calliope asked, bouncing her knee, unable to keep still even when sitting.

"Let's start from the beginning. Everything we know. Grim can fill us in on anything we're missing," Thalia said.

"It's been the Petridis' sacred mission to protect the Dark Oak as long as we've been in Gold Springs. But Mother never really talked about our grandmother or our ancestors." Dissy tilted her head, gray eyes wide and wondering.

"And what about Mother's warnings? How much of them can we actually trust if she'd lost most of her memories?" Thalia said.

"Her warnings only ever came when she was herself," Calliope said, her hackles raising slightly. She wasn't sure why she was defending her mother after she'd abandoned them, but still, the desire was there.

"Never trust a Shadowcrafter," Dissy said.

Thalia nodded. "Protect our string of fate and stay away from the Dark Oak."

"Where did the Dark Oak *come* from, though?" Calliope asked. "We know nothing about the curse or the enchantments or what it contains."

"Two hundred years of Petridi women keeping the enchantments in place with their string of fate. Always three sisters."

"Wait a second. How did Mother do magic if she was the only sister alive?" Calliope asked. "She never spoke of her sisters, and weren't they already gone before I was born?"

"Their string was broken then?" Dissy asked. "That . . . makes sense." Calliope remembered the glassy look Penelope's eyes would get. It seemed like a prophecy of her own future.

"Aunt Lyra and Aunt Daphne died after you were born," Thalia said to Calliope. "But you were so little you wouldn't remember them."

"Do either of you remember them?" Calliope asked. "Because if we can find out how Mother continued to do magic despite their string being broken, we can do the same thing!" Her voice pitched higher as she spoke, a spark of hope flaring in her chest.

"I remember Daphne was the youngest," Dissy said, "but that's about it."

"She used to read me bedtime stories," Thalia said. "And Aunt Lyra would play hide-and-seek with me for hours. If I found her, she'd teach me a spell."

"Do you remember how they died?"

"I . . ." Thalia shook her head as though to clear it. "I can't remember," she whispered.

"Grim?" Calliope asked. "Do you know or remember anything about our aunts?"

At this, Grim stilled, falling open to a blank page.

I don't remember, it wrote, the letters appearing almost reluctantly.

"Don't remember, my foot!" Calliope cried, placing her hands on the pages to stop the book from snapping closed.

"There's magic at work here," Thalia said. "I can feel it. Some kind of memory block."

"Great," Calliope muttered. "Just what we need. More secrets we don't understand."

Grim didn't answer, and Calliope knew there was nothing more to be done other than the thing she dreaded. Inviting the Shadowcrafter to dinner. Roz would be arriving any minute, too, and she bounded up the stairs before she lost her nerve.

"Lucien," she said, finally in the quiet of her room. Nothing happened. "Lucien!" Still, he didn't appear. And then she started saying his name in her mind. Over and over again. She yelled it and sang it and shouted it in the confines of her own head.

Still, when he materialized in front of the fireplace, she screamed, slapping a hand over her heart. His hair was rumpled, and the few buttons he'd done up were mismatched so his shirt hung crooked. She looked away from the slice of chest and tried to ignore the image of pressing her lips there, but it was seared into her mind.

"Do you have a death wish, little muse?" he demanded, breathing heavily.

"Is that supposed to sound threatening? You can't even button your shirt properly," she said, gesturing to the shirt in question. Her words were calm, but her heart was hammering, and annoyingly, her palms began to sweat.

"Have you found a way to break the bond?" he asked.

"I've run through a dozen different ideas," she said. "A spell to nullify the bond, sacrificing a memory to replace it, an elemental confluence, lunar rituals. But I don't know how your stupid magic works, so I don't know how to cut through it. My sisters want to meet you and see if we can find the solution together."

Lucien stood silently, and Calliope was about to tell him she'd changed her mind and he could go to hell when he finally spoke.

"I just want to be clear," he said slowly, taking a step toward her and enunciating each word so that his accent was harder to detect. "That what you're saying . . ." He paused again, took another step so he was towering over her, and Calliope stood her ground even as her pulse skipped and her throat was suddenly parched. "Is that you need my help."

She stared at him. Open-mouthed.

"You are the most—" She stopped, searching for the right word. "Arrogant. Infuriating. Annoying human being to ever walk this planet!"

Lucien watched her splutter, his mouth twitching in a strange way. And then, like he couldn't quite help it and wasn't sure he wanted to anyway, he laughed. It was a deep, rich sound that tickled Calliope's ears.

"What is *wrong* with you?" she demanded, shoving him hard in the chest, which only made him laugh harder. It was so at odds with his stoic demeanor that she didn't quite know what to do with it. "Why are you laughing? Are you hexed or something?"

"The only curse I have, little muse, is being bound to you," he said, still smiling. "Though it does provide a certain entertainment value. So perhaps it's not all bad. And yes, before you hurt yourself trying to hurt me, I will help you. However I can."

"Oh," Calliope said. It wasn't the answer she'd been expecting. She'd thought there'd be more pushback. Had been prepared to threaten or, at the very most, ask nicely. "Well, then, I guess it's time for you to meet my family."

Lucien followed her downstairs. In the kitchen, Dissy was busy at the stove while Roz pulled down ingredients for drinks and Thalia laid out plates. When Lucien cleared his throat, they all stopped and stared. But before Calliope could introduce him, Grim flew in and began to beat Lucien about the head with its binding.

"Control your book or I will rip the pages from its spine," Lucien growled, swatting at Grim.

"Grim, if you're going to attack him, at least do it where it'll bring him to his knees," Calliope said jokingly.

Grim dive-bombed toward Lucien's groin, and Calliope screeched, not thinking the book would actually do it. She grabbed its binding at the last second, her hand grazing dangerously close to Lucien's crotch. Grim beat its pages, trying to escape, but Calliope held it fast. "That's *enough*," she said. The grimoire relaxed in her hands. "You know very well I was teasing. Now, can I trust you to behave yourself?" Grim gave a noncommittal flap of its binding and then flipped its pages, the leather bookmark flying out like a tongue, so it looked like it was blowing a raspberry at Lucien.

"Welcome to Lethe Manor," Thalia said with a wicked gleam in her eyes. "We're not used to receiving Shadowcraft visitors."

"You're aware, yes, that if not for the little witch binding herself to me, she would be dead?"

"Prejudice is a finnicky thing," Thalia said with a shrug of her thin shoulders. "It often spits in the face of truth."

"That's Thalia," Calliope said with a sigh. "That's Dissy, and this is Rosalind. And I think you've met Grim," she added, gesturing to the book.

"I'm making sage and brown butter gnocchi," Dissy said, and Calliope smiled inwardly. Sage was known for its truth-telling properties. If Lucien had anything to hide, it would soon be out. Roz, meanwhile, was pulling the cocktail shaker and highball glasses down from the shelf.

"I think it's time for a drink," Roz said genially. "And if we're going to drink, we're going to drink properly, darlings. Now, get me the rosemary, Calliope. Thalia, fetch some ice, please," she added as she collected the bottle of simple syrup.

A few moments later, the clinking sound of ice against

metal and the fresh smell of gin and rosemary filled the kitchen. If they weren't there to discuss what felt like the end of the world, it might be a nice moment.

Roz poured the rosemary gin fizz into the highball glasses while Dissy browned the butter and set a pot to boiling.

The atmosphere was tense, but soon, the nutty smell of the browned butter rose in the air with the earthy, sweet scent of sage. Calliope ladled bowls of gnocchi and sliced a loaf of crusty cottage bread while Dissy pulled a bowl of salad from the fridge, and they all, save for Lucien, grabbed something and carried it over to the table. He stood off to the side, eyes tracking their movements. There was curiosity in his gaze, something almost wistful as he watched the women move seamlessly around the kitchen.

"What?" Calliope demanded, when she caught him staring.

"Do you do this . . . often?" he asked, his voice strained.

"A few times a week," Calliope said, tilting her head as she regarded him. "Why?"

"I've never . . ." He paused, cleared his throat. "This was not a common occurrence in my household. Or indeed, an occurrence at all."

"There's a first time for everything. Sit," Dissy said encouragingly. "Eat."

There was only one empty chair, and Lucien took it, which placed him directly next to Calliope. His broad shoulders entered into her space, and even over the scent of dinner in front of her, she detected his smell of apples and amber and something else, a smoky, decadent note she couldn't place.

Trying to ignore him, she took a bite. The butter and sage played across her tongue like a silent symphony, and she tried to contain her groan at how delicious it was, not realizing how ravenous she'd been. Calliope ate and ignored Lucien as he stared at the sisters as though they were creatures he couldn't quite understand. And she smiled inwardly when Dissy frowned at him and he dutifully began to eat as well. As the pasta warmed her stomach, and the gin fizz burned a delicious path down her throat, her head cleared.

"You added rosemary," Calliope said, her eyes narrowing at Dissy.

"Of course I did. Better?" Dissy asked.

"I'm not sure," Calliope answered, her eyes darting toward Lucien.

"Now that we're being civilized, can we get back to the topic at hand?" Thalia asked haughtily. "Why are you in town, Lucien? What could Gold Springs possibly hold for a Shadowcrafter like you?"

Lucien shifted uncomfortably, his eyes on the table. Calliope thought he would refuse to answer, but then he cleared his throat.

"I came here for my grandfather," he said plainly. "He wanted me to come visit Gold Springs, but I didn't know why. Always said he had some kind of connection to this place. Then when I saw you and your sisters, knew you were the only witches in town, I wondered if maybe your family had something to do with it. That's why I followed you, but I didn't know how to approach you because of this prejudice between Shadowcrafters and Lightcrafters."

"So, why now?" Calliope demanded.

"My grandfather died recently." He shrugged nonchalantly, but it looked a little too forced to be casual. "I suppose I wanted to honor his wish. He never left France. He was something of an eccentric, an experimentalist, if you will, and spent most of his time locked in his study. So now here I am, in his stead, trying to figure out what his connection to this place was."

Calliope stared at Lucien in shock. It was the most he'd ever uttered in one conversation.

"You'll forgive us, of course, if we question the truth of this story," Roz said amiably. "You see, there's coincidence, and then there's fate. And while the two aren't exclusive, you understand that your presence aligning with the Dark Oak awakening seems a little, shall we say, steeped in destiny."

"You don't have to trust me," Lucien said carefully. "I know you're protective of them and that their prejudices run deep. But I bear no ill will toward the Petridis and know nothing of what that tree holds."

Grim, who'd been sitting on the kitchen counter, flew to the table and opened to a blank page. They all leaned over as the ink began to flow.

I may not trust Shadowcrafters, but what's done is done. He must be brought in so he understands how dire the situation is.

Calliope looked at her sisters, who, after a brief pause, nodded. And then, Grim went on.

For generations, the enchantments were the only thing stopping witches from seeking the power of the Dark Oak. To keep those enchantments active, the sisters must use their string of fate. But your bond with Calliope renders that impossible.

"And those enchantments also conceal the Dark Oak, so the fact that a Shadowcrafter even knows it's there . . ." Calliope said, trailing off with a frown. "No one else can know."

If you truly bear them no ill will, Grim continued, *help Calliope break that bond so they can stop whatever evil is coming.*

"I will do what I can, but the bond is rooted in our respective magic, and in order to unravel it, I need to know more about yours," Lucien said gruffly.

"All magic comes from a well," Dissy said softly. "Light-craft practitioners draw on the well of nature, pulling from the earth's power."

"But ours is more convoluted than that because we're cursed," Calliope interjected with a frown. "Most Lightcraft witches can access that well of nature by will, but Petridis must sacrifice a memory to gain access to that same power."

"A memory curse," Lucien said, his eyes boring into Calliope's. And for some reason, the heat of his gaze was nearly too much to bear. She could see him unraveling her history, the questions burning away behind his dark eyes. But she refused to look away. "Very well," he continued. "Shadowcraft draws on the well of self, your soul. In a way it's like your memory curse. We use what's inside of us to fuel our magic, except our memories stay. But because of the way we draw on that well, our magic is intrinsically tied to us. Nature will only give you so much. It likes balance, knows when to stop you. But Shadowcraft? It imprints on our soul."

Calliope leaned back in her chair and huffed out a breath of air. A well of magic that came from your soul. Power without limitations. She wondered what it must be like, and part of her craved the endless possibilities.

"It's not what you're thinking," Lucien said flatly, cataloguing Calliope's wistful expression. "The balance rests with us, and if we tip the scales too far, the magic consumes us completely."

"Have you heard of anything like this happening before?" Dissy asked. "A bond between Lightcraft and Shadowcraft?"

Calliope remembered the words that had followed her through the Forgotten Forest, what seemed like so long ago now. *Shadow and Light shall never align.* What if this bond was impossible to break? What if, in one swift, foolish motion, Calliope had doomed them forever?

"I have not." Lucien frowned. "And you?"

They all shook their heads.

"Grim?" Calliope asked. "Is there any history of bonds between Lightcraft and Shadowcraft? Something we missed?"

Grim flipped open to a blank page and began writing.

There is something here, but I cannot reveal it. It feels . . . hidden.

Lucien stood, hovering his hand over the book.

"Être délié, montre toi." He spoke the words, his voice deep and low, and a breeze sang through the room, ruffling the grimoire's pages.

And then, the cover slammed closed and Grim stood straight up on its binding before flying off. Calliope jumped up and followed it, the others following suit, until they all stood in the living room.

"What did you do?" Calliope cried. "If you hurt this book, so help me goddess, I will—" She stopped when Lucien pointed to the grimoire, which had fallen onto the coffee table and opened to a page Calliope had never seen before. The paper looked older, the ink faded in places, with what seemed to be tear stains in the margins.

Petridi Family History, bound until needed. Read with caution.

Calliope looked to her sisters and Roz, and without so much as a hesitation, they all bent back over the book and began to read.

Once upon a summer moon, Alexia Petridi fell in love with a Shadowcraft practitioner. He took her heart as his, though in secret, he was promised to another. When Alexia discovered the truth, the very stars trembled at her rage. And in her heartbreak, she convinced her sisters to help her cast a spell that would curse this man and all future generations of his family. It was a formidable curse, and they needed power to fuel it. In the Forgotten Forest, there grew a tree, slumbering with ancient magic. They woke it up with promises and secrets. But the beacon of it, that magical surge of power, resounded through the land and brought all manner of creatures seeking its strength. Shadow- and Lightcraft users alike, as well as wraiths. And so, instead of powering their curse, they unleashed chaos. The sisters were forced to use the very power of the tree to create enchantments that would hide its power from those who would seek it. But magic seeks balance, and those actions had consequences. They bound the enchantments to their own descendants, to ensure they stayed intact. And Petridi memories became the price of the town's protection. With every spell they cast, with every ounce of magic they wielded, a memory would be sacrificed so that they would forget their bid for revenge and never try anything so foolish again.

Something was missing from this story, Calliope thought, though she couldn't put her finger on what. The words swirled in her mind like ink in water. Their curse, the Dark Oak, it all led back to Shadowcraft and Lightcraft. Thalia was the first one to speak.

"Why keep all this a secret?" she demanded. "If this is the truth, why have we never heard any of it before?"

"Probably because they knew others might try to exploit it," Calliope said. "The original sisters wanted to protect the town from their mistakes and the darkness they unleashed."

"They made the ultimate sacrifice to ensure the safety of Gold Springs, even if it meant condemning their future generations to bear the burden," Dissy said sadly. "And if the protections are weakened or broken, it will release that magic again."

"Yes, yes. 'Where magic gathers, there will be those who

seek to claim it,'" Calliope recited. "Why does everything always go back to Shadowcrafters?" she muttered.

"You can't blame him for the sins of his ancestors, just like we can't blame ourselves for Alexia's," Dissy interjected, her voice gentle but firm. "What matters now is what we do with the knowledge we have."

"And that's what, exactly?" Thalia asked archly.

"Rectify our ancestors' mistakes however we can," Calliope said.

"We can do this," Dissy said. "Can't we? Put aside our differences, our pasts? It's the only way we can get our magic back, all of us *together*. And maybe in the process we can break the curse that ties our memories to our magic." Dissy was sitting on the edge of her seat, her hands clasped in her lap.

The grimoire's pages fluttered again and returned to Grim's script.

The magic inside the Dark Oak has only increased over time, it wrote. *You may be containing it, but it still grows. That kind of magic feeds itself. And if it's let out, the wraiths will come. Power calls to power.*

"What are these wraiths? Why have I never heard of them?" Calliope asked.

"You should know all about them," Lucien said darkly, and there was a note of anger beneath his words. "It was Lightcraft witches, after all, that cursed Shadowcrafters in this way."

"You lie," Calliope said, narrowing her eyes.

"After the Great Rift, Lightcrafters were terrified of us actualizing our full power. They banded together and cursed us so that if we use too much of our magic, we turn into wraiths and lose our souls. Wraiths exist only to consume more power. They eat other souls to grow even stronger."

Sounds like a fitting punishment for what they tried to do, Grim wrote.

Lucien scowled at the words while dread squeezed Calliope's heart. "Why did you never tell me this?" she asked the grimoire.

I told you as much as I knew about your string of fate and the Dark Oak.

"So, this is what we've been guarding," she said, her voice low and flat with fear. "And the only way to ensure it stays imprisoned is to reconnect the string of fate that binds us."

The room went silent as they all took the measure of one another.

That's not all, Grim wrote. *The spring equinox, Ostara, is coming. The veil grows thinner with each passing day. If you can't restore the string before then, the wraiths will come seeking, and it will be easier for them to get through. And you will have little magic left to stop them.*

"So we have less than two weeks to break the bond, restore our string of fate, refortify the enchantments, and find who or what's trying to break into them in the first place?" Calliope said frantically.

All while your magic grows weaker.

"Right, plus that," Calliope said. "Excellent, thank you so much, Grim."

And all with a Shadowcrafter in our midst, she thought, worrying her bottom lip with her teeth. He might have had an explanation for why he was here, why he'd followed her, but after years of sacrificing her memories, Calliope knew when something was missing. And something didn't line up. She would use whatever knowledge he had, but she refused to trust him.

"We can do anything as long as we do it together," Dissy said firmly. "One in three, three in one."

"I know you don't trust me," Lucien said, as if reading Calliope's mind. "But I will do everything in my power to break this bond and restore your string. I have no need to prove my worth, but you will see it proven nonetheless."

"Even when you're offering help, you're arrogant," Calliope said.

"And even when you're in need of help, you balk at the prospect of accepting it. It rather seems to me that you are possessor of both pride and prejudice." His eyes had darkened to coal, and his accent had thickened in his anger. They were facing each other now, the air charged with fear and hope and . . . something that tasted deliciously like desire. Somehow, the toes of their shoes were almost touching, like their anger had propelled them toward each other. Noticing it, he took two steps back and blew out a long-suffering breath.

That was when Calliope noticed that the sky outside, which had been a dusky robin's-egg blue, had turned dark.

Without warning, the glass in the high arched windows shattered, and the ground trembled, shaking the frames on the wall and forcing Calliope to clutch at the nearest thing to stay upright. She felt muscles and the soft fabric of a shirt before she realized she had Lucien's arm in a vicelike grip.

"What's happening?" Calliope demanded.

A deafening roar filled the air, and Calliope opened her mouth to shout. But the next thing she knew, the ancient, mottled mirror over the fireplace crashed to the ground and shattered, slivers of glass exploding in every direction.

Lucien yanked her behind him to take the brunt of the shrapnel-like glass, but she still felt the scrape and tear of skin along her forearms and cheeks, felt the blood trickling down.

Lucien met her eyes, blood running from a cut in his forehead. "The second enchantment," he said grimly. "It must have broken."

CHAPTER 13

THE EARTHQUAKE LASTED ONLY MOMENTS. BUT the damage was done, and when the roaring died down, it was replaced by an eerie silence that slithered over Calliope's skin like oil, leaving a film in its stead that made her want to scrub her body clean. Her heart beat too fast, and sweat beaded down her spine as the clouds grew darker and rain began to pelt the roof. The smell of damp earth and broken magic gagged her and made her head spin.

And then, Calliope's stomach heaved, her throat burned raw, and she struggled for air. Her chest spasmed and a coughing fit claimed her. She fell to her knees, dimly realizing her sisters had done the same.

Viscous shadows poured out of Thalia's and Dissy's mouths.

Calliope opened her mouth to scream, but instead, a column of shadows streamed from between her lips, catching on her teeth, gagging her as they pooled on the floor.

Calliope watched in horror as the shadows slithered across the ground, seeking one another, gathering and forming into the shape of a creature with eyes that glowed red as hot coal. Ten feet tall and terrifyingly solid, the creature moved, tendrils of darkness lashing out, reaching hungrily toward her sisters and Roz, who were huddling in the corner. Calliope knew she would do anything to save them. Even if it meant her own death.

She stepped away from Lucien.

"What the hell are you doing?" he barked.

"Saving us," she said with a confidence she didn't feel. Then she called, "Hey, over here, dipshit!"

The creature snapped its glowing red eyes onto hers, and she stuck up her middle finger.

Before she could blink, much less run, a shadow whipped out and wrapped around her ankle, slamming her into the glass-covered ground. It yanked her closer, pain searing her skin, and she screamed.

A yawning black hole opened in the center of the creature, like a screaming mouth, as if it meant to drag her directly into its body.

"Calliope!" Lucien shouted, but she could barely hear it over the sounds of her own screams and her sisters shrieking her name.

Another shadow whipped out toward her sisters, and then Lucien was moving, grabbing her sisters' hands and shoving them roughly behind him next to Roz, shielding them. An unnatural wind tore through the room, deafeningly loud.

As the creature dragged her across the floorboards, Calliope sacrificed the memory of Danny's birthday dinner last year, of the laughter late into the night until they were silly with it. She muttered a spell through gritted teeth, her vision blurry with pain. A burst of light shot toward the creature and pierced through its shadows, right into the hole in its massive chest. It screamed in rage, the sound pulsing in her eardrums until she thought they might bleed. But a moment later, another tendril shot out, wrapping around her other ankle.

Calliope tried to fight back, searching frantically for another memory to sacrifice, but the longer the beast held on, the more it seemed to be leaching her magic from her. Over the sound of the wind, Calliope heard Lucien's voice. Words poured from him, spells in Turkish first, then English, and finally French. But nothing worked. Calliope twisted, hands scrabbling against the floor as she tried to get away, crying out in agony at the burning flesh of her ankles where the creature still held her.

Consume, it said, the word echoing in her mind. *Crunch the bones, feed the flesh, sinew will be mine. Give us your magic, putrid witch.*

Calliope's cheeks flushed with rage, but her vision was fading, blackness closing in. Time slowed, and finally, the memories she'd sought came rushing in without invitation. Building sandcastles on the beach in Milos, her mother's bright laughter, Dissy carrying a basket of fresh strawberries from the garden, the red juice already staining her lips. Thalia tucking her into bed and singing to her when she couldn't sleep.

She was almost at the creature's yawning mouth now, its eyes narrowed on her with a sinister glee.

Her hands stopped their clawing, her eyes closing of their own accord. Tears tracked down her cheeks, and though the air was still rank with the putrid smell of dark magic, Calliope's mouth tasted sweet, the overripe fruit of old memories bursting across her tongue.

"No!" Lucien shouted.

She wanted to tell him it was okay. To say thank you for protecting her sisters and friend, but the words refused to come. The pain was ebbing now, and she thought that perhaps this was a fitting end. She'd tried to heal the broken enchantments, and they'd come back to haunt her.

"Enough of that," Lucien said firmly, his voice close to her ear. He wrapped her hands in his, his fingers gripping her wrists. "You will not give up, little muse."

Calliope whimpered, struggling to open her eyes, to find any crumb of willpower that didn't want to succumb to the shadow beast. Lucien tightened his grip, and the pain grounded her once more. Her vision was still hazy, her head pounding from where it had slammed into the floor, her magic a thin wisp, but when she looked at Lucien, she saw the blurry shapes of Dissy, Thalia, and Roz behind him.

"Together," Lucien growled, keeping Calliope's hands tight in his. "Unir et lier," he said, holding up their joined hands and angling them toward the beast. His own shadows snaked out, keeping the creature at bay even as it thrashed against the constraints.

His palm was rough in hers, and over the smell of rotten phloem and darkness, she could detect the scent of his apples and amber, and it was that, more than anything, that grounded her. She opened her mouth, and the bitter taste of bad memories burned her tongue. She coughed and dragged in a ragged breath.

"Unir et lier," she said weakly, holding out her left hand toward the creature. She sacrificed the first memory that came to mind. The feeling of sand between her toes as she walked along the shoreline of Sarakiniko Beach in Milos, her sisters laughing and her mother dancing in the waves. The power flowed through her, and a burst of bright light flared from her palm.

"Unir et lier," Lucien and Calliope chanted, and the shadows screamed, a low, keening sound that vibrated her bones.

Together, their light and shadow wrapped and bound the creature. It reared back with a roar, and Calliope winced as Lucien's foreign magic flowed into her through their joined hands, searing and electrifying. The dream mark on her wrist throbbed in pain, and rage made her skin prickle.

This was *her* house.

The rotten scent of shadows and death faded as her magic pulsed brighter.

She squeezed Lucien's hand tighter, her words coming out in a shout over the turbulent wind. She screamed the words *unir et lier,* not even knowing what they meant, but taking Lucien's lead.

And with a final burst of magic, the shadow demon screamed again, the life in its red eyes snuffed out as its body began to fold in on itself. Its limbs collapsed until it was once again a pool of shadows on the floor, and then finally, even those dissipated, leaving the air clear and bright. The wind died immediately, and then there was nothing but silence and destruction.

Calliope dragged in a shuddering breath, turning to make sure her sisters and Roz were okay. The air was still heavy with the scent of magic. But now it was the smell of faded memories, orange syrup drizzled over baklava and long nights under a canopy of shooting stars when sisters were friends and secrets were shared. The magic felt like moss pressed softly beneath bare feet.

"I think," Calliope panted, her voice reedy and thin,

"that you're right, Lucien. Another enchantment was broken." Thalia's eyes were wide while Dissy's were still pinched closed. Roz was weeping quietly. Calliope felt Lucien's gaze on her and turned to find that she was still clutching his hand. She dropped it quickly. "Thank you," she said quietly.

He only nodded, his eyes lingering on her, and she had to suppress a shiver. Her thoughts were muddled, her head pounded, and her ankle burned, but one thing was clear. He'd protected her sisters. He'd been beside her the whole time, so it couldn't have been him weakening the Dark Oak. Confusion threatened to derail her, but then her sisters were hugging her.

A sob burst from Rosalind, her chest heaving.

"It's okay," Calliope said soothingly. "We're all here. We're all safe."

"It's not that," Roz whispered now. "I remember everything." Roz stood and placed a hand on Calliope's cheek and squeezed Thalia's arm with the other while she looked at Dissy with tears still tracking down her cheeks. "When the enchantment broke and that . . . that *thing* was released, something happened, something . . . I don't know, lifted. All the things I'd forgotten, who I was, it all came rushing back." Another sob burst out of her. "I remember it all."

"Remember what?" Calliope breathed, fear squeezing her chest. What else were they about to be bombarded with?

But then Roz spoke again, gathering the sisters in her arms.

"I'm your aunt Lyra," she said.

CHAPTER 14

As Calliope sank into her embrace, ques-
tions fell away, and the rightness of the moment, the truth
of it, settled over her like silk. She didn't understand the how
or why or when of it, but none of that mattered. All that mattered was that the space inside of her, that echoing hole that
had opened when her mother left and had kept growing ever
since, shrank ever so slightly.

"I don't understand," Thalia said, pulling back, ever the
logical one. "One of the enchantments over the Dark Oak
broke, a shadow demon ruined our living room, and Roz is
our *aunt*? I know we're witches, but this is a little much even
for us." And though she was leaning away, Calliope still saw
the ember of hope burning in her eyes.

"My impossible girls," Roz said, her eyes crinkling as she
smiled. "There must have been a geas," she continued. "Some
kind of spell Penelope did so that I forgot, couldn't speak of
it. The only thing I can think is she tied the magic to the Dark
Oak, and when the enchantment weakened, so too did the
spell that bound me."

"Tell us everything, right now," Thalia said. She tried to hide the tremble in her voice, but Calliope heard it nonetheless.

"Please," Dissy pleaded, wiping her eyes. "If this is true, how did it come to be?"

"A rebirth spell that transformed me from Lyra into Roz. Advanced, complex magic that's incredibly dangerous," Roz said, a touch of reverence in her voice.

"What about Aunt Daphne?" Calliope asked.

"I . . ." Roz started and trailed off. "I don't know. There's still some kind of block there." She frowned as she tried to remember.

"Roz—I mean, Aunt Lyra," Calliope stumbled. "I mean . . . what should we call you?"

"Call me Roz. I've rather gotten used to it," she answered with a smile.

"You can help us now! Tell us everything you know about Mother and the curse and this string of fate that binds us together."

"I don't . . ." Roz started but trailed off, her eyes squeezed shut. "Some information is still misty. There's something about only three Petridi sisters being able to use magic at a time, but I don't know why. I wish I could be of more help, but it feels like I've just come out of a hundred-year sleep and there are so many patches."

"Another mystery," Calliope said. "There's nothing else you remember? Why we have this curse? Where it came from?"

"The only thing we really know is that it started with a Shadowcraft family."

Calliope groaned. "It always comes back to Shadowcrafters."

At this, Lucien cleared his throat. All four women turned, and Calliope flushed at the sight of him, having forgotten he was there.

"Let's go to the kitchen," Dissy said, squeezing their aunt's hand. "I'll make tea and warm some lemon poppy seed bread and you can tell us everything."

"I'll join you three in a moment," Calliope said.

"Darling girl," Roz said, holding out her arms. And Calliope walked into them, sighing as Roz's arms wrapped around her and she was enveloped with her signature scent of bergamot and grapefruit. "We'll get through this," Roz murmured against her hair. Calliope nodded mutely, and in spite of everything, her heart felt lighter. Because here was her aunt. Her *aunt*! Hugging and consoling her.

"I can't believe this is real," Calliope whispered.

"I always knew there was a reason we were drawn to each other." Roz smiled. "Spells and curses can't keep blood apart. We'll always find our way to each other."

Roz and her sisters left and Grim followed, soaring through the air and knocking hard into Lucien's shoulder on the way out.

"Why does that damn book have it out for me?" Lucien growled.

Calliope turned and advanced on him, her eyes narrowed, lips pursed. The light was still dim, and it gave the air an intimate feel that did not match the tension between them.

"I still don't completely trust you," she said quietly. "But I will do anything for my sisters and this town."

"Are you about to threaten me, little muse?" Lucien said, taking a step toward her.

"I might if I didn't think you'd get off on it," she answered, and her hand warmed at the memory of it pressed into his.

"You have no idea what I get off on," he growled, taking another step closer. "But I'm certain you'd love to find out." His eyes were pitch black as he stared at her, like he could eat her with his gaze, and she shivered under that dark look.

"You wouldn't know how to handle me," Calliope countered, hating the way her heart sped up at his nearness.

They were breathing the same air now. He reached out a hand, tentatively at first, and then threaded his fingers through her hair. With his palm cradling her head, he drew her forward, and she refused to acknowledge the pool of heat gathering in her core.

"I would know exactly how to handle you," he whispered in her ear.

"I bet you're all talk," she said, forcing her voice to remain level. "I think you talk a big game and women just fall at your feet, but when it comes down to it, you have no idea what you're doing."

"You talk far too much. Cease, before I'm tempted to find another use for that mouth."

Calliope stopped talking, practically stopped breathing.

"Good girl," he said, releasing his hold on her.

And damn the man, but she shivered, her body trying to chase the warmth of his as he stepped away.

"Tomorrow, we'll begin our research. Tonight, get some rest. I refuse to work with you if you're depleted before we even start. And though I'm sure you'll be dreaming of me, try not to call for me in your sleep again."

By the time Calliope opened her mouth to answer with a scathing remark, he'd already disappeared.

CHAPTER 15

LUCIEN APPEARED IN HIS COTTAGE AND STOOD stock-still. His hand flexed at his side as he remembered the way her silky hair had slid through his fingers. He'd gone too far. He was supposed to be gaining her trust, but something about that witch got his blood boiling. She was too brash, she talked far too much, and if he wasn't careful, he'd do something he'd regret.

Lucien was never one for getting sidetracked. With this goal in particular, he wouldn't rest until it was completed. And yet, he thought of the fire in Calliope's eyes. The way she'd rallied despite her fear, her dark blond hair billowing out around her on that phantom wind. She had been fearsome to behold, and her small hand in his had anchored him. Even now he felt the imprint of it on his palm. He'd thought her magic was weak? She'd proven him wrong, and he realized what a fool he'd been. He . . . respected the hell out of her.

Behind her recklessness was sorrow and emptiness. Oh,

she hid it well. But like calls to like, and despite himself, he wondered what hole she was trying to fill, what wrong she was trying to right.

He knew their Lightcraft was muddled. Had done enough research and spying to see it. But it all made so much more sense now. She was sacrificing one thing for another, her past for her present, and losing herself in the process. The thought hit a little too close to home. For though she irked him, he was, loath as he was to admit it, drawn in by that brokenness in her. What would be left of her when he was done, his goal reached?

He shook the question off. It was of no consequence. She was the architect of her own misery, same as he was. After all, he'd spent years laying the scaffolding of pain and sorrow, engineering the very path he was on now. Defying his family's power-hungry ways, running from his father, starting his own coven. There was blood on his hands, it was true, but he would bathe in a vat of it if it meant protecting Eléa.

Sounds of commotion drew him to the kitchen, where Sarai looked on with hearts in her eyes as Eléa pulled a mixing bowl down from a cupboard and lined up ingredients—flour, salt, sugar, vanilla—neatly on the counter. Her long dark hair was pulled back, and pride bloomed in Lucien's chest as he watched her. Meanwhile, Malik was reading a book, studiously ignoring both women, but he looked up when Lucien entered.

"Hello, sister mine," Lucien said quietly. Eléa started and then her eyes grew large with guilt before flashing with defiance.

"Time to go," Malik said to Sarai.

"Oh, you can stay!" Eléa said as she took butter from

the refrigerator. "Shortbread cookies don't take too long to make." Her heart-shaped face was wan, her delicate features pulled down into a pout.

"Shouldn't she be resting?" Lucien asked Sarai.

"I tried; she wouldn't listen," Sarai said in a long-suffering voice that was filled with love. Lucien hadn't expected the friendship between Eléa and Sarai, but it was a bright spot he wouldn't dare muddy.

"If I stayed in bed another second, I was going to dig my eyes out with a spoon," Eléa said merrily.

"I'll walk you out," Lucien said to Malik and Sarai. "And then you and I"—he pointed at Eléa—"are going to have a discussion."

Eléa rolled her eyes at him, and Sarai gave her a wink and a wave.

"The earthquake, that was you?" Lucien demanded when they were in the small entryway and away from Eléa's ever-prying ears.

"One enchantment down," Malik said instead of answering Lucien's question.

"Next time, warn me so I can ensure their safety," Lucien said, his words calm and measured though there was rage simmering just beneath them. "A wraith appeared, drawn by the release of power, and almost killed the witches. I've never seen anything like it before. If something happens to one of them, it ruins our entire fucking plan. We can't undo the final spell without them." He didn't say the rest. The truth that had hounded him from the moment he left the Altar that night, when the string connected to that witch stretched thin. His life was now inextricably connected to Calliope's. If she died, he did, too. And the reverse was also true. Life or death, they were bound together. But he hadn't told Malik. He didn't trust the coven, and that information was too dangerous even for an old friend.

"You'll find a way to protect them regardless of the enchantments," Malik said dismissively. "You may be an asshole. But you're a chivalrous one. Why do you think Ahmed tried so hard to beat it out of you? Goes against your family ethos."

"If you mention my father again, I'm going to rethink your position as my second-in-command."

"You couldn't spare me, brother," Malik said with a grin, clapping Lucien on the shoulder. And Lucien, against his will, was reminded of their youth when it was them against Ahmed. Hell, it was them against the world.

"How'd you fare afterward?" Sarai asked, chewing her bottom lip.

"We'll find out tomorrow. The sooner I help her, the sooner we can obliterate this bond and get what we need." And the sooner he could stop worrying about his safety being tied to hers. The witch was far too reckless for her own good.

"Go easy on Eléa," Sarai said, laying a hand on Lucien's arm before she turned and left.

When Malik and Sarai had gone, Lucien inhaled deeply before he headed back to the kitchen.

"Why did Sarai tell me to go easy on you?"

"She's so lovely, isn't she?" Eléa said, mixing the dough in a metal bowl. "I mean, yes, she worries too much, but that's kind of part of her charm, isn't it?"

"Just like evading questions is yours." Lucien frowned. "You're overmixing that."

"I am not!"

"You're making shortbread," he said flatly. "You're mixing it too much."

"Don't be such a know-it-all, Lucien, it's unbecoming."

"You read too many old books."

"Okay, Mister Fuddy-duddy," she said, with a mocking smile.

"Why did Sarai tell me to go easy on you?" he asked again.

"Fine." Eléa sighed. "I went into town today. But—" She held up a hand before Lucien could launch into a tirade. "Everything went fine! See? Here I am, overmixing short-bread dough."

Lucien rolled up his shirtsleeves and walked over, nudging his sister out of the way as he took the bowl from her hands, scattered flour on the counter, and dumped the crumbly dough on top of it.

"Did you add orange zest to this?" he asked, sniffing the dough.

"Maybe," Eléa said defensively.

"Good choice," he said, and a smile bloomed on her face. "Tell me about the town. And get me a rolling pin while you do."

"It was *adorable.*" Eléa launched into a detailed description of the town and how different it was from their estate in the French countryside. "I feel like the colors are different here, you know? And everyone is so friendly! Nothing like Lucida," she added with a frown. "Do you ever miss it there?" she asked, finally finding the rolling pin and handing it over. Lucien didn't miss the way she casually leaned on the counter, trying to hide her labored breathing.

"Sit," he commanded.

"I'm fine," she said, rolling her eyes.

He glared at her, and she sat on the high stool at the counter, making a face at him as he began to roll the dough out.

"I don't miss it," he answered tersely. "There's nothing but bad memories there."

"*Only* bad memories?" she challenged.

"You're an evil little thing." Lucien laughed despite himself at the cajoling look on Eléa's face. "Fine, one good memory. You."

"What about Serein?" she asked, naming the river that flowed through their estate and ran alongside the French village. "You used to disappear for hours out there in your little boat."

"Only to escape Grandfather and our parents," Lucien answered. "You were the darling of that village. Everyone there hated me."

"They didn't hate you," Eléa argued. "That's just the French. You simply spent too much time in Turkey to remember that your French blood means we don't say hello to everyone we pass. It's not *Beauty and the Beast,* you know."

"That, dear sister, is the understatement of the century," Lucien said darkly, which made Eléa laugh. And it was true. When he was at Château d'Ancy, with its harsh lines and gilded opulence, he longed for the messy bustle of the Grand Bazaar and the chaos of Istiklal Street on a weekend, where more than three million people walked daily. In Lucida, there were perhaps three hundred pairs of feet treading its cobblestone streets per day.

And nestled on the far side of the village was their estate. Chateau d'Ancy was surrounded by emerald grass cut so sharp you could bleed from it. The Renaissance palace was a piece of history, stunning in its symmetry and elegance. But his parents treated it as their birthright. Stolen with magic and kept with the same, it was a place of cold beauty that harbored too many bad memories and broken dreams. Meanwhile, the village itself had been frozen in time. Half-timbered houses built on archways in the medieval style lined the cobbled streets. The village square with its weekly open-air market could very well have been taken from *Beauty and the Beast*, despite what his sister said. And the crumbling stone walls running along the River Serein with ivy choking away the mortar had been his only escape, the mossy green water a soothing lull to the hardships at home.

The little town of Gold Springs reminded him too much of Lucida. And perhaps that was why he felt suffocated by it. His father was an ocean away, but he still felt under his thumb. Still felt the need to prove himself, all these years later. Prove that he was different. More than. Better than. And then there was this strange itch that plagued him, pushed him forward, and kept getting worse every time he went near the girl with honey-wheat hair and storm-swept eyes.

"I went into a shop called Tea and Tome," Eléa said after a moment of silence.

Lucien looked up from where he was molding the dough into a pan.

"Of course you did." He sighed. "And?" He thought of Calliope surrounded by books and enveloped in the scents of bergamot and black tea. Imagined her defiant expression and the fire in her eyes if he were to walk through that red door he'd contemplated entering multiple times these past few days.

"It was like a little slice of dreams." She smiled.

Lucien shook the thoughts of Calliope out of his head and used the tines of a fork to make the marks on the top of the shortbread while Eléa told him about all the magic teas they had there. She was the only one he could listen to prattle on for hours. They had at least fifteen years between them, and they were opposites in every way, but he loved her the way spring flowers love rain, desperately and unable to survive without it.

"They had tea for clarity and energy, and they had Serenity tea and"—she paused and wiggled her eyebrows—"Seduction tea."

Lucien choked on what seemed to be his own spit, and Eléa laughed delightedly.

"I don't need to hear my teenage sister talking about seduction," he said.

"Don't be such a toad," she said airily. "Anyway, I ordered the Healing tea. So spicy, lots of ginger. And nobody knew who I was, so you don't need to be cranky."

"I'm not cranky," he said with a frown, sliding the baking tray into the oven.

"You're always cranky. But anyway, the tea had all this beautiful symbolism, so that's why I added orange zest to the shortbread. For a burst of brightness and hope even amid the darkness. And it made me think of how you used to teach me to cook. I miss that."

"We'll have plenty of time for that yet, princess," he said, and tried to believe his own words. "Now, how about I make you some tea for sleep and we play a card game."

"It's going to be okay, you know," Eléa said quietly.

"I know," he said gruffly.

"You don't. But I do. And I just wanted to remind you. Now, tell me everything about this witch that's gotten under your skin, dear brother. I think I like her already."

Lucien frowned as he gave her the barest details. She didn't know the whole plan and would balk unnecessarily if she did.

"If you hope to gain her trust, you'll need to be nice to

her," Eléa said, as though this were the most obvious thing in the world.

"I'm nice," he countered.

"You're nice to me. Usually. But come on, I'll detail the finer points for you while I beat you at gin rummy."

He watched as his sister counted out the cards, her dark curls swept over one delicate shoulder. She'd grown thin, and he hated it. Hated the dark circles under her eyes and the way her breathing grew labored after so much as a gentle walk.

He would burn the world for her.

CHAPTER 16

CALLIOPE WOKE WITH THE SUN, ANGER UNFURL-
ing as she remembered the dream that had played on repeat
last night. Though she'd deny it to her dying day, it had to do
with Lucien's large hands and the way he leaned in to whisper
that he'd know exactly how to handle her. She shivered and
brushed those thoughts under the rug where they belonged.
Instead, she thought of her aunt. Her *aunt*! They were family
no matter what, but finding out they were blood helped all
the puzzle pieces slide into place.

She sacrificed the memory of Danny's laughter. She would
hear it again, after all. And with a few muttered words, the
candles strewn around her room flickered to life before
quickly dying out. She frowned, closing her eyes and searching the hum of magic that filtered through her. It was . . .
thinner. But that made sense. Last night she'd healed the
wounds on her head and ankle as well as the cuts from the
shattered glass. Then, she'd spent hours restoring the living room back to order, repairing the windows and mirror
with magic after the wraith had nearly made a meal of them.

And to top it all off, she'd tossed and turned all night while dreaming of the Shadowcrafter who'd protected her family.

Now she sent out a tendril of connection, drawing on the energy of the plants she kept in her room: peace lilies and marble queen pothos, snake plants and string of pearl succulents spilling over their terra-cotta pot. The tendril moved on to the crystals on her desk: amethyst for stability, carnelian for creativity, jasper for grounding. Her magic flared, and she sacrificed another memory. The candles lit once more, their flames casting warm shadows in the gray light.

Dread formed a heavy knot in her stomach. If she could barely light candles, how was she going to break the bond?

The smell of lavender and orange filled the air from the scented wax. Pouring candles was something the sisters did every summer solstice, and those balmy evenings seemed like another world in the cold, misty morning of spring.

As if sensing her distress, Astro padded over and crawled into her lap. Her claws poked through Calliope's leggings as she kneaded her thighs. The sun rose higher, and the mist began to clear, rays of light painting her walls golden. She idly ran a hand down Astro's fur and thought, again, of how Alexia's failed attempt at revenge had doomed their family for centuries. These *sacrifices* were the reason her mother disappeared, the reason Lyra was reborn into Rosalind. It was the very reason Marigold had left her. It was too early for such sorrow, but it barreled into her, anyway. Took up the space she'd been trying to heal and made her hollow again, forcing her mind to other past loves. Or at least, the memories that remained of them. Holly, the girl she'd dated all of her junior year of high school, with her cascade of jet-black hair and a laugh that sounded like chiming bells. Matt, the white water rafting guide from Brazil that she'd been glued to all summer after she'd turned eighteen. All of them meant little compared to Marigold, but perhaps it was because she'd sacrificed so much of them that all that remained were fleeting images of a past barely remembered.

Tears were threatening, and she was finally ready to give in to them when she let out a startled yelp as Lucien appeared in front of the fireplace. Rain speckled his hair, glinting in the dying embers like falling stars. He held two cups of coffee in his hands.

"Stop *doing* that," she shouted, her heart pounding from the scare. But still, a smaller, quieter part of herself sighed in relief. He was here. He'd kept his word.

"I brought you coffee," he said by way of greeting. "May I approach your majesty?" And then, as though realizing what he'd said and the sarcasm with which he said it, he continued, "That is, I think we've got off on the wrong foot. And I wanted to apologize."

Seeing the chagrined look in his eye, Calliope couldn't help herself. "For what? Being a complete and utter ass? Looking down on us because you think our magic isn't as strong as yours? Testing my patience? Teasing me?"

"All of it," he said tightly. "Except for the last two."

"You're infuriating."

"Look," he said, holding out the coffee. "I know you don't trust me, but I didn't poison it."

Her hand rose of its own volition and took the coffee cup he offered. She took a sip and made a face at the bitterness.

"Kremalı şeker," Lucien muttered quietly, drawing his finger in a circle.

Calliope took another drink, the coffee now with cream and just the right amount of sugar.

"You are good for some things, I suppose." She tried to

look away from him, but Calliope liked beautiful things, and for all his infuriating qualities, she didn't mind admitting that he was, indeed, beautiful. She was growing used to his presence, and that irked her. Where would he go when their bond was done? Her eyes traveled up from his polished loafers to his charcoal jeans. Up, farther still, to his perfectly pressed white button-down shirt. The inch of skin from the one button undone, up to the strong column of his throat, and to his sharp jaw, which clenched as Calliope continued her perusal. He must have healed himself of the cuts as well, for his skin was smooth as carved marble, though he still retained a shadow of stubble. An image of his face roughing the soft inner skin of her thighs as he kissed his way up her leg rose unbidden in her mind, and her cheeks grew warm.

"See something you like?" he asked drily.

"Yes," she admitted unabashedly, taking another drink of her coffee.

He frowned, clearly not expecting that bit of truth. He cleared his throat, and Calliope laughed.

"Am I embarrassing you?"

"I think I like it better when you're mean," he said. "Now, get dressed and let's begin. I will meet you downstairs."

"Just because you warded the damn place doesn't mean you can act like you own it," she called after him, but he was already halfway across the house.

She was irritated with herself for liking his presence there, for the little nagging voice that said she was looking forward to meeting him downstairs. Despite their bickering and verbal sparring, or perhaps because of it, he was beginning to grow on her. And in the back of her head, in a little dark corner she didn't like to look at, was his accusation that her mother had poisoned them against Shadowcrafters. How many of her mother's warnings and lessons had she taken as gospel merely because Penelope was an adult and she was a child? How many of her prejudices were inherited, and why had she never examined those doctrines that had guided her life? But she knew the answer. It was because she'd never been challenged to. They lived their sleepy little routine in a sleepy little town, their days governed by books and tea and gossip. She detested Lucien for planting this seed of doubt in her. For rocking the balance of her world with razor-sharp words that cut into the safety net she'd happily been living in.

Still, Calliope took her time getting dressed, opting for a pair of velvet leggings and a sweater that always fell off one shoulder. As she deliberated over socks, she thought again of the memories she could sacrifice to try to break this bond.

Knowing Lucien was waiting for her and taking savage pleasure at making him sweat, she opened Grim and began writing on a blank page.

In case I end up sacrificing my memory of Lucien just to annoy him, here's what I've learned and what I surmise about the Shadowcrafter in our midst . . .

She wrote several hastily scrawled pages, sipped her coffee, and decided on her socks. One had a cauldron pattern with green potion bubbling out, and the other was stitched with repeating lines of IT'S ALL JUST A BUNCH OF HOCUS POCUS. She added a pair of combat boots, preparing for battle.

She found Lucien pacing the library when she got downstairs. The sconces on the wall were dim, and the towering windows with their brocade curtains let in an eerie light from the misty grounds beyond. Candelabras lined the long table, with black taper candles dripping hot wax. It was like stepping back in time or into another world, and though Calliope had always loved the library, she never spent much time there. It was too quiet. Even now the silence bathed her in its musty essence, and it made her skin itch. She inhaled the scent of dusty old books, the burning logs from the fire, and, underneath it all, the warm, spiced smell of Lucien, cinnamon and apples and cozy winter mornings. She was reminded of the melomakarona they made every Christmas. The sweet, spiced, honey-soaked cookies were a Greek staple, and she could almost taste the grated apple and crunch of walnuts.

He turned to glare at her when she entered, and she met him with a challenging stare, daring him to comment on how long she took. He pursed his lips with the effort of keeping the words in before his eyes fell to her bare shoulder. His jaw clenched, and Calliope had to hide her smile.

"Where do we start?" she asked.

"I presumed you would be coming to the table with an idea or two."

"If I knew how to fix this, I wouldn't need you, now, would I?" She smiled sweetly.

"And you've yet to provide any useful ideas."

"You're being condescending again. Péfto apó ta sýnnefa."

"I beg your pardon?"

"It means 'I fall from the clouds,'" she said archly. "An English translation would be 'I'm shocked.' And not in a pleasant way."

"Fall from the clouds all you want, little muse. I'll be forced to catch you until this bond is broken."

"Fine, and I suppose you have all the answers then?" Calliope demanded, her voice rising slightly. She thought about telling him of the words she'd heard that night on the way to the Dark Oak. *Shadow and Light shall never align.* Perhaps he could decipher their meaning, but somehow, the words felt personal, and she wasn't ready to trust him with them just yet.

They glared at each other, both of them breathing hard, fists planted on the large oak table that was scattered with ancient tomes and scrolls. They were leaning toward each other, and the air was charged. No matter how beautiful he was, he still got under her skin. And, loath as she was to admit it, she liked it. Liked that he challenged her, didn't hold back any punches, and said whatever he wanted. It was refreshing.

The sconce lights flickered, and the fire licked the grate. The sweet apple smell grew stronger. Lucien straightened, his eyes clearing.

"I apologize," he said stiffly. "I don't want to fight with you. I just want to find answers."

"So you can get back to whatever nefarious Shadowcraft activity you have planned?"

"Shadowcraft is not inherently evil simply because it draws on the power of self instead of nature," he snapped. "And you're a hypocrite if you don't see that your curse requires you to sacrifice *of yourself,* which is, essentially, Shadowcraft."

"Fine," Calliope huffed. And she felt again that phantom itch at the back of her neck that felt too much like guilt. "Fine. No more arguing."

"What's this I hear?" Thalia asked, bustling through the library doors, holding a tray of tea. Dissy followed her, carrying a plate of muffins. "My sister isn't going to argue anymore? Which news outlet should I contact first?"

"Hilarious," Calliope deadpanned.

"Let's focus on how to break the bond," Dissy said gently.

"The first we should try is obvious, I think," Lucien said. "Try to sacrifice a powerful memory to restore your string of fate."

"And when that doesn't work?" Calliope asked.

"We find out everything we can about it. Why and how you're connected. And how to purify it when it's been tainted."

"If only I hadn't bound myself to you." She sighed.

"Then you'd be dead and much less of a pain. But you also wouldn't know the truth. If you fix the string, maybe you can find out how to break the memory curse. Is it not better to face the hard truth than to go on blindly?"

"Oh no," Calliope said blithely. "I find it's much easier to forget."

"Perhaps that's why your sisters didn't believe you when you told them what was coming."

"We believe her now," Thalia said with a disapproving look at Lucien. "I'll look for anything pertaining to Alexia and the curse. Dissy, you research wraiths and find any information you can on defeating them. Opie and Lucien, you look for ways to break your bond and restore our string of fate. Roz will be here later to help. But there are centuries of knowledge here, both mundane and magic. If there's something to find, we'll find it."

CHAPTER 17

CALLIOPE WANDERED THROUGH THE STACKS. EVEN with the curtains drawn back from the high windows, the stained glass meant the light filtering through was muted. Dust motes danced in the air, and the rustle of pages called to her. She loved being among the books, trailing her fingers along spines, and that strange dusty scent of history and fable alike. The books hummed as she walked past them. And she remembered why she loved the whimsy of this place. Some books hid themselves, others traded dust jackets so what was inside wasn't what was on the cover. Still others found homes in sections where they didn't belong. Calliope remembered a particular series that refused to leave the biographies even though they were fiction.

"Are you planning on reading any of these or making love to them?" Lucien asked drily as Calliope ran her fingers over a thick leather tome. He stood behind her, too close, so that she felt his words on her neck.

"Is that a note of jealousy I detect in your voice?" she asked, her throat dry.

"If I wanted your fingers trailing over me like that," he said, leaning down lower, his breath coasting over the shell of her ear and making her shiver, "I would have them." Calliope swallowed hard as her head was filled with the image of a shirtless Lucien, her fingers tracing over the hard planes of his stomach and up through the light smattering of chest hair. When she looked up at him, his eyes were hooded and dark, and she stepped away before her hands betrayed her and did something foolish of their own accord.

For hours they pored over old family journals and flipped through countless tomes of spells and curses. Unable to stand the silence, she opened some of the windows to let the birdsong in. But it wasn't enough. She muttered to herself, hummed odd snippets of songs, and read aloud quietly as her finger trailed down dusty old pages.

"Do you have to do that?" he asked shortly.

"Yes." She didn't even look up from the book she was reading.

When Calliope pulled out *A History of Craft,* Lucien scoffed.

"Written by a Lightcraft witch, no doubt," he said.

"And what's so wrong with that?" Calliope challenged, thumbing through the pages.

"When you hear only from the side of the victors, it doesn't leave much room for interpretation." He frowned.

"You think we won?" Calliope asked, astonished.

"You are believed to be the pure practitioners of magic while we are painted as the villains, so I believe that answers your question."

"Only because Shadowcrafters solely care about power," Calliope said.

"Look," he said, pointing to a passage. And Calliope leaned over to read, remembering the nights when her mother would tell these stories to her and Dissy and Thalia while they drank hot chocolate and practiced tying witch knots.

Once, there was a time when no delineation between magic existed. There was no Lightcraft. No Shadowcraft. There was only the one Craft. Magic that drew on both nature and the power of self. It was a time when magic was widespread and common, when witches worked together. But as civilization grew stronger, their magic grew weaker. And so, they sought to grow their power through a spell that required cooperative magic. But as they powered the spell, the magic grew too strong for them to contain. The very earth began to shake with the weight of it. And the covens fought, some of them wanting to continue and others wanting to stop. The spell went wrong, separating them into those who could access nature and those who could access the well of power within, but not both.

The aftermath of this magical catastrophe was swift and profound. Accusations flew between Lightcraft and Shadowcraft practitioners, each blaming the other for the disaster. Lightcraft accused Shadowcraft of seeking too much power, while Shadowcraft accused Lightcraft of arrogance and meddling beyond their comprehension. Prejudice grew between them, mistrust abounding in the chaos, and the effects of this rift are still felt today.

"Both sides sought power," Lucien said. "Or they would not have done cooperative magic. But we are the ones believed to be evil."

"All stories have a kernel of truth, though," Calliope said, her brow furrowing.

"Or perhaps that is what people tell themselves when they can no longer remember why they hate someone in the first place."

And Calliope could not deny the truth of his words.

✳

As morning lengthened to afternoon, they moved around each other cautiously, as though a single wrong step might set them off. The air grew thicker as their shoulders brushed when they passed each other down a row of books. As their fingers grazed when they went to turn a page at the same time.

It was a delicate dance, a tenuous balance as the bickering faded and every glance and touch turned heavy. It mingled with the hopelessness that was beginning to creep in and put Calliope on edge.

She was having trouble concentrating on the words in front of her when, out of the corner of her eye, she saw him get up from the table and walk down a dark, narrow row. Dissy and Thalia were nowhere to be seen, so she followed him, not wanting to be left alone with her thoughts. The air was cooler back there away from the heat of the fire, the light even dimmer. He was stretching to the highest shelf, reaching for yet another book, and she ducked under his arm, but before she made it past him, he brought his other arm up, caging her in.

She straightened and turned to face him, his warmth pressing in on her.

"I think I'm capable of walking down a row of books without your supervision," he said, his face getting closer.

She wanted to retort, but the words in her brain were muddled. Lucien's eyes narrowed, and he reached forward and laid the back of his hand on Calliope's forehead.

"What are you doing?" she said, swatting his hand away.

"You didn't insult me, so I'm checking for fever," he answered seriously.

"Stop it," she said, batting his hand again when he brought it back up. "I'm fine. I'm just . . . tired."

"Go take a break then," he said, his voice terse. He was still caging her in, and she smelled his now-familiar scent of apples.

"I can't," she said after a beat. "Don't you get it? I'm desperate. I have to find . . . something." Her voice fragmented on the last word.

"We will," he said gruffly.

"What if we don't?" she whispered, not looking at him. "We only have until Ostara. That's less than a week and a half away now."

He bent down, his eyes level with hers, and she finally glanced up.

"We will find something," he repeated. "If ever there was a witch determined to find a way, it's you." It sounded like the words cost him something to admit. Maybe she was imagining it, but her fear seemed to penetrate that shield he kept raised at all times.

"Is that admiration I hear in your voice?" she teased, even though her heart hammered at his closeness.

"It . . . might be," he said reluctantly.

"Lucien," she said, not even knowing what words to follow it with, only knowing she wanted to taste his name on her tongue.

"Little muse," he answered, leaning forward until his nose ran the length of her jaw and into her hair, where he inhaled. He was barely touching her, and yet it felt like he was touching her *everywhere*.

She laid her hand on his chest, his crisp white shirt cool against her palm. His sleeves were rolled up now, the black ink peeking out on his forearms. She trailed her hand over to his shoulder and down his arm, where her fingers traced the tattoos.

"What are these?" she asked. A spring storm had rolled in, but they were so far back in the stacks that she could barely hear the rain beating against the windows. For some reason, she didn't mind this silence.

"Memories," he answered. "A way back to myself. Ironic, isn't it? You sacrifice yours and I ink mine on my body, so I can remember them forever."

"Opposites in every way." She laughed quietly. "What kind of memories are they?"

"Regrets, mostly," he said.

"Tell me," she said, and watched as a war played out on his face. She didn't know what this was, but it felt like the beginning of trust. He was here. He'd shown up. He was helping. Sharing pieces of himself.

Calliope was walking on the knife's edge of caution and desire, those old prejudices trying to remind her why this was a dangerous game to play. But those were paltry warnings that died in the heat of his gaze when he stared at her. When he was about to spill a secret she could tell he wasn't ready to share.

Finally, he said, "It took a long time for me to realize that the power my parents want, that my whole family has strived to uphold for generations, isn't something worth fighting for. Not at the cost they pay. But then, my sister got sick, and the only way for me to help her was to use that very same power. I will gladly turn myself into the monster everyone fears to save her."

"Is that such a bad thing?" Calliope asked. She was tired of fighting him, for now, at least, and this new, softer version of him was breaking down her barriers.

"It is when the consequence is greater than the sacrifice," he said, his voice low. "Save one and destroy many? Give myself over to Shadowcraft at the risk of becoming a wraith and having my sister hate me forever?"

"She would never hate you for saving her, no matter what you became. The world isn't so black-and-white, Lucien. Love doesn't work like that." She wasn't sure she liked this shift between them. It was soft as quicksand. She'd formed her opinion of Lucien, but these admissions were pulling her feet down, knocking her off balance.

"I wish I saw the world the way you do," he admitted.

"I don't think anyone wants that." She laughed softly.

"I was wrong before. I think I like this even better than the fighting." His eyes dropped to her lips and desire surged through her. When he inhaled, his chest expanded and brushed against hers. "You are . . ." He paused, and his voice came out strangled. "Very irritating."

"Is that the French way of saying you're turned on?" she asked, her own voice coming out breathy.

"I speak three languages fluently and two more passably. I don't need to use any of them for you to know that I'm turned on."

"Insufferable," Calliope muttered, her hand fisting in his shirt, pulling him closer.

"I think," he said, his voice low, "that I am beginning to tolerate you. Barely."

She leaned forward, her free hand snaking around his neck and up into his hair. It was softer than she expected it to be. This whole moment, it felt like something . . . more. And that terrified her, but not enough to stop.

"Calliope?" Dissy's voice called from the main area of the library.

"If we're very quiet," Calliope whispered, "do you think she'll leave?"

"You need to see this," Thalia said loudly.

Calliope groaned and leaned her forehead against Lucien's chest. She could hear his heartbeat, feel it pulse against her skin. This, whatever this was, had been building since the first morning she woke up at the Altar of Fate. Even then, knowing what he was, she'd felt that pull, the promise of it, no matter how hard she tried to cover it with harsh words and mistrust.

His hands dropped from the shelf above her, and when he placed them on her cheeks, she looked up, startled. Where his words were always sharp, his hands were gentle as his thumbs caressed her skin. Her heart stammered, and the smell of apples and cinnamon tickled her nose.

"This mouth," he murmured. His eyes shone like obsidian as his thumb brushed over her lip.

"You want it?" she breathed. "Take it."

A low growl escaped him as his hands left her face and fell to her waist, where he pulled her roughly against him.

"Opie!" Dissy called again, panic infusing the single word.

With what appeared to be great reluctance, he stepped back.

"Let's go, little muse, before I forget what I'm doing here." And with that, he turned and walked toward her sisters, leaving a trail of desire in his wake.

Calliope followed, swallowing hard and willing her heart to slow, her palms to cool. Goddess bless her sisters, but whatever they wanted had better be good. Because though she'd been lying about her attraction to Lucien, it was the softness behind his hard exterior, the pain he kept so carefully hidden, that had her wanting to give in to it.

When Calliope walked out from the row of books, Dissy's

face was pinched with worry and Thalia's was luminescent with rage.

"You," Thalia said sharply, eyes directed at Lucien.

"Yes?" he asked archly, crossing his arms.

"You said your grandfather, a renowned Shadowcrafter, had some kind of connection to Gold Springs," Thalia said, her voice hard as granite.

"I did," he said with a nod.

"And Grim said that it was a Shadowcrafter who started this whole mess with the Dark Oak, with our curse, the enchantments, all of it."

Lucien didn't respond, but his skin turned pale in an instant, his full lips pursed into a frown.

"Care to explain this?" Thalia tossed a book onto the low table in front of the fireplace. Calliope leaned over it to see what appeared to be a genealogical tree. She'd seen the book before but never opened it, though she knew it was a magical tome that filled in the family tree when a member died or was born. And there, near the bottom, was Lucien's name. What was his name doing in a Petridi book? A pit formed in Calliope's stomach as she followed the line up to the top. And there, in a black banner, was the family name. Deniz. It wasn't just any Shadowcraft family who'd started this conflict.

It was the family of the man she'd just been about to ravish in the library stacks.

CHAPTER 18

LUCIEN'S FEATURES REMAINED IMPASSIVE. CALliope whirled on him, rage clouding her vision and making her ears ring. How foolish she was. She'd allowed herself to be hoodwinked. To be drawn in by him. Disgust made her blood boil as she thought of his hot breath on her ear, his hand on her cheek. Traitorous tears burned hot behind her eyes.

"*Your* family is the one that started this whole mess with the Dark Oak?" she demanded, pointing at the book. "Explain, now. Our magic might be weak at the moment, but we will use every last ounce of it to destroy you if you don't tell us the truth." Calliope was breathing hard, her very blood luminescent with fury. It took every ounce of willpower not to launch herself at him. Rake her nails down his cheeks until he was bleeding.

"The story your grimoire told last night," Lucien said tightly. "It wasn't the whole story. But there are pieces of it I'm missing, so I can only tell you what I know. It's true that my grandfather was obsessed with his connection to Gold Springs, but there was a reason for it. Here," he said, pulling the book forward. "Witch genealogies like this can't lie, but your grimoire can. Look." He pointed to the top of the tree, and there was Alexia Petridi, but then he dragged his finger across the horizontal line that indicated marriage. "Alexia didn't just fall in love with a Shadowcrafter. She married him. Bayram Deniz. I come from his line, a descendant of Bayram's brother. But Bayram, he already had a daughter from a previous marriage, here." He pointed again to a small rectangle with the name Isra Deniz. "Alexia had three other daughters from her own previous marriage, there." He dragged his finger down and to the left. "This is your ancestral line."

Calliope knew Lucien was right and that witch genealogies couldn't lie; it was ancient bloodline magic. But that didn't mean the betrayal hurt any less.

"You lied to us about this," she spat. "Why are you *really* here? Why was your grandfather so obsessed with this place?"

"He knew some of the history, knew there was a source of power here, though he could never figure out where it came from or how we were tied to it. I was curious." He shrugged. "I should have told you. There is no excuse for it save that I knew you would trust me even less. I apologize for that. But here's the truth. While we are bound, I cannot harm you and you cannot harm me. If you die, I will die. So, you see, I have a vested interest in helping you. Protecting you. We are tied together, Calliope, whether we like it or not."

"Bound or not, I don't trust you. Mother warned us, she *warned us* about Shadowcrafters," she said, turning to her sisters now. "It went deeper than the normal prejudices that came from the Great Rift. This wasn't just about Lightcraft versus Shadowcraft. It was personal to her. We just didn't know why. Now we do."

"Regardless of her warnings," Lucien said before Dissy or Thalia could answer, and there was frustration lacing his words now, "I could have let you die that night. I could have walked away. I did not."

"This isn't some fey court where I owe you a life debt," Calliope ground out, rounding on him.

"You're right. And yet I saved you knowing I placed my life in *your* hands, Calliope," he said. And she winced. It was, she thought, the first time he'd used her name. "You don't owe me a life debt, but you hold the power here. Until we break the bond, my time is yours. My skill is yours. My magic is yours."

Dissy inhaled a sharp breath.

"That's it," she said.

"What's it?" Calliope asked.

"Hello?" said a singsong voice as Roz entered the library. "I brought backup!" And Danny entered right after her.

"Oh," Danny said, staring at Lucien, their eyes going wide. "Damn. Shadow daddy, indeed."

"Excuse me?" Lucien frowned.

"Um, nothing," Danny said, clearing their throat. "Just, you know, hi. Nice to meet you?"

Roz looked back and forth between Lucien and her nieces. Their defensive stances, their eyes cold and hard with anger.

"Dearie me," she said. "What *have* we walked into here?"

"I think," Dissy broke in, "that we need a, ah, family quorum. Please excuse us, Lucien." And she grabbed Thalia's hand and then Calliope's and began to drag them out.

"He's nothing but a liar; you don't have to be polite to him," Calliope snapped, throwing him a scathing look over her shoulder as she let herself be pulled by Dissy.

"Yes, yes," Dissy said. "Roz, Danny, come *on*."

They followed her to the kitchen, where she began pulling down ingredients.

"We're . . . cooking?" Calliope asked, confused. "And this is supposed to help how?"

"I need to think, and to do that, I need my hands to be busy. Fill in Roz and Danny in the meantime."

"I love it when she gets like this," Calliope said to Danny. "Thalia, you fill them in. If I speak about him, I'm liable to break something. Probably his face." She threw herself onto the stool at the high counter and quickly offered up the memory of choosing her clothes that morning. She tried to summon a steaming cup of tea in front of her. And while the teacup appeared, the tea did not. Grumbling in frustration, she tried again, sacrificing a bigger memory. Tea filled the cup. The rosemary and peppermint were meant to help her focus, and the fragrance, as it wafted up, cleared her head, though her anger remained.

Grim flew in and settled on the table, and Calliope tuned out as Thalia recounted their revelations. The smell of the tea reminded her of her mother making it when Calliope couldn't stop talking long enough to focus on her homework. It had been fifteen years. She shouldn't miss her mother anymore. And yet, she'd wished on a thousand shooting stars that somehow, some way, she would come back. Calliope could picture her mother, ready with a quip or a joke to lighten the mood. But, as always, there was only the ghost of her. The memories turned into a haunting history that begged not to be repeated.

Calliope tuned back in as Thalia finished, and the smell of garlic and fresh-squeezed lemon filled the kitchen.

"The good news is, my darling, that he can't harm you," Roz said.

"The bad news," Calliope retorted, "is that I can't kill him. Because if I do, I'm gone, too. Although at this point, I'm wondering if it might be worth it."

"What's the plan then?" Danny asked. "I say we break this bond and then shank a shadow daddy."

"I have an idea for that," Dissy said. "The, um, breaking the bond, I mean. Not the shanking."

"No, no, you're far too good and pure for that. You leave the shanking to us," Danny said, patting Dissy's arm.

"Well, your magic is weakening," Dissy said, turning to Calliope. "You can barely summon a cup of tea." She gestured to the cup in front of her.

"An astute observation." Calliope frowned. "Already loving where this is headed."

"You need to use Lucien's."

Calliope only stared at her sister.

"Channel his magic and see if you can break the bond and restore our string. We'll be there, too, connected, so you can see if it's working."

"A Deniz," Calliope said flatly. "You want me to channel a Deniz's Shadowcraft magic. The man who lied to us about his family's connection to ours and probably why he's here. I'd rather unleash whatever's in the Dark Oak."

"That will happen anyway if this doesn't work," Dissy said softly. "Three in one, one in three. We can do this." She was grating cucumbers now, the light, aromatic scent filling the kitchen. "Remember our summers on Milos?" she asked. "Mom would make yogurt-marinated chicken skewers and tzatziki. Thalia would use her magic to heat up pita bread, and we'd sneak in when we thought she wasn't looking and dip it in." She was mincing garlic now, and the smell of Greek yogurt, cucumber, and lemon juice brought back memories of running into the ocean at night from their little house on the beach, the black sand still so hot from the summer sun that they had to dance over it.

"I remember," Calliope said. She had just turned nine the last time she'd been back, the summer before their mother left. Penelope would whisper secrets and spells and stories as she tucked them in, all three sisters sleeping in one bed.

"I—" Thalia started, her head tilted, eyes straining. "I don't remember."

"What do you mean, you don't remember?" Calliope demanded, turning to her sister.

Dissy mixed the cucumber, yogurt, and garlic into an earthenware bowl filled with lemon juice, dill, and olive oil. But her hand stilled as she looked at Thalia, her eyes wide with fear.

"The longer your string is broken, the more your memories fade," Roz said sadly.

"By the goddess," Calliope breathed. "We're turning into Mother."

"I'll remember for you," Dissy told Thalia. "Every time I taste tzatziki, I think of those summers. Back when we thought the world belonged to us. We can do this. *You* can do this, Opie," she added, turning to her other sister.

"Fine." Calliope sighed, taking Dissy's ember of hope and letting it bloom in her chest. "Fine. Let's do it. But even though I can't kill him, it doesn't mean I can't hurt him. I won't be held responsible for my actions."

"When have you ever?" Thalia muttered.

"I think the Denizes and Petridis have been tied together

for generations for a reason," Dissy said. "And I think this is the reason. Everything is interconnected; we just have to see it through to make sure everything follows the way it's supposed to. I know you're mad, Opie. But there's more to this story we don't know yet. And from what I can tell, both families are at fault."

Calliope didn't answer that. Didn't think her sweet sister would like the vehemence with which she denied that claim. Instead, she followed them back into the library, where Dissy shared her idea. Calliope had expected Lucien to balk when they told him the plan. But he merely nodded.

"It is a good plan. And I told you, my magic is yours," he said. Calliope only scowled at him. Her skin crawled being in the same room as him, and the thought of accessing his magic, channeling it, almost made her physically ill. But for her sisters? For the town? She would do what was necessary. Even if she wanted to strangle him in the process.

"We'll do it at the Altar," Thalia said.

"And we'll be there for moral support," Roz said, linking her arm through Danny's.

The sun was sinking when they all trailed out of Lethe Manor. It was the coldest, foggiest end of winter that Calliope could remember. And she hoped that wasn't a sign, even though she knew things like that usually were.

The Altar of Fate welcomed them with a hum that reverberated in Calliope's bones.

In the quiet of the clearing, she recognized a hollowness that was usually filled with the sweet, gentle buzz of magic. That, combined with her last two spells going poorly, made her realize how weak her magic was getting. But it wasn't the magic she missed; it was the connection to her sisters.

Thalia directed Dissy to the southernmost point of the

Altar, where she knelt, her eyes closed in supplication. Wearing a look of grim determination, Thalia took up her post at the northernmost point. Roz and Danny stood back, huddled together in the mist.

"And here we are again," Lucien muttered, eyeing the Altar with something that resembled trepidation. "I admit I underestimated you in the beginning," he said to Calliope, circling closer. "But you misjudged me the same as I did you. And I can admit my mistakes. Can you?" Lucien gave her a challenging stare. She looked away.

"I'll let you know when we're finished here. Candles, now," she said, gesturing to the Altar.

With a wave of his hand, Lucien conjured white candles in a circle around the Altar and lit them with an incantation. They sat facing each other, the flames blowing gently in the evening air. Her sisters' presence on either side anchored her. The only sound was the symphony of crickets, and the stars were beginning to peek out, the air still and waiting. Nature sensed magic more than humans ever could, and it was for that reason, perhaps, that witches had survived for so long. For they were too connected to the natural world not to notice the signs of new life and old dangers.

Calliope let the power and magic and memories of her ancestors flow through her. Generations of fierce women who'd flouted convention through wars and witch hunts and everything in between. They would break this bond and together meet whoever or whatever was coming. In spite of the lying, conniving Shadowcrafter in front of her.

Calliope drew a small dagger from her pocket and unsheathed it, but before she could prick her finger, Lucien grabbed her wrists. She whipped her head to glare at him with hatred in her eyes, and he quickly released her.

"Once the gateway is opened . . ." He paused, struggling for words. It made Calliope uneasy.

"Cat got your tongue?" she asked. "Or are you trying to come up with another lie?"

"I never pretended to be anything other than what I am," he said. "But you disarmed me. Your fearlessness has led you here, and I admire that. I know you hate me now. Just, please, be careful, little muse."

Calliope nodded, any words she might have said sticking in her throat. And before she could second-guess herself, she sliced the tip of her finger, hissed as her skin tore, and dabbed a smear of her blood on either side of Lucien's temples.

She handed him the knife and waited for him to do the same. But she should have known by then that Lucien was never one to meet expectations. Instead, he took her finger and inspected it. His eyes found hers in the dying light, and he held her gaze as he licked the last drop of blood that pooled on her fingertip. And despite his betrayal, despite her confusion, her cheeks flushed, and the whole world centered on the feeling of his tongue on her skin. Before she could yank her hand away, he released her, and then he was speaking low, a verse in Turkish, and the torn skin sealed back together. Only then did he quickly slice his own finger and dab the blood gently on her temples.

Heart beating fast, willing her hatred to remain at the surface, she closed her eyes and focused on the bond between them, coaxing it to open a path for her. She let the silence of the clearing settle into her, that damp, earthy smell rising, the cold stone of the Altar beneath her, the warm hum of their magic tangling.

As the connection deepened, she slipped into his mind, his memories, his past, every little piece that made him who he was. She could feel his magic enveloping her, had expected it to feel different from hers, but the powerful pull was a twin flame to her own.

Lucien's memories unfolded before her like a tapestry, and she searched through the tangled strings for the source of his magic. As soon as she found it, she could divert its path, lead it into her.

But it was as if she had stepped into another realm.

In a large French manor house, cold and imposing, a young boy wandered the halls, alone. He entered a study where two adults were conversing, but they waved him away. His face fell, and he instead found solace in the vast library and the secrets it held.

She was supposed to be channeling his magic, not losing herself in his past, but it was too tempting. She pushed deeper, needing to see his secrets and lies.

An older man stooped over a table filled with beakers and phials. Dark smoke shrouded the room. His grandfather, perhaps? A bond between them. It didn't feel quite like love, but it was better than being alone. And then, a new presence in the house. A young boy named Malik. She felt Lucien's mistrust and then watched as it shifted to friendship. Finally, he had a confidant. But even that was tainted when his father pitted them against each other in tests of power. Lucien wanted his father's approval, but he wanted that boy's friendship more.

As she delved further still, the scene shifted.

Now he was a young man, perhaps eighteen, and he held what was unmistakably a baby bundled in swaddling blankets. The echo of his voice from so many years ago was so close it was as though he'd whispered it in her ear. Sister.

Images flickered before her like a flip-book, each one telling a story from pages out of time.

Running the halls with his sister. Malik chasing them. Joyous laughter. Years passing; the girl looked perhaps ten. He fretted over her starting school, a first boyfriend. Still, their parents were mostly absent. Only the grandfather in his study, the young man, the friend, and the little girl.

But then, darkness loomed in the memories.

The little girl's laughter faded, and she was a teenager now. Her skin was sallow, dark circles under her eyes. She'd grown painfully thin.

Calliope watched helplessly as Lucien struggled to find a way to save his sister, his desperation and pain evident in every action he took. As Malik helped him until his father forbade it and their friendship deteriorated even more.

The images shifted again, and now Calliope saw the version of Lucien she knew today. His face was stoic, frown lines etched around his mouth, his demeanor commanding. She could feel the weight of the responsibility he carried as though it were her own. He stood before a group of witches; Calliope could feel their magic through the memory as they bowed before him.

A Shadowcraft coven leader.

Confusion and concern clouded Calliope's mind. These were not the memories she'd expected to find. The sacrifice. The burden. They settled on her as if they were her own and choked her. She could sense the darkness, that hidden pain he'd buried deep within himself. It was a shadow she recognized from the depths of her own soul—a pain she tried to forget and leave behind. She didn't want these memories. Didn't want to see him as a human who'd suffered loss and fear and would do anything to set it right.

She shoved his memories away and tried to refocus on drawing his magic into herself. The bond that connected them was different from the string that connected her to her sisters. Instead of the gentle hum of comfort she had with Thalia and Dissy, Lucien's was white-hot and searing.

She reached out to Thalia and Eurydice in her mind. Searching, searching for a way to purify their string of fate. Sweat broke out on her brow, and her mind began to fracture as the doorway opened and the magic pushed against her. She saw their string, tangible, glowing a soft golden hue, connecting them to one another. But there were cracks in it. Pieces of string that were muddled with darkness. She let Lucien's magic fill her and tried to heal those shadows with light. Hope bubbled like the waters of a clear spring when the strands began to heal.

But then Dissy's scream rent the night air.

CHAPTER 19

THE STRAIN WAS IMMENSE, LIKE TRYING TO PUSH a boulder uphill, as Calliope tried to hold on to Lucien's magic. A roaring wind picked up as thunder sounded overhead, and Calliope was breaking, bit by bit. Through her hazy vision, she saw Lucien swaying, the power draining from him as Calliope pulled more and more of his magic into herself.

"I'm okay," Dissy called. "Keep going!"

"Dissy's string is fighting against Lucien's magic," Calliope shouted over the roaring wind and thunder, her voice barely audible amid the sudden tumultuous storm. She gritted her teeth, sweat beading on her forehead as she struggled to maintain control.

"Try mine," Thalia yelled.

She turned to Thalia's portion of the string, praying she could fare better there. But hers had even more cracks. Fissures that wept shadows. As Calliope bled her light into them, Thalia screamed in agony and fell to the ground, the string pulsing so bright it blinded all of them. As Thalia's scream died away, the light went with it, and Calliope saw

Thalia, her body convulsing. With a cry, she broke the connection to Lucien and rushed to her sister's side, Dissy and Roz following close behind.

The wind whipped around them, tugging at their hair and clothes, as the thunder continued to rumble menacingly overhead.

"What do we do?" Calliope shouted, her voice laced with desperation as Thalia thrashed and her eyes rolled back.

"Hold her shoulders while I hold her head," Roz replied, her own voice nearly drowned out by the howling wind. Magic and emotions were colliding like thunder and lightning. Finally, the storm began to abate, the winds calming, the thunder receding into the distance. Thalia's convulsions ceased, and she lay still on the ground, her breaths ragged but steady.

"I'm fine." Thalia coughed, struggling to push herself up.

"Of course you are," Calliope said, her chest so tight with fear she couldn't take a deep breath. They huddled close, holding each other in the quiet, energy drained from their failed attempt to restore the string.

At first, there was only the symphony of night. The crickets and birdsong, the smell of damp grass and wet earth. But then, a voice sighed on the wind. It was softer than a whisper and drifting from the Forgotten Forest, sweet as a siren song and just as dangerous. A gentle melody that sang of spells, strings, and forgotten things.

Come, sisters, it called. *Come seek me where the shadows sing.*

They stilled, waiting for more. But nothing more came.

"Does it mean us?" Calliope whispered.

"What other sisters are there?" Dissy asked.

"Lovely, now we have bodiless whispers beckoning us to our doom." Thalia frowned.

"Maybe it's beckoning you to a lake of cotton candy, you don't know," Danny said, and somehow, they all laughed.

"What does it mean? Where does it want us to go?" Dissy asked.

"Let's not find out. Rule number one, don't follow voices into the forest at night. I already tried that, and look where we ended up," Calliope said, trying to make light of it.

"Let's get you back to the house, darling." Roz helped Thalia to her feet.

"I'll be fine, trust me," Thalia said, laying a hand on Calliope's arm. "I need to rest. And you need to check on Lucien. Remember, what happens to him happens to you."

Calliope glanced behind her to see Lucien, his shoulders slumped as he leaned against a moss-covered outcropping of rock. And she hated that her sister was right.

"Buddy system?" Danny asked Calliope, who squeezed their hand, loving her friend for offering to stay with her.

"I've got this one," she said darkly, fighting the fatigue that was threatening to pull her down. "I think it's better we have this conversation alone."

"That way no one hears his screams?" Danny asked with a laugh. "Don't go too hard on him. He looked like he was about to pass out the whole time you were, you know, doing your thing." They wiggled their fingers, presumably to indicate doing magic, and Calliope smiled. "Hey," Danny called over to Lucien before Calliope could stop them, their voice ringing loud in the quiet clearing. "Don't be a dick to my best friend, okay? She's been through enough." Lucien didn't deign to answer.

Calliope watched them go, her heart splintering into slivers of guilt and love and fear. This was all her fault. If she'd never gone to the Forgotten Forest, they'd never have been set on this path. Shame pricked at her like a disease that threatened to take over every limb, every vein, insidious and creeping. No matter how much she promised herself they would prevail, the anxiety of what would happen if they failed burned into her skin like a brand. Without Lucien's magic, her own was weak once more. And Ostara was marching ever closer.

She turned to Lucien now, all his memories flooding her own again. She'd seen more of him than he would ever have revealed willingly, and it formed a tenuous wall between them.

"I must be a fool," she said.

"I've been trying to tell you that since the night you almost killed yourself in the forest," Lucien remarked drily, though his voice was thin and didn't pack his usual punch. And in the fading light she saw that his skin looked pale, the corners of his mouth tight as though he were holding in a grimace. He looked even worse than she felt.

"Shadowcraft coven leader," Calliope said, her own voice tight with anger. "First, you lied about your family, our connection. And now this?"

"I'm sorry, Calliope, but I couldn't tell you everything about me. And you fault me for this? From the very moment I met you, you've spewed your disdain of my kind."

"From the very moment I met *you*, you've proven me right! Who are you, really?"

"Someone who will do anything to help the ones I love. You, of all people, should be able to understand that."

"But why didn't you just tell me the truth about your sister?" she demanded, her words thick with emotion she tried and failed to stem.

"We were forced together, Calliope. You hated me for *what*

I was without knowing *who* I was. Would you have believed me? Would you have cared? Or would you have thought it was just another ploy?" His accent was growing thicker with his fatigue. If there was one thing she'd learned through this failed attempt to break their bond, it was that Shadowcraft and Lightcraft did not mix for a reason. The words that had trailed her in the Forgotten Forest echoed in her heart. *Shadow and Light shall never align.*

"Where is she now?"

He paused, ran a hand through his hair.

"She's here. In a cottage I'm renting on the other side of town."

"What's her name?"

He hesitated once more, as though his sister's name were the secret that kept his dark heart beating.

"Eléa," he said, finally.

"Eléa," she breathed.

And maybe it was his ragged face, maybe it was the fatigue clouding her thoughts or the vestiges of his memories still eating away at her. But in spite of it all, she understood him. He was right. He'd withheld information, yes, but he had told her up front that he was a Shadowcrafter, a Deniz. She just hadn't known what that meant to her family. And Calliope's heart ached for him, knowing the lengths he was willing to go to for the one he loved. She saw a reflection of her own dedication to her sisters in his actions.

"You'd do anything to save her," Calliope said.

"Just like you'll do anything to save your sisters. Your town."

"Where is your coven?" she asked.

"The coven is not your concern." His voice was hard and tired.

"How am I supposed to trust you?" she said, her heart sinking. "You're not telling me everything."

"Little muse," he said darkly, taking a step toward her. "Remember that I am still bound to you. I cannot harm you."

"You may not be able to physically hurt me, but that doesn't mean you can't lie." She wanted to trust him, wanted to believe him, wanted to give in to this pulsing thing between them that refused to die out. But it was too much of a risk. And that fueled her anger even more.

"Look at me, Calliope," he said, taking another step toward her just as rain began to fall. He looked up at the sky with a growl. "We should go."

"I'm not going anywhere until you tell me everything I want to know," she shouted, planting her feet and crossing her arms.

Without a second of hesitation, he strode toward her, breathing hard. He pulled her to him, his hands searing hot against her cold skin. In a flash, darkness engulfed her, and when she opened her eyes, they were back in the library. The fire was low, her back pressed against the long table.

"We're out of the rain," she said, hopping up onto the table. Her clothes and hair were damp, and she shivered despite herself. With an idle wave of his hand, the fire was once again roaring. Even depleted as he was, his power still emanated from him.

He looked at her in the glowing light as the storm outside grew louder. It seemed to be reflected in his eyes as he took her in. He took a step forward, and Calliope's breathing picked up.

"This bond we're stuck with, use it," he growled. "Feel the truth of me."

He took another step, and though she told them not to,

her knees fell open as he filled up the space between her legs. He was so warm she was surprised steam wasn't coming off his skin. His palms settled on her knees, and she inhaled sharply as he ran them up her thighs.

"Do it," he said. "Feel the bond with your mind. Your soul."

She closed her eyes, reaching for the connection she'd been trying to ignore. And his desperation flooded into her. The resolve that meant he would shake the clouds from the sky if it meant saving his sister. The shame and rage and longing he felt toward his family, his father in particular. Her skin grew hot as she felt his desire for her, even as it warred with his frustration and pride.

"I still can't figure out if you're the villain or the good guy," she said on a whisper, and her eyes closed of their own accord, her head tilting back as his hands reached her hips and pulled her forward against him.

"Isn't it possible to be both?"

"No," she breathed.

"Is this really what you want to discuss right now?" His voice was velvet and amber, and if she could only swallow it, she knew it would heat her up from within. But he was trying to distract her, and damn it all, it was working.

"Yes," she whispered. But when his hands trailed up, over her waist, brushing the sides of her breasts, skimming over her throat and then threading into her hair, her unsaid words were swallowed in a wave of desire.

His thumb caressed her neck, and her whole body shivered.

"I'm here. That's all I can give you right now."

She thought of Lucien as a young boy, wandering the halls of that great house. Could still feel the tendrils of his loneliness wrapped around her heart. It was so different from her own childhood with laughter echoing down the hallways and sisters to fight and make up with, the way her mother would open their doors a crack every night, just to peer in and check on them. True, all that had vanished when Penelope had. But she'd *had* it. They were woven into her, those memories, and they had shaped so much of her that it was hard to begrudge the bad without also acknowledging the good.

"Fine," she said tightly. "I trust that you believe you're doing what's best for your sister. I don't trust that you're a good person."

"I never claimed to be," he murmured in her ear. She turned her head so that his nose grazed hers. Their foreheads were touching, and she could almost taste her heartbeat, the heat of his body pressed against hers making her forget everything else. His thumb traveled from the pulse at her neck to her bottom lip. He leaned back, a question in his eyes, and when she answered by leaning forward and tilting her head up, his gaze burned with intensity. Their lips hadn't even touched, and she was panting.

He kissed her temple and her eyes closed. He placed another kiss on each lid and her knees tightened around him. One hand squeezed her hip through the damp fabric and the other threaded through her hair, fisting it, tilting her head back even farther so the column of her throat was stretched taut. And when he licked a path from her collarbone to the spot just below her ear, she thought she might pass out.

Then, his lips were finally on hers.

It was a delicate kiss. A promise of what was to come. He tasted like coming home, like rain and stormy nights and lost dreams. But when she slipped her tongue into his mouth, it turned bruising in the best possible way. He moaned into her, his hips moving restlessly against her center as their tongues danced a battle that echoed through her core. Her fingers ran through his hair, over his shoulders, down his back until she gathered his shirt in her fists to pull him closer.

"If you keep this up, we're going to desecrate the hallowed grounds of this library," he whispered against her skin.

"Sounds like a blast," she said breathlessly.

"It does," he agreed, his voice rough. "But I refuse to give you anything but my best, and I'm nearly depleted. And you're exhausted, too." He began to move his fingers across her scalp, massaging until her eyes closed again. With a slight pressure to the back of her head, he brought her forward, so her head was resting against his chest.

She smelled apples and amber.

Fatigue warred with the ache to feel his lips replace his thumb on her neck.

No sooner did she have the thought than he transported them to the couch.

"I'm not some delicate flower that will wilt just because I'm tired," she said grumpily, though it didn't stop her from curling up against him, her stomach still dipping at the memory of his kiss.

"You may not," he said. "But I might." He reclined, his head resting against the back of the couch, his arm snaking around her shoulders to pull her closer.

"Another enchantment could break any moment." Her eyes closed, the heat and Lucien's solid chest against her cheek making her sleepier by the moment.

"Let them break then, little muse. We'll deal with it in the morning."

"Tell me about your family," she said, yawning in full this time.

"You can't even fall asleep without talking," he said, and

there was laughter in his voice. But he did. He told her about their house in France, his parents and their bid for power, always more power. Anything to break the curse that had plagued them since the Great Rift.

"My father always hated that I didn't care enough about the family name," he said, and she could hear the frown in his voice. "My grandfather was even worse. They were both obsessed with finding a way to fix the curse of the wraiths. And my mother, she went along with it all. I still don't know if she stands with my father because she believes in his cause, or because she's terrified of him."

"Tell me about your sister," Calliope said, listening to his heartbeat through the fabric of his shirt. And so he told her about Eléa's arrival and how she'd shifted his whole world. How, after years of bowing to his father's every whim and edict, he found that the role of Shadowcraft coven leader left a strange taste in his mouth, a heavy mantle he never wanted. And though he hated his father for what he'd done, he was grateful for the power he'd forced him to hone, the weapon he'd forged him into. The hours and days of torture, pushing him to the brink, exploring just how far he could go and then yanking him back from the edge before the Shadowcraft consumed his soul and he turned into a wraith. How sometimes he longed for it, that shadow version of himself, soulless and mindless.

In turn she told him about their summers in Milos. Visits to old archeological sites, stealing their next-door neighbor's boat and joyriding around the island. She told him about her first love, a boy named Georgios who lived in the village there. He stiffened at the mention of this, his fingers curling around her shoulder. What she didn't mention was that after meeting Georgios's sister, her feelings for the girl's brother paled in comparison, and she realized for the first time what it was to be attracted to a woman. Instead, she shared about her family's late-night dinners under the stars.

"Those are my favorite memories of my mother," she said softly. "Whenever we couldn't sleep, we'd have midnight feasts on the beach. She taught us how to make baklava and our fingers would get sticky with honey." She held up her hand in the light of the fire as though she could still see the golden strands that had stuck there. "She told us she wanted us to have summers like she and her sisters used to have."

Her head was in his lap now, his tree-trunk thighs hard against her head, but she was unwilling to move. A second later, a soft pillow appeared under her head and a quilted blanket was tucked neatly around her.

"Tomorrow we can resume our bickering," she said, yawning again.

"Tomorrow. For now, sleep." His voice was honey in her ear, and when he closed his eyes, hers closed, too.

She dreamed of kisses that tasted like apples and shadows that wrapped around her throat.

When she woke, he was gone.

CHAPTER 20

THE SKY THAT MORNING WAS SO BLUE IT SEEMED almost translucent. Calliope left the library and followed the sound of clinking dishes and the smell of croissants to the kitchen.

Seeing Thalia sitting at the table, drinking her tea, brought tears to her eyes when she remembered the way her sister's body had spasmed, the glazed look that had taken over her features. Without preamble, Calliope wrapped her arms around her sister.

"I'm glad you're okay," she whispered.

"Me, too," Thalia said with a shudder.

"Where's Dissy?" she asked, grabbing a croissant from the counter and tearing it in half. The butter coated her fingers, and flakes scattered on the floor as she took a bite.

"In the garden," Thalia answered, narrowing her eyes at the mess Calliope was making. Calliope laughed. "Having a crisis because channeling Lucien's magic was her idea."

"She couldn't have known." Calliope frowned. "It was a good idea. And we're all okay."

"Try telling her that."

"She's honestly the strongest of the three of us, but I'm still worried about her. I don't want her to think we blame her."

"I'll go talk to her again." Thalia sighed. "Come with me?"

"Of course, I'll be right out. Just going to finish my tea and talk to Grim for a minute."

When Thalia had gone, Calliope flipped through Grim. Generations of spells and recipes and potions. Tucked between the pages were old photographs, pressed flowers that inexplicably still smelled fresh, and drawings of various ingredients.

Now, as she was looking for a blank page, a sketch she'd never seen before caught her eye. It was crudely done in broad charcoal strokes but arresting in the way the artist had caught the movement of the girls. There were four of them, wearing long dresses. Three of the girls were grouped together and the fourth stood apart, looking toward the trio with a face of longing. Their names were written in faded ink below the sketch. Selene, Rhea, Ariadne—all named in the Petridi tradition of women from Greek mythology—and Isra. She let the page flutter past, picked up a pen, and began to write on a blank page.

She'd meant to write only a few brief sentences about last night, the soft moments they'd shared, but she wound up writing two pages about Lucien. How he irritated and fascinated her in equal measures; how she strangely desired to trust him, though she knew she shouldn't; how she'd been glad he was gone in the morning so she had space to catch her breath; how their kiss had shaken her world, and she wasn't ready for that yet. With an angry slash, she crossed out the last line she wrote and shut Grim with a thud, hating that she was acting like a schoolgirl with a crush.

She drained her tea, polished off the croissant, and went upstairs to change before joining her sisters in the garden.

She was riffling through her sock drawer when Lucien appeared.

"Don't you have anything better to do?" she demanded, her heart beating fast. Whether from the jump scare or his presence, she wasn't quite certain.

"Better than breaking this bond? I think not," he said crisply.

"What about your sister?" she asked, holding up a magenta velvet sock and considering it before tossing it back into the drawer.

Lucien began to pace.

"What about her?"

"Is she still sick?" She held up another sock, this one with cauldrons, bats, and tarot cards on it.

"They'll be covered by your shoes," Lucien said, irritation coloring his voice as he stopped his pacing. "You won't even see them."

"But I'll know they're there," she answered sweetly. "And you didn't answer my question."

"Eléa is safe."

"That also doesn't answer my question," Calliope said, narrowing her eyes as she settled on one sock that had neon psychedelic mushrooms on it and another with honeybees. She pulled them on as Lucien watched silently, his eyes tracking her every movement. "I want to trust you, Lucien." She laced up a pair of combat boots. "But you've got to give me something to work with. Last night I found out that not only are you the head of a *coven* of Shadowcrafters, but your family is part of why we're cursed in the first place."

"You didn't seem to have any qualms about it last night," Lucien said smugly. And the memory of that moment hung heavy in the air between them, unacknowledged and yet tangible: the visceral feeling of their lips crushing, tongues tasting, skin heating—until Calliope's cheeks were flushed as she stared at him. The intimacy of the evening was almost unbearable to think about. How Calliope was feeling things she was not ready to feel.

"Can we please just pretend that never happened?" she said, and the words tasted bitter in her mouth as she broke the spell between them.

His eyes flickered with something before a smile twisted his lips. "Well, I can't sacrifice it like you can." Her heart twisted painfully, but before she could say anything more, he waved his hand. "Consider it forgotten." The lines around his mouth tightened, and he continued, "Anyway, if you must know, my coven has access to Shadowcraft magic that is more powerful than anything I could achieve on my own . . ."

"Oh," Calliope said softly. She certainly couldn't judge him for that. She'd have made a deal with the devil himself if it meant keeping her sisters alive.

"Oh, indeed," Lucien said archly. "Now, if we're finished with this little heart-to-heart, can we move forward with our plan for the day?" He was speaking to her, but his eyes were on the chaos of her sock drawer, which she'd left open.

She laughed. "Does this bother you?" she asked innocently, picking up a few socks and dropping them onto the ground. "You must love lists and organization. You probably have a plan for the day before you open your eyes. Maybe you need to let go a little bit."

"I'm perfectly content with my grip on reality, thank you very much."

"Come on," she said, rolling her eyes. He followed her downstairs and into the morning sunshine, to the sprawling garden where her sisters were pulling weeds and pruning. There were lush hedgerows, a small garden shed, and a pebble walkway that wound through the herb and flower gardens.

"I'm taking Lucien to Tea and Tome," Calliope announced.

"You're what?" he demanded, scowling.

"We searched the library and came up empty. We need a change of scenery."

Calliope could feel her sisters' eyes on her as she and Lucien volleyed back and forth. Dissy was wearing a wry smile, and Thalia sat back on her heels, her eyes darting between them like she was watching a tennis match.

"Very well," Lucien said finally, his tone short.

"Excellent." Calliope smiled in triumph. "Shall we drive or walk, or will you use your magic to—" The words weren't even out of her mouth when Lucien grabbed her by the arm and darkness consumed her vision. By the next blink, she was standing in a dark alley at the top of Front Street.

"You couldn't have taken us all the way there?" Calliope said, breathing hard. She wasn't sure she'd ever get used to that kind of magic.

"Would you have preferred to appear out of the ether where anyone might have seen?"

"Fine, fine," she huffed. "Let's go."

They walked down Main Street and a sliver of peace returned. The air was cool and bright, and the town was fresh and welcoming. But she didn't miss the way Lucien's eyes darted around the street. His shoulders were squared, and he gave off a menacing air as though anyone might attack them at any moment.

And then, Calliope's heart skipped a beat when she saw a short figure on the opposite side of the street. Calliope didn't need her to turn around to know it was Marigold. Her pixie-short hair, now dyed a luminescent, neon green, was like a beacon. She flounced down the walkway of Timeless Treasures and disappeared inside.

A little piece of Calliope's heart went with her. Everything seemed to come undone. Her emotions unraveled, choking her. The façade of bravado and brash actions that she'd constructed to hide her fear and guilt was beginning to crumble. She wanted to weep. And why shouldn't she? Wasn't it fair, when she'd been carrying so much on her shoulders? Wasn't she allowed one moment of weakness?

"Little muse?" Lucien asked. He was a few paces ahead of her. Calliope hadn't realized she'd stopped walking.

"What happens if I can't break the bond?" she whispered, panic scorching along her veins. "What happens if I can't protect the Dark Oak? The town?"

Lucien regarded her. Saw the tears shimmering in her eyes. And he did not look at her with pity or scorn, but with understanding. Calliope recalled his memories, the heavy weight he felt of leading his coven, of saving his sister.

"Tell me what you need," he said, walking back and standing in front of her, toe to toe.

"The truth," Calliope said, and then hiccupped.

"The truth? The truth is that you do not have to do any of those things. Not alone. You have Rosalind and Danny and your sisters. And me," he added as an afterthought. "The burden will not change, but it will grow lighter if you can let someone in to help you carry it."

"You're saying everything is going to be okay?" she asked with a choked sound.

"I am not," he answered simply.

She stared at him and couldn't help the laugh that bubbled out of her. He didn't coddle her with false words and promises, and she appreciated him all the more for it. Wiping the tears that had trailed down her cheeks, she nodded.

"Right," she said, feeling somehow lighter. "Right then. Let's march on, shall we? To death or victory."

They continued their walk to Tea and Tome, and as they neared Autumn's Attic, Calliope waved at Maya Johnson, a middle-aged Black woman with a kindly face and the most fashionable wardrobe Calliope had ever encountered, who was adjusting the window display of vintage clothing. When she saw Calliope, she beckoned her over and met them outside. Her long locks swayed as she moved.

"You'll be at the Moonlight Masquerade next week?" Maya asked.

"We have a lot on our plate at the moment," Calliope answered, her heart twisting painfully. "I'll have to talk with my sisters."

"You do that," Maya said, strong-arming her into a hug. "We need you there. Women like us are the backbone of this community." And with another hug, Maya returned to the shop.

"This town is very strange," Lucien noted as they reached Tea and Tome and the red door swung open of its own accord.

"We all care about each other," Calliope said. "This town is everything to us. It's more than a home. It's family. You should see the Moonlight Masquerade next week," she added with a small, sad smile. "Everyone out in the streets together, dressed up and laughing and celebrating. It's like something out of a movie."

"What are you dressing up as?" Lucien asked, the words tight, as though the question unwillingly left his mouth.

"I'm not . . . we're not going this year. Too much going on. Have to save the town and all that," she joked, but it fell flat. When Lucien stepped over the threshold, she waited for the witch bell to ring and grimaced when it remained silent. "Now, flip the sign on the door and help me take these chairs down," she said.

It was strange having Lucien in the shop. But between customers they practiced small spells to see how much Calliope's magic was weakening (a lot) and bounced around theories about the original curse and how they might break it. They bickered and baited, but there was none of the usual bite.

Dissy stopped by with several caramel apple crisps for the store, and when she'd left, Lucien looked at the crisps and then at her.

With a laugh, Calliope cut two pieces, and the rich, comforting smell filled the shop. Cinnamon and caramel and sweet apples. Lucien's eyes closed when he took the first bite. Calliope watched him chew, entranced, until he caught her staring. She hurriedly took a bite of her own slice.

As she savored a spoonful of the crisp, she tasted not just the sweetness but the richness of life itself—a delicate balance of knowledge, warmth, and sweet surrender to the unknown.

She'd barely swallowed her second bite when the bell over the door chimed, and she nearly choked. Marigold stood at the threshold. Calliope glanced away quickly, trying to gather her wits, attempting to act normal. Did she have caramel on her chin? She tucked a wayward strand of hair behind her ear; Marigold still hadn't spoken. She felt Lucien tense beside her and finally looked up.

Calliope's heart thundered as she took Marigold in, the white Converse shoes hand-painted with purple flames, the short lavender skirt, the purse in the shape of a piece of cake slung over her shoulder. But when her eyes reached Marigold's face, she realized something was deeply, terribly wrong. Her lids were hooded, the pupils blown so large her icy blue eyes looked black. Her features were slack as she stumbled into the shop.

"Mari!" Calliope cried, rushing forward. But as she got closer, she smelled something rotten, like a dead animal left too long to fester on the side of the road.

Lucien flew to his feet, the air in the shop turning heavy and ominous.

"Mari? What's wrong? What happened?"

Lucien tried to grab Calliope and hold her back, but she shook him off. Calliope reached Marigold and took her by the shoulders, giving her a gentle shake. But when Mari looked up, Calliope saw that her eyes had gone completely black, a deep void that sent shivers down her spine.

She tried to step back, but Marigold's hand snaked out and grabbed her in a movement that seemed preternaturally fast.

And then, she opened her mouth on a silent scream and shadows poured out of her throat in a torrent.

The air in the shop turned black, thick and viscous, as a high-pitched keening wail echoed deep in Calliope's bones.

A tendril of shadow flowed toward her like the craggy branch of a tree, and she gasped as the cold of it stole her breath, the rotting, festering smell of it making her gag.

She could hear Lucien shouting, but it sounded far away. She reached for her magic, for some memory to sacrifice, but the shadows began to inch around her throat and toward her mouth.

Her eyes began to water as the stench seeped into her pores. It was more than the smell of death. It was hatred and fear, decomposing like it had been buried too long in a shallow grave, and now that it was free, it sought to infect all in its treacherous path.

The shadows circled her arms, drawing tighter as Marigold's fingers dug into her skin. She couldn't move, could barely breathe for fear of those shadows inching closer and closer to her lips. "Mari," she whispered, eyes filling with tears.

And then Marigold's mouth opened once more. It was not her voice that spoke, but a bone-chilling whisper, the words like a strange caress that made Calliope's stomach churn with fear.

"Time is running out and the magic wears thin. I will be free."

The proclamation settled as the shadows around the room pulsed blacker still. It was ancient and waiting, and she struggled against it even as the fingers of shadow around her neck curled tighter.

And then there was a warm hand in hers. Lucien's calluses were rough against her palm, and she let him anchor her. He spoke low and menacing, and her magic stirred as it pulled from her and into Lucien. A blinding white light filled Tea and Tome and sang through the room.

The shadows recoiled, the tendrils around her neck loosening, and she poured more of her magic through the bond until, finally, they dissipated from Marigold's mouth with an anguished scream.

Marigold slumped forward, and Lucien darted to catch her.

Her eyes opened, and they were back to their normal vibrant blue.

"What . . . what happened?" she choked out, her voice hoarse. "Calliope?" she asked, confused.

Calliope swayed where she stood, shock and fear silencing her.

"I think Calliope's tea was a little too strong for you," Lucien said, his deep voice a balm to Calliope's frayed nerves. "Are you feeling all right?"

"Tea?" she said, dazed. "Who are you?" she asked, looking up at Lucien and then at his hand that still rested on her shoulder.

"A friend of Calliope's," he said tightly, removing his hand just as the door opened again and Tamir entered. She looked among the three of them, her eyes wide and suspicious.

"Mari?" she asked. "What happened? One second you were there, and the next you'd vanished. Maya said she saw you come in here. Is everything okay?"

"I . . ." Marigold started but clearly couldn't find the words. Meanwhile, panic was clawing up Calliope's throat like acid.

"Everything's fine," Calliope said, forcing her voice to remain calm. "Mari just wanted to say hi."

"Right, yeah," Marigold said, nodding even though none of it made sense. But that was how it always went. People wanted to accept the simple explanation, and magic was far too complicated.

"Okay," Tamir said slowly. "Come on then, let's finish loading your stuff."

"Yeah," Mari said, rubbing her throat, her blue eyes curious and a little scared. "Good to see you, Opie."

They watched them go, the bell jingling merrily as the door swung shut, and Calliope leaned against the counter, breathing hard.

"That's what happens . . ." Her voice was barely more than a whisper.

"If the Shadowcraft gets out," he finished for her. "It infects. Seeks more power. And the only way to get it is to possess and consume."

"How did you—" she started, but he knew her question and answered it.

"I drew your Lightcraft into me through our bond." He laid the back of his hand gently across her forehead. "You're warm," he noted, his touch and voice in stark contrast to the anger slashing across his face like lightning at midnight.

Calliope batted his hand away, panic rising again. "This means another enchantment is broken. We have to keep it locked away," she said, her own voice stronger now. "We can't let that . . . that *evil* out. And we have less than a week until the equinox."

The counter was biting into her back, but she didn't feel the pain, only the threat of what was coming.

CHAPTER 21

HE HADN'T INTENDED TO SHARE SO MUCH ABOUT himself with her. But once he started, the words kept coming. And then he convinced himself that's what needed to be done. That the only reason he cracked his past open and laid the ashes of it at her feet was because time was running out. The equinox was growing ever closer, and he needed to rebuild their tenuous trust.

But he couldn't get the feel of her off his skin. The weight of her head in his lap as she fell asleep.

He'd seen her face when that green-haired woman had come into the shop. The quick succession of emotions that painted themselves across her skin. He wanted to ask what they meant to each other. But he had no right to know, and she didn't offer any explanation. And so, he simply watched as the light flared in her eyes and then died just as quickly. The desire to reignite that light with a kiss was a visceral reaction that threatened to undo him. And he wasn't sure what it said about him that he loved that she wore her heart on her sleeve. It was so completely opposite of everything he'd ever known. There was a purity to her emotion he longed to consume like whiskey. Wanted to mull over the flavors and nuance and notes of it.

But it changed nothing. He paced around the living room of the small cottage he was renting. Couldn't stand it. Changing into athletic wear with the snap of his fingers, he went out for a run and kept a punishing pace, forcing himself to remember the real reasons he was here. And yet, with every footfall, his mind conjured images of golden-blond hair and ocean eyes.

By the time he returned, he was dripping sweat, breathing hard, and no closer to getting that confounding witch out of his head. He followed the smell of food cooking to where he found Eléa reading a book as she leaned against the kitchen counter.

"Running away from your demons, brother mine?" she asked with raised eyebrows.

"What are you making?" he asked, pouring himself a glass of water and draining it.

"Why do you never answer my questions?" She pushed her long, dark hair behind her ears.

"Why do you always ask questions you know I won't answer?" he countered. "Now, what smells so good?"

"Sarai took me to the bodega." She sighed happily. "I got an organic frozen pizza!" Lucien laughed at the look of utter delight on her face. They'd both grown up with a private chef, and their parents would never have let something like a frozen pizza disgrace the freezer they never actually opened themselves.

"Imagine what Chef Matthieu would say," Lucien said in mock horror. And this, this was easy and safe. Slipping into the mask of older brother. Teasing, protective, loving.

"Alexandre once smuggled me a frozen chocolate moelleux," she said thoughtfully. "He'd never made one, and Chef Matthieu had told him it was too decadent for 'the family' so it was pointless to waste money on the ingredients."

"Good to know we weren't the only ones with overbearing fathers. And how was it?"

"Delicious. But Alex took notes. Saved up his pocket money for weeks until he could buy his own ingredients. And I snuck down to the kitchens when he finally made his own version. We sat in front of the oven and burned our mouths when they finally came out because we couldn't wait for them to cool." Her eyes turned thoughtful. Wistful. "It was like the first moelleux never existed. That's how good his was. Like I'd only ever read about chocolate before and finally got to taste it." She sighed at the memory, and Lucien felt an uncomfortable pull in his chest where those words resonated. Calliope was his moelleux. It was like every other woman before her never existed. He shook the thought off as Eléa pulled the pizza out of the oven and began to slice it into uneven pieces. She was about to take a bite when Lucien spoke.

"Maybe we should . . ." He cleared his throat. "Should we sit at the table?"

"How civilized!" Eléa said delightedly, putting her slice on a plate and getting another one for her brother. He pulled out her chair and then sat beside her. "What brought this on?" she asked with a sly smile.

"Just thought it would be a nice change of pace," he lied as he thought about the Petridis' kitchen table, the wood worn smooth from countless dinners. He wondered if that wood held memories. If he could charm them out of it and see an image of a young Calliope, no doubt with wild hair and wilder eyes, elbows and knees scraped from climbing trees.

"You're allowed to be happy, you know." She tilted her head as she said it, as though regarding him like something under a microscope.

"My happiness is ensuring your happiness," he grumbled, taking a bite of the pizza.

"I'm not your job, Lucien." She frowned, but he couldn't tell her just how wrong she was. "I don't want you to do anything you'll regret," she said softly now, laying a hand on top of his. Her skin was cold against his, and as he curled his fingers around hers, he saw that the circles under her eyes were growing darker. Rage burned through him. Anger at his grandfather for what he'd done. At his father for allowing it. At himself for not seeing the signs. The equinox was just over a week away, and he shuddered at the thought of what would happen if he failed. With a silent vow, he strengthened his resolve to break this damned bond, so he could do what needed to be done.

There was a knock at the front door. Brisk and impatient.

"Come in, Malik," Lucien called with a sigh. He'd sent a missive requesting his presence just after he'd returned from his run but had expected a little more time before Malik arrived.

"Well, well, well," Malik crowed. "What a pretty picture this is. Not quite up to Chef Matthieu's standards, though, is it?" he asked, leaning over the table to look at the pizza with an aggrieved face that had Eléa laughing.

Orphaned young, Malik had run from the French foster care system and was wandering the streets of Paris when Ahmed had used a location spell that sought out potential powerful Shadowcrafters. He'd embraced Ahmed's invitation quickly and arrived at their French estate with nothing but his wit and charm. He used those traits to endear himself to Lucien's father and became something of a protégé to him.

Together, Malik and Lucien grew in both talent and power, always trying to outdo each other in impressing Lucien's father. But when Ahmed began to stoke that rivalry, pitting the boys against each other, Lucien realized he valued their friendship more than empty words of praise from a man who sought only to profit off their strength. Because that was all his father ever wanted, more and ever-increasing power. A way to break the wraith curse and in the process eradicate any Lightcraft he came into contact with. But by then, Malik was in too deep. He longed for that fatherly approval more than he cared for Lucien. Still listened to Ahmed's honeyed words that their work was to be rid of their curse, so they could increase Shadowcraft magic for all. And so, as Malik's good nature drained away under Ahmed's tutelage, they drifted apart.

Lucien didn't completely trust Malik, knew he wanted the power of the Dark Oak so he could finally make Ahmed proud. Still, he trusted him more than anyone else. And that would have to do. Their truce was uneasy, the ghost of their past echoing in unsaid words, even as being together again brought back memories of their youth. Despite it all, Lucien hungered for that old root of friendship. And away from Ahmed's influence, Malik returned to his charming self, and Lucien felt himself being pulled into it, lulled into what he feared was a false sense of security. But he'd lived his life trusting others only insomuch as they could serve his goals. It was too like his father, and so he'd vowed to try, really try, to repair his friendship with Malik.

"You finish up," Lucien told his sister, grabbing her book

from the counter and depositing it next to her plate. "Malik and I will be in the next room. We have some business to discuss."

"I can discuss business, too, you know," Eléa called after her brother, but he was already through the door.

"New developments, boss?" Malik asked, making himself comfortable on the couch, leaning back and crossing an ankle over his knee.

"Where are we at with the enchantments?"

"Sarai and Feng are working on the next one. They're sticky," Malik said. "Feng said something about the enchantments being woven with traps. It's slow going, but it's better that than one of the spells rebounding and killing him outright."

Lucien ran a hand through his hair. He needed to take a shower. He could magic the sweat and dirt off, but he never felt quite as clean. He thought of Calliope's clothes strewn in piles around her room, the haphazard drawer filled with mismatched socks, and shuddered. Lucien needed clean lines and organization because it soothed the chaos in his head. And now he had Feng to worry about on top of everything else. When Feng was ten, his father had died in a horrific train accident. He'd witnessed the whole thing and afterward dedicated himself to learning and perfecting protection spells. His mother was all he had left, and the boy was consumed with getting more power so he could protect her the way he wasn't able to protect his father.

"The kid's fine." Malik bristled at the look of worry on Lucien's face. "Just let him do his thing."

"If the flow of magic gets too strong—" he started, but Malik cut him off.

"He knows the risks, Luce. Stop babying him. Jesus, stop

worrying about everyone. We've got this handled. You just keep the sisters away from the forest," Malik said with a shudder. "Everything goes dark and silent and lifeless the closer you get to the Dark Oak. Eerie as shit. But if they get so much as a whiff of what we're doing . . . it won't be good for them or us."

Lucien swallowed hard and nodded tightly.

"You okay?" Malik asked, furrowing his brow. "The sisters got you spooked or something?"

What could Lucien tell him? The old urge was there. The desire to share that he was terrified of what would happen if they didn't succeed. But right behind that fear was the one of what would happen if they *did* succeed. What would happen to Calliope and her sisters once they were disentangled from the generations of enchantments that had bound them? If his Shadowcraft coven couldn't contain what was in the Dark Oak? He heard the clink of dishes being placed in the sink in the kitchen and pictured Eléa's face, the hollows and dark circles, her ever-growing illness.

"I'll keep them busy," Lucien vowed, his words taking on a sharp edge. "There's something called the Moonlight Masquerade coming up. Calliope said they wouldn't be attending, but I'll convince them to go. Use that time to do what needs to be done."

CHAPTER 22

THE NEXT FEW DAYS PASSED IN A BLUR OF RE-search as the eve of the Moonlight Masquerade drew near. Every mention of wraiths said only that they were dangerous beyond measure and to stay far away from them. Perhaps no one who'd ever encountered them lived to tell the tale. Calliope and her sisters grasped on to anything that might mean something, but their magic was growing weaker by the day, and Calliope's in particular was temperamental at best. She offered memories like pieces of gold, but nothing was worth the price she needed to pay. Even Thalia, who hated using magic, was sacrificing memories in an effort to find something, anything, that might help them. But there was nothing on wraiths they could find. Nothing on purifying their string. Just dead end after dead end. Calliope had even reached out to Alice and the Lightcraft coven in Aurelia to see if they had access to information the Petridis didn't. Calliope received a note back from Alice saying she didn't know how to fight wraiths or break Shadowcraft bonds, but that she and her coven were looking for answers. She didn't ask questions, only signed off with a kind reminder that she was there if Calliope needed her.

She fought with Lucien, who remained steadfastly, annoyingly, by her side. And the more time she spent with him, the more she was able to hone her aptitude for irritating him. His wards around her house remained strong, and she did not ask him where he went when he was not at Lethe Manor. Or why sometimes when he would arrive, he would be in such a quietly foul mood she found herself irritating him even more, just to replace his scowl with a look of soft annoyance.

One afternoon, he asked again about the Moonlight Masquerade. "If it's your favorite day of the year, why aren't you going?" he asked with a frown. Calliope was overcome with a desire to use her fingertips to drag the corners of his lips up. But then her eyes snagged on those lips, full and pouting, and her traitorous stomach did a somersault.

"Impending doom?" she said with a shrug.

"Seems like the right time to let loose," he said.

"When have you ever let loose?" she scoffed. "Do you even know how?" His eyes were dark when he turned his gaze on her.

"Wouldn't you like to know," he said with an almost teasing note to his voice. Their eyes locked, and his smirk died away. There was something ravenous in his stare, and Calliope's skin tightened, as though he might just take a bite out of her.

"Fine," she huffed. "We'll go. A last hurrah, as it were." Goosebumps sprouted on her arms, and she tried to hide her shiver as she tore her gaze from his.

With each day that passed, the veil grew thinner, tempers rose higher, and hope was a fragile thread that began to fray.

With mere days until the Moonlight Masquerade, Calliope sat with her sisters in front of the sitting room fireplace, Dissy sipping tea and Thalia eating a scone as they continued to pore over books and ledgers and journals. Danny, a saint among humans, was keeping them company in comfortable silence. Hope seemed as elusive as a wisp of smoke, dancing just beyond reach and extinguished with the barest puff of air.

Calliope startled when the front door banged open. Roz crossed the threshold, and her face grew dismayed as she took in Danny and the sisters sitting around in despair.

"This simply won't do," she said. "If you let them steal your joy, they've already won. Up." She clapped her hands with a resounding echo. "Thalia, get the vodka. Calliope, squeeze some lemon juice, please. We're making basil lemonade martinis."

The sisters stared at one another, but when Roz clapped her hands again, they scurried into action. Roz's martinis were famous. When each sister had turned twenty-one, she'd thrown them an elaborate themed party at Tea and Tome after closing. Fairy lights were involved, costumes were required, and, always, there was dancing.

Now Roz reached for her phone and connected it into the Bluetooth speaker disguised as a wireless vintage radio.

Michael Jackson's "Billie Jean" floated into the room, and the corners of Calliope's mouth lifted as the fresh scent of lemon wafted toward her. Roz grabbed Danny's hands and pulled them to their feet.

"Come on, now," Roz wheedled, pulling Danny behind her as she danced over to the shelf and pulled down five martini glasses.

"I've got the basil leaves and simple syrup," Dissy said, and her face was softer, the stress lines around her mouth disappearing.

"Good girl, darling. Now . . ." She reached for the martini shaker and filled it with the ingredients. She shook it above her head and passed it to Calliope, who laughed and shook it as well before handing it to Dissy.

When they each had an ice-cold martini in their hands, Roz held hers up.

"Whoever is trying to break those enchantments, they can go to hell. To never letting those bastards steal our joy," she cried, and the group echoed her. The tart lemon and sweet syrup mixed with the sharp bite of vodka. It was clean and crisp and spicy and warmed Calliope's throat with a delicious burn.

Roz turned up the music and pulled Calliope into a dance. Dissy laughed and held up her martini in a salute as she swayed to the music. Danny, always on board with Roz's wild antics, grabbed Thalia's hands and spun her around. Calliope watched as Thalia reluctantly gave in, her body moving stiffly. Danny rolled their eyes, placing their hands on Thalia's shoulders and shaking the tension out of her. Thalia laughed, her cheeks blooming with color, and Calliope was shocked when her sister finally slipped an arm around Danny's waist and began to dance.

"Look at that," Danny said drily. "She does have a pulse."

"Why must you always tease me?" Thalia demanded with a little frown. Calliope tried not to gape when she noticed that Danny couldn't take their eyes off of her sister.

"Because you make it so easy," they said with a laugh. "And there's just nothing like getting a pretty woman's panties in a twist." They spun Thalia out and then back in, and Calliope nearly choked when she heard Thalia's answering giggle. A *giggle*. From her *sister*.

Calliope watched them out of the corner of her eye until, a few minutes later, there was a loud knock at the door and Thalia pulled away, laughing breathlessly as she went to answer it. When she came back, she brought Sean Zhao with her. Sean's eyes were wide as he took in the scene before him, like he wasn't quite sure what he'd just walked into.

"I'm, uh, just here to deliver the final report on that fire," he said, almost shouting over the music. "No cause could be identified, but we recommend creating a more defensible space. I brought pamphlets." And indeed, he pulled several foldouts from his pocket.

Roz took the pamphlets and tossed them into the air, where they rained down like confetti.

"Right now, we're dancing," she said.

Sean laughed his deep, rich laugh, and Dissy blushed prettily.

"Well, then," he said. "May I?" And he held out a hand to Dissy, who, to the shock of everyone in the room, slipped her hand into his.

They danced around the kitchen as the Bee Gees' "Stayin' Alive" filled the room, and soon they were all laughing.

"To staying alive," Roz said, toasting the second round of drinks.

"To staying alive," they echoed her.

"Thank you," Calliope said quietly to Roz as she twirled her close, the martini spilling over the side of her glass and making her fingers sticky with lemon juice and sugar. It was the lightest she'd been in days.

"Anything for my girls," Roz smiled, pulling Calliope into a hug. "My nieces," she whispered into her hair.

"I don't know what we'd have done without you all these years." Calliope felt tears prick the backs of her eyes. "And if there's only one good thing to come out of this whole mess, it's knowing that you're here. As family."

"I know you're not my daughters. But you saved me as much as I saved you." Roz placed a gentle hand on Calliope's cheek, and her heart swelled with love.

The night wore on as they danced and laughed until they collapsed in the sitting room, draped across couches and the thick, plush rug.

"I should go," Sean said, clearly not wanting to. And when Dissy looked up at him with pleading eyes, he made a strangled sound. "I guess I could stay a little longer." He sounded breathless. "But if anyone asks, I was here lecturing you about fire safety." The sound of Dissy's answering laughter was the sweetest thing Calliope had heard in ages. There were only four days left until the equinox, but Calliope couldn't begrudge the thrum of life that threaded through that room.

"Your mother would have loved this," Roz said, flopping down into a chair and pulling her long sheet of silver hair up to cool her neck. Calliope listened eagerly, always hungry for any crumbs of her mother. "She adored noise and chaos and magic."

"Do you miss it? Doing magic?" Calliope asked quietly, glancing at Sean to ensure he wasn't paying attention.

"It's like a phantom limb." She smiled sadly. "I can almost feel it. But this." She twirled a finger to indicate all of them. "This is its own kind of magic, don't you think?"

"We used to dance on the beach in Milos," Calliope remembered.

"Our mother took us there when we were girls, too," Roz said. "Before she passed away. There's no place like it. Milos is in our blood, our bones. Did you know there's an old Petridi family legend that the Dark Oak actually started out on that little island? We've never been able to confirm it. But I think that's why every generation goes back. Like it calls to us and we're restless until we pay our homage."

"I didn't know that," Calliope said softly. "But every summer when my feet finally touched that sand, I wanted to cry. Even though I was young, I knew it just felt *right*."

"Penelope would spend hours out there," Roz said, her eyes turning glassy with the memory. "Always in her own world. Our mother would send Daphne out to drag her back in at dinnertime, and she'd have sand in every crevice, her hair crusted with salt."

"What happened to your mother?" Calliope asked, feeling foolish for not knowing the answer.

"Your grandmother and her sisters were killed while protecting the Dark Oak," Roz said quietly as she watched Eurydice dance with Sean and Danny pour another drink for Thalia, all of them blissfully out of earshot.

"What?" Calliope choked.

"Oh, yes." She sighed. "Shadowcrafters. I don't know the story, darling. I was too young for the details. But one day she was there, and the next she wasn't. No, don't be sad," she said, tapping Calliope's cheek as a tear fell. "We didn't have the same relationship with our mother that you had with yours. Anyway, our magic came fast after that, mine and Daphne's and Penelope's. We were lying in bed one night, the three of us together, because we were sad and somehow being close let us share the sorrow between us. The lights were all on, but none of us wanted to get up. And Daphne just dragged her fingers together like this"—she showed Calliope—"and whispered, 'skotádi—' "

The word was barely out of her aunt's mouth when the room was plunged into darkness. Calliope felt a hand clutch her arm, Roz's fingernails digging into her skin. Thalia swore. Dissy let out a little yelp.

"The hell?" Danny called.

"A power outage," Sean said, his voice calm and sure.

"Fos," Calliope whispered as she sacrificed the memory of her first taste of baklava. And the lights sputtered back on, the room bathed in that amber glow. Sean had one arm wrapped protectively around Dissy's shoulders. Thalia was standing next to Danny, their fingers grazing in the inch of space between them. The song had faded to Fleetwood Mac's "Silver Springs." And Calliope was staring at her aunt, breathing hard.

"Strange," Sean said, his brow pinched in confusion. "Must have been a surge."

"A surge," Calliope echoed, her heart pounding. Roz had just done *magic*. Which meant . . .

"I'd better go," Sean said, regret laced through every word. He looked at Dissy, but she was looking at Roz. She tore her eyes away from her aunt and whispered something in Sean's ear. Calliope watched as he blushed and walked out of the room like he was in a dream.

"What?" Danny asked. "Why is everyone being weird all of a sudden? Is it Fleetwood Mac? I can change the song," they joked, eyes nervously darting among the sisters.

"How?" Calliope asked. "How did you just do magic?"

"I don't know!" Roz said, her eyes wide as she stared at her hands. "This can't . . . I don't understand."

"That was you?" Thalia whispered. And when Roz nodded, Calliope's stoic sister clapped a hand over her mouth. Dissy, white as a sheet, sat down abruptly, which Calliope thought was a good thing since it looked like her legs were about to give out.

"They're alive," Calliope whispered. "Somewhere out there, Mother and Daphne are *alive*." The tears pooled and began to fall before she even knew she was crying.

"*What?*" Danny demanded, running their hand through their short hair. "Explain, please."

"Petridi sisters can only do magic if their string of fate is still intact," Calliope said, and though she knew it was her saying the words, she felt like her body was suspended. She was a specter, weightless, and though she tried to grab the strings, her mind was floating away. *Alive alive alive.* The word tasted foreign. And when she closed her eyes, bright sparks of color flashed on the backs of her eyelids. Something was burgeoning in her chest, growing, spreading, until her very blood sang with it. *Hope.* Her mother and Daphne were alive.

"We'll find them," Calliope promised. "Somehow, some way, when this is all over, we'll find them."

"Alive," Roz whispered. And the five of them laughed and cried and danced and poured another round of drinks as they toasted the news that sang of a different kind of future.

But amid it all, Calliope's spontaneous promise whispered through the room, and she tried not to think about what fate had in store for them.

CHAPTER 23

THE NEXT EVENING, WITH ONLY THREE DAYS LEFT until the equinox, the moon hung like a silver coin in the dark sky, casting an ethereal glow over the town of Gold Springs as the Moonlight Masquerade began to unfold. The festivities were in full swing by the time Calliope and her sisters arrived, and the air hummed with excitement. The townsfolk, adorned in their finest spring costumes and masks, swirled like leaves in the breeze. Flower crowns and ribbons were everywhere, a true celebration of the changing of the seasons as they said goodbye to winter and welcomed the soft days of spring.

"I've been waiting for this since—" Calliope started.

"Since last year," Dissy said with a laugh, looping her arm through Calliope's and giving it a squeeze. She reached out with her other arm to Thalia, who reluctantly gave in and allowed herself to be pulled to her sister's side.

They were dressed to match, which took some wheedling on Dissy's part to get Thalia to agree, but they cut a striking figure. Diaphanous white dresses floated ethereally around their bodies. In years past, Calliope would sacrifice a simple memory to make the fabric appear always in motion, but her magic was waning too much even for that. Their honey-wheat hair was braided intricately in ancient Greek fashion and woven with narcissus. They dressed as the muses they were named after and wore the same outfits at each Moonlight Masquerade, strolling among the crowd and doling out destinies and death with mock-serious voices. Calliope loved the crush of bodies, the buzzing chatter, but Dissy hated it. Oftentimes, she'd leave early, unable to stand it for too long. Even now her eyes scanned the streets looking for the emptiest path. Calliope squeezed her sister's arm with her own.

"Let me know if it gets to be too much," she whispered.

Dissy nodded and smiled tightly. "I'm sorry I'm like this."

"Don't you dare apologize for being exactly the way you're meant to be," Calliope said with passion.

As the crowd thickened, Thalia, sensing Dissy's rising anxiety, stepped in front of them and acted as bulwark, cutting through the people. They stopped by the Potion Tasting booth, which was really a themed bar put on by the Piano Rouge on High Street. Calliope ordered them each the moonlight elixir, a concoction of vodka, blue curaçao, and orange bitters served in a tall plastic glass with glowing plastic ice cubes and dry ice that made it smoke like a real potion.

Calliope drank hers too fast and was about to force her sisters back to the booth when Danny showed up and held out another.

"You know me so well," Calliope said with a sigh, pulling Danny in and planting a kiss on their temple.

"You should keep a clear head," Thalia warned with a frown.

"What could possibly happen at the Moonlight Masquerade, dear sister?" Calliope demanded, finally feeling the layers of stress peel away, her throat delightfully warm from the vodka.

"That is not the kind of question to ask in our current climate," Thalia whispered.

"You sound just like Lucien. I'm surprised you two don't get on like a house on fire," Calliope said.

"And where is the shadow daddy?" Danny asked. They were wearing wide-legged pants and a long collared shirt that they buttoned only halfway so the lower half flared open. Their mask was made of intricate swirls of black and white.

"Do *not* let him hear you calling him that. His head is already big enough."

"Come on then, let's forget about him," Danny said, and they made their way into the throng of people.

"Where's Roz?" Dissy asked, craning her neck to try to see through the crowd. "She's supposed to meet us here."

"We'll find her," Calliope said, swaying down the street as the stars pulsed brightly in her vision.

Stilt-walkers towered over the crowd, their billowing pants blowing in the breeze as they bent down to drop lollipops into the hands of waiting children. Lanterns bobbed like fairy sprites, adding to the mesmerizing scene as the procession meandered through the streets that had been blocked off for foot traffic only. And the street was indeed packed. Children and adults alike held sticks with ribbons attached, swirling them through the air until there was color everywhere.

They caught sight of Sean Zhao, who was wearing his firefighters' uniform. He saw them and waved. Calliope started to walk over, but Dissy, blushing hard, tried to steer them in the opposite direction.

"Go on," Calliope said, nudging her sister.

"Go where?" Dissy asked quietly, trying and failing not to glance back at Sean. Calliope smiled inwardly. It was so rare for Eurydice to show interest in anyone, if blushing in someone's general direction could be called showing interest.

"I honestly can't remember the last time you dated anyone," Thalia said.

"Usually keeping you two from killing each other is a full-time job," Dissy joked.

"Which means you have no excuse right now because Thalia and I are being absolute angels to each other, right?" Calliope said, looking to Thalia.

"Indeed," Thalia said, leaning her shoulder into Calliope's. And it was true. They still had their spats and irritated each other as only sisters could, but there was a levity there now. It had been so long since they were united in a common goal.

"Go on, go," Calliope said, drawing out the vowel in a sing-song voice until Dissy laughed and gave in. Calliope watched Dissy go and said a silent prayer that she and Sean would hit it off.

"What?" Thalia asked Danny sharply when she noticed them staring.

"Do *you* ever date?" Danny asked.

"What's it to you?" Thalia raised an eyebrow.

"Goddess spare me," Calliope groaned.

"You're just so different from Calliope. I mean, I see the family resemblance, but you're like creatures from two different planets. And you're so cool, calm, and collected about everything."

"Hey," Calliope cut in. "Are you saying I'm *not* cool, calm, and collected?"

"That is literally exactly what I'm saying," Danny responded drily.

"Oh, shut up." Calliope laughed. "And come on, I smell something delicious."

The scent of cotton candy and caramel corn made Calliope's stomach grumble. Her head was buzzing just a little from finishing her second moonlight elixir, and it gave the night a delightfully misty quality. A live band played jaunty music, and dancers dressed like goddesses of spring waltzed in a choreographed dance. Danny's niece Anika, wearing a deep purple dress and mask to match with purple flowers threaded through her dark curls, ran up to them as they watched. She pulled on their hand, trying to drag them onto the makeshift dance floor, which was really just a stretch of pavement.

"This isn't dancing music, Anika," Danny whined. "I need strobe lights and techno beats."

"Please," Anika pleaded, and Danny gave in with a laugh.

"Catch you later," Danny shouted as they let themself be pulled by the ten-year-old.

"Where *is* Roz?" Calliope wondered aloud as they weaved gracefully through the crowd, the revelry moving around them like water. Calliope was so lost in the enchantment of the night, she didn't notice Lucien at first.

He wasn't dressed up, of course, but the tall, broad cut of his figure stood out. He was wearing his ubiquitous dress shirt, but the sleeves were rolled up again, and even from a distance, Calliope could see his tattoos snaking around his forearms. His dark hair was mussed, and she could practically see him running a hand through it in the singular irritated fashion he had. One hand was in his pocket and the other held a cone of pink cotton candy hanging loosely at his side.

He stood preternaturally still, only his eyes darting around, as though looking for someone. Between that and the pink cotton candy, he looked lost, until his gaze landed on Calliope like he could feel her stare. When he saw her, his eyes narrowed, all traces of the lost look gone, and he drank her in hungrily, eyes roving from her braided crown down to her sandaled feet in a way that made her stomach dip.

She left Thalia in line at the Fairy Cakes booth run by Whisk and Spoon bakery, the table filled with spring cakes, moonlit meringues, and macarons shaped like Easter eggs.

"Little muse," Lucien said by way of greeting.

"Why do you call me that?" she asked, eyeing the pink cotton candy still dangling in his hand.

"I thought that would be obvious."

"Humor me then," Calliope said, rolling her eyes.

"Calliope was called the 'Chief of all Muses.' It seemed fitting. Though she *was* the Muse who presided over eloquence and poetry, and your wanton disposition to narrate every mundane moment could never be called that."

"Ah, your costume for the evening finally reveals itself, I see. You've dressed up as an uptight asshole," she said. "How *fitting*. Is it possible for you to give a compliment without following it up with an insult?"

"Yes," he said. Only that, and nothing more. His tone was flat, but his eyes were sharp as they locked on hers.

"Go ahead then, try." Calliope laughed. Two drinks deep, she wasn't offended by his impudence anymore. There was an oddly endearing quality to it, as though he'd never quite learned how to behave in polite society. She grabbed the cotton candy from his hand, tearing off a piece and letting the sugar dissolve on her tongue.

"Are you angling for a compliment?"

"Absolutely and without shame. My life has fallen to pieces, and I'm managing it wonderfully, all things considered. So, go on, praise me. Tell me how marvelous I am. I dare you."

He paused, feigning concentration. "It could be said that there is something . . . charming about your incessant chatter."

"You're horrible at this. Try again." The crowd swelled and jostled Calliope closer until she could feel the warmth emanating from him. Almost unwillingly, he lifted a hand and trailed his finger down the long column of her throat. And then, with deliberate slowness, he wrapped those fingers around the halter neck of her dress and used his grip around the fabric to pull her closer, closer, until she was pressed up against him. It was more than she'd bargained for, and between his closeness amid the crush of people moving around them and the alcohol making her reckless, she knew a very foolish decision was coming on.

"You want a compliment?" he whispered in her ear, his breath warm against her skin. "Every time I look at you, I see the allure of a thousand wistful dreams. You vex me every moment we are together and even more so when we're apart, but I would be remiss to let that color the truth of you. Your stubbornness and loyalty are the very things that dare the universe to be daring in return. And I find myself fantasizing of a dozen ways to use that clever tongue."

Calliope's stomach dropped; her breathing turned heavy.

"That's better," she rasped. "Could still use some work, but better." She was fuzzy and deliciously hot all over.

He was still holding her dress, staring hungrily at her lips when a loud chorus of cheers went up near the dancers. His eyes cleared, and after glancing over her shoulder, he stepped back, releasing her and putting some distance between them. A moment later, Dissy and Thalia walked up behind her.

"Still no Roz?" she asked her sisters.

"Maybe she's still at her shop," Thalia said. "You know how she loses track of time."

"Let's go find her," Calliope said with a sigh.

As they turned and walked away, thunder cracked and forks of lightning seared purple across the night sky. A loud *crack* rent the air as a looming elm was hit and split in two, and the smell of burning wood reached Calliope's nose. People near the tree screamed, and the band stopped playing as fat raindrops began to fall. Hurricane-force winds ripped the tops off tents, knocked the stilt-walkers over, and buffeted people into one another.

More screams tore through the air as the rain turned to hail. Fat, ash-toned ice the size of quarters rained down, and the crowd scattered, seeking cover.

"What the hell is happening?" Calliope said, gasping. Though California was known for temperamental weather, the forecast had been clear, and Calliope had never seen hail like this. It smoked as it hit the street and then melted instantly into a puddle of black.

"Time to go, little muse," Lucien growled, grabbing her firmly by the arm.

"It's the enchantments, it must be," Calliope shouted over the din, yanking her arm out of Lucien's grip. Her white dress was already drenched and sticking to her curves, her braids heavy on her head.

They ran with their arms over their heads to Roz's shop. The wind was screaming now, the hail falling nearly horizontal. Townsfolk rushed into shops or huddled beneath what remained of the awnings. Limbs tore from trees, and branches littered the pavement. Somewhere, a child was wailing. And Lucien was beside her the whole time.

They were panting by the time they reached Roz's tarot shop and barreled through the front door. Slamming it shut behind them did little to dim the noise. The moment Calliope caught her breath and swiped away the tendrils of hair clinging to her face, her heart lurched. The air smelled wrong, and an energetic residue coated the walls. The shop was a large, open room with a round wood table in the center and half a dozen chairs. Roz's chair, at the head of the table, was pushed out. It was dark save for the candles burning, the wax dripping over the sides and pooling on the black tablecloth.

"Roz?" Calliope called, walking forward, eyes scanning the dark corners and the staircase that led up to her flat above the shop. A tarot deck sat on the table with a spread laid out. There was Death and the Knight of Swords, portents of change, both. The cards were singed around the edges, and Calliope knew, without knowing how, that her aunt had been channeling magic for this reading. Had she been trying to find Daphne and Penelope? Calliope looked for the third card in the spread, but it was missing. There was also a small bowl of what looked to be black ink, a scattering of crystals, and bird feathers laid out in a geometric shape. Had she been attempting a spell? Would she have been so foolish when her magic had been dormant for so long and they didn't know what she was capable of?

"Roz!" Thalia shouted now.

Lightning flashed outside the window and illuminated the shop for the barest moment, and that's when everything happened at once.

Calliope let out a muffled cry when she saw Roz's boots on the ground, sticking out at an awkward angle. The sis-

ters surged forward, and Calliope fell to her knees beside her
aunt's too-still body. She was laying on her side in a heap,
partially under the table, as though she'd fallen sideways off
her chair.

Dissy and Thalia were there beside her, and Thalia gently
turned Roz's shoulders. Her eyes were open but unseeing.
Glassy as she stared at nothing.

"No!" Calliope cried. "No, no, no." Her own body felt
foreign, strange, with her skin stretched too tight over her
bones. She couldn't tell which way was up and which was
down. The whole world tilted on its axis as she stared in horror at her aunt's slack face. "Roz," she said, shoving Thalia's
hands away and shaking Roz by the shoulders. "Roz!"

Dissy slipped out the front door saying she would go get
help, and Thalia sat back on her heels with her head in her
hands.

"Please wake up," Calliope whispered now, leaning forward and pulling Roz's body into her arms. "We need you.
We need you. Please."

And with her aunt so close, she saw the marks. Swirls of
shadow burned into her skin that started below her ears,
traveled down her neck and chest, and disappeared beneath
her shirt. Death had left its calling card. Her soul was truly
gone.

As Calliope laid her gently back down, a scream lodged
in her throat. She gently closed Roz's eyes. And when she
moved her arms to rest beside her, she noticed the third tarot
card clutched in her hand. Calliope pulled it out and stared
down at the Ace of Pentacles. An inheritance card. But it
didn't make sense. The Ace of Pentacles was a positive card,
one that meant something *good* was coming. That a new opportunity would appear out of nowhere and extend its hand

to you, if you only possessed the wherewithal to take it and turn it into something meaningful. But what could possibly be good and meaningful about this?

"Fix her," Calliope begged of Lucien, who still stood by the door, his face drained of all color. "Fix her!" she screamed. "You're the only one with the magic to do it. Please, please, Lucien. Never do anything else for me. I'll break our bond and you'll be rid of me forever. I'll do whatever you want. Anything!" Her words were frantic, voice hoarse as she clutched Roz's shirt in her hands and tears poured down her cheeks.

"I can't," Lucien said softly. "I'm sorry, little muse. I may be powerful, but even I cannot bring people back from beyond the veil."

Calliope screamed and then closed her eyes. If he wouldn't try, she would. She would channel both of their magic and bring Roz back. She couldn't lose her so soon after finding out they were family. Couldn't lose all she had left of a mother figure in her life when that chasm inside her was just starting to close. She placed her hands over Roz's heart and began to chant.

"No," Lucien said darkly, pulling Calliope away from Roz, shaking her by the shoulders. "Look at me," he barked. "This will kill you and you'll still fail. Then we'll both be dead because we are bound. And where will that leave your sisters?"

"He's right, Opie," Thalia said.

"Right?" Calliope shouted. "*Right?* There is nothing right about this! We have to fix it. Fix *her*!"

The door of the shop slammed open, and Dissy entered with Sean.

"He's a paramedic," Dissy said, her eyes wild, chest heaving.

Sean shot into action, kneeling beside Roz, testing for a pulse. Finding none, he tilted her head back and blew into her mouth.

"It's too late," Thalia said, and she was crying now.

"Don't say that," Dissy said, shaking her head, shoulders trembling. "Don't."

Sean began chest compressions. But there was no reviving her. The sisters held one another, and it seemed that a hundred years passed inside the span of a minute. And then another. And another. Until finally, Sean sat back with pursed lips and shook his head. The storm raged on outside, the candle flames flickered, sending shadows creeping up the wall, and Calliope wept with her sisters.

CHAPTER 24

LUCIEN'S STOMACH TWISTED. HIS HEART HAD been consumed with Eléa for so long, he didn't know there was room in it for anyone else until Calliope entered it without asking. Now, though? Now her grief was screaming down the thread of their bond. It assaulted him, the wave of sorrow so bitter it nearly gagged him. He felt every barb and slice of it as though it were his own. He couldn't bear to see the pain in her eyes. Couldn't bear knowing he was the likely cause of it. He'd done unspeakable things, first in his futile quest to make his father proud, and then in keeping his sister safe. Betrayal and blood, death and lies—these things coated his veins until his heart pumped poison. And still, with every beat, it seemed to whisper her name. A purification. A calling. She'd bewitched him with her fearlessness and strength, beguiled him with her brokenness and beauty. There was no more denying it. No other way to suppress the lies he'd been telling himself. He might be a monster, but he was *her* monster now.

He had to find a way to heal his sister *and* protect Calliope.

When he appeared at the estate where his coven was staying, they were celebrating. Feng was grinning wildly, and even Luna's usually stern face seemed lighter than usual. The others were talking and laughing, clinking glasses together and raising them in toasts. Sarai, he knew, would be with Eléa.

"Another enchantment broken," Malik said with a grin. "We're getting closer. What's wrong, Lucien? I thought you'd be happier." There was a challenge to his voice, and Lucien wanted to tear him down where he stood.

Malik was testing him. Testing his loyalty.

"Their aunt is dead," Lucien said.

"I—shit," Malik said, running a hand down his face. "How did it happen?"

"I don't know, do I?" Lucien growled. "Maybe she was channeling magic when you undid the enchantment. But she's gone."

"I know you wanted no bloodshed, but you've gone soft if you think we can accomplish this without getting a little on our hands," Malik said.

Lucien's jaw clenched, and his gaze turned cold.

"We didn't know what kind of hell breaking those enchantments would release," Lucien said, running a hand through his hair.

"It's nothing we can't handle. I know we need those witches, but it seems you've become a little too invested."

"You'd be wise not to command me in that imperious tone, Malik." He hated the steel edge to his voice, hated who he had to become to maintain control.

"You were supposed to distract her, keep her away from the protection spells, not fuck her!" Malik snapped, his fury growing. "We've been watching you. You're not just trying to help them restore their string of fate. You're beginning to care too much, Lucien."

"Don't be an idiot, Malik. We need their string restored. I'm playing the long game. While you're gallivanting around causing chaos, I'm helping those insufferable witches." The insult tasted bitter on his tongue.

"She's distracting you from our main goal, Lucien!"

"Our *goals* differ greatly, Malik," Lucien said quietly.

"You're right." Malik's laughter was sharp. The room was pulsing with tension as Lucien and Malik faced each other. "You've let her cloud your judgment, your loyalty to the coven and to the mission. A mission you guaranteed us would end in success. You care more about keeping your hands clean than doing what needs to be done. But that changes now."

"And don't forget it's our magic keeping that sister of yours alive," Feng said. "Without us, she's dead."

"I care about Eléa," Malik said. "We all do. But the time is growing close. Betray the sisters if you must, force them if you have to. But we will undo the final enchantment no matter what." The threat pulsed in the air, and the room quieted as the rest of the coven listened intently.

"We need them to break the final spell," Lucien said, his rage barely controlled.

"What if we just offed all three of them?" Feng said. "Wouldn't their deaths release the enchantment, too?" There were murmurs around the room.

Rage filled Lucien until it seeped out of his pores. He didn't try to stop it, didn't try to contain it as it unfurled in a cloud of black fog that enveloped the room. The savage pleasure of it crept over his skin as he stretched out his hands, power flowing from his fingertips as his magic wrapped around their throats and squeezed.

"Lest you forget," he said, his voice booming into the silence, "who wields the *true* power here." He curled his fingers, and the room was filled with the sounds of coughing and choking as the coven gasped for air. "The sisters' bond must be restored so they can undo the final protection. Therefore, you will continue your work."

Feng was on his knees now, clutching at his throat, unable to access his magic to fight back, just like the rest of them. Lucien pulled from the well of misery and pain and betrayal inside of him. It was deeper, he thought, than any of theirs. Between that and the years of training from his merciless father, his well ran very deep indeed. He pulled their magic into him until he nearly choked on it. The darkness enveloped him, the threat of what was waiting on the other side baiting him. Sweet oblivion. He could give in to it now. Turn into a wraith. Seek only more power and exist on a hunger for souls. But his sister's face stopped him. He was doing this for her. And so, he released their magic back to them and stepped back from the precipice.

"I will continue mine. And the next time one of you threatens or challenges me, they will be the last words you ever speak."

Feng nodded. "Sorry, boss. Insensitive of me."

Malik, meanwhile, was glowering with barely controlled fury. He never did like looking a fool. But he was wise enough, at least, to keep his mouth shut.

"If the sisters die," Lucien snarled, "the power of the Dark Oak remains locked away. Eléa dies. And *you*"—he looked at the room at large—"don't get the power you seek. We must work together if we are to succeed."

"There's a simple solution to all of this that you're overlooking if you'd only—" Malik started, but his voice was cut off when a far-off screech filled the air, piercing through the walls. An unnatural wind picked up, and the shutters slammed against the house.

"Wraiths," Lucien growled with a curse.

"Good." Malik scowled. "Let them come."

"Calliope's magic is weak," Lucien barked, frustration rising. "The wards I put in place go only so far. Initiates, head to Lethe Manor. Keep yourselves concealed. Malik, Feng, Luna," Lucien commanded, "we're going to the Forgotten Forest."

The four shadow-walked to the center of the forest where three wraiths circled the Dark Oak. They were feral. Grotesque and twisted, these were not the elegant and alluring creatures of legend; these were the true face of their malevolent nature. They were skeletal and ghostly, their eyes glowed with a sickly green light, and their movements were jagged and unnatural.

The air around the Dark Oak was charged with anticipation, a tension that matched the storm clouds rolling in overhead. Lucien stood at the heart of the clearing, flanked by Malik, Luna, and Feng, their faces grim with determination. Their eyes locked on the Dark Oak, the ancient tree of power that had drawn them here, and the hideous beasts trying to claw their way through the enchantments.

Lucien moved like a predator stalking his prey. Every movement was calculated, every muscle tense. The wraiths were too focused on the Dark Oak to notice the four figures closing in around them. Luna created a protection shield and then, with a surge of power, Malik swept his hand, drawing a circle of salt in the air that glowed with a pale light. Feng mirrored his actions, and Lucien followed suit, completing the circle that sealed the wraiths within.

The wraiths, finally sensing their presence, turned in unison and darted forward with preternatural speed. But when they reached the salt barrier, they were blown back to the center, the air filled with unearthly screeching. Lucien silently thanked Luna, who'd been researching how to fight the wraiths. Her role as Scholar of the coven suddenly filled him with gratitude. If it were a paid position, he'd give her a raise.

The wraiths' faces contorted with rage as Lucien, Malik, and Feng threw vials of moon-blessed water that sizzled when it touched their skin. Their unnatural screams filled the air, their forms writhing and flickering as if they were being burned from the inside out.

Lucien's voice rose above the chaos, his words resonating with power. A Shadowcraft spell flowed from his lips, fueled by the well of anger and hatred within him. The ring of salt erupted in flames, and the wraiths' screams reached a crescendo. The flames licked out like whips as Lucien and Malik chanted and Luna and Feng held the barrier in place.

And then, with a final burst of power, the wraiths erupted in a pillar of eerie green flames. Their screams echoed through the forest like a living nightmare. It was a haunting symphony of despair and agony.

Silence settled over the clearing, broken only by the crackling embers that remained. Lucien, Malik, Luna, and Feng stood together, their chests heaving with exertion, their eyes fixed on the scorched ground where the wraiths had been.

"Looks like salt, moon-blessed water, and fire work after all." Malik coughed, wiping sweat from his forehead.

"Luna was right about that, at least," Lucien said darkly.

"Moon-blessed water," Feng said. He was bent over with his hands on his knees, and Lucien was reminded again how young he was. "Need more, yeah?"

"Yeah," Lucien said with a somber nod as the acrid smoke spread into what looked like a low-level fog.

"Right. Come on, Luna. We'll make more. And boss?" Feng said, staring at the ground. "Sorry 'bout before. My mom. She's all I have left. Want to keep her safe. You know? That's why I want this power so bad."

Lucien nodded. He already knew this, of course, from Malik's report. All the members had been interviewed extensively. All had their own reasons for wanting this power. An ability to do greater magic without risking becoming the very thing they'd just fought. But first, he had to draw that power into himself. Once he held it, would the wraiths come for him? Would the power contained inside that tree be enough to stop them if they did? He took a deep breath, trying to calm himself. The only reason he was doing this was for Eléa. He'd told himself he would cross any line, he would betray, tell any falsehood, unleash a thousand monsters if he had to.

Now he stood alone in the clearing, wondering why that felt like a lie.

CHAPTER 25

CALLIOPE WAS STARING OUT HER WINDOW WHEN she felt it. Someone out there, several someones, watching her. Watching the house. Their magic tasted different, an imprint she'd never come across before, and she idly wondered if Lucien had sent them to guard her. She willed herself to care, but nothing came.

A dense fog crept over the grass despite the warmth of the evening. And then an unearthly scream rent the air, raising the hairs on the back of her neck and sending a shiver down her spine. Another scream. Spectral and eerie. Calliope's throat went dry, her hands clutching the velvet curtains until her knuckles turned white, her heart beating fast. She wished, somewhere in the depths of her jaggedly broken heart, that those screams would come for her. Drag her away. Put an end to the ceaseless misery that choked her.

She waited, but nothing came. The screams stopped. And she was still hollow. Still numb. The fog receded, and in the stillness of the night, echoes of Roz's voice haunted her memory. Grief was a ghost that clung to her soul and broke her scars open, weeping regret and helplessness and despair. She turned from the window. Wherever those screams came from, they were gone now. The only thing coming for her was sorrow. If her sisters heard the screams, they didn't make it known. She was alone.

She didn't remember walking to her bed, but then the comforter rose to meet her, her cheek pressed into soft linen. And though she ached to sacrifice a memory and slip into slumber, the pain was the only thing keeping her grounded. She feared that if she slept, she'd never want to wake. So she lay there with a symphony of heartbreak playing inside her chest until the sun rose and her eyes were rimmed in red and her skin was itchy with fatigue. The air was heavy and suffocating, but she couldn't bring herself to leave her room.

She spent the day in her bedroom, unable to face her sisters. Dissy's quiet sobbing or Thalia's hard stare. All of them useless, their magic neutered against forces Calliope had never even imagined. She gave in to the grief until time stretched on and the shadows lengthened, and with the growing darkness came an anger that consumed her. She shoved her grief into a tight corner in her mind and let rage and revenge take over.

Dissy knocked on her door, and Calliope couldn't bear to answer it.

"I'm leaving a tray of food outside," her sister called. "You need to eat something. And there's a cup of motherwort tea."

But food was a foreign concept. Her skin was stretched too tight over her bones, an invisible boulder sitting on her chest making every breath painful, and she wondered if she'd ever remember what it felt like to be human. She didn't want the bitter motherwort tea that was meant for grief. Her heart was bitter enough. For the first time in her life, she didn't want to skip past the discomfort. Didn't want to sacrifice the memory of this pain. She wanted it to tear her apart.

Exhaustion consumed her as she paced her bedroom, her eyes red-rimmed and puffy. She still saw Roz's vacant eyes every time she closed her own. Her stomach roiled, and she leaned on her old rolltop desk, feeling the grained wood beneath her palms. Of all the whispers in her mind, the echo of regret was the loudest. She could feel the weight of lost memories, like fragments of a forgotten self, scattered in the abyss. She'd spent her whole life sacrificing those little moments, offering pieces of herself like discarded trinkets. Nothing was sacred. But now, as she stood at the precipice of her past, she realized that the true essence of being human, of being *alive*, lay in those little moments, the threads that wove the tapestry of her soul. Each memory was a star in her own constellation, and in her quest to protect, she had forgotten the most important magic of all—self-preservation. Something Roz would never be afforded again.

She had just resumed her pacing when Lucien appeared.

"You'll wear a hole in the floor," he said, breaking the silence.

Calliope didn't even jump at seeing him. It was almost as if she'd gotten used to his sudden appearances, as though he always came when she needed him most, though she'd never admit it. It was probably just the bond, she thought. Nothing more.

Still, she could never quite get used to the way he towered over her, or the way his quietly commanding presence filled her with a peace that usually came only after sacrificing a memory she'd been longing to let go of. Loath as she was to admit it, she liked having him there, but his presence was a reminder that she'd failed at protecting Roz. That another enchantment had been undone. That the string of fate was still broken, and the whole town was still at risk.

"You shouldn't have stopped me," she said, anger making her heart race, her chest heave.

"There was nothing you could have done," he answered, his voice gentler than it had ever been, and that enraged her even more. She didn't want his pity, his sympathy. She wanted to crush the world with her fury. And she wanted his help to do it.

"I could have tried," she shouted, her anger cresting.

"You would have died," he said calmly. "And the string between you and your sisters would have been completely broken. You wouldn't be able to protect the Dark Oak, the town. And isn't that what you care about most? You can stand here and mourn, or we can do something about it."

At his words, she attacked him, looking for an outlet, a way to get the grief and rage out of her body. She sacrificed the memory of a Milos sunset and released a spell to knock him back. But her magic was thin, and he felt what she was going to do through their bond. He threw up a shield that crackled with light, and the spell bounced off, knocking a mirror off her dresser. She let out a disgusted sound of rage, and instead of sacrificing another memory, she pulled from him, reaching for that bond, that damned bond, and opening herself up to it. She let the shadowy pull of his magic suck her in as she drank from that font of power.

His eyes widened in alarm, and Calliope felt a sick twist of satisfaction as she used his own magic against him. Her next spell knocked him off his feet, and he flew back against the wall with a thud. He righted himself at once and opened his arms.

"Come on then," he growled. "Let's see what you're made of, little muse."

She fired spell after spell and watched, enraged, as he blocked and deflected every single one. And then, sparks began to fly as he absorbed the magic coming his way, the room glowing in shades of emerald and sapphire. Sweat poured down her temples as she let her rage free, released the anger and bitterness and regret. He stepped closer, wincing at the bright light, but not firing back any spells of his own, which enraged her all the more.

He took another step toward her, and she felt the moment he opened up his side of the bond even further. Felt his calm presence, cooling her feverish rage. She gasped as the room effused a humming that vibrated against her skin. She tried to shove his magic away, step away from the bond that threatened to undo her, cling to every hated emotion that swept through her blood like a tidal wave.

She flicked her wrist, and the plant on her desk lengthened its vines like growing snakes until they wrapped around his ankles. He kicked free of them, and suddenly she felt hot tears coursing down her cheeks.

"Fight back, damn it," she yelled at him.

He didn't answer, and he was standing in front of her now as they were bathed in the glow of spent magic. He reached out a hand to her and she shoved it away, swiping angrily at the tears.

He stood there as her fists pummeled his chest and her tears came harder and her hands grew weak. Lucien took her hands, and when she resisted, he pulled her against him, gathering her in his arms as he slid down to the floor and pulled her onto his lap.

She could barely breathe as she clutched his shirt in her hands, her face buried in his chest. His hand rubbed up and down her back, a soothing motion, as he locked her into the tight cage of his arms, and she thought that maybe he was trying to hold her together. But she didn't want to be held together. She wanted to split apart. Ached to forget everything and remember it all at once.

As her sobs turned to quiet hiccups, the steady rhythm of his heart calmed her own. Outside, rain tapped quietly against the windowpane, creating a quiet symphony that soothed her more than words. Life. Life was what she was fighting for.

"Why are you being so nice to me?" She looked up at him, not caring that she was still in his lap and trying to ignore the way she wanted to stay there.

"I'm capable of niceness when the situation warrants it," he said, almost affronted at her words.

"You could have fooled me."

"No, I couldn't." He laughed darkly, one hand moving to cup the back of her neck.

"Maybe I don't want kindness. Maybe I want to forget," she said, daring him as her eyes darted to his lips. "Maybe I want to *live*."

His hand moved from her neck to her jaw, his thumb brushing over her bottom lip. His breathing hitched when her tongue darted out, her fingers wrapping around his wrist to hold it steady as she sucked his thumb into her mouth.

"You want me to fuck you, little muse?" he said roughly, turning her head so he whispered in her ear. "You want me to make you come so hard you forget your own goddamn name?" He licked a path from her neck to the spot just below her ear, where he bit down hard, making her core clench in anticipation, her breathing turning to panting. She ached for friction.

"I will," he said, and then he groaned when his hands fell to her waist and she moved so that she was straddling him on the ground. She could feel his hardness pressing against her, and goddess above, but she wanted this. Had been aching for it. Wanted to see what he tasted like when he came undone for her. Her hands ran up his hard chest, wrapped around his broad shoulders. "But not when you're grieving," he said, his voice strained, holding her hips still in a vicelike grip as she tried to move against him. "Not when you want it because you want to forget."

She growled in frustration, needed his lips on hers. His tongue in her mouth, claiming her. She leaned forward, her honey-wheat hair falling in a curtain around them. The scent of her lemon verbena mixed with the lingering smell of apples that always seemed to trail him.

"Bold of you to think you know what's best for me, what I need right now," she said.

"It's for my own sanity as much as yours," he said darkly.

"Lucien," she whispered. But she didn't get any further because a knock sounded on the door.

"Eurydice sent me up to check on you," Thalia called.

Calliope swore under her breath, then cleared her throat. "I'm fine," Calliope called back.

"I made dinner. Do you want any?"

"No," Calliope said, shivering as Lucien trailed a finger down her throat.

"Does Lucien want any, since I know he's in there, too?" Thalia asked archly.

Lucien let out a low grumble of laughter.

"He's not hungry," Calliope answered.

"Not for food," he murmured in a tortured voice.

"Fine, but you'd better tell Dissy I tried."

Thalia's footsteps receded down the hall, and then he was pulling Calliope to him and his lips were on hers, crashing into her like a wave, soft and warm and salty from the tears she'd spilled on him. It was fast and desperate, and just as she threaded her fingers through his hair to pull him closer, deepen the kiss, he pulled back. His eyes shone like onyx, his pupils blown wide.

"Come," he said, and, scooping his hands beneath her backside, he stood in one fluid motion. Her legs wrapped around him as he carried her to the bed and laid her down before climbing in beside her. "I'll stay with you."

"Why?"

"Because you're sad," he said simply.

The moment of desire passed, and grief clawed its way back through. She pulled the covers up to her chin but still shivered. Out of habit, she reached for a memory to sacrifice and began to speak a spell.

"No," Lucien said firmly, covering her lips with his fingers. "No more of that. Tell me what you were going to do with that spell." His voice was low and warm against her ear, and she shivered again, though this time for a different reason.

"I was going to summon a thicker blanket."

She could practically hear him roll his eyes. A second later, a fur blanket covered them.

"Better?" he asked.

"Better," she said reluctantly.

"Why would you sacrifice a memory for such a small thing?"

"It's always been so easy for me to sacrifice my memories.

What are they worth, really? What's any of it worth? What's the point?" Her voice trembled slightly. "My mother left us, my father died when I was young. Thalia distanced herself, Dissy buried her head in the sand. The love of my life left me."

"If she left, she wasn't the love of your life," Lucien said gruffly. And Calliope stared at him as the words fell from his mouth. She hadn't told him about Marigold, but he must've seen the way she reacted in Tea and Tome and connected the dots. And the fact that she didn't have to explain her sexuality or field any judgment, that he accepted the truth of her without question, sent a cascading warmth through her. A silent moment of acknowledgment passed between them before she spoke again.

"But she should have been. I wasn't honest with her. She didn't know I was a witch."

"Would she have believed you if you'd told her? Accepted you for who you are? *What* you are?"

"Marigold believed in whimsy, but not magic. I think she would have been terrified, but maybe . . . she might have stayed," Calliope answered, her voice colored with sorrow, the truth of her words a sting to her heart. "But I never gave her the chance."

"I'm not saying what you had wasn't real, but if you can't share the truth of yourself with someone, if they don't know the core of you and welcome it with open arms, then that relationship is bound to hit some road bumps."

"Sounds like you're speaking from experience," Calliope said, nudging him in the shoulder.

"I spent years trying to build that kind of picture-perfect life with my parents, but it was always on their terms. And when I finally showed them who I was, that I had no interest in furthering the Shadowcraft agenda, they cut me off."

"They don't know what they're missing," Calliope whispered.

"Neither does your ex."

"She thought I was cheating on her," Calliope said haltingly, "thought I was lying, because she'd ask me a question about our first date or our anniversary and I wouldn't have a goddamn answer. I was so in love with her, but I still sacrificed memories of her. All to save a legacy I didn't really know anything about."

"Maybe it wasn't love then," Lucien said with a frown.

"No." Calliope shook her head. "I've sacrificed memories of my sisters, and I love them more than life. But Marigold, she was this ideal. And I think I thought . . . that maybe I wasn't worthy of her. And giving up pieces of our time together was my subconscious trying to punish me for having something good in my life. Because what am I really good for? Other than this? Protecting the Dark Oak and losing pieces of myself in the process. It's the only thing I ever had control over, and now I don't even have that. I couldn't even protect Roz."

"Failing to protect the ones we love is the greatest burden to bear. It eats away at your soul, if you let it. But failing doesn't affect your worth."

"That's a little ironic coming from a Shadowcrafter whose magic is dependent on your soul. And how many times have you told yourself that?" She laughed, and it came out cold. "Do you actually believe it? Wouldn't you sacrifice all your pain, if you could?"

"Never," Lucien answered without thinking. "The pain is

how I hold on to those moments. It's what drives me. It's what's made me who I am. You can't heal if you keep pushing it away."

"I don't want to heal. I just want revenge," she said quietly, and her words were laced with the poison of grief and regret.

"You're lying to yourself," Lucien said. "You know what you're fighting for. You know it's worth the pain. But you're too afraid to actually feel. You sacrifice your memories to get a sense of control when everything is spiraling." His fingers were drawing lazy circles on her shoulder that ignited her skin.

"What's so wrong with that?"

"When you guard yourself against the potential of emotional damage, it's fear that's in control, not you. You don't think I've been fucking terrified that my sister is going to die? That the only person who's ever meant anything to me could abandon me here, alone? I live in fear every day. But I don't let it control me. I force it to drive me."

"Sometimes it feels like too much," Calliope whispered, staring out her window at the waning moon that glowed with secrets. "I'm a whole-ass adult, and I still don't know what I'm doing half the time."

Lucien laughed, actually laughed. Not his typical low chuckle, but a deep, full-bodied laugh, and it rocketed through Calliope's system like adrenaline.

"Are you—did you just laugh at me?" Calliope cried indignantly.

"Come here," he said gruffly, pulling her closer.

"So, what happens now?"

"Now, we sleep."

"It seems like you're trying to distract me," she said. "And I must say, you're doing an excellent job."

"Did I not mention that sleeping is typically a silent affair?" Lucien asked.

"Did I not mention that you are stuck with my neurosis?"

"Talk me to death tomorrow, little muse." His palm cradled her cheek and gently pulled, so her head nestled in the crook of his shoulder. His other hand lay heavy on her waist, and she was deliciously anchored. "But for now, we sleep."

And, for the first time in a long while, Calliope drifted into a peaceful slumber.

CHAPTER 26

CALLIOPE DREAMED OF THE BEACH IN MILOS. OF her mother on the shore, her long hair whipping in the wind. She was in the ocean, watching as her mother called to her, but she couldn't make out the words. Her arms ached with the effort of keeping herself afloat, the waves growing bigger and bigger as they crashed over her, until something grabbed her foot and pulled her down, down. She woke choking on phantom seawater.

The sun was already high in the sky—midafternoon, she thought. And Lucien was gone. But he'd comforted her. Held her when she thought she might break apart and reminded her that the grief and pain were the price she paid for loving someone so dearly. He didn't promise everything would be okay or try to distract her or treat her like a porcelain doll. And it was that, perhaps, that intrigued her more than anything else. For here was a man who painted himself in the hues of a monster but wiped her tears so tenderly they might have been diamonds. She wasn't sure what it meant.

She reached inside herself, testing the string of fate. Her

magic was even thinner now. She could feel it floating away like dandelion seeds on the wind. Now that she was alone, her body was heavy with the weight of grief and fear and anger. It seeped into her muscles and tensed her shoulders. Her jaw ached from clenching. And though her stomach rumbled, she wasn't inclined to eat. Her thoughts were sticky, each one clinging to the last until everything was muddled and she couldn't sort through them.

Astro padded over to her. She'd slept on Lucien's feet, but Calliope couldn't quite blame the feline for her traitorous actions anymore. Calliope ran her fingers through Astro's fur, and the cat purred like a sports car engine. It was an anchor, one she desperately needed. And it gave her enough gumption to get up, even though she'd rather bury her head in the pillow and wake up years from now when the grief of losing Roz wasn't serrating her soul.

With heavy feet, she approached her dressing table and ran the brush through her hair. The silver filigree handle was weighty in her hand, and she wondered if it would keep her from floating away. Everything felt strange and mechanical. The sun was too bright through her window, the birdsong too loud, and even the air tasted different, sticky on her tongue. But if she could just get through one part of her routine at a time, maybe she would feel better. She rummaged in her drawer for a box of matches, not wanting to waste a single memory, and lit the lavender candles, hoping it would chase away the stench of heartache.

Finished with her hair, she stripped naked and stood in front of her closet. Dresses hung from one strap, shirts spilled out of the shelves where she'd hastily shoved them instead of folding them. A smile tested the corners of her lips when she thought of what Lucien would say at the mess. She reached for a black dress, but her hand paused before it touched the fabric. Black was for mourning, and she could only imagine Roz's response if she covered herself in a shroud and allowed herself to melt into a puddle. Instead, she put on an ochre dress that hit just above her knee and then grabbed the burgundy duster she'd gotten from Maya. She cinched a wide leather belt around them both, the round pewter buckle etched with a crow.

"Okay," she said on an exhale. "Doing good. The ground isn't swallowing you up. You're doing this." She pulled on a pair of socks, one of them patterned with honeybees and the other with stalks of lavender, and then added knee-high leather boots. There was no point trying to conceal the dark circles under her eyes, but she layered on mascara and painted her lips a deep wine red. Crystal rings went on every finger. Citrine and rose quartz, garnet and amethyst, healing stones, all. She slipped her pyrite necklace around her neck, where it settled against her heart. Astro wove between her legs, rubbing against her leather boots. Her life might be completely unraveling, but at least she had her cat, candles, and crystals.

She called and searched for Grim, but the book was nowhere to be found, and she gave up after pulling out every drawer and looking in every dark corner.

It was late in the afternoon when Calliope set out with no sense of purpose but needing to get out of the house. Feel the gentle kiss of the breeze against her cheeks. And her steps led her first to the heart of the town she loved. As she passed Rosalind's tarot shop, her heart sank at the sight of the CLOSED sign. The memory of that night flooded her mind, and her grief resurfaced like a relentless tide. And yet, Gold Springs seemed to pulse with life.

Her brows furrowed as she observed the townsfolk going about their business, a stark contrast to the grief still suffocating her soul. And yet, somehow, it was also a balm. A reminder that life marched on in spite of tragedy. A long banner was strung across the street, announcing the seventy-fifth annual Gold Springs Easter Eggstravaganza, when businesses hid eggs in their shops and children and adults alike were welcome to join the hunt. Participants were encouraged to decorate their baskets, and at the end of the event, a winner would be chosen and presented with a three-foot chocolate egg painted in edible gold dust.

She paused outside Autumn's Attic, where she saw Maya bustling about inside. The shop's window was dressed in a delightful array of spring-themed attire, from pastel dresses to flower-patterned pants. Calliope stepped inside, the soft jingle of the bell above the door announcing her arrival.

Maya looked up from her counter, a warm smile gracing her lips. "Calliope, dear! What brings you here today?"

Calliope returned the smile, though her thoughts were still caught up in the unexpected vibrancy of the town.

"I . . . I just wanted to see how everyone's doing after . . . well, you know."

Maya's expression softened when she understood the unspoken words behind Calliope's question.

"It's been a heavy blow for all of us, honey," she said, reaching out a hand to Calliope, who nodded, her gaze drifting to the street beyond the window.

"I expected to find the town quieter, more somber. I was so scared," she chattered on nervously, "of what I would find. I've been so lost in my own world, and—" Calliope inhaled a deep breath, forcing her words to stop before they took over and she spilled too much. "Sorry, got carried away there."

Maya's eyes sparkled with a quiet determination.

"Sometimes, in the face of darkness, people find strength they never knew they had. We're all grieving with you, in our own ways. And we'll honor her passing by celebrating every little moment of life we're granted. No one knew where Roz came from, but she made herself a staple in this town, and we all loved her for it. You know, I see her vibrancy in you," Maya said, tilting her head to inspect Calliope.

A sense of pride and warmth filled Calliope's heart at those words.

"Thank you," Calliope said sincerely.

She hugged Maya and left the shop, running straight into Sean Zhao.

"Sean," Calliope said, and immediately she was slammed with guilt. She'd been so consumed with the Dark Oak, her sisters, and Lucien, she hadn't checked on him, hadn't thanked him for what he tried to do.

"Hey," Sean said with a quiet, sad smile.

"I'm so sorry I never thanked you . . ." Her throat grew tight, and she had to clear it. "Never thanked you for what you did for Rosalind."

"I wish I could have done more," Sean said, his voice gentle and filled with kindness.

Calliope nodded, unable to speak around the lump in her throat.

"And anyway," Sean continued, "Dissy has been checking in on me. Doesn't seem to believe me when I tell her I was just doing my job. She keeps bringing me food." He frowned, but there was a glint in his eye, like he was secretly pleased about this. And she glowed at his use of her sister's nickname and the familiar way it rolled off his tongue.

"Dissy believes food can heal just about anything."

"It usually does," Sean said. "My mom used to make me yan du xian soup anytime I so much as sneezed. Actually," he said thoughtfully, his brows furrowing, "she still does that. Anyway, you and your sisters reopening Tea and Tome soon?"

"Yes," Calliope said. "Yeah, I think we will."

"Good," Sean said with a pat on her shoulder.

As Calliope continued on her way, the energy of the town around her was a reminder that they were more than just a collection of individuals—they were a community that stood strong. She walked into the gazebo, the sound of the fountain in front and the birdsong overhead soothing her nerves. Her eyes closed as she inhaled the fresh spring air. Her mother had vanished. Her aunt had died. But she thought of her sisters and Grim and Danny. Of Lucien. They were a strange sort of family, but strange was a comfort in the face of magic and love and loss. And Lucien had indeed, somehow, in some way, become part of their family. They'd been through too much for him not to be. And wasn't that what family was? A constant path of navigating boundaries and betrayals and grief? Family was walking away but always coming back, challenging one another and accepting apologies even when you weren't sure you wanted to. And as terrifying as it was to let him in, *really* let him in, she found herself wanting to. His arms had become a safe place that blocked out the world when she couldn't handle it anymore and needed a break.

The sound of footsteps on gravel had her opening her eyes. And she knew who it would be even before she saw the flash of neon green.

"Hi," Marigold said, slowing her approach. Her voice was soft and lilting, just like Calliope remembered it. Just like she'd heard in her dreams for so long after Marigold had left. Calliope tried to reach for the first moment she met Marigold, tried to remember the flutter in her chest or the sense that they were about to embark on something great. But she came up empty. Where those memories should have been, there was nothing.

"Hi," Calliope said, the single word sticking in her throat. She'd always thought Marigold looked like she'd been carved from marble with her sharp cheekbones and straight nose. She was wearing an emerald-green sweater that complemented her hair over a short lace dress and combat boots on her tiny feet. Her septum piercing winked in the sunlight. Calliope waited for the longing, the yearning, the heartbreak. Only it didn't come.

"I heard about Roz, and I just wanted to say I'm so sorry. I know how much she meant to you and your sisters."

"Thank you," Calliope said. "It's been . . . hard." She settled on the word because no others in the English language could convey the way the grief was starving her soul.

"You're doing okay? Other than that?" Marigold asked, and there was so much warmth and sincerity in her voice. It was one of the things that had drawn Calliope to her, but again, when she reached for that memory of the first time she knew she was in love with Marigold, there was nothing. Just like so many other moments in her life, she'd sacrificed it for what had once felt like a greater purpose and now felt like a weight around her neck.

A wild laugh escaped Calliope. Was she doing okay? No. And what was the point of lying now?

"I'm surviving," she said. "You?"

"Yeah, I mean, Portland is great. I met someone—that is, I mean . . . yeah, it's great. I love it there."

"That's . . . great." Calliope nodded, the awkward silence enveloping them. So, Marigold had found someone but didn't want to rub it in Calliope's face in the moment of her grief. Same old Mari. Sweet to a fault. Calliope searched for the jealousy but found only happiness for Marigold's new life instead.

"Right, well, I'll see you around, maybe?" Marigold said with no conviction, but as she turned and walked away, Calliope called out to her.

"Wait, Mari," she said, her voice cracking. "I'm sorry. I'm sorry I couldn't be everything you wanted."

Marigold turned around, her head quirking to the side as she regarded Calliope.

"You *were* everything I wanted, Opie," she said sadly. "You just weren't everything *you* wanted. It's like you thought you had to be perfect for me to love you. But you never let me all the way in to see the whole of you." She shrugged her delicate shoulders.

The truth of those words crashed over Calliope like an icy wave, dragging her down into the undertow and making her struggle for breath. She'd been trying to fill the yawning void in her chest left by her mother's absence with love and lost memories and reckless choices. Anything to make her *feel*. But it never worked for long, always left her aching. She'd never come to terms with Penelope's disappearance. She didn't think any of them had. And she didn't know where to start. But she knew she couldn't keep treating people like Band-Aids just to make herself feel better the way she had with Marigold. Knew that real love wasn't walking on eggshells, hiding your true self while trying to be perfect so that maybe, maybe they wouldn't leave this time.

"I'm sorry," Calliope said again. "You deserved better." And she did. Because even as Calliope tried to remember when it had started to go wrong with Marigold, she found there were just fragments. Where the memories of Calliope's greatest love should have been, there were only holes. She'd been hanging on to the ghost of that love for too long.

"It's okay." Marigold smiled sadly. "We're all on our own path, you know? You just have to find yours. And I hope you find someone that makes you feel, I don't know, like you can be yourself with them. Mess and all. Because we're all a mess in some way, Opie. The point is to find someone whose baggage goes with yours."

Marigold twirled her fingers in a wave, and Calliope was left standing in the gazebo, the sun warming her back, as confusing thoughts of Lucien filled her head. Overcome with the sudden need to see him, she knew where she needed to go. He'd mentioned staying at a cottage, and there was only one in Gold Springs that was available for rent. Knowing everyone's literal business was another perk of living in a small town.

And so, she walked away from her past, from the fragmented memories of her broken love for Marigold, and toward something that felt dangerously like her future.

Chapter 27

By the time Calliope reached Lucien's cottage, nerves were getting the better of her. It was a small but charming property. There was a stone pathway leading up to the cottage that cut through swaths of cheery green grass on either side. Rosebushes surrounded the front windows, and for some reason, she had a hard time picturing Lucien staying there. The front door, painted a deep, burning orange, was low, and she wondered if he almost hit his head every time he walked through it. She raised her hand and knocked.

The door flew open, but it wasn't Lucien who stood there. A girl appeared, tall and thin with dark hair and darker eyes that sparkled with mischief despite the purple circles beneath them.

"Oh," the girl said in surprise, twinkling eyes going wide. And then, the apples of her cheeks bloomed as her lips drew into a knowing smile. "I thought you were my brother, and I was wondering why on earth he'd knock, but I see I was wrong. You are very clearly *not* my brother, but I remember you. Calliope, yes?" She spoke fast, her French accent far more pronounced than Lucien's.

"Yes," Calliope said with a smile. "That's me. And you're Eléa." Calliope held out her hand, and Eléa looked at it before stepping forward and pulling Calliope into a brief but tight hug.

"Well, come in, come in. My brother will have an aneurysm when he finds out you're here without him present, but honestly, he could do with some shaking up, don't you think?"

Calliope followed Eléa into the cottage, which was stiflingly warm.

"Can I get you something to drink? Tea, perhaps? It may not be up to your standards, what with that exquisite shop you have. But I don't think you can really go wrong with a simple cup of Earl Grey, can you?"

Calliope laughed. She couldn't help it. There was a light about the girl that bled into the room.

"Earl Grey sounds wonderful, thank you."

"Let's not stand on ceremony," Eléa said, beckoning Calliope with a nod before bustling into the kitchen and turning on the electric kettle. "You're wondering why I don't just do a spell," Eléa said, noting the way Calliope watched her. "Well, that's a whole other story, I'm afraid. Instead, I want to hear about Tea and Tome. What's it like running a business with your sisters? Who chooses the recipes?"

"That's mostly my sister Dissy," Calliope said, smiling at Eléa. It was refreshing to talk about something other than the constant horrors that had been plaguing her.

"The middle sister." Eléa nodded. "The peacekeeper, yes?"

Calliope laughed, wondering just how much Lucien had told her. "That's the one. A lot of the recipes we grew up with, others are from our family grimoire, and others we've come up with ourselves." At this, Calliope was reminded of the excitement all those years ago. Hours spent in the kitchen as the sisters tested and retested recipes, trying to inject their Greek heritage into the sweet and savory concoctions. The days and weeks they'd spent poring over design choices for the store and favorite books to stock while their creations baked.

The kitchen was never cold then, always filled with the yeasty scent of focaccia olive bread or the sweet smell of honey cakes or, Thalia's favorite, cardamom-rose baklava. Calliope could never stand the rose flavor.

"What's your favorite thing you've come up with?" Eléa asked, drawing her back to the present.

"Orange fairy tea cake," Calliope said without hesitating. "It was our inaugural cake." She smiled remembering it. "We'd thrown out dozens trying to perfect the recipe, until one afternoon, we all took a bite and just looked at each other and started laughing. We held hands and danced around the kitchen like kids."

"That sounds so marvelous." Eléa sighed. "I'd have loved to have had a sister. Not that Lucien isn't wonderful, but you can't exactly see him dancing around the kitchen, can you? I was already a . . . *surprise* for my parents, though," she said, and a shadow passed over her face. "Anyway, orange fairy tea cake sounds like heaven. Lucien spent a lot of time in Istanbul when I was growing up. Our father owns a shipping business there, and I think Lucien relished being out from under his thumb and focusing on the numbers and logistics. But whenever he was back in France with me, we'd cook together."

"Lucien?" Calliope asked, her eyebrows shooting up. She

tried to imagine him with his sleeves rolled up, the muscles in his forearms flexing as he kneaded dough, and the image sent a flutter through her stomach.

"I know." Eléa laughed. "He did it for me. My best friend and I had always wanted to go to Le Cordon Bleu in Paris. It was our dream. But our families would never allow such a mundane future to befall us." She smiled, but there was a tightness behind it.

"I think pursuing your dream is its own kind of magic," Calliope said, frowning. "There's nothing mundane about building a future that makes your soul sing."

"You know," Eléa said, "my brother's keeping me locked up in here because he's afraid a strong breeze might knock me over. But now I'm thinking he just wanted to keep you all to himself." She laughed, a dainty sound like bells chiming.

Calliope smiled inwardly. She'd finally found someone who liked to fill the silence the way she did. No wonder Lucien always remarked on her own propensity for chatter.

"Now, tell me everything that he's been trying to hide from me," Eléa finished.

"There's not much to tell," Calliope said, watching as Eléa's movements began to slow. The motion of her hand bringing her cup to her lips was sluggish, and her skin grew more pallid.

"I don't believe that for a moment. The horror that happened the night of the Midnight Masquerade—I'm so sorry for your loss, by the way. And the things I hear my brother whispering about when he thinks he's being discreet. I may not be able to use magic, but I can still *feel* it. And it's all my fault we're even here, anyway. I probably shouldn't have said that," she added, her lips pursing.

"I thought you were here because your grandfather had

some mysterious connection to Gold Springs that you wanted to investigate," Calliope said, inhaling the sweet smell of bergamot as Eléa poured the tea.

"Is that what he told you?" Eléa sighed. "You know, I've found that concealing the truth never does anyone any favors. Lucien thinks I don't know everything that's happening here. But I know more than I let on, and Sarai fills me in on the rest because she respects my desire to know the truth. Lucien is overprotective." She frowned, wrapping her hands around her mug and blowing steam off the top.

"Overprotective and controlling," Calliope noted drily.

"Exactly!" Eléa said, her eyes brightening again. "He really will lose it that you're here. But you know he's absolutely fallen for you."

"What?" Calliope spluttered, choking on her tea. "No, it's not like that between us." Lust? Yes, that was there in spades. But lust was different from catching feelings.

"Isn't it?" Eléa asked with a sly grin. "I know my brother better than I know myself. He won't want to admit it, but you completely derailed his plans."

"What plans?" Calliope asked, her stomach once again dipping with nerves.

Eléa studied her for a moment, her head cocked to the side. The shadows beneath her eyes seemed more pronounced now, her already pale skin a shade paler.

"You know I'm, I'm . . . sick?" Eléa asked.

Calliope nodded.

"Us being here, it does have to do with my grandfather in a way. But not to honor his dying wishes. I'm surprised Lucien got those words out without choking on them. That's how much he hated our grandfather. The Denizes, you see, have a reputation to uphold. We're known for being quite powerful. Ruthless, even. But my magic, well, it never quite fit in with the rest of the family." She paused for a moment, choosing her next words, and then seemed to change subjects. "Shadowcraft magic isn't inherently evil, you know. But there is an end to it. It draws on the power of self, and if you get too close to the end of that well within, that's when you start crossing over. Become taken over by the thirst for power. Ultimately, if left unchecked, you can turn into—"

"A wraith."

"Exactly. My family, they only respect one thing. Power. And I didn't have much of it." Eléa paused, her features turning thoughtful as she traced the rim of her cup.

Outside, the wind began to pick up, and the oaks swayed like a song. Calliope took a sip of her tea in the sudden silence, wondering where this story was going.

"My grandfather experimented with me," Eléa finally said, her features turning from thoughtful to determined. "With my magic. He wanted to see how far he could push me. Turns out, my body didn't react well. Over the years, the magic started slowly taking over until I got weaker and weaker, sicker and sicker." Her eyes turned sad, and she chewed on her lip nervously.

"But, what about your parents?" Calliope demanded, aghast. "What about Lucien? And there was a boy who grew up with you. Malik? None of them did anything?"

"My father approved it. He didn't have time to deal with me himself. My mother supported my father in anything he said. And Malik . . ." She laughed sadly. "He would never go against my father himself. He wanted his approval too badly for that. But he was the one who finally told Lucien it was happening when I began . . . slipping further away. Until then we were forbidden from telling him."

"But why, Eléa? Nothing is worth that."

"You clearly had at least one parent who loved you unconditionally," Eléa said with another sad smile. "But when you have none, you think maybe, maybe you can earn their love. So, I let it happen. I was a willing participant. At first, anyway. I wanted that power. Wanted my family to respect me. To love me. Of course, it wasn't until I was actually dying that I realized a family who only accepts you for what you can do for them isn't really a family at all." She took a sip of her tea. "Lucien, he's much older than me, a cross between brother and father. You must understand, he'd do anything for me. And when he found out, he killed our grandfather." She said the words fast and they came out flat, like she couldn't bear the taste of them in her mouth.

"Eléa," Calliope said, reaching out a hand across the countertop. She didn't know this girl, but she could feel her in her bones, a mirror to her own brokenness.

"It's the only thing we've ever fought about," Eléa continued. "Well, that, and how to keep me alive. See, he'll stop at nothing. But I don't want a life if it's tied to his downfall. And that's exactly where he's headed. And I think . . . I think you're the only one who can stop him."

CHAPTER 28

"I DON'T UNDERSTAND," CALLIOPE SAID, HER HEAD spinning.

"I think you do," Eléa said.

Calliope sat there, staring at this girl who seemed so unlike her brother save for the stubborn set of their eyes, the hard line of their mouths when they were displeased.

"The Dark Oak," Calliope whispered. Eléa nodded.

"Before Lucien killed our grandfather, he tried to barter information for his life. The real reason he was experimenting on me. Grandfather told my brother of the connection between the Petridis and Denizes. That there was a tree whose power was locked away. Our power. Only it was guarded by Lightcraft witches. Lucien killed him anyway, but it was enough for him to form a plan."

"A plan," Calliope murmured. So much about Lucien was coming into clearer focus. His rage. His need for control. The self-hatred. What would Calliope have done if she'd found out Thalia or Dissy had been tortured for years? Forced to contort themselves into a specific shape to fit a family agenda? Her blood boiled to think of it. "What plan?" she asked now.

"It started with the coven. They performed a tethering ritual to keep me alive, but it's not enough. And so, he scoured our library and found out about our ancestors, about Gold Springs and the Denizes and Petridis. He promised the coven that if they helped him break the enchantments of the Dark Oak and take the power for himself, he would give them what was left when he was done with it." Here she swallowed hard and seemed to force her eyes to Calliope's. "Lucien believes the power of the Dark Oak is the only thing that can cure me. Light for darkness. Darkness for light. A trade that's been generations in the making." Tears were streaming down Eléa's face now, and Calliope's own throat was tight with the pressure of holding back an anguished cry.

"Why not just kill us outright then?" Calliope asked. "Get us out of the way for good."

"My brother may have killed, but he is not a killer." Eléa frowned. "You know the old prejudices as well as I do. Shadowcraft doesn't make one evil. Can it be used as a conduit by evil people? Absolutely. But so can Lightcraft. Aren't you tired of all the bigotry?"

"Yes," Calliope said, surprising herself. She wasn't sure when it happened, but she'd started seeing Lucien as a person instead of just a Shadowcraft practitioner. And Marigold had been right. Everyone had their own mess, their own wounds that shaped the way they perceived the world.

"He didn't want more bloodshed. But you should know that my grandfather said that the final enchantment can only be broken by three Petridi sisters," Eléa said sadly. "The enchantments protect the Dark Oak, but they stop you from accessing it, too. That's why he was supposed to gain your trust. So that when he fed you some reason as to why you needed to dismantle the final spell, you'd listen to him. I've told him from the beginning I don't want it," she continued. "That I'd rather pass in peace than start a war just to live. But he won't listen. And he didn't bet on you." She laughed weakly. "My stubborn, stoic brother who carries the weight of the world on his shoulders finally found someone to help him carry it."

Anger began to unfurl inside Calliope like a living, breathing entity.

"He lied to me," she said.

"Wouldn't you have?" Eléa asked. "To save your sisters?"

Calliope made a choking noise and cursed the clever girl because she was right.

"He's doing what he thinks is right. But he's wrong and too stubborn to see it. To see that if we can just set aside our prejudices, we could work together." Eléa's shoulders slumped, and Calliope could see how much energy this conversation was costing her. "I wouldn't tell you any of this, but I'm tired. Tired of fighting and tired of watching Lucien slip further into something that will turn him from brother to enemy. Every day I'm afraid that he'll go too far. Turn into a wraith. So, what, I get to live, but at what cost? I'll lose my brother."

"He won't listen to me," Calliope said angrily. "He's never listened to me."

"Sometimes the heart hears better than the mind, and only love can make you truly listen."

"How old *are* you?" Calliope demanded.

"Almost eighteen, but I've read a thousand books and lived a thousand lives," she answered with a small smile.

Calliope was trembling with rage and sorrow and hurt. Her chest was too tight, and when she tried to draw in a deep breath, it wouldn't come. Rain began to fall against the window, and the kitchen grew darker as the storm clouds moved in.

Lucien had been right. She'd hated him from the beginning because of what he was instead of getting to know him for *who* he was. They were both at fault.

"I don't know you," Eléa said, her words coming quicker now. "But I do know my brother would never fall for someone who wasn't worthy. We've been tied together for generations. There has to be a reason for it." There was conviction in her words, and it reminded Calliope of Dissy saying almost the same exact thing. "Fate drew us together," she was whispering now, hunched forward over the counter and clutching Calliope's hands in her own. "Now it's up to you to make sure we stay that way."

The front door opened, and the sound of angry, thundering footsteps echoed. At once, Eléa straightened, plastering a serene smile on her face.

"Brother," she said, as Lucien came stomping into the kitchen. "Look who's come for tea."

"What do you think you're doing?" Lucien demanded, staring between Eléa and Calliope, who'd pushed her chair back and was now standing, her chest heaving as she breathed hard. She couldn't quite decide if his features held more rage or fear.

"I'm sorry," Eléa said sweetly, "to whom are you speaking?"

"Both of you," he thundered. His broad form filled the kitchen, his dark hair shining with raindrops as he glowered at them both. He hadn't shaved, his eyes were wild, and, inexplicably, Calliope could think only of what his stubble would feel like scratching against her soft skin.

"You see," Eléa said in a falsely dulcet tone, "I don't think you are. Knowing full well that my *brother* would never address me in such a manner and knowing that Calliope would tear down any man who dared use that tone, I can only imagine you've lost your head for a moment. We'll wait while you find it." Her words were clipped as she leaned back in her chair and crossed her arms.

And despite everything, Calliope had to hold back a laugh as she watched the war play out across Lucien's features. As this giant of a man with his three-day beard and his head nearly brushing the ceiling was cowed by his young sister, who wore a waiting expression.

"Calliope, Eléa," he said finally, struggling through the words as though someone were choking him. "I see you've met." His tone was short but civil, and Calliope loved Eléa in that moment, for the way she stood up for herself, and for the way she brought Lucien to heel.

"Excellent," Eléa said. "Or, at least, passable." She stood up, dumped her mostly unfinished tea in the sink, and then said, "I'll be going with Sarai."

Just then a beautiful woman stepped out from behind Lucien, her dark blue hijab spattered with wet spots from the rain. Her face was a mask of concern as her eyes darted among the three of them. Lucien turned to glower at Sarai.

"I'll take care of her," she promised, her voice musical and lilting.

"Thank you," Eléa said, wrapping her thin arms around Calliope and squeezing.

"For what?" Calliope said, surprised.

"For not killing my brother on sight," she said with a small laugh. She kissed Lucien on the cheek, and Calliope watched, mystified, as his hard eyes turned soft at the gesture. And then Eléa was pulling Sarai by the hand, leaving Lucien and Calliope facing off in the dim light.

Every line of his body was taut. Calliope only stared at him, trying to arrange her thoughts, but they were too messy. She'd always needed to process verbally but didn't want to give him the satisfaction.

"Now you're finally silent?" he demanded, taking a step closer to her.

"I don't even know you," she said, taking a step back. Her fury grew like a weed. Fury at the fact that he'd used her, that she would have done the same exact thing if she were in his shoes, but most of all, fury at herself for wanting him despite everything she now knew. Thunder cracked overhead, and Calliope jumped, her heart racing.

"You know exactly who I am," he said on a growl, advancing another step. "And that's what scares you."

"You used me," she said, fingers curling into fists at her side, lips flattening to a thin line.

"Just as you used me, only for different reasons." He strode forward, and Calliope stepped back until she was pressed against the counter and there was barely a breath of space between them. He loomed over her, and as a flash of lightning lit up the kitchen, she saw the lines around his eyes, the deep brackets around his scowl. He wore his age like a fine wine, and she hated his harsh beauty.

"The difference is, you pretended to care," she said. His eyes darkened like an encroaching storm.

"*Care*, little muse, is far too tender for my taste. Nevertheless, I concede to its partial truth."

"What do you concede?" she asked, her anger a vortex threatening to pull them both under.

"I concede that despite your incessant chattering . . ." He leaned forward, his tone a mix of gall and passion. "Despite your weakening magic, the barbed words, the very fact you've bound me to you unwillingly, I have found myself"—he paused—"entangled in the web you've spun. I've tried, unsuccessfully, to diminish it. It pulls at me and makes demands I'm not ready to meet."

"Demands," Calliope echoed, her heartbeat staccato at his nearness, the scent of amber and apples and rain and something else that was simply *him* threatening to overpower her.

"Despite the chaos and the contradictions, I find myself . . . wanting you," he admitted, his features twisting into an expression of anguish as though the words were poison on his lips.

The countertop was digging into her back as Lucien pressed against her front, anchoring her when she felt like falling.

"You insult me and tell me you want me in the same breath," she snarled. "Get away from me." She shoved him hard in the chest, but he placed his hands on the counter behind her, boxing her in until all she could see and smell and feel was him.

"My plan was to distract you," he said, leaning forward and grazing her ear with his nose as he inhaled the lemon verbena scent of her hair. "Have I done a good job, little muse?" His voice turned hard and brittle as he pressed against her. "I placed myself in that forest with the intention of binding us together. Do you hate me for it?"

"You're an asshole," she breathed. "And I wish I hated you." *But I don't* echoed between them.

"Wrong answer," he growled. He took her chin in his hands, tilting her head so she looked into his eyes, his gentle fingers in stark contrast to his hard words. "The only reason I've worked so hard to keep you alive is because I need you to undo the final enchantment." His fingers tightened against her chin, and Calliope gasped but refused to turn away.

"That may have been true once, but it's not true now," she said.

"You should hate me," Lucien said, his words laced with acid. "You should fear me. Know that I will stop at nothing to save my sister."

"Neither would I," Calliope panted, his thumb tracing up her cheek making it hard to think. "You're scared," she said. And she saw the alarm in his dark eyes as she said the words. "You think the things you've done make you unlovable. Well, congrats, I've spent my whole life there. I see your broken-ness, and I raise you. You need Lightcraft magic to heal Eléa. I'm right here." She dragged her nails down his chest. "Fuck the coven. Fuck the Dark Oak. I'll restore the string of fate and we'll heal her ourselves. We've lied to each other and our-selves enough, let our prejudices dictate our path. No more. You hear me? Stop pushing me away." She didn't even hear the words that were coming out of her mouth. She was in a fugue state, his presence overwhelming her senses. The way he grounded her and challenged her and, yes, scared her. But not because of what he'd done. Because he stripped away her armor and never asked her to be anything other than exactly what she was.

He lifted her by the waist to set her on the counter. They were nearly eye level now, and he devoured her with his gaze.

"They think you hoodwinked me," he said. "They think you're a distraction. And you are. My god, you've turned me inside out, little muse. I'm tired of pushing you away." His hand came up to cradle the back of her neck, the gentle pressure so at odds with his harsh words and storm-tossed face. There was agony and hope and sorrow etched into every line.

Calliope leaned forward and pressed her lips to his like it was an inevitability. It was gentle at first, their lips sliding together in a greeting, a promise, an apology. But then his hand on the back of her neck tightened and he angled his head. His tongue skimmed against hers and he groaned into her mouth and the world faded away. The grief and anger and fear of the future were still there, under the surface, but they were overshadowed by the desire electrifying her skin.

In the next moment, darkness enveloped them, and by the time she opened her eyes, they were standing on the Altar of Fate.

"In case Eléa comes back," he said, staring at her with devouring hunger. He reached forward, his fingers curling around her belt and pulling her close. He didn't move his eyes from her as he unfastened the buckle and it fell to the ground with a thud.

The spring air had a bite to it, and dark clouds still filled the sky even though the rain had stopped. Calliope tried to breathe evenly, but Lucien's nearness, the desire pulsing through her and making her legs tremble, made it impossible.

His fingers brushed her shoulders as he pushed the duster off and down her arms. It floated to the ground and pooled around her boots. Goosebumps feathered over her arms as the night air kissed her skin.

"Right," she said. "Yes, we're doing this."

He spoke a few quiet words, and a thick layer of bedding with down pillows appeared on the Altar.

"I know it will be difficult for you, since you can't seem

to let thirty seconds of silence settle into your bones before speaking whatever crosses that mind of yours." He stepped closer to her, invading her space in a delicious way. "But this is where the talking stops," he growled.

"You're infuriating even when I want you to kiss me senseless," she said, giving him a light shove.

"Don't start a war you can't finish, little muse," he said, grabbing her wrist.

"I may not like silence, but at least I know how to use my words." She tried to twist her wrist out of his grip, but he only held on tighter, her skin burning. She moaned at the feeling and his eyes darkened.

"You want me to use my words?" he asked, dragging her closer. "Or do you want me to use my tongue?" And he picked her up and laid her gently on her back, and then he was on top of her, pinning her wrists above her head, his weight deliciously heavy against her until she wanted nothing more than for her imprint to be left in the stone for generations to come.

"Perhaps you need a lesson in how satisfying silence can be," he said, his nose grazing the sensitive skin below her ear, and just that made her stomach clench. She looked up at him, an invitation in her eyes.

"I feel certain you'd be an excellent tutor," she said breathlessly, arching her back so her hips could press closer to him, needing the contact, the friction, the heat of him.

"But you'll need to follow directions," he murmured. "And you are notoriously stubborn." He took both her wrists in one hand and used the other to drag her dress up, his fingers grazing hot against her calf, her thigh, her hip as he went higher, higher.

"You're more stubborn than I could ever—" she started,

but he silenced her with a kiss, his tongue slipping into her mouth like it was always meant to be there.

She could drink from the fountain of this kiss forever. It was slow and languorous and torturous, and she melted into it, into him. But then he deepened the kiss, his head angled, his tongue sweeping into her, and she fought back. They kissed the way they fought, with abandon and fire.

He finally released her wrists and threaded his fingers into her hair, his palm cradling her head, crushing her to him like he was afraid she might slip away.

She reached for his shirt, and he pulled back just long enough for her to unbutton the top few buttons and then draw it over his head. And goddess above, but his skin, his body. He practically glowed in the moonlight, every rippling muscle inviting her to taste, to touch. And so, she did. Her fingers trailed across the wide expanse of his chest and up to his shoulders, where her fingernails bit into his flesh, and she moaned as he fisted her hair.

His hand tried to push higher, but the bodice of her dress stopped his path.

"Take it off," she panted, desperate to feel him against her. He muttered a few quick words, and she lay naked beneath him. "That's quite a trick," she said, her chest rising and falling as he stared at her, drank her in in the moonlight. "Do you use that on all the—" She sucked in a breath as he leaned down and began to lick a path between her breasts, her nipples stiffening as he buried his head like he'd been born searching for that very place and finally found it.

He sat up, his hips still straddling hers. His hands trailed over her curves, exploring every inch of soft skin, worshipping the dips and valleys. His tongue traced delicious paths until she was panting and writhing against him.

"Off," she said, tugging at the waistband of his pants, but he tsked and shook his head.

"Not tonight," he said. "This isn't about me. This is about you." His voice was gruff, and even in the moonlight, she could see the way his eyes darkened as he took her in.

She was naked beneath the night sky. The smell of damp grass and the sharp, cold air enveloped them like a dream. Cradled them in a world where there were no nightmares, no Dark Oak, no death, only this. The movement of him against her, the trail of his fingers down her thighs.

"I've been dreaming about this," he groaned against her stomach, his breath hot on her skin. And when his knuckles brushed against her sex, she swore she tasted starlight. Longing morphed into something stronger, something feral as he teased her. She shivered as he touched her, and when he entered her with two fingers, she clenched around them. When she gasped, he swore, and in the grass beside them sprouted a host of snowdrop flowers.

He was demanding and domineering, and Calliope demanded right back. She wanted to cry with the beauty of it, their bond pulsing around them. He was in tune with every groan of pleasure, every arch of her back as he worked her.

"Look at me," he growled, his fingers pumping harder while his other hand pinched her nipple. "Let me watch you come," he said, his voice quieter now, almost pained with longing as his eyes never left her face.

Calliope lost herself as he brought her closer to the edge. The ceaseless voice in her head had finally muted, and now it only cried *more, more, more*.

"Küçük ilham perisi," he growled against her ear when she cried out. "Hepsini bana ver. Give it all to me."

She did, crying out as the wave of desire crested and

crashed into her, and she was happy to drown in it. She lost herself, and, though her eyes closed, she could still see the stars. When she opened them again, she'd found a way back to a small piece of herself.

Afterward, she lay sweaty and breathing hard, her heart tightening when he pulled her close.

"Was I silent enough for you?" she asked, and her voice sounded dreamy and far away. Her limbs were loose, and her problems were distant.

"I believe you still have some lessons to learn," he said, kissing her temple and pulling the blanket up. Calliope shivered despite the warmth that enveloped her and swallowed hard as he kissed her temple. After all her mother's warnings, she was starting to fall for the very Shadowcrafter she'd been warned against. And yet, despite it all, a smile tugged at the corners of her mouth as she slipped into a dream.

CHAPTER 29

LUCIEN WAITED UNTIL CALLIOPE'S BREATHING deepened and the crease between her brows smoothed out to transport her to her own bed. Her honey-wheat hair cascaded over the pillow, and he called himself a hundred different names as he leaned down and placed a gentle kiss on her forehead. The moonlight from her window slashed across the bed, and half her face was cast in shadow while the other was bathed in a glow that made her look angelic. Even though he knew she was anything but. Fierce, messy, fearless, powerful, protective, and smart? Yes. But angelic? Not a chance.

He willed himself to leave, but his feet remained motionless. He glanced around her room. The open drawer with socks spilling out, shoes scattered all over the floor, crystals jumbled in a mess across her desk. And there, thrown carelessly over the back of a chair, was the starlight dress she'd worn at the club. He'd studied the Petridi line for years. Still remembered the first moment he'd seen her through the window of Tea and Tome. He couldn't say why he'd chosen to follow Calliope instead of Dissy or Thalia. But something had called him to her. And her chaos had sunk into his bones. He should have known, that first night, her long hair in a wild tangle down her back and her body luminescent as her dress shimmered like shooting stars. He hadn't known how she'd get under his skin. Hadn't been prepared for her defiance or beauty or brokenness. A groan escaped him as he looked down at her again, and then he vanished before the desire to linger could pull him in again.

Still, when he arrived at the cottage, he was almost . . . smiling.

The house was dark and smelled of puff pastry, apples, and warm spices. Eléa must have baked tarte tatin, which made his smile grow even broader. He'd arrived in this town desperate and angry and lonely. Now an ember of hope glowed inside him, thawing his soul, which he'd kept carefully iced for so long. After all, what was his soul really worth? Just like Calliope and her memories, it served only as something to give him more power.

His plan had worked, albeit not the way he'd thought it would. He'd tied himself to a Petridi, built up their trust, and kept them distracted while his coven broke the enchantments. Now it was only a matter of time until the sisters figured out how to break the bond and restore their string of fate, and then they'd be able to break the final enchantment. Something he couldn't help them with no matter how much he wanted to. He was, dare he even think it, buoyant with hope. He pictured his sister glowing with health, the coven with their respective power, the Dark Oak freed, and maybe, just maybe, a way to rid the Petridi sisters of that memory curse. It wouldn't bring Roz back, but it would ensure they'd never have to sacrifice any of their memories of her.

Forcing himself not to hum, he walked toward the kitchen for a midnight snack of his favorite dessert but stopped short in the doorway when he saw a broad form outlined in the dark, sitting on a stool at the high counter.

His heart turned to concrete. *No,* he thought. *No, no, no. Not when we are so close.*

A light flicked on, and there his father sat. The bastard was using the tines of a fork to pick up the last crumbs of the tarte tatin. When the man turned to look at Lucien, that familiar face sent rivers of ice roaring through his veins.

Thick eyebrows and shrewd eyes, lips that were capable only of speaking cruelty. Even in the dead of night, he wore a crisp suit, his Hermès cuff links glinting in the low light. His leather Gucci dress shoes gleamed, shined to within an inch of their life. Argyle socks peeked out from under the hem of his pants, and Lucien thought of Calliope, her mismatched socks and wild hair and messy drawers and how she was the antithesis of everything he was raised with. She was warm and fiery and strong but still so, so soft. And he would not let this man anywhere near her.

"Merhaba, son," he said. His voice was low. Bass drums and thunder and bad memories.

"What are you doing here?" Lucien demanded. And though dread formed in his gut, his tone was level. His hands remained loose at his sides though he ached to curl his fingers into fists and see what crushing his father's skull felt like.

"Is that any way to greet your father?" he asked conversationally, licking the crumbs from the fork.

"You are no father of mine," Lucien spat.

"Ha," Ahmed said, wagging a finger. "Interesting comment from a powerful witch who can literally make things so by wishing them. You were always willful and stubborn, but you've never been delusional."

"Leave this house at once," Lucien said, forcing every ounce of command he could into his voice.

Ahmed ignored him.

"Let's get down to business, shall we? I've already gotten to work on the enchantments. No need to thank me. This . . . little coven you put together," he said condescendingly, "they're good. But clearly, no match for me. Not with what I'm capable of." And at that, the stone in Lucien's gut grew even heavier. He knew what his father was capable of.

"The wraiths," Lucien said.

"Oh, I'm sure they'll be arriving soon. They're drawn to Petridi blood, or haven't you noticed? It was so easy to give them the scent of that two-bit tarot card witch," Ahmed said with distaste. Lucien choked, but his father kept going. "You see, your problem is you're far too careful. Too slow. Trying to preserve everyone's safety and plan for all the variables. It's pointless, son. If you know what you want, what you need, you take it with no apologies and let the consequences be damned."

"No," Lucien breathed. "That's *you*. Not me. Not anymore."

"Haven't you heard the expression that blood is thicker than water? You are who you are *because of me*." Ahmed's voice boomed through the kitchen.

Lucien's eyes darkened. If his problem was being stubborn and willful, his father's was ignorance and arrogance.

"Everything I am is in spite of you," Lucien said, breathing harder now.

"In spite of, because of, they have the same end result, do they not? You think I haven't kept tabs on you? Wasn't aware of your every move? I thought this might be when you re-deemed yourself and I could welcome you back into the family fold."

"I want nothing to do with the family fold," Lucien said darkly.

"Be that as it may, I was wrong. Not something I enjoy admitting at the best of times." He pushed the tart pan away from him and dusted his hands together before standing. "You took your sister into your care without my permission."

"Because grandfather was killing her!" Lucien shouted, and Ahmed's eyes darkened dangerously.

"And you killed him for it," he said softly. "One of the few things you've done that I'm truly proud of. When you finally claimed your birthright as a powerful Shadowcrafter who took his revenge without mercy. But that's where my pride ends, son. Eléa is not safe with you."

The room narrowed, and Lucien's vision was edged with black. He was a fool. A *fool*.

"What have you done with her?" Lucien said, seething, his chest heaving.

"The coven is under my control now," he said, not answering the question. "Malik has ensured from the beginning that they hold no allegiance to you."

"Malik," Lucien said, confusion warring with the unfettered fear of losing Eléa when he was so close to saving her.

"You didn't think he'd walked away from me," Ahmed said with a sinister smile. "No, no. He's here at my behest. Who do you think led him to Feng? Who put Luna on your radar? Sarai—"

"No," Lucien whispered.

"Sarai was in Egypt because *I* hired her. Didn't trust you, even then, to complete the job. Not when you found out that the snake would unleash devastation on the town. *She* brought me the canopic jar. And *you* failed the test. Lied to me about it." Ahmed shook his head. "You've always been a bleeding heart beneath that stern exterior. And there's simply no place for that in what needs to be done here. I told Sarai to stay in touch with you, to answer your call when you decided to embark on this little quest."

"And the initiates?" Lucien asked, his throat dry.

"All mine." Ahmed smiled with savage pleasure. "Was it convincing when they cowered in fear of you? I certainly hope so. I've paid them well enough for it."

"Why?" Lucien asked. But, of course, his father didn't answer.

"You hate me so much it's made you blind. But it's okay. All will be as it should be now that I'm at the helm. Your sister is with us."

"You say Eléa isn't safe with me, but you were the one who sanctioned grandfather's torture," Lucien growled.

"There are bigger things at play here," Ahmed barked, losing his patience now. "Plans that have been generations in the making. Now I will keep Eléa until you've ensured that the Petridis can do their job."

Unbidden, Lucien's magic rose to the surface and shadows shrouded him, filled the kitchen until the light was nearly blotted out. Rage was making his ears ring, and fear was making him foolish.

But Ahmed merely laughed. He snapped his fingers once and the shadows vanished.

"Move against us in any way, and I'll ensure those wretched Lightcraft witches are dead when this is all said and done."

This time, it was Lucien's turn to laugh. Underestimating

the Petridis would be his father's gravest mistake. One he looked forward to immeasurably.

"My empire could have been yours," Ahmed said with a frown. And then he vanished.

But Lucien had never wanted his empire. He wanted to tear it down to rubble and dust, so it never had an opportunity to rise again.

Lucien stood in the silence of the kitchen, his father's musky cologne lingering in the air. He picked up the dirty plate and threw it against the wall, where it smashed with a satisfying shatter. But it wasn't enough. Lifting his arms and letting his magic flow through him, he forced the cabinet doors open, and he bellowed with rage as every single dish flew out and smashed to the ground with a deafening clatter.

Someone was calling his name, but he couldn't hear it. He needed to get Eléa. But how? He couldn't fight the whole coven and his father and win. His head fell forward into his hands. Malik had betrayed him again. And for some reason, it hurt more this time. And Sarai. How could he have been so stupid?

"Lucien," the voice said again.

"You," he growled when he looked up and saw Sarai.

"Me," she said, worry etched around her eyes. "I heard everything Ahmed said, but he's only partially right. I *was* in Egypt on a job for him. But I stayed in touch because I wanted to, and I said yes to this coven because once I met Eléa, I knew I'd do anything to save her. She's *good*, Lucien. She's pure goodness and light. So, when we fight, I fight with you. I fight for her because she's become my best friend."

Lucien regarded her carefully, felt his father's poisonous words being drained out of him.

"Malik and the rest?" he asked.

"I can't speak for them," Sarai said.

"Very well." Lucien nodded. "We need to get the moon water. The wraiths will be coming soon."

His father had said that blood was thicker than water. But he'd misquoted it. It was actually, *The blood of the covenant is thicker than the water of the womb.* And now Lucien would have to rely on his father's arrogance. On his refusal to accept that chosen bonds could be far stronger than the ones forced on you by birth.

CHAPTER 30

CALLIOPE WOKE BEFORE THE SUN, BACK IN HER own bed, and couldn't go back to sleep. Lucien was gone, Astro curled in his place. The candles he'd lit had burned low. The smell of fasolada wafting up the stairs through her open door meant at least one of her sisters couldn't sleep, either. A looming threat was working its way under her skin, making her antsy.

When she entered the kitchen, Dissy was pulling a loaf of crusty cottage bread out of the oven, and Thalia was ladling the Greek bean soup into bowls. Dissy's eyes were red and puffy, and Thalia's mouth was in a perpetual frown, her shoulders drawn up. But there, on the table, sat Grim. The book flew up and crashed into Calliope's chest, and she wrapped her arms around it, inhaling that familiar scent of leather and ink and parchment. Fresh, hot tears tracked down her cheeks, but these tears, they were a gift. Of shared grief and memories and love.

She was given extra time. Your mother made sure of that, Grim wrote after she settled him back on the table. *The greatest gift is remembering her. So, we will. We'll talk and laugh and honor her the way she'd want us to.*

They were all silent as they sat at the table. The soup symbolized unity and harmony, and as they dipped their bread and let the flavors play across their tongues, a measure of peace returned to them.

Finally, Calliope told them about Eléa's news and Lucien's confession.

"The plot thickens," Thalia said with a sigh, using a piece of bread to wipe her bowl clean.

"But did you tell him how you feel?" Dissy asked.

"I don't even know how I feel," Calliope said, moving the carrots around the bottom of her bowl with her spoon. She'd always hated carrots.

"Opie," Dissy said softly.

"Don't 'Opie' me, Dissy."

"I'm just saying you've spent your life sacrificing your memories. Don't you think it's time you face your own fears? Live a life worth remembering?"

Calliope scowled at her sister as she buttered another slice of bread and sprinkled coarse salt on top. Because when all else failed, bread fixed everything.

"Life is nothing but a collection of memories, you know," Dissy said. "If you don't tell him how you feel, you're lying to yourself as much as you are him."

"Sounds like the pot calling the kettle black," Calliope said, pointing her spoon at Dissy.

"What do you mean?"

"Sean?" Calliope said archly, raising an eyebrow. "You're telling me to spill my guts, but you haven't spilled yours."

"Actually," Dissy said, her cheeks turning pink as she

averted her gaze from Calliope's sharp stare. "I went to see him yesterday."

"You didn't," Thalia said, while Calliope just looked on in shock.

"I did," Dissy said, and a giddy laugh escaped her. "I was shaking, I was so nervous. But I asked him out, and he said he'd been wanting to kiss me since the moment he saw me in Tea and Tome."

Calliope gave a low whistle. "Touché, sister," she said, raising her glass to salute her.

"I'm proud of you," Thalia said quietly, placing her hand on top of Dissy's and giving it a squeeze.

"I think this calls for dessert," Calliope said. She cut a violet tart and set the plates on the table. They were quiet as they ate, the buttery crust and creamy, floral custard dancing in a marriage that tasted like heaven.

The fire crackled in the hearth, and the wind buffeted gently against the windows. Dissy had lit candles, and the flames swayed merrily as the sound of fork tines scraped across plates. And as the scene sunk into her like a warm hug, the shadows loomed, and Calliope's thoughts swayed with the candle flames. All her life, it was in the moments of peace that the fear would set in. For never were the stakes of loss higher than when the good was highlighted so prettily. If they succeeded, she could lose all of this. But if they failed, she'd lose everything. Already, the threat of it loomed, stealing the joy of the moment.

"Whenever I cook," Dissy said thoughtfully, "or bake, the string of fate inside me pulses brighter. I can *feel* it. It's tied to more than just me. It's tied to memories of us. To the nostalgia of our past. To meals we shared on Milos or midnight snacks when we were kids or things we've made for Tea and Tome. Can't you feel it?"

Calliope closed her eyes and searched for that string inside her, that ageless thing that had tied her to her sisters for time beyond remembering. She reached out, following the string, and found Thalia easily. Could feel her brashness and stubbornness, knew it would taste tart as rhubarb but with a hint of earthiness and a touch of sweetness. But there, faintly, she could feel Dissy. The steady thrum, warm and comforting like cinnamon, that she hadn't experienced since that night at the Altar.

"I can feel it," Calliope whispered.

"Me, too," Thalia said.

"What if," Dissy said quietly. "What if it's not our magic that heals the string?"

As she spoke the words in the silence of the kitchen, the string pulsed brighter. Thalia had just opened her mouth to say something when the windows and doors slammed open on a gale-force wind. Glass shattered. The candles winked out. Their fragile string snapped, the connection gone. And whispers filled the house. What sounded like dozens of them all speaking over one another. The hairs on the back of Calliope's neck stood on end, and then a shrill, keening wail rang from outside, so loud the sisters clapped their hands over their ears, and the ground began to tremble. Wordlessly, they ran outside, looking toward the forest. A haunting sound reached their ears, drifting from the woods.

The wind began to howl, sharp and slicing into their very skin. Calliope's mouth opened on a silent scream. Another enchantment had broken. The wraiths were coming.

As if nature itself recoiled from the unfolding chaos, the

sky darkened further, and shadowy forms filled the air. They circled overhead, their grotesque hybrid bodies casting eerie silhouettes. Their wings beat like a foreboding omen as they circled closer and filled Calliope with a haunting dread. Their faces were pale with hunger, and as they flew lower, Calliope could see the long, sharp claws protruding from their fingers.

The sisters stared in terror and then, like a bolt from the heavens, Lucien appeared. Smoke was swirling from his body, rage etched into every line of him as though he'd been chiseled from stone. A moment later, a woman appeared behind him. *Sarai,* Calliope remembered.

"Get back," he yelled. The wind whipped his hair, his white dress shirt pulled taut across his body as he faced the forest, eyes to the sky. His usual composure was gone. Instead, raw energy poured from him until he seemed to vibrate with it. The wraiths flew faster, and Lucien raised his arms. Turkish poured from his lips, and his eyes grew darker as the spell took over.

When he unleashed the lightning, the very earth seemed to cry out. The bolt shot across the sky, illuminating the terrors above.

"Inside, now!" Lucien's voice rang out urgently, the force of his words shocking them into movement.

They were barely inside before they slammed the door, the sound of wings beating against the wood sending shivers down Calliope's spine, her heart racing in tandem with the storm winds outside.

Lucien and Sarai faced the door, both of them speaking quiet words as their hands moved deftly, and then, a glowing light filled the entryway.

When he was done, Lucien sagged against the door.

"My father," he said, his voice heavy with anguish. "He's taken Eléa. As leverage to ensure you undo the final enchantment."

"He'll stop at nothing." Sarai looked tormented, her eyes bright with unshed tears. "He wants the power of the Dark Oak for himself."

"He sent the wraiths after your aunt," Lucien said. "He's responsible for her death."

"No," Calliope whispered.

"We will fight the wraiths and we will win, and then we will get Eléa back," Sarai said.

"I'll fight with you," Thalia said.

"Lucien," Calliope said, stepping into his path as he paced back and forth, anger emanating from him like a beacon. She wanted to tell him it was all her fault, that they would get Eléa back. But the words stuck in her throat and instead she said, "I'll fight, too."

"They will steal your magic and then eat your soul if they get hold of you," Lucien said darkly. "Our magic calls to theirs, and they'll stop at nothing to consume it."

"But how do we fight them?" Dissy asked, chewing her lip. "We never found anything in the library."

"Moon-blessed water and fire," Lucien said.

"You've known how to fight the wraiths this whole time?" Thalia demanded.

"What she said," Calliope said, her eyes narrowed.

"My coven has been working on it, and I had the displeasure of learning that it does indeed work. Trust me when I say, you don't want to know how I found that out. But we already stashed jugs of it outside. Let's go."

Calliope, Eurydice, and Thalia stood behind Lucien and Sarai, and when he opened the door, the skies were a maelstrom of wraiths and shadows as though chaos itself had been unleashed.

They hurled spell after spell, Sarai holding a protective field of magic energy around them. The sisters drew on what power they had, but Lucien possessed the vengeance of a fallen angel. He threw his magic like sharpened knives, corralling the monsters ever closer.

With a roar of rage, Lucien stepped outside of Sarai's protection and unleashed a stream of fire. It catapulted toward the sky, but one of the wraiths' bladelike feathers sliced across his arm, and blood began to pour.

Sarai let out a cry and dropped the protection. She ran forward, her arms flung wide as a string of Arabic left her lips. Her body went taut as the spell released and the moon-blessed water formed into arrows that sailed through the sky toward the wraiths.

Their screams filled the night, and she looked back to Lucien with a triumphant look on her face.

And that was when the remaining wraiths descended upon them in a fury.

Their ghastly talons slashed the air, and Sarai was ensnared by the wraiths. Her bloodcurdling scream pierced the chaos, the sound reverberating through the air.

Calliope, Thalia, and Eurydice watched in horror, their strength faltering in the face of such unspeakable darkness. Their string was too weak, their magic thin and faltering.

And yet, Calliope's feet seemed to move of their own accord. Slowly at first, and then she was breaking into a run, throwing herself into the fray as she concentrated every ounce of her weakened power. She had to do *something*. Couldn't let Sarai be consumed. She reached into her cache of memories, but before she could sacrifice one, Lucien let out a savage roar.

Calliope barely recognized him. His eyes blazed black as he plumbed the depth of the well within, drawing on the darkness there. Daggers made of fire materialized in thin air, and with a flick of his wrist, they pierced the wraiths' hearts. The monsters began to fall to the earth, and as they did, he bound forward and picked Sarai up, cradling her in his arms like she was nothing more than a doll.

"The water," Sarai whispered, and she was close enough now that Calliope heard her.

She rushed forward, grasping at any memory she could find as the creatures began to slowly pull themselves closer. Their faces, once human, were haunting: cheeks hollowed out, gaping mouths lined with razor-sharp teeth, and red coals for eyes. These ones had shadowy, translucent wings, the bones visible as they beat them with powerful strokes.

Calliope shook as she called forth a simple fire spell. But it wasn't enough. Her magic was too weak.

Thalia stepped forward, linking her hand with Calliope's, and together they sent a pillar of moon-blessed water, half of the wraiths screaming as they burned. They were panting, shaking, and it still wasn't enough.

"Both of you get back in the house," Thalia said through gritted teeth.

Instead of answering, Dissy, panting and pale, stepped forward and linked her hand with Calliope's.

The surge of power nearly knocked them back.

"Three in one, one in three. Even without the string of fate," Dissy whispered, tears tracking down her cheeks.

And together they chanted the words that burned the last of the wraiths.

The five of them stood there, breathing hard in the silence, until the sound of slow clapping rang through the air. A figure had been watching from the tree line. And as he emerged, Lucien swore.

"Do you hear that?" the man asked as he got closer. And when Calliope could make out his features, there was no mistaking who he was. Lucien's father. Same height, same build, same fire in their eyes that spoke of being burdened with glorious purpose, though their purposes differed greatly. Lucien, still bleeding, stepped in front of the sisters and Sarai, who lay on the ground, drained of color, her features twisted in agony. The man wore a suit so perfectly creased you could cut your finger on it, and his leather dress shoes squelched through the mud.

"Listen," he said now, cocking his head and holding up a finger toward the Forgotten Forest. Calliope listened, and over the field came an enchanting song, sung by voices braided together through time and memory, that raised the hairs on the back of her neck and sent a shiver down her spine.

Come, it sang.

Come seek us where the magic was bound,
You'll find your fate within our sound.
Let us reveal your histories past,
So you can be free, free at last.

"That's your destiny calling," Ahmed said. "Yet you seem hesitant to answer it. Perhaps you need an incentive, like my son did."

And then everything happened at once.

CHAPTER 31

LUCIEN'S SHOUT OF RAGE RATTLED THROUGH THE clearing.

His father held up a hand, and the sisters fell to their knees, writhing in agony. Calliope's chest constricted, and though she tried to draw in a ragged breath, the air wouldn't come. Pain seared every inch of her skin, and she couldn't even find her voice to cry out. It felt as though she were combusting from the inside, fire consuming every vein.

"I cannot kill you, of course," he said conversationally. "But I can, how shall we say, *encourage* you to heal your silly little string of fate so that we can get on with our business."

Lucien unleashed his magic on his father, a fury of shadows that launched like arrows. But Ahmed only laughed, and, with a flick of his hand, the shadows dissipated.

"You have gone up against me before and lost, my son," he said, and with a wave of his arm, he unleashed a shield that Lucien's magic couldn't penetrate.

Ahmed's power surged again, and Calliope fell forward onto her hands, coughing blood. She didn't have room to wonder how or why he was torturing her because her vision was fading to black, and nothing seemed sweeter than the sweet oblivion that beckoned her.

"No," Dissy croaked out, her voice ragged as she struggled to her feet.

"No?" Ahmed released his hold on them a fraction.

Dissy grabbed Calliope's hand and pulled her close, whispering hurriedly in her ear. She could barely hear the words through the pain lancing through her, but when they registered, they shocked Calliope to her core, her eyes going wide as everything clicked into place. But before she could respond, Ahmed began his torture anew even as Lucien fought against the barrier and failed.

"You want another bargaining chip," Dissy said, releasing Calliope's hand and stepping forward. Her voice cracked through the air. "Take me."

The shadows and pain stopped abruptly.

As though in a trance, Dissy moved forward. Thalia and Calliope struggled to their feet, tried to hold her back, but she pushed them off. And now Calliope watched, helplessly, as her sister sacrificed herself. As she walked toward Ahmed's shield. As he smiled ruthlessly and grabbed her roughly by the arm and they disappeared, taking his shadows with them. And all that was left behind was a series of broken souls, panting and shattered beneath the purple sky.

The night was their witness as the world outside Lethe Manor mourned the carnage that had happened there. The sun began to rise, but Calliope couldn't feel its warmth. Her sister's last words to her were coursing through her veins.

"He's a bastard, but he won't kill her," Lucien said, and it was a shock to hear his voice. Calliope's whole world had narrowed to Dissy's retreating back. Lucien was moving his hands over Sarai's wounds, speaking healing spells in Turkish.

"Enough, Lucien," Sarai said, and though her face was wan, her voice was strong. "We don't need another wraith on our hands. Protect your magic. I'm okay, I promise."

Lucien rocked back on his heels, every line of his face hardened into rage.

"How do you know?" Thalia asked, her voice broken. "How do you know he won't kill her?"

"Only three Petridi sisters with their string of fate can undo the final enchantment," he reminded them. "He'll keep her until you restore the string of fate because he won't be able to access the full power of the Dark Oak until that final spell is broken." His words were hard, his voice hoarse, and he looked as desperate as Calliope felt.

"How do we get her back?" Thalia asked.

"There are two enchantments left. We undo them, and I will use the power of the Dark Oak to destroy my father once and for all," Lucien growled.

"What?" Calliope said, her eyes going wide.

"You want Eurydice?" he said, rounding on her. His dark hair was in disarray, and blood soaked through the sleeve of his shirt. His eyes were wild, and, in that moment, Calliope was a little afraid of him. Not for herself, but for what he might do. "They'll know when you're at the Dark Oak," he continued, "and they'll bring her there. But we'll be faster. They won't be expecting you to cooperate."

"This is what we've been fighting against this whole time!" Calliope shouted, her throat raw from screaming. "Our family has spent generations protecting that Dark Oak. It's the very thing that caused this memory curse in the first place!"

"It's the only way we'll be able to fight the wraiths and the coven. The only way we can get Eléa back."

"How can I trust you're not the same as your father? What if you only want the power for yourself?" she cried.

"Watch your words, little muse," Lucien said, and his own words held a dangerous quality to them, but Calliope was past heeding warning signs. His father had stolen *her* sister now, too—would stop at nothing to get what he wanted. Who was to say that Lucien was any different? What if he and his father were working together in some twisted, intricate game?

"You said it yourself," she said, and her voice trembled slightly. "I knew you were supposed to distract me, but I didn't realize what a good job you'd done. We're not breaking that last spell. We will guard the Dark Oak as dozens of Petridi women have before us. Protect it from people like *you*."

"Calliope," he said, and now there was a pleading note to his words. "I am on your side."

"We don't need you," she said. And at this, Thalia stepped forward to stand by Calliope's side. All the moments with Lucien flashed before her eyes. In her mind, she saw the snowdrops that had sprouted at the Altar of Fate when he'd made her see stars. And it wrecked her. She knew she wasn't being fair, but fear drove the words from her heart, and it was too late to pull them back.

Lucien stared, his gaze boring into hers, and she knew. Knew he could see that fear written so plainly on her face. She felt him plumbing the depths of who she was. She could sense his unspoken words. And then he helped Sarai to her feet and they both vanished. Calliope's knees went weak, and she wanted to fall to the ground. To scream that the world wasn't fair. Instead, she stared at the place where he'd stood, as though that patch of trampled grass might hold the answers she sought. And even as her heart was breaking, she turned to her sister.

"Dissy told me how to restore our string of fate," she whispered into the cold air, her breath forming into mist.

"What?" Thalia demanded sharply. "How?"

"Right before the wraiths came, we all felt it in the kitchen, remember? It's not magic that heals the string. It's a choice. Though I guess that's a kind of magic all its own, isn't it?"

"But if that's true, why wouldn't Mother have chosen to heal her string?" Thalia asked.

"Maybe she didn't know. Maybe theirs was broken beyond repair. But this bond with Lucien that muddles ours? I think I was holding on to it. Holding on to all the anger and hurt and fear that had been pushing the three of us apart."

"And now you're not?" Thalia asked quietly.

"Ever since I went to the Dark Oak, we've been set on this course. So much has happened—" Calliope's voice broke, but she kept going. "But look at Dissy. She told Sean how she felt. She just sacrificed herself to keep us safe. She's standing up for herself now. And you? You've taken care of us for so long. And I know part of it was because you were afraid we'd leave you, too, but—"

"But you never would. I know that now," Thalia said. "I was scared. So scared that you'd leave me behind. You've always been this supernova, and goddess above, that terrified me, Opie," she said with a choked laugh. "But you burn so bright for a reason. So, fix it. Do it."

"But we need Dissy *here* to heal it. All three of us, together. But how? We can't get Dissy back without our magic— Lucien's gone. And even with him and Sarai, we barely beat back the wraiths. And if the coven breaks the other enchantment?" Her eyes were frantic and pleading. "How do we protect the town? We couldn't even protect Roz! Could barely protect Sarai. How do we win?"

"By not collapsing on the ground in tears when things go to hell," Thalia said, gently now.

"I've spent years sacrificing my memories only for it to end in *this*."

"This is how they win," Thalia said, her voice low and urgent. "We fight among ourselves and they have the upper hand, you understand me? Look at me, Opie." And there was such command in her voice that Calliope raised her tearstained face and looked at her sister. "You've been sabotaging yourself for so long because you think it's all you have. And that's bullshit. The only thing I've ever seen you be afraid of is yourself. So, you have two choices. Sit here and wallow, or get up and *do something*."

"I can't," Calliope cried.

"You can," Thalia said.

"I'm not strong like you."

"We're only as strong as each other," Thalia said. "One in three, three in one. We lean on each other. That's what sisters are supposed to do. You're not strong enough? Fine, take some of my strength. And when I feel like giving up, you give me some of yours."

"Everything feels so hopeless," Calliope whispered.

"Hope doesn't have to be a blazing fire," Thalia said, her voice growing gentler. "Sometimes, it's just a flicker in the darkness, but it's enough to guide us through."

Calliope sniffed and nodded, using her shoulder to wipe the tears from her face. And when Thalia leaned forward and wrapped her arms around her sister, they sank into each other. Calliope could feel Thalia's strength seeping into her, warming her, stoking the flicker of hope until it burned just a little brighter.

"It's time to stop running, Opie. Stop running from the hard things just because you don't want to feel the pain."

Calliope was silent, letting her sister's words run over her like cool water on a burn.

"Okay," she whispered.

"What was that? I couldn't quite hear you," Thalia said, cupping a hand around her ear, making Calliope laugh.

"I said, okay." Her voice was louder now, stronger.

"Come on then," Thalia said, dragging Calliope to her feet and then back to Lethe Manor. The house was cold, colder than normal. And her legs were numb as she followed Thalia to the kitchen. Always the kitchen. As if the memories there were strong enough to sustain them.

"Do you really think he's like his father?" Thalia asked.

"No," Calliope groaned. "Of course not, but everything is so muddled, and I can't think straight."

"What would Dissy do?"

"She'd make us a cup of tea," Calliope said with a manic laugh. "She'd turn on all the lights to chase away the darkness and tell us that together, we can figure it out."

Just then, Grim flew into the kitchen at an alarming speed and landed on the table with a thud. The pages were a blur as they flipped open to blank space and words began to splash across the parchment.

Another secret has been lifted with the weakening of the enchantments, it wrote.

"Bad or good?" Calliope asked, swallowing hard. "I don't think I can take any more bad news right now."

Lyra was given a new body with the rebirth spell, Grim wrote quickly but then stopped, as though unable to decide how to continue.

"Go on," Thalia said impatiently.

Lyra was trapped in Roz, but I . . . I was trapped in a grimoire.

No more words appeared. Calliope stared, open-mouthed. "No way."

"Aunt Daphne?" Thalia asked in shock, her eyebrows so high on her forehead Calliope would have laughed if she wasn't so shocked herself.

Hello, darling nieces, the grimoire wrote.

CHAPTER 32

"BUT HOW . . . *WHY?*" CALLIOPE ASKED. SHE laughed. It was a wild sound that rushed through her. The way you laughed when you got good news and couldn't contain the joy that bubbled up inside of you.

Penelope was always the most powerful of the three of us, Grim wrote—or no, *she* wrote.

It was I who called you when you were a child, Calliope. I had to wait until your mother was gone. The more her memory failed, the more the sight of me sent her into an episode.

"What? How?" Thalia asked.

From the moment you were born, Thalia, Penelope became a woman possessed. She became obsessed with breaking the curse that stole our memories. Because there's a second part to the curse you've never known about.

"No," Calliope said, shaking her head vehemently. She couldn't possibly stand to hear more bad news, not after everything that had happened. "No, no, no. I don't want to hear this. I can't."

Thalia reached over and squeezed her hand.

"Tell us," she said grimly.

There can only be three Petridi sisters with magic. When a new witch steps into her power, the older witch begins to die until the transfer is complete. When the second-born begins to come into her power, the cycle repeats. The only way to stop this is for the string of fate to be broken completely. But if that happens, the enchantments over the Dark Oak die as well unless the next generation takes over before the magic has had time to fade.

Calliope let out a small cry, the walls of the room closing in around her. The joy she'd felt only moments ago turned to ashes in her mouth. A fire sprang up in the grate, and the air turned insufferably hot as hives broke out on her arms.

We don't know why this is, Daphne wrote. *But as Thalia got older, your mother grew more desperate.*

"But why didn't Roz tell us this? She must have known!" Calliope said, her voice coming out raspy, her throat raw.

Perhaps it was part of the curse. Or, more likely, she sacrificed the memory of it. It's a terrible burden to bear. By the time Calliope was born, Penelope was crazed with the thought of it. She didn't want the three of you growing up having to sacrifice pieces of yourselves. She wanted to save you. And save us.

We were happy to help her. We ourselves ached to be rid of the sacrifice. What would it be like, we wondered, to do magic so freely? And we loved you. You were too little to remember us well, but we loved you dearly and wanted you to grow up free of this, too.

So, when your mother came up with a spell the likes of which we'd never seen, well, she worked on that spell in secret for twelve moons. When she showed it to us, we were so hopeful. We didn't question her. But we should have known there was a risk. We waited until the hunter's moon. A time that traditionally marked the hunting season. We brought the grimoire to the Altar of Fate and began. But we didn't know her true mission. That she was going to sacrifice everything.

Calliope was crying soft tears now, and Thalia was breathing hard. Whatever information was coming, she knew, would change the course of their lives forever. Her fingers trembled, and her eyes were locked on Daphne's script as she continued to write.

She figured out that if she broke our string, there would be no threat to us. We wouldn't have our magic, but we'd be alive, even though the enchantments would be broken. She was willing to set the Dark Oak free to save us. She enchanted the grimoire to hold my memories and did a transference spell on me so my body became fused with the book. And you know what she did for Lyra, or Roz, as you called her.

"But then, how was Roz able to do magic?" Thalia demanded with a frown.

Perhaps changing bodies tricked the curse, I do not know. There are too many questions and not enough time to answer them all. But, my darling nieces. I am here. And your mother is out there somewhere. I may be just a book at the moment, but if I had my body, I'd say I felt it in my bones.

"You've never been just a book," Calliope said softly, patting Daphne's pages. "And when this is all over, we'll get you out somehow and maybe, together, we can find Mother."

"Wait until Dissy finds out." Thalia was shaking her head as she pulled down the tea cannisters.

We'll get through this, my darling nieces, Daphne wrote. *Together.*

Calliope was reeling, too many thoughts and questions racing through her mind. And she wanted to sit down and demand answers, beg for them, actually, but saving Eurydice came first. There would be time for explanations later, she'd make sure of it.

Five minutes later, Thalia and Calliope sat at the small kitchen table, the smell of chamomile rising in the steam from their cups. Dissy's absence was a visceral thing, the shadow of which not even the light of Daphne's revelation could chase away. But Thalia was right, Calliope would not cower in fear.

Daphne lay open on the table between them, and the three plotted ways to get Dissy back, break the bond, and protect the Dark Oak. And with every dead end, Calliope's plan continued to form. Finally, she sat back.

"Nothing we can think of will work. So . . . we bring the battle to them," she said quietly, her fingers wrapped around the mug, its warmth spreading through her hands.

Thalia's head snapped up, eyes locking on hers, something like fear shining there. Fear at what her wild sister was going to bring down on their heads this time.

Calliope could feel her mask slipping. The one she'd worn for so long. The one that hid her even from herself.

What was she, truly? Could she bear to know? To look the truth of herself in the eyes and not cower before it? A tempest was brewing, poised to shatter the illusion she'd spent so long weaving and reveal the storm beneath. And she vowed to face it head-on.

"Móno oi nekroí échoun dei to télos tou polémou," Calliope said, and there was a wolfish gleam to her eyes now. *Only the dead have seen the end of war.*

CHAPTER 33

AS THOUGH DAPHNE KNEW WHAT CALLIOPE would say next, she wrote one word in all capitals.

NO.

"Do you have a better plan?" she asked the book, who stayed blank save for those two letters. "I didn't think so."

Calliope, bone-weary and hopeless only moments ago, was energized as her spirit came alive again. The sun was rising higher in the sky, and she could hear birdsong through the open kitchen window. The tea was still warm in her hands, the smell of lavender and rose mixing with the smell of the grimoire's vellum pages.

"Are you going to share your harebrained scheme or keep it to yourself?" Thalia demanded.

"Ahmed wants the power for himself. Lucien does, too. But we take it for ourselves. We break the enchantments, just like they want us to," Calliope said, and Thalia's eyebrows shot up. "Restore our string and use the magic hidden there before they can. It's the only way we'll be strong enough."

Thalia only laughed humorlessly.

"How else do we beat the coven and the wraiths? And if they really have Eléa? Lucien may be . . . Lucien, but that doesn't mean his sister deserves to die. Aunt Daphne doesn't have a better plan. Do you?" Calliope huffed.

"I—" Thalia spluttered. "I don't have a plan, but *this* cannot be it. You've spent your life protecting that stupid Dark Oak, and now you want to throw it all in the trash?"

"This is about our *family*," Calliope said in a scathing tone. "About the town. What happens when the Dark Oak is laid bare? When all the wraiths come seeking the power that's been held in that tree for generations? How do we protect everyone?"

Calliope stared down at Daphne's writing, her stomach in knots.

"Opie," Thalia said, laying a hand on her arm. Her voice was softer now, cajoling. "We can't."

And Calliope was reminded of the nights that Thalia would let her crawl into bed with her after a bad dream. She was reminded of a young Thalia, with apple cheeks and a strained smile, as she made breakfast for her and Dissy. Packed their lunches and listened patiently, if a little impassively, to Calliope's chatter about crushes and grievances, homework and tests. She was reminded of the way Thalia had come up with the idea for Tea and Tome. A way for the sisters to be together and work together. Of how she'd given up her dream of attending the Culinary Institute of America and instead enrolled in the Aurelia community college. She'd explained it away by saying that a business degree would be more beneficial for the shop. Calliope had thought nothing of it at the time. Had never considered trying to talk her sister into chasing her dreams. Had even agreed with the decision. But now it made her wonder just what else Thalia had given up.

And in all of these memories, she knew there was more she was missing. She had only fragments of her sisters, of her own life. She'd spent so long giving away pieces of herself that she couldn't quite remember what her life was actually made up of. And it had gotten even worse since their string had broken. She'd built a shrine around the altar of sacrifice for so long she'd forgotten what it meant to be whole. And she wanted it. To be whole. To see her life for what it was, and not for the memories she'd let go of. It was all a tapestry with missing threads, the whole picture always just out of reach. It was time she stopped trying to fill the hole her mother had left and started living for herself. She was worthy in spite of that abandonment.

"We can do this," Calliope said. "I've always been wild. So different from you and Dissy. But when Mother left, I . . . I turned self-destructive. Threw away my memories for magic because it was easier to forget than to remember I wasn't worth staying for. But now we can actually *do* something about it." And as she spoke the words, she knew they were true. That the moment had finally come when she realized her life was worth remembering, with or without magic. She knew what the knots in her stomach meant, the tightness in her chest that made her heart race and her palms sweaty. She was scared. Scared of not having an excuse to live life on her terms. Scared of remembering. Fear told her she couldn't. And if there was one thing Calliope hated, it was being told not to do something.

"We need to get Dissy back, that's what we should be focusing on," Thalia said.

"But what then? How do we *do* that? I'm telling you, this is the answer."

I can't believe I'm writing this . . . but I think I'm beginning to agree with Opie.

Thalia was silent as she regarded Daphne and Calliope, who silently begged her sister to trust her. It was that lack of trust—between the witch who never used her magic and the one who used it so casually it had eaten up whole chapters of her life—that had started this whole mess in the first place.

"Okay," Thalia said finally, taking a deep breath. "I guess we're doing this. Let's save the town. Banish the coven. Get our sister back. Our power back."

Calliope launched herself at Thalia and buried her face in her shoulder. With Thalia's trust, another small piece of her healed.

"And maybe Lucien, too?" Thalia asked slyly.

"Yeah," Calliope said, chest growing tight again as she pulled away from Thalia. A bubble of laughter escaped her. "I may have been a bit hasty with my words."

"You?" Thalia asked in feigned shock.

"Very funny," Calliope said, smacking her on the arm. "But Dissy *had* just sacrificed herself, and goddess above, why did she *do* that? Anyway, I was a little . . . harebrained. Do you think he'll forgive me?"

"For accusing him of kidnapping his own sister?" Thalia asked. "Honestly, yes. I think you've bewitched him body and soul and he'd forgive you just about anything."

"Here's hoping." Calliope sighed, closing her eyes and calling for Lucien, pleading with him, sending the urgency down the bond. "Aunt Daphne?" she asked, turning to the grimoire. "Perhaps while we wait for Lucien, you could try to find out where Dissy is being kept?" The book snapped closed and zoomed out of the kitchen, out the door to the backyard, and off into the clear morning.

"Hope nobody sees that," Thalia remarked drily.

"Do you think there's a way we can get her out of there? When all this is said and done?"

"One thing at a time," Thalia said in a businesslike tone.

"What's the plan then?" a deep voice asked from the doorway. Calliope startled and looked up to see Lucien and Sarai. His arm was still bleeding, and he was still wearing the same sweat-soaked white dress shirt. His hair was still mussed, and there was a wild glint in his eyes. "I presume you do have a plan? If, that is, you've decided to trust me." There was no malice to his words; he spoke earnestly, calmly.

"I see you got my message," Calliope said, willing her heart to slow. "I always forget about your little teleportation ability." He only stared, waiting. Calliope cleared her throat. "Can we, um, talk? Privately?" she asked.

"We'll tell Sarai and Lucien the plan when you're done talking," Thalia said. "Go."

Calliope led Lucien to the sitting room, where he stood, staring at her. Her heart beat hard at the sight of him, and she took a deep breath.

"I'm sorry," she said. "Sorry for everything, Lucien. I was scared. Scared and angry, and I didn't want to believe you because I didn't want to let go of what little control I had left. My mother leaving me, constantly sacrificing my memories . . . I have trust issues, Lucien. My prejudices were inherited, and that's not an excuse. I'm fighting them every day because I want to trust you now. I do, and—" She would have kept going, but Lucien pulled her into his arms.

"Little muse," he said, and despite it all, there was the hint of a smile in his voice. "Save your apologies."

"But I accused you of being like your father, that, that . . . *monster.*" She groaned into his chest.

"I have had worse accusations leveled at me," he said.

"Then why did you leave?" she asked, pulling back and looking up at him.

"I thought you did not want me there," he said simply, his hand running down the length of her hair.

Calliope mumbled something into his shoulder.

"What was that?" Lucien asked.

"I said, I always want you here," she answered, her eyes meeting his. "Even when we're fighting. Which is most of the time. But I like you being here. You make me feel grounded."

"Well, then," he said. "I will stay. We will fight together."

His words bloomed inside of her, vines curling out and wrapping around her heart. But the words of that eerie voice played over and over in her head. *Shadow and Light shall never align.* She shook them off. *Later,* she thought. They'd talk about it later.

"Now," he said, kissing her temple, "let's discuss this plan of yours."

She walked back to the kitchen with Lucien trailing after her to find Sarai and Thalia drinking steaming cups of tea.

"How are your wounds?" Calliope asked Sarai.

"Healed," she said. "I'm ready to fight."

"Thank you for what you did. For what you both did," Calliope said.

"It was only the beginning," Lucien told her. "My father will not hesitate to use Dissy. He has the whole coven under his command. He . . ." Lucien paused, running a hand through his hair with an aggrieved look. "He has from the beginning. He's orchestrated everything." And he told them about Malik and Feng, Luna and even Sarai.

"But I chose to side with you, Lucien," Sarai said now, her voice earnest even as her face paled. "I know what your father is. I don't think he started out as a bad man, but he became that way. His morality rotted through when his drive for power became all-consuming. He's so obsessed with breaking the wraith curse that it'll be his downfall. You of all people should know it's more complex than good and evil. He's been caught in a vicious cycle of generational curses and hatred, but this is a new era. And men like your father have no place in it."

"You think there are others in the coven who might side with us?" Calliope asked.

"I do," Sarai said even as Lucien shook his head. "You don't give yourself enough credit, have let your father get in your head. Maybe he thought he was pulling the strings, but I believe some of them followed you because you're worthy of being followed. Some of them want power for power's sake, but most of them have reasons for wanting it. Feng to protect his mother, Luna to study the limitations of magic without the threat of turning into a wraith, Malik—"

"Malik seeks only to serve my father," Lucien growled.

"Fine, but the initiates? You don't know their stories. I do. Your father has dirt on them. Or he's threatened them into submission. They're loyal out of fear. But what if they were given another choice?"

"Then we'll call them all to the Dark Oak," Calliope said, her voice resolute. "With Dissy there, we'll be able to restore the string of fate, and we take the magic. Rewrite our legacy. Shadow- and Lightcraft working together."

"That doesn't solve the problem of getting Eléa back. He will keep her as leverage to ensure I don't interfere." His jaw clenched, his anger palpable.

"What if you trade us for Eléa?" Calliope asked.

"What?" Lucien snapped, his lips immediately pulling down into a frown.

"We can't fight them. Not while they have her. We don't know who's on our side. So, threaten to kill us unless he gives you Eléa. He knows how much you love your sister. He'll believe it. You hand us over to the coven and get Eléa away. While we're in their clutches, we'll heal the string of fate. Then put up a protective shield over the Dark Oak, so we can undo the final enchantment to fight your father."

"I don't like it," Lucien said darkly.

"This isn't about what you like. It's about what'll work and keep your sister safe," Calliope said. "Thalia?"

"It's a good plan," she said, almost reluctantly. "But if the protective spell doesn't hold, if the coven gets to the Dark Oak . . ."

"We won't let them," Calliope said as her eyes met Lucien's, determination burning within her.

"And what will you do with Ahmed?" Sarai asked. "Once you have all that power."

"If the wraiths don't get him first? Banish him, I guess?" Calliope suggested. "Make it so he can't come back."

"It's not enough. He will always come back. One way or another," Lucien said darkly.

"Then once we've unleashed the magic in the Dark Oak, we use it to trap him inside of it," Calliope whispered. "He wants the magic so badly? He can have it. We'll drown him in it. We lock him away. And we are the only key."

Sarai and Thalia stared at her. Lucien stared at her. Until a slow smile began to blossom on his face. It was cold and cruel and sent a shiver down Calliope's spine.

"Little muse," he said quietly, proudly. "You've stopped hiding from the darkness."

CHAPTER 34

CALLIOPE WONDERED IF HE WAS RIGHT OR IF SHE could simply no longer distinguish between desperation and darkness.

"When we undo the final enchantment, your father and whoever fights with him will try to take the power. Can you and Sarai cast a protective shield to keep them out?"

"Yes," he said resolutely. "I will protect you with my life. All of you."

"You can't step in, no matter what," Calliope said sharply.

"My days of saving you are over, little muse. You're the one with all the power now. Just like you've always been."

Calliope's throat grew tight at the words, and she wanted desperately to believe him.

"There are so many things that could go wrong with this plan." Sarai frowned, chewing on her lip. "But it's the only option we have."

"We're doing this then," Calliope said. Her pacing ceased as she faced her sister and Lucien. "We're fighting back. We're taking your father and the coven head-on, dismantling the enchantments, and healing your sister."

As the three of them exchanged determined glances, the weight of the impending battle seemed to hang in the air. In the midst of darkness, hope flickered, fragile yet unyielding. The Dark Oak had bound them, and now it was up to them to break its chains. They would forge a new destiny—one that would finally break the curse that had bound their family for generations, or damn them all to whatever lay inside the Dark Oak and the wraiths that would come calling when it was released.

"But first, we sleep. We're no good to anyone if we can't access our full power," Thalia said forcefully.

"You've lost it." Calliope laughed darkly. "We start now. We do this *now*."

"Our energy is drained, sister. I know you can feel it. And tonight is Ostara. The veil will be thinnest, and our magic will be stronger."

Calliope didn't want to admit it, hated that her sister was right. They had a plan, and she wanted to enact it *now*.

"Dissy is safe," Thalia added gently. "He needs all three of us. And you're right. I don't think your father will hurt Eléa," she said to Lucien. "Not when he could use her as bait."

"I agree with Thalia," Lucien said tersely. "We use the time to rest."

"Fine." Calliope shook her head. "Fine. You sleep, I'll see if Daphne has anything that could help us." But Lucien stepped forward, and Calliope's body locked up as he wrapped his arms around her. And then, the light of the kitchen faded to black as pressure hit her from all sides, squeezing her through the fabric of space until, when she blinked again, she was lying in her bed with Lucien next to her.

"That's unfair," she panted, her body decompressing.

"I never promised to fight fair," he said, his voice close to her ear, his arm underneath her shoulders.

"How do you even do that?" she asked grumpily.

"I can only take someone with me for a very short distance. And this seemed like a necessity to get you to stop talking."

"Your arm is like a rock," she said, rolling her head back and forth across his bicep.

Instead of responding, he rolled her toward him, so her head was nestled against his shoulder.

"Sleep, little muse."

"I can't," she huffed against him. "And you should really take a shower. I can smell the blood from your arm."

In the next second, she was standing in her shower with Lucien before her.

"May I?" he asked, gesturing to her clothes.

"Yes, fine," she grumbled.

"You're grumpy when you're tired."

"I'm grumpy because the world is ending," she said, her full lips pulling down into a frown.

"The world is not ending, little muse." He slowly pulled her shirt off over her head, his calloused fingers dragging up her waist. "It's just beginning." He pulled her leggings down, and as he crouched, he placed a kiss on the front of each of her thighs. He stood, his eyes hungrily drinking her in, and then, with a few muttered words, his clothes were off, her underthings gone, and they stood staring at each other.

His tattoos stood out in dark contrast like shadows painting a story across his skin, and her eyes raked over his body.

That night on the Altar of Fate had been dark, but now, now she drank him in, too. The black ink formed figures that looked like deities mixed with symbols of magic and power. He filled up the small shower with his size and presence. There was a smattering of dark hair on his chest, and a darker patch trailed down from his belly button. She could drag a finger through the lines separating his abs, and she did just that. Following the trail of her finger with her eyes, she groaned when she took in his hard length. Her sex clenched, her stomach dropped, but before she could reach for him, he turned the water on, so hot it was scalding.

"If you keep making noises like that, we'll both leave this shower dirtier than we entered it. Turn," he said, angling her so the water cascaded over her. He picked up the bar of lavender-and-mandarin-scented soap and slowly, methodically, began washing her. She closed her eyes as his hands massaged the soap into her shoulders, down her back, his fingers digging into her skin in a deliciously painful way that grounded her. When he reached her breasts, he growled low in his throat. She turned and met his eyes, dark and shining in the steam.

"Wars have been waged for less than this," he said darkly, his fingers trailing over her nipples, down her sides, wrapping gently around her waist as he pulled her to him and kissed her, his tongue claiming hers. The cold tile against her back as he pressed her to the wall made her gasp.

"I worship you," he whispered against her lips, one hand leaving her waist and reaching up to gently caress her cheek. "I am bound to the very gravity of your presence." He kissed her eyelids. "You make me reckless with hope. With abandon." His fingers dug into her hips now, as though he really were anchoring himself to her.

"I'm sorry I was scared," she whispered.

"Never be sorry for going at your own pace," he murmured, turning her again so her back warmed up under the spray of water. "If your feelings do not match mine, only tell me." His hands were gentle once more as he gathered her honey-wheat hair, which tangled over her shoulders, and swept it back.

"I hated you," she said, looking up at him, searching his face for any sign of a lie, any vestige of truth. "And it wasn't even my own hate. It was a grievance built into me and passed down through generations. But more than that, from the moment I saw you, you saw through me. Into me. And I hated that even more because it scared me. You were bound to me, yes, but then you started showing up. Helping us. Protecting me even when you didn't need to."

"Everything I've done, I've done for Eléa," he said, and his arms fell to his side now as he stared at her. "And now it's for Eléa and *you*. You're all that matters to me."

"Well, then," she said, placing her hands on his chest, her palms brushing up to his shoulders until they linked behind his neck, and she stood on her tiptoes and kissed him. It was a sweet kiss. A sealing of fate and a long-awaited promise. It seared through her soul like a lightning bolt, and she finally stopped fighting the bond that connected them. It pulsed bright, a living thing inside her skin, and the lights in the bathroom flickered. His soul was singing to hers through their bond. They were singing to each other, and it was a melody that orchestrated the symphony of her very existence. The silent song that poured forth from them was a tune that had been present since the beginning of the world and would exist long after it was gone.

"Speechless, at last?" he asked, breaking the kiss and

pressing his nose against the soft spot beneath her ear. His voice rumbled through her, and she hoped her bones would hollow out, so his deep timbre could live there forever.

"In your dreams." She laughed. And somewhere, guilt was beginning to grow in her veins. Guilt that she was here with Lucien, eating his kisses and drinking his desire, while her sister was held captive. While the town was under threat. And sweet Eléa was a hostage of the coven.

"I can see you spiraling," he said, his finger tilting her head up, so she was forced to look into his eyes. "Very well. Here," he said, switching spots with her. She watched as he quickly washed the dried blood off his arm—he'd already healed the cut—and rinsed. He turned off the water, and in the next blink, they were dry, dressed, and once again on her bed. The covers were pulled up over them. He lay on his side facing her. Even her hair, soaking wet only seconds ago, was now dry.

"Very handy," she murmured, running her fingers through the smooth strands.

"I would say 'I'd die for you,'" he said in a low voice, tracing her cheek, the line of her jaw, outlining her lips. "But what's the point in that? I would *live* for you. I've done monstrous things, little muse. I don't know if I'm worth it. But for you, I'll try. So yes, I'll dry your hair and bring you coffee with too much sugar. I'll buy you mismatched socks and organize your disastrous drawers. I'll fight for you. With you. Because you gave me a reason to piece myself back together."

Calliope's heart pounded faster and faster as he spoke, and there were no words she could formulate to match that kind of declaration. So instead, she pressed her lips against his in a long, hot slide. She intended it to be sweet, a kiss of gratitude. But when he swept his tongue into her mouth, claiming her, it turned filthy. The kiss in the shower had been slow and languorous, but this was frenzied, as if time were running out and this kiss was the only thing that could stop the clock. He fisted her hair in one hand and angled her head back, her scalp tingling deliciously, while his other hand rested gently against her throat. His skin was hot against hers, his apples-and-amber scent making her dizzy.

"You should sleep now, little muse. If you don't, I'll keep you up with my tongue and you'll be too tired to walk, let alone fight," he growled.

"You said you'd live for me," she panted against him, placing her hand over his on her throat and squeezing his fingers so that his grip tightened. "So, live for me." They were both burdened with the task of saving their sisters, but she didn't know what tomorrow would bring. And this was one memory she wanted to keep forever.

"Tell me what you want," he demanded, sliding his thigh between her legs to spread them apart.

"I want you to fuck me," she begged without hesitation, her hips writhing against the hard muscle of his thigh, the friction making her ache for more.

"How do you want me to fuck you, little muse?" he whispered now, squeezing her throat tighter as his other hand dipped beneath her shirt and played over her breasts, squeezing one pebbled nipple between his fingers until she cried out with pleasure and he moved to the other. "Tell me," he said, licking the shell of her ear. "Do you want it rough, or do you want it slow? Either way, I'll worship you every fucking second."

"I want it all," she said, drawing his head down and branding him with a kiss that had her head spinning. His tongue licked into her mouth and she tasted apples. His thigh pressed firmly against her center as she rubbed herself against him, and his hard length pressed heavily against her hip. She could have come just like that, but he pulled back, and with a few muttered words, they were naked again. Her skin was burning, feverish, and she needed all of him.

"Then you will have all of me," he said against her mouth like he'd heard her thoughts through their bond. "But first, I will have you." His fingers trailed down her stomach, and she shivered at the light touch, panting for more. And then he was moving, settling himself on his knees between her legs. He stared directly at her, his eyes dark as pitch, as he grabbed her ankles and placed them on his shoulders.

"Have you thought about this since the last time?" he rasped, his fingertips trailing lightly up and down her calves. One touch. And then another. Until she was vibrating with the need for him to do *something*. Anything.

"Yes," she panted. There was no room for lies here; her heart was too full for that. He didn't look away as he dragged two fingers through her center and groaned when he found them wet.

"Fucking dripping," he growled, bringing those fingers to his mouth and licking her arousal off. Calliope whimpered, or at least she thought she did. She couldn't be sure. Because when he entered her with two fingers, her mind turned into a kaleidoscope. How had she lived since the last time this happened? Why were they not doing this every second of every day?

"Yes," she whispered as he stretched her. Groaned. "Yes, yes, yes." And then he dipped his head and his velvet tongue, hot and wet, licked her core, and suddenly she didn't just smell the apples, she tasted them. Like he was infiltrating every pore. She writhed as he worked her in a slow, steady rhythm that drove every coherent thought from her mind. It wasn't supposed to be like this. Not this perfect from the first time. But their bond meant he was aware of her every desire, every little move she made that cried *more, harder, faster* until she came against his tongue, clenched around his fingers, and he worked her through every moment of it, milking every last drop of pleasure until he sat up on his heels. Wiped the back of his hand against his mouth and moaned.

"That was the slow," he said, his voice rough with promise in the still of the night. "And now—" He grabbed her by the hips and yanked her down the bed, turning her so she was face down, and then pulled so she was on her knees.

"Yes," she panted, still shaking from her orgasm. "Lucien," she breathed. A plea. A prayer. And his name in her mouth did something to him. She felt him tremble, sensed the way he was barely holding back. He ran a hand over her ass, squeezed, and she nodded into the mattress, giving him permission. "Do it," she said breathlessly. And he drew his hand back and gently slapped the soft skin of her cheek. She moaned so loud it was obscene. "Harder," she begged, looking back over her shoulder. He had one hand wrapped around his length, lining it up at her entrance. Drawing in a ragged breath, he muttered a contraceptive spell. And when he entered her, his hand came down again and she screamed in pleasure, her fingers fisting into the sheets as she pushed to meet him.

"Little muse," he groaned and stilled as she adjusted around him. "I've been waiting for this since the night I first saw you." And then he began to move, his angle from behind allowing him to go so deep that Calliope could only moan in response.

The world slowed, her back arching as she urged him harder, faster. They were both broken, but the jagged pieces fit together. Each razor-sharp edge, every painful memory softened until they pressed together like a puzzle box creating something new and beautiful. Calliope's chest squeezed at the release of it, and when she came, he followed, and her very atoms were rearranged. Flares of light raced across the night sky as he filled her, shooting stars that left trails of shimmering dust.

He kissed down her spine as they caught their breath, his careful, soft lips such a contrast to the way he'd just taken her with abandon. Calliope shivered, unsure why her cheeks were wet. Why it seemed that the light of those shooting stars had fallen to earth and found their home in her chest. She knew he felt it, too, could feel it through their bond. She flexed her fingers, stiff from clutching the bedsheets so tightly, as Lucien got up and padded, naked, to the bathroom. She watched him go, and when he came back with a warm washcloth to clean her up, she watched his movements, enraptured. He could have done it with magic. But she could feel that he wanted to do it with his own hands. Wanted to see the evidence of his claiming. And the thought made the light in her chest glow even hotter.

She should tell him, she thought, as he lay down next to her. Tell him that her soul had found a new home in his. That this burning orb in her chest glowed for him. That she loved him. But the words wouldn't come.

"Little muse," he said gently, softly, as he tucked a wayward strand of hair behind her ear. His fingertips traced down her jaw to her chin, where he used two fingers to turn her face toward him. "Don't leave me alone here. Not after that. Tell me what's going on in that beautiful head of yours." He kissed her then, a decadent kiss that felt like the sealing of fate, a metal stamp pressed into hot wax.

His thumbs brushed her tears away, and she discovered that while taciturn, growling Lucien was devastating, gentle, loving Lucien might be the death of her. She only shook her head in answer, and she felt the soft shaking of his chest as he rumbled a quiet laugh.

"Very well," he said, kissing her temple and pulling her close so that her head rested against his shoulder. "Take your time. I'm not going anywhere."

And it was those words, the promise and threat and draw of them, that began to heal those old wounds. Minutes passed by as she tried to work up the courage to tell him.

"Lucien," she whispered finally, swallows swooping low in her stomach, her breath coming shorter. He didn't answer. "Lucien?" she said, louder this time. But the only response was the steady rise and fall of his chest. His lips were slightly parted, but his hand was still curled protectively around her waist as he slept. Calliope sighed. It was better this way. She would tell him later. When they emerged victorious on the other side.

And as she nestled against his side, her eyes closed. They would save their sisters. Unravel the final enchantments around the Dark Oak and then contain it anew. Protect the town. Banish the wraiths. And they would do it together. Sleep claimed her quickly, and she dreamed of him, singing quietly in Turkish.

CHAPTER 35

BY THE TIME SHE WOKE, DARKNESS HAD FALLEN.
And Lucien was gone.

Her stomach dipped pleasantly at the memory of him in her bed. Her cheeks heated as she remembered the way his touch had felt, like the first time you learn a new spell, the rush and thrill of it. But it was Ostara. She thought about what the day held, the battle to come, and the pleasant dip turned into a restless churn. Fear had chased her for so long that it had become more of a friend than an enemy. She would sharpen the blade of dread against a whetstone of rage and wield it to cut down their enemies.

But first, she needed to pick out her socks.

Naked, she padded over to her dresser and riffled through the mismatched pairs. She chose one that had a pattern of constellations on it, a reminder of the vast universe of possibilities that lay before them today. The other had a pattern of hedge mazes, an intricate labyrinth to symbolize the paths they had to navigate to emerge victorious. From there, she pulled on a pair of black jeans painted with large white magnolia blossoms and tucked them into her combat boots. She had just thrown on a heather-gray sweater and swept her hair up into a topknot when a sweet scent wafted under her door.

Bougatsa, Calliope thought.

She raced downstairs to find Lucien and Sarai at the counter and Thalia cutting the pastry into squares.

"Good morning, little muse," Lucien said, looking up. His eyes raked her from head to toe and heated at the sight of her. He wanted her again, right then; Calliope could feel it pulsing down their bond like an electric shock.

"It's almost night," Thalia corrected him, blind to the tension simmering between Lucien and her sister. Sarai, meanwhile, was staring between her coven leader and Calliope with wide, awestruck eyes.

"It is a figure of speech." Lucien frowned at her.

"Good morning," Calliope said, smiling despite herself and drinking in his features in the fresh light of day. The orb of starlight in her chest pulsed, bright and alive and thrumming with love. She glanced away quickly, trying to stuff the feelings away so he wouldn't see them, feel them. Even though she knew it was too late for that. "You made bougatsa," she said to Thalia, pouring herself a cup of coffee, trying to keep all the words she hadn't said last night from spilling out. *Later,* she reminded herself. *When we get through everything.*

"I thought it was fitting," Thalia said, putting three slices on three plates.

"Dissy usually makes it," Calliope said quietly, the back of her neck tingling as she felt Lucien's gaze on her. The cinnamon and butter wafted up and made her mouth water.

"And she will again. But we needed the extra boost."

"'By the essence of cinnamon's transformative magic, as I dust this sweet creation, may change align with my intentions and unfold in harmony with my will,'" Calliope quoted softly. She could practically see Dissy at the counter, her hands hovering, palms down, over the pan of bougatsa as she said the affirmation in her sweet, melodic voice. The creamy custard wrapped in crispy golden-brown phyllo dough was meant for bringing your will to fruition. And Calliope supposed her sister was right; they could use all of that they could get.

"So," she said. "Today, we go to war."

And the words hung between them like a thin bridge. One wrong move and they'd slip, fall into a ravine of despair. But one foot in front of the other, and they might make it across. To hope. To victory. To revenge.

*

THE FORGOTTEN FOREST loomed eerily in the muted afternoon light. Storm clouds threatened, and a mist hung about the grass.

They stopped a dozen feet away, staring into the depths of the forest, where the light grew darker.

"Everyone knows their role?" Lucien asked.

"Lucien," Calliope said, laying a gentle hand on his arm. "We've been over it a dozen times."

"Dissy and Eléa are the priority," Thalia said.

"And then we unravel the final enchantments and use the power of the Dark Oak's magic. No more keeping it locked away. We've protected it for generations; now we see what it can really do," Calliope said with grim determination.

"Very well," Lucien said darkly. "Let's begin."

He tapped her wrists, and Calliope groaned but held out her hands.

Lucien murmured a spell, and there was a subtle shift of power emanating from him as his magic snaked around her wrists, binding them. And then she watched as he did the same thing to Thalia. Her expression was stoic, but Calliope knew her sister hated this as much as she did. No matter that it was a ruse, they were bound. But they looked at each other, determination in their eyes, before stepping into the Forgotten Forest.

She hadn't gone two steps before Lucien grabbed her by the back of the neck and brought her back to him, spinning her around with his fingers digging into her skin until his mouth was devouring her. His tongue claimed hers, and the slick heat of it, his possessive hand around her neck, anchoring her to him, made her dizzy. His hand snaked up to fist in her hair, and he tilted her head back, deepening the kiss until she was consumed with it.

He tasted bright and fresh like summer. Like the crisp crunch of watermelon and the sweet, cold tinge of mint leaves. It reminded her of their summers on Milos. Sleepy eyes and sandy feet and the freedom that comes with youth. The way it stains your soul and makes you believe that anything is possible. She was panting by the time he pulled away, and even then, it was too short.

Too many thoughts were at war within her head, each one fighting for dominance. But then, she reminded herself that confidence was a made-up construct. That no one actually knew what it was or if they had it. It wasn't based on her *actual* ability to succeed but on her *belief* in her ability to succeed. And so, she chose, then and there, to be confident.

To lay her demons to rest, to chase away the ghost of her mother's disappearance once and for all, and to believe, fully, that they would get through this no matter what.

Birdsong followed them through the woods. The rattling call of the western tanager, the jumbled warbling of the European starling. Through the branches she saw a descent of pileated woodpeckers, their red crests like flames among the leaves.

And then, a great buck with eight-point antlers emerged from the trees. He looked at them with his large, intelligent eyes, and began to walk alongside them.

As they moved deeper into the dense woods, Calliope's heart began to pound in sync with the distant rhythm of the Dark Oak as it reverberated through her. It was as if the very heartbeats of the forest echoed the pull of the magic that had drawn them here. The darkness grew heavier and became suffocating, shadows moving like specters around them, whispering secrets to the night. Everything became a blur of greens and browns, the trees like towering sentinels guarding secrets of centuries past. Her skin tingled with anticipation.

She reached down and squeezed the small pouch she'd added to the pocket in the side of her leggings. While Lucien, Sarai, and Thalia had consulted Daphne for spells, charms, and curses that could combat the coven and the wraiths, Calliope had made a charm bag for success. She'd gathered a green candle, quartz crystal, mint leaves, and a few other ingredients and, in the quiet of her room, spoke words of power and intention over each item as she placed them into a cloth drawstring bag. The weight of it in her pocket anchored her now, her fingers tracing over the clear quartz. They would be successful.

She looked back at Lucien and in the dim light saw his hardened features, the suppressed anger in every line of his face. He didn't meet her eyes, only stared forward.

And then, they were breaking through to the clearing, and she and Thalia both stumbled as Lucien shoved them hard in the back. The coven, a dozen of them, were surrounding the Dark Oak. It looked even more sinister than it had before, straining against the few invisible strings that still held it. What would happen, Calliope wondered, when that darkness was let out? Even now shadows were seeping from it like smoke, curling inward, beckoning them forward.

Ahmed stood at the front of the group with Malik beside him, his hand clamped around Eléa's arm in a vicelike grip. Eléa struggled against him the moment she saw her brother. She was shouting, struggling against his grip, but Malik yanked her back. Eléa's dark hair fell over her eyes, but she wasn't crying. Her features were painted into a mask of rage that made her look so much like Lucien that Calliope could barely stand to look at her.

The girl's skin was ashen, and even as she struggled, her movements were weak. She appeared smaller, more vulnerable than Calliope remembered. Her heart clenched at the sight.

"What will it be, Lucien?" Ahmed called. "Your sister or hers?"

Ahmed snapped his fingers, and Dissy floated forth. Her ankles and wrists were bound by shadows, her body suspended in the air with her feet barely touching the grass. Her head lolled forward, her honey-wheat hair creating a curtain over her face. Calliope swallowed a scream. Thalia tensed beside her.

Lucien twisted his hand and produced two blades forged

of shadows and sharper than any man-made steel. These were daggers to cut through soul and sinew, and he directed them toward Calliope's and Thalia's throats.

Ahmed's laughter was sandpaper against Calliope's ears.

"I see you've come to your senses then," he said.

"I will trade the Petridi sisters for Eléa," Lucien said, his voice clear and cold as midnight stars. "Take them and do what you will. But if you try to move against me, if any harm comes to Eléa, I will slit their throats where they stand, and you will never get what's inside that tree."

Ahmed's eyes darkened, his lip snarling in fury.

"Are you fast enough, Father?" Lucien asked quietly, though his voice carried in the dense silence of the forest. "Will you risk it?"

Ahmed nodded once, and Malik released Eléa and she staggered forward. And Calliope may have been imagining it, but she thought she saw a glimmer of relief pass over Malik's face, but it was gone before she could be sure.

"Take her then," Ahmed snarled, pushing his daughter forward. "Little use she is to me, anyway. But I told you, didn't I? Blood is thicker than water."

Lucien didn't answer, and Calliope could feel the tension rolling off him. When Eléa had made it halfway across the clearing, Lucien shoved the sisters forward. Calliope's gaze darted back to him. His features were marked with a darkness of his own, a mask of calculated fury. The raw power emanating from him was palpable. She could sense the weight of his suppressed anger like it was her own.

Ahmed's eyes were burning with triumph.

Eléa fell into Lucien's arms just as the coven encircled Thalia and Calliope. Standing next to Dissy with her hands still bound, Calliope laid her head against her sister's side.

I heard you, she said to Dissy in her mind, trying to wake her sister up. *I know how to heal our string. Together.*

Dissy's head shifted, and her eyes cracked open.

"He won't give you what you're after," Lucien said to the coven. "You think he's unstoppable now? Wait until he gets his hands on the power there." He pointed to the Dark Oak behind him. And he continued, trying to sway them while his father laughed. But Calliope had more important things to do.

While Lucien spoke, she found the string that connected her to her sisters. It was frayed and dull, and sections of it were overtaken with shadows from her bond with Lucien. But she let it guide her and followed it back. Back to when they'd started planning Tea and Tome, united in a common cause. And back further still until the memories of their youth surrounded her. When their love was unfettered, and their mother was there to tuck them in every night. Those memories always burned the brightest. And she'd been running from her mother's absence for so long, she'd forgotten the strength of her presence. She'd let her become a ghost when, all along, she could have been a guardian angel.

Together, she thought into Thalia's and Dissy's minds. *Please, hear me.*

And she spoke over their string. Words of healing and kindness, forgiveness and grace. Pleading and hope. She poured the warmth of every good memory into those threads. Dancing with Roz and laughing at Daphne's antics when she'd still been Grim.

Sister. She heard Dissy's voice in her head and nearly sobbed with relief. But she forced her face to remain neutral. The coven was focused on Lucien, his bid for their loyalty. They didn't have long. She felt Dissy through their bond. The way she'd embraced her power, her voice, in a way she hadn't done since their mother left. How she'd stepped out of the shadows and into her true self.

The string was glowing brighter, her connection to Lucien fading and the one with her sisters growing stronger. Her magic began to pulse once again in her veins.

Sister, she heard again, and this time it was Thalia's voice. And again, she felt her sister's power. The way she was finally at one with her choices. How she'd released the fear and welcomed where it led her. Gone were the bitterness and sorrow, replaced with purpose and gratitude.

Please, she thought, pouring her words and intention over their string, her eyes closed.

And then, she heard another voice in her mind. One that didn't belong to either of her sisters. One that set her heart to beating like a bird's wings against a cage when it wanted only to be free.

Let go of your grief. I will always be here. Her mother's voice was the same as she remembered it. Tears spilled hot down her cheeks as she surrendered the grief she'd been carrying, white-knuckled, for so long. She let it go, and the strands healed—no trace of shadow, only a pure, glowing thread that poured its warmth down Calliope's soul until she shone with hope.

Opie, Thalia whispered in her mind.

Can you hear us, Dissy? Calliope asked.

Yes, she answered. And they were all there. Fully restored, their magic intact, their string luminescent. *How are we able to do this?*

Our bond, Calliope said. *It's never been stronger. We've built a bridge between us.*

That was when Calliope told Eurydice the plan.

CHAPTER 36

"So, I ask you," Lucien continued his speech, and Calliope was listening now. "Who among you will join me?"

Feng looked torn, his eyes wide, barely daring to look at Lucien. Luna stared at the forest floor, pushing her glasses up her nose where they kept slipping down. Malik looked on with pity in his eyes, as though Lucien had already lost.

"Your grandfather didn't tell you the whole truth, son." Ahmed laughed, and it made Calliope's blood run cold. "Once the sisters undo the final enchantment, if you take all that power into yourself to heal your sister, you'll die. Why do you think I sent you and Sarai on that job so many years ago? For this." He held out a hand, not taking his eyes off Lucien, and Luna reached into the satchel bag on her shoulder. And when she placed an ancient stone canopic jar in his hands, Calliope could hear Lucien's growl even from where she stood. "I told you this was generations in the making. This power is *ours*. It belongs to us," he barked, growing agitated now.

Calliope caught Lucien's eye and nodded. He'd been stalling. But they were ready. A powerful surge of magic burst forth among the sisters. With a twist of her wrist, they freed themselves from their bonds, and in the span of one blink to the next, Lucien and Sarai's protective shield burst forth. The Shadowcraft coven members stumbled back, their faces uneasy as they looked to Ahmed.

Ahmed's features turned from triumphant to enraged. He was caught off guard. He had been expecting them to be weak, which was exactly what they'd wanted.

Dissy held out her hands, and each sister took one.

They closed their eyes, letting the hum of magic infiltrate every pore, flood every vein, until their hands began to glow with it. The sky overhead, what could be seen of it through the thick trees, grew even darker.

Calliope had spent her life strengthening these spells. And now she sought to break them.

"Memories at the ready," Calliope said.

"One in three, three in one," Dissy said, squeezing their hands.

"Where magic gathers, there will be those who seek to claim it," Calliope recited. "But we won't let them. And we won't let them leave this forest. We're the shield that guards the town."

"Time to break the last enchantment and see what we've been protecting," Thalia rasped.

And then they delved into their magic, plumbing the depths until they found their string, and the connection sprang alive among the three of them.

It sang a tune Calliope had not heard in years. A gentle melody, delicate with sisterly love, and as the song carried, it morphed into something else. Something harder. It sang of the ways they could break the world with their love. But also, how they could put it back together. And she knew then that when you couldn't bear the world a moment longer, that's when it was time to make a new one.

They began to chant old spells in ancient Greek that came to them on the wings of memories that did not belong to them. The strings of enchantment began to pulse, glowing bright as a dying star. Their hands grew slick with sweat as they plucked the strings and broke them, sacrificing memory after memory to fuel their magic.

And as another string snapped, a roar filled their ears. The limbs of the Dark Oak trembled violently as shadows bled from it like sap.

Thalia dropped to her knees, concern filling her eyes until her own body convulsed.

And then, Daphne appeared. As though she'd been waiting.

"No," Calliope croaked, her lungs seizing with pain as she coughed blood onto the ground. The metallic tang filled her mouth.

"Do it," Dissy cried, her voice barely audible, her skin paler than death.

Calliope pushed to her knees, grabbing her sisters' hands as her vision began to blur. Her skin was hot with fever, her head pounding as she tried to bring the memory of Daphne to the forefront.

She pulled from Thalia and Dissy, and they fed their magic into her. Though she was screaming in pain, Calliope could still feel the power of their magic just below the surface.

And with an anguished cry, she used the memory of the grimoire to power the spell that would break that final string.

"Na katanalotheí," she whispered even as her skin felt like it was being flayed from her body. *Be consumed.* Her hands curled into fists, and she pulled hard. And the strings began to burn hot as the magic gathered inside them.

With Calliope's final scream of pain and fury, the magic rose up, and the very ether cried out in a burst of light and power that rippled toward them and knocked the sisters back with a shock wave. There was a sound like an explosion that thudded in their ears, and then all was silent.

Calliope waited, her heart beating fast in that quiet space like the beat of a war drum. She waited for the horrors to be unleashed, for the magic that had been contained in the Dark Oak for so long.

But it had gone still. A faint light began to shine from beneath the bark. The eerie eyes in the trunk closed as though in pain. Or perhaps it was sorrow. The Dark Oak hummed, and it seemed to Calliope that it was waiting, though for what, she didn't know. Power emanated from its black leaves, from the roots that snaked over the ground. Power they couldn't access unless it released the magic it held. But still, nothing happened.

And then, Calliope saw a book on the ground by her feet.

It scuttled across the dirt, and she scrambled back, a look of horror on her face.

She had seen this book before. When she was five, she'd crept into her mother's room one night. She'd meant to scare her for a lark but stopped in the shadows when her mother started speaking, this very book open on her vanity.

Its leather was tooled with intricate designs. Ivy and irises etched in careful detail. Her mother had been speaking to the book like an old friend. As though the book were talking back. And at the thought, five-year-old Calliope had giggled, her mother's eyes finding her in the shadows.

"Why are you talking to a book?" she'd asked.

"Sometimes books are the only ones who understand," her mother had said, gently closing the pages.

"Can I talk to it?"

"Not yet, Opie."

"What kind of book is it?"

"It's our family grimoire. Full of spells and potions and recipes," her mother had said, eyes dancing with light. "One day, this book will find you when you need it most. It will reveal things to you when the time is right. And you will come to understand what I've done. How I would do anything to protect you."

Calliope had asked more questions, her eyes continually drawn to the leather cover of that beautiful book. Even now, as the book hovered before her, its pages flipping in the breeze, she was drawn to it.

"Daphne," Dissy cried, and the book turned toward her, landing in her hands.

"I'll deal with the sentient book later, I suppose?" Calliope asked, and then Ahmed's voice cut through the shield.

"Drop your magic, son, or I force the coven to sever their tie with Eléa," he growled.

Lucien and Sarai strained as they fought to keep up the shield that protected the sisters. Lucien's face twisted as he was faced with the decision to save his sister or the woman he loved. Eléa lay on the ground near his feet.

"No," she whispered. "Don't drop it."

"Lucien, drop it, damn it!" Malik called. "He'll kill her."

"Do it," Ahmed said, his voice sharp as a blade. "Sever it!" he screamed. And Calliope watched as, before her eyes, Eléa began to fade. She whimpered, her skin growing paler, death claiming her with too-quick fingers.

And Calliope refused to let this be how her story ended.

With a glance, the sisters communicated wordlessly. They moved like water, fluid and graceful, as they formed a tight line, their shoulders pressed together.

"Lucien, move!" Calliope called.

His eyes darted back over his shoulder, and even in the dim light, Calliope could see the fear written there as clearly as words on a page.

"Trust me," Calliope said quietly, behind him now. "Drop the shield . . . *now*."

Without hesitation, Lucien dropped the shield, the spell fizzling out.

And then the sisters linked hands and crafted a shield of their own. Stronger, bound by their united power, it rippled out like a shock wave, blasting Ahmed and the Shadowcraft coven back, leaving only Eléa, Lucien, Sarai, and themselves on the side closest to the Dark Oak.

Lucien gathered his sister up in his arms as she cried out for him. Her voice was thin, her skin paler than Calliope had ever seen it. Even her dark hair looked leached of color.

Behind the shield, Ahmed paced, his face filled with rage as the coven tried to tear down the shield, but the sisters held it strong.

"You have to let me go," Eléa cried.

"Don't be absurd," Lucien said into her hair.

"I love you," she said, and then she turned to Calliope. "Lucien came here to save me, but you saved him instead." She coughed, and blood spattered on the ground. "Thank you."

Calliope's throat tightened, and she didn't trust herself to speak. Instead, she broke from her sisters and kissed Eléa on the cheek before turning to Lucien. She placed her hands on his cheeks and forced his eyes to hers.

"I love you," she said. Plainly. Simply. And then she kissed him. A hard crush of her lips to his, and then she returned to Dissy and Thalia.

She looked at her sisters, and Thalia nodded without hesitation.

"Are you sure?" Dissy whispered.

In answer, Calliope held out her hands and entwined her fingers with theirs once more.

She looked at Lucien with pleading eyes.

"Make me remember," she said softly.

And then she closed her eyes and began to pull her magic from the shield. The words of an ancient purifying spell took shape in her mind, and she drew all the memories of Lucien to the forefront.

The night on the Altar of Fate.

Lying in his arms in her bed.

The way he washed her body.

How he held her together when she didn't know where all the pieces of her had gone. But more than that, he wasn't just a Band-Aid; he filled her with the fire to put those pieces of herself back together again.

The challenge and fire in his eyes.

All her love, all the memories, she funneled them through her magic and directed it at Eléa. The light of love to wash away the stain of her grandfather's magic that had tainted her. Tears poured down her cheeks, but she wasn't afraid. She'd spent her life sacrificing her memories for menial things, trying to forget the pain and heartache. Now she used it to heal, to save not just Eléa, but Lucien, too.

"No," Lucien roared when he realized what she was doing. He laid Eléa gently on the ground and rushed forward, trying to stop Calliope. But Thalia and Dissy used their free hands to send him back, their shield glimmering in the dark.

His fists beat against the shield, but Eléa was right. He was weakened. And the power of three was far too strong for him to break through.

The tendrils of Calliope's spell slithered forward, wrapping around Eléa's body, pulling her up off the ground, suspending her in the air. The strings pulsed and glowed as they leached the Shadowcraft from her.

But then, a low rumble shook the ground, and the Dark Oak woke up.

CHAPTER 37

CALLIOPE CALLED FOR HER SISTERS, REACHING blindly for them, but it was not her sisters' voices that answered. It was the shadows.

Come seek us where the magic was bound, they sang.

You'll find your fate within our sound.
Let us reveal your histories past,
So you can be free, free at last.

"No," Calliope shouted, her magic connected to Eléa, who was still suspended in the air. The light of Calliope's magic wrapped around Eléa's slender body was beginning to fade. She had to save her.

Closing her eyes, Calliope drew on the power of the Dark Oak, which was still trembling so violently that the ground shuddered beneath her feet. But as she tried to harness that magic, a blast of fury rang out from the Dark Oak that nearly knocked her off her feet. Anger poured from the branches, bitterness wept from the bark, and it pushed back against her, a violent, visceral thing.

Thunder cracked overhead, and the clearing flashed bright white with lightning, and Calliope tasted sorrow and regret on her tongue, bitter as chicory. She took a shuddering breath and pushed harder, pouring her magic out, trying to draw from the power.

And then shadows began to pour forth from the Dark Oak, sweeping from its branches, the roots, the bark and leaves, until the clearing was black as night.

Calliope stared, confused and terrified, as the shadows flickered like black flames and then shifted into memories, shapes.

"You can't marry him, Mother!" one of the girl-shaped shadows cried. She looked perhaps seven, though it was hard to tell. "He's a Shadowcrafter. You're the one who told us the stories of the Great Rift. They're dangerous."

"I was wrong," her mother said. "I was blinded by those stories, but that's all they are, Selene. Stories that have been twisted over generations, so we don't even know what's true and what's not. But there's nothing more dangerous than not following your heart," the woman said. "Bayram Deniz will be my husband, and his daughter will become my daughter. She will be your sister." She tried to take the girl's hand, but she yanked it away.

"Rhea and Ariadne are my sisters," she said angrily. "I don't want a third."

"You will learn to love Isra," her mother said. "She's only four, but full of life."

"I won't," Selene vowed.

The shadows dissolved and re-formed.

The girl, Selene, was older now. She was in the forest with three other girls. Two were walking with her, their hair the same light color. The fourth trailed behind, her hair black as night.

"Leave the freak," Selene commanded. "The center of the Forgotten Forest is for Petridis only. We do not accept Shadowcrafters."

"Please," Isra called.

"Don't you get it?" Selene demanded, whirling on her, her livid features evident even made of shadow. "We don't want you here. You're a threat. Your magic, everything you could possibly do and become, is the exact opposite of what we stand for."

And so it went. Scenes shifted, and the girls grew older and the animosity turned fiercer, though they always hid it from their mother.

As Isra grew into her magic, Selene, the ringleader of her trueborn sisters, grew more fearful and meaner. And always, Isra only begged to be one of them. When the sisters did magic under a full moon, Selene would turn up her nose at Isra. And so, Isra turned to more powerful spells, trying to impress her sister, to gain her respect and show that she was one of them. The Petridi girls would draw Isra's burgeoning shadows into their light, mutilating her magic until frustration drove her home. When their mother caught Isra crying, Selene pretended it was a game. But never had a game cut so deep.

When Isra would use her Shadowcraft to cook, Selene refused to touch the food. When Rhea broke her arm falling from a tree, Selene refused to let Isra fix it, claiming that she'd rather her sister have a broken arm than evil magic tainting her bones.

Isra chased after the scattered crumbs of her sister's love like a starving cat. But the crumbs were never enough, and bitterness began to take root.

"We have to stop her, or she'll turn into a wraith," Selene told Rhea and Ariadne. "Shadowcraft can only lead to a life consumed by darkness. It's a poison that will suck everything good from your life. That's what the stories say."

And so, they devised a plan to trick her. They were in their twenties now, and such schemes seemed too young for them, but fear made fools of any age.

They invited Isra for the first time to the Forgotten Forest, where Selene promised a binding spell that would tie them together as true sisters. Isra went willingly to the tree in the center of the clearing.

But when Selene, Rhea, and Ariadne began to chant, it was not a binding spell they spoke. It was a spell of forgetting. They planned to curse Isra to forget her Shadowcraft, to protect themselves once and for all. After all, they'd grown up filled with stories of the evil of Shadowcraft. Wasn't it always wraiths that witch mothers would threaten their children with? *Behave or they'll come snatch your souls and eat your magic.*

Yet Isra had grown too powerful. She heard the words of that wretched curse and dove into the well of darkness that had fermented over years. All the rage and bitterness spilled forth as she fought off her sisters' magic.

"You never loved me," Isra shouted. And at this, Calliope felt more than saw the Dark Oak tremble. "You never wanted me. Don't you see you've forced me to become the very thing you feared?" Isra cried.

Selene stumbled back as Isra's voice swelled darker and louder, shadows spilling from her fingertips like smoke.

"You want it to be just the three of you? Fine. Then that's what it will be forever."

Her words were a hiss of anger and sorrow, and they filled the clearing, the echo imprinting on Calliope's heart generations later.

One in three, three in one.
When new power rises, the old must wane,
Memories forgotten, your fates are spun,
Your hatred twisted to your pain.

Isra screamed as she powered the curse, but Selene and her sisters fought back. Shadow clashed with Light.

Rhea and Ariadne clasped Selene's hands and fought to contain the Shadowcraft magic that poured from Isra.

Their magic tangled together, threading through the forest as love and hate collided with fear, and the trees bowed toward them, begging for them to stop. But it was far too late for that.

Selene, Rhea, and Ariadne bled Isra's magic from her body, shadows leaching from her skin as she screamed in agony. The darkness tore through the air, reaching toward the sisters, who began to chant in unison. They funneled Isra's magic into the great oak at the center of the clearing. Immediately, it began to come alive with Shadowcraft while Isra still writhed on the ground.

Strings of enchantment wove around the Dark Oak, locking the magic in, imprisoning it with their fear and hatred.

Isra's body stilled, but instead of trying to hold on to her magic, she used it to steal one last thing from the sisters who should have trusted her. The light faded from Isra's eyes. But the Dark Oak pulsed with life. Shadowcraft lived with the stolen pieces of her sisters' Lightcraft.

Isra's bodiless echo whispered through the forest.

One in three, three in one. Let this be your curse.

A blast emanated from the Dark Oak, knocking Selene, Rhea, and Ariadne back and rendering them unconscious.

When they came to, they had no recollection of their lost sister or what they'd driven her to do. They saw the Dark Oak, blackened and scorched, its branches hanging heavy with Shadowcraft magic, and surmised that they'd trapped a great evil there. They vowed to protect it, keeping the shadows locked away. Little did they know that their magic would ever after come at the price of sacrificing their memories, as a side effect of what they'd tried to do. That when they had children of their own who came into their magic, theirs would start to fade until death claimed them. One in three, three in one.

The shadows dissipated, the memories fading as the blackness swirled around them.

The coven remained behind the wall of shadows. They were a warbled mist beyond it now, their forms barely visible. The forest was hot and humid, and sweat trailed down Calliope's skin, but the shadows were ice-cold as they licked up their legs and coiled around their arms. The magic was trying to consume them, biting at their flesh with gnashing teeth, and Calliope couldn't fight it off.

Calliope could barely take it all in. The memories, their past, the hatred and anger. It all swirled around them like a black hole, sucking them in.

Eléa was on the ground, gasping and choking on shadows. Calliope's magic hadn't healed her, but it had kept her alive long enough for this, and that meant there was hope. Thalia and Dissy were on their knees, reaching for every last vestige of magic to stave off the darkness. And as the Dark Oak shuddered again, pouring out more memories, more shadows and hatred and fear, Eléa cried out.

My sister, Calliope thought. The words came fast and unbidden. But she realized, in a sense, that it was true. Not by blood, but by spirit. Lightcraft was glowing around the girl's body as the sisters tried to save her.

"Together," Calliope cried out in the darkness. "It's the only way." Shadow- and Lightcraft, both of their bloodlines were in this ancient tree. She reached for Thalia's and Dissy's hands, their palms sweaty in hers, and they moved forward to Eléa. The air was viscous as they pushed through it, but finally, they were at Eléa's side. There was a man kneeling next to her whom Calliope hadn't seen before, but there was no time to pay him any mind.

"We have to trust each other," she said, and her voice came out hoarse. She was panting with the strain of so much magic.

Eléa, weak but determined, pushed herself to her feet. And together, the four of them clasped hands and formed a circle. They opened themselves up, poured their power into the girl even as her Shadowcraft seeped into them. And beyond them, Malik and Luna, Feng, and several of the initiates broke away from Ahmed. They stood shoulder to shoulder, enhancing the shield held by Lucien and Sarai.

Calliope could feel the connection form, a bridge that made them whole. And instead of fighting the Dark Oak's magic, they began to absorb it. Calliope's body trembled, dark and light chasing each other, the power so great it seemed to stretch her skin until she cracked apart. And when she came back together, she was a new person.

And Eléa was the one who bonded them all together.

That old whisper returned, repeating the words she'd heard the first time she'd journeyed to the Dark Oak. But this time, two lines had been added, and now it was whole.

Through each enchantment's whispered lore
Three sisters guard, forevermore
But when darkness comes, a curse is spoken
And all is lost if their bond is broken
The air ablaze with demon's calls
At last, at last, the Dark Oak falls
With magic woven, strings so fine
Shadow and Light shall never align.
Unless the past with its prejudice is healed
And pride with its poison forever sealed.

CHAPTER 38

THEY DIDN'T USE WORDS, FOR THIS KIND OF magic came from the soul. It wasn't Shadow- or Lightcraft anymore, but something between the two. Something that spoke of a time before the Great Rift when the Craft rang true and free and bright. And the Dark Oak began to tremble again.

The magic tasted bitter at first, so acrid it began to sting Calliope's eyes. The ground trembled beneath her feet as the smell of power swelled, a scent that choked her with its iron tang. But then the last of the shadows unfurled from the Dark Oak, and the magic stretched its wings, shook off that ancient mantle of hatred and darkness, and let itself be seen for what it really was.

It was the thing they'd feared for so long, the magic their ancestors had tried to curse away, and when they couldn't, they locked it up like some dark and dirty secret. The string of their magic pulsed; the layers of enchantment began to converge. They braided together, a tether, an anchor, and the whisper they sent forth was full of light and love and truth.

The magic was sticky with age, soft in places, brittle in others. The strings themselves seemed to carry memories. They echoed in the silence, a mirror into the past. Screams and cries and pleas resounded quietly in the confines of their minds as they plucked, their deft fingers moving fast, like they were strumming the very strings of fate.

"It's coming," Calliope whispered.

"I can feel it, too," Thalia said, voice strained.

The bond was unbreakable, a shared purpose driving it. Their combined magic surged forth with an explosive burst of energy that resounded through the woods as the shadows and light entered them, filling up their very souls.

Calliope cried out as the full force of her magic, not bound or constrained by memories to fuel it, flooded her. It was raw and terrifying and freeing, and she laughed.

The branches curled around them protectively, a silent farewell, the leaves tickling their shoulders like a kiss of gratitude.

As one, their heads tilted back, and they fed themselves with the power of generations. Perhaps Ahmed was right, and the power of the Dark Oak would kill a man. But they were not men. The magic of the Dark Oak, Isra's magic, free at last, flowed through them until they glowed with it. The strings that had once held the enchantments now twined with the fabric of their skin. There was an ancient sigh of relief from the sisters' spirits. A shuddering exhale of love that sounded like: *finally.*

When Calliope's eyes opened, her gaze landed on Eléa. Her color was back, the light had returned to her eyes, the luster to her hair, and she stood tall and strong.

The wall of shadows that separated them from the coven dissipated, and Calliope saw Ahmed's face contorted in rage.

Once, she would have been afraid. But now, with her sisters and Eléa by her side, the fresh magic coursing through her veins, she sought vengeance with glee. Vengeance for Roz, for kidnapping Eléa, for threatening their town and attempting to steal something that did not belong to them.

The sisters and Eléa strode forward as though the winds of fate called them forth, the infinite echoes of abandon clanging in their ears.

Ahmed and the remaining initiates scrambled back, calling on their own power. But Calliope and her sisters merely flicked their hands, and they flew back.

Power swept from them like a tidal wave, and they took the strings within them and sent them out. Tendrils wrapped around Ahmed and the others who still stood with him, choking them, binding their hands and feet. The canopic jar fell from Ahmed's hands and shattered. They struggled, but their magic was no match for the sisters' unfettered power.

"You wanted the Dark Oak," Calliope said, and her voice shook the air, vengeance emanating from her every syllable. "It's yours."

But as they began to bind them to the very essence of the Dark Oak, Ahmed bellowed with fury.

"This is not over," he called. And, summoning the full force of his magic, he tore free of the bonds and vanished.

Let him go, Calliope thought. For him, defeat was greater torture than death.

"And the rest of you?" Calliope called. "What fate do you choose?"

Most of them ran. And the sisters let them go, refusing to lock more magic away and start a new feud. Malik stayed. So did Sarai. Feng. Luna. The sisters felt their intention, knew they were on their side, and let them stay without consequence.

The sisters, breathing hard, let go of the surplus of magic they'd drawn. They fed it back into the earth, left only with what they were meant to have. But it was no longer ashen. It had been cleansed as they'd absorbed it, and flowers sprung up from the dirt, covering the ground like a fresh promise. No longer was it used as a weapon. Instead, it fed the earth. The Forgotten Forest around them drank in the power.

And as the last tendrils seeped into the air, the hum of the Dark Oak finally quieted. No longer would others come seeking its power. It was slumbering, ancient and ethereal. Never again would it be a reminder of fear, but a beacon of reconciliation. Of moving forward.

Calliope stared up at the branches, the sky barely visible through the thick leaves. The eyes on the trunk were now fully closed, and she thought about how sometimes the things we fear have the power to break us, and sometimes they empower us. For so long, that fear had driven her: sacrificing memories to avoid the pain, to avoid confronting her own life. Now she'd taken the first step. And sometimes, that was all it took. She would embrace her emotions, her memories, her past. She would reclaim her power. Not magic, but the power of looking generations of prejudice and fear in the eyes and telling it to go to hell. She was finished running away from hard things.

Calliope turned to her sisters, tears glistening like diamonds on their cheeks as they sank into one another's arms.

"We did it," Calliope said, shock coloring her words.

"And we're alive to tell the tale," Thalia said.

"I knew we could," Dissy added softly.

"That makes one of us," Eléa said with a laugh.

"I'm so glad you're okay," Calliope said, her love for the girl a bright, warm light that glowed between them.

They sagged against one another, exhausted but exhilarated. Calliope's bones ached with the weight of a missing piece. Something she couldn't quite put her finger on, but that seemed like a problem for later. Now she drank in the silence. The warm pressure of Dissy's hand in hers. Of Thalia's arm hooked through hers. Of Eléa's head leaning against her shoulder. How Sarai joined them and slipped her hand in Eléa's. Together they had recombined their magic and set it all right. Both Shadow- and Lightcraft, healing generations of trauma and prejudice.

The man she'd seen earlier walked forward. Calliope wanted to say she'd nearly forgotten he was there, but his presence was too commanding to forget.

He was heartbreakingly beautiful, with joy, sorrow, and rage battling on his face. Without a word, Eléa turned to him, and the light in her eyes as she looked up at the beautiful man could have blinded the sun. She ran and launched herself toward him. He picked her up off the ground as she threw her arms around his neck and sobbed.

In a daze, Calliope touched her cheeks. Her fingers came away wet, and she wondered why she was crying. What had she done? What had she sacrificed? The echo of it painted itself across her skin as she watched Eléa cling to this man. Her heart was brittle, like it was settled on a precipice and couldn't quite decide which way to fall.

When he set her down, holding her at arm's length, he inspected her face. Her color had returned; the dark circles beneath her eyes had vanished. She looked young and healthy, and there were tears glistening in his eyes as he took her in.

As Eléa's eyes searched his, her joy faded at seeing the pain there, and she looked at Calliope. Calliope, who stood there staring.

Calliope could feel his magic and the way it called to hers. It was like an echo of something, an imprint on her soul. For some reason, when she looked at him, she tasted apples and mint like a memory on her tongue. She tried to follow the shadow of that memory, of how they were tethered together. But instead she saw only the bright, shining thread connecting her to her sisters.

His face shone with pride as he looked at Eléa, and it made Calliope's chest tight.

Sarai pulled Eléa into a hug and cried into her shoulder. Eléa laughed and patted her back as Malik was looking anywhere but at them.

"And you," Eléa said to Malik. "You helped."

"A bit," Malik said with a grin. "Though I should have helped sooner. I was a fool. We all were." He nodded to Feng and Luna. "Drawn in by his promises. And I . . . I wanted his approval, Lucien. But not at the cost of Eléa's life. I didn't think he would really . . ." He shook his head, his eyes filled with sorrow.

"All is forgiven," Eléa said, standing on her tiptoes to kiss him on the cheek, and then she looked expectantly at the dark-haired man, who cleared his throat.

"I'm glad you got there in the end," he said. He held out his hand, and Malik shook it.

"Sorry, but . . . who are you?" Calliope asked.

"This is my brother, Lucien," Eléa said. Her voice was sly, and she was trying to contain a smile. "You—" she started, but the man cut her off.

"There is time for all that yet," he said.

"Right, yes, of course," Eléa said, still smiling.

"Lucien," Calliope said quietly, her head tilting to the side, testing the shape of his name on her lips.

"Let us leave the sisters to celebrate in their own way," Lucien said. He spoke to Eléa, but his eyes were on Calliope.

"But—" Calliope started, and Eléa stepped forward and hugged her.

"Don't worry," she said. "I'll be back. I promise we'll be seeing a lot of each other."

The sisters hugged, and Calliope was shocked when Dissy wrapped her arms around the tall, brooding man. Eléa's brother. *Lucien,* she thought.

"Thank you," Thalia said, offering her hand to him. "For everything."

He nodded once as they shook.

"Until we meet again, little muse," he said, turning to Calliope with a strained nod, his deep voice imprinting on Calliope's skin. His eyes lingered on her, cataloguing her features, giving her a heated, longing look that was tinged with a sorrow Calliope could feel down to her toes. And then he and Eléa vanished on the spot.

Birdsong was beginning to return. Leaves rustled. The air, which had been hot and humid with magic, cooled to the natural temperature of a crisp spring night.

Overhead, in the small circle of sky, the stars shone as they'd always done, a witness to all that had happened.

The Dark Oak was dormant.

The town was safe.

The darkness had been defeated.

The curse was broken.

And still, something nagged at Calliope.

"Let's go home," Dissy said.

They walked slowly through the Forgotten Forest, letting the night sing its ageless song, and for the first time, Calliope didn't mind the silence. She let it wash over her, her sisters' presence a soothing balm to the thoughts creating a maelstrom in her head.

Always, when she'd sacrificed a memory before, there was a small hollow space where it once lived. A small piece of herself chipped away. She had never gone searching for those pieces, knowing they were the currency for a life half-lived, constantly forgotten. But now, though she was more comfortable in her skin than she ever had been before, there was something missing. The small, hollow space seemed bigger than usual.

"I think," she said as they neared the tree line, "that I sacrificed a memory that was too big."

"You did what you thought was right to save Eléa," Dissy said reassuringly. "And it worked."

"It doesn't make sense, though," Calliope said. "How did I fuel such a powerful spell?"

"I think you'll have to find that out in time. Now, come on, I'm starving," Thalia said, pulling her sisters forward.

They passed the Altar of Fate, the old stone sitting innocently in the night, a monument to all they'd overcome.

As Lethe Manor came into view, Calliope sighed.

The kitchen welcomed them, and Dissy looked excitedly at the fireplace.

"Watch this," she said. And with a snap of her fingers, flames danced merrily in the grate. "I keep forgetting we don't have to sacrifice a memory!" she said, and Calliope laughed at her eagerness.

They moved around the kitchen, using their magic for every little thing. One knife was chopping an onion on the cutting board while another was dicing a butternut squash. A large cast-iron pot flew gracefully through the air and landed on the stovetop.

The smell of garlic and carrots and celery filled the space and then married the scent of ginger, cinnamon, and nutmeg. When all the ingredients were simmering, Calliope grinned.

"Why wait?" she said, and she waved her hand over the pot. The butternut squash soup was done in moments.

They sat around the table, eating in silence, until Dissy spoke.

"What do we do now?" she asked.

"Now we live," Thalia said with a soft smile.

Dissy and Thalia went up to bed soon after, but Calliope, though fatigued, wasn't sleepy. Her skin was too tight, and the hairs along the back of her neck stood on end and she kept looking over her shoulder for something, though she knew not what.

So many pieces were missing. There was something about the family grimoire and her aunts. Something about the way the man had looked at her after she saved Eléa. The forgotten memories piled up until they filled her.

She fell asleep in the library, chewing on rosemary as she tried to bring back any remnant, but nothing came.

Nobody, neither book nor human, knocked on the door.

✳

OVER THE NEXT week, the sisters reopened Tea and Tome. Being back among the intoxicating smells of oolong and jasmine and books brought a sense of peace Calliope hadn't known she'd been missing so fiercely.

They dedicated a tea blend to Roz.

Calliope still couldn't walk by her shop without tears welling up. But as the days wore on, the tears turned happy. To be loved so fiercely was an honor, and she knew Rosalind would disapprove of too much sorrow.

Dissy went on her date with Sean Zhao and came home beaming so widely that Calliope thought her cheeks might split.

Thalia, to Calliope's utter shock and secret joy, said yes when Danny asked her on a date of their own. They'd all been in the kitchen, waiting for Dissy's return, and Danny couldn't take their eyes off Thalia. They were evenly matched, Calliope thought, as Danny wouldn't let Thalia get away with much.

Life fell into a stable rhythm as the Easter Eggstravaganza event neared along with the end of March. Spring garlands were strung with care across the trees, and the air was filled with shouts of laughter and the smell of apple pie from Whisk and Spoon. The sisters donned their Fates costumes once more and handed out violet candies wrapped in wax paper.

The Dark Oak remained quiet. And though the pain of loss still lingered, Calliope no longer had the urge to sacrifice it. She didn't want to give up any of it. She wanted to hold on to the hurt, the sadness, the grief as it shaped the hard parts of her and made the good that much sweeter.

Calliope thought of the tarot card that Roz had been clutching in her hands when she died. The Ace of Pentacles. She framed it and set it on her bedside table. Because they had inherited something after all. A new legacy. One free of fear and old prejudices. One where the type of magic you used didn't dictate the kind of person you were. One that was filled with love and the healing of generational trauma. The Ace of Pentacles meant something good was coming. And though Calliope never would have believed it at the time, something good *had* come. Their string was restored, the Dark Oak was free, and her relationship with her sisters was thriving once more.

And yes, okay, Eléa's father was still out there somewhere. But that was a problem for another day. For now her new life had appeared and was extending its hand to her. All she had to do was possess the wherewithal to take it and turn it into something meaningful. And that, she thought, was what she'd spent her whole life building up to.

If you let them steal your joy, they've already won, Roz had said. And Calliope was determined to find that joy. A joy worth remembering. A life worth living. Where magic danced with light and the three Petridi sisters' love grew fierce and wild.

EPILOGUE

By mid-May, the wounds of the past were healing of their own accord. And though Calliope charged toward her new life with abandon, she knew something was still missing. Some intricate piece of her past that no amount of her new magic could bring back. She'd tried potions and spells and food steeped in symbolism, but the echo of what had been lost trailed every moment.

Dissy continued to grow in confidence, finally relinquishing her tight-fisted grip on the title of peacekeeper. She and Sean could often be found in the sitting room with the three cats of Lethe Manor draped between them.

Thalia, meanwhile, was having fun, perhaps for the first time in her life. She knew now that they were able to live their own lives and still be part of one another's. The sisters relearned how to share responsibilities as they processed through all that had happened and who they'd become.

But always, there was the pull. It tugged from Calliope's core, different from the string of fate that connected her to

Thalia and Dissy. This cord wasn't the warm, soft love of her sisters, but a bright, pulsing thing that threaded through her veins, leaving a trail of icy heat and longing in its wake. Every day, she ate mnimi soup, hoping to restore some semblance of what she'd sacrificed, but nothing would come.

One morning, she followed that pull out into the early dawn. The first tendrils of sunlight were painting the sky a delicate gold, and a mist hung about the grounds. She was barefoot, and the crunch of grass against her feet anchored her. The smell of dry leaves and freshly sprouting flowers swirled around her, and she thought, if she stuck out her tongue, the air might just taste like sweet summer honey.

And there, in the distance, across the field, stood the man from the Forbidden Forest. Her heart lurched at the sight of him. He'd disappeared that day in the woods, and the look of pain in his eyes was one of the only things that lingered clearly in Calliope's mind.

He was staring at the Altar of Fate but looked up and locked eyes with Calliope, as though he sensed her presence.

The hairs prickled again on her neck, and for some reason, butterflies took flight in her stomach.

He strode toward her with something in his hands, and she tried not to quicken her steps to meet him. She'd run the memories over and over in her head. Her mother warning them away from the Deniz family. The summoning and binding. His sister. And still, she knew something was missing.

When he stood before her, she saw he was holding the Petridi family grimoire.

He drank her in with his eyes as though she were an oasis and he himself was the desert.

"Little muse," he said, his voice a low rumble. There was stubble on his cheeks, and his hair was a mess. "You saved my sister."

"I did," she said, though the details were fuzzy.

"And you don't remember what you sacrificed for it," he said. It wasn't a question, but his words were filled with anguish.

"I don't."

"Would you believe me if I said you sacrificed your love for me?"

She stared at him, and then she laughed. It was a clear, bright sound that was swallowed up by the mist.

"I thought so," he growled.

"You're telling me I fell in love with you?" she asked, her cheeks warming. "I'm sorry," she said. "It's not you, I just remember swearing off love a long time ago."

"I was under the impression you might say that, so I brought you this." He handed her the grimoire, and it lay heavy in her hands. "Read for yourself."

She opened the old leather book, and it fell comfortably to a spot that seemed to have been read many times before. Her eyes lingered on his for a moment before they dropped to the pages.

In case I end up sacrificing my memory of Lucien just to annoy him, she read, *here's what I've learned and what I surmise about the Shadowcrafter in our midst . . .*

And then there were pages and pages of writing. Her eyes scanned the different dates written in different colors of ink. Sometimes the letters were formed carefully and thoughtfully; other times they were scrawled hastily, each word bleeding into the next.

She read, by her own hand, how she'd slowly and almost unwillingly fallen in love with this near stranger who stood before her.

And that wasn't all; she read about her aunt Daphne being trapped in the grimoire, and about Roz. She remembered Dissy and Thalia talking about Daphne and Lyra in the days following the events in the Forgotten Forest. How they'd wondered where Daphne had gone and why she hadn't come back. She'd longed for those memories. Longed for a connection to the women who had helped them. Who could make their family whole.

She flipped the pages and read about Eléa and the way her chatter and light had filled the room. About arguments with her sisters and the fear, the ever-present fear, that it wasn't going to be enough. But it had been. And they'd won.

And as every line bled into her soul, the last little hole inside her began to fill up. New pieces locked into place like she'd been waiting for them.

Tears filled her eyes as she looked up at Lucien, who waited, his face filled with yearning.

"I guess you're going to have to prove it," she said finally, her voice quiet but strong and sure. "Make me fall in love with you all over again."

"Little muse," he said. "Why do you think I've stayed away so long?"

"What do you mean?" she asked breathlessly.

"That book you're holding used to fly around and hit me in the head," he growled.

She laughed. "Perhaps you deserved it?"

"Be that as it may, you'll notice it's now quite still. Malik helped. It was the least he could do."

Calliope's heart flipped as she stared down at the grimoire.

"At this very moment, Eléa is introducing your sisters to your aunt Daphne. In the flesh. That infernal woman didn't make it easy, but you must understand that though my heart is dark, it belongs to you. Only tell me if you'll give me a chance to prove it, over and over again, as many times as you need."

At his words, something bloomed between them, and suddenly she was overwhelmed with the scent of apples and amber.

Calliope's heart raged against her chest as her body seemed to lean toward him of its own accord, trying to get closer to his warmth, to that strangely familiar smell that was making her blood race. She may have forgotten him, but her body had not. He filled her senses, and a delicious shiver raced down her spine as he took a step closer to her.

"I know you don't remember me," he said, his voice deep and full of a quiet longing that made Calliope want to cup his cheek and whisper words of reassurance in his ear. "But I remember you. I remember your mismatched socks and the chaos of your clothes spilling out of drawers," he said, and Calliope let slip a small laugh at the look of anguish on his face when he spoke of her messiness. But he kept going. "I remember the weight of your cat on my feet. The fire in your eyes when you're irritated with me. The crease in your brow when you're determined. The texture of your skin is imprinted on my soul," he said, his voice full of anguish. "The way you moan when I kiss your throat is a dream I'll be chasing for the rest of my life."

Calliope's heart was racing faster now, his words burrowing into a deep, hidden part of her that ached to be seen. To be chosen. This, she knew now, was the thing that had been missing. The piece of herself that she'd sacrificed.

"I know that I am a stranger in your eyes," he continued, his accent growing thicker with emotion. "I will not touch you until you ask me to, impossible as that is when I'm in your presence. I only need you to see that my heart beats for you, my soul calls to yours. That my mind is consumed with you and will be until time has claimed me."

Calliope swallowed hard, past the lump in her throat, refusing to squeeze her eyes shut to stop the flow of tears. They fell down her cheeks like liquid diamonds. She saw the way Lucien's fingers clenched at his side and knew he wanted to wipe them away, but he was true to his word and didn't touch her. She didn't remember their love, but she felt it. It resonated in her bones, her very blood. All at once, a dim memory filtered in. It was hazy, as though she were seeing it through a room filled with smoke. Lucien was holding her in his arms. *I would say I'd die for you, but what's the point in that?* he'd whispered. *I would* live *for you.*

She reached out with her free hand and unfurled his fingers from their fist. He watched her movements as though he was entranced. Watched as she took his hand and laid his palm on her cheek. He stared at her in wonder, his thumb tenderly wiping away the tears that still fell.

Her aunt was alive. And with Daphne back, the hope of finding her mother was rekindled. Together, she knew, they would go to the ends of the earth to find her. She stared at Lucien, the one who'd made it all possible. And the rightness of it, of him, blossomed inside her.

"Well, then," she said, placing a hand over his where it still rested on her cheek, and the look of relief in his eyes was so potent that it bloomed as an echo inside herself. They still had to find her mother, and Lucien's father was still out there somewhere, but those problems faded away when she drew his hand away and kissed his knuckles, his eyes closing. "I think I'd like to meet my aunt. And see your sister. And then . . . Then I'd like to learn exactly how to love you."

And just like that, a new chapter began.

Acknowledgments

I'm a little bit in awe that I get to sit here and write the acknowledgments for my second book. First, thank you, God, for bringing this long-standing dream to fruition. Every single day I write out my affirmations, manifestations, and prayers, and I'm full of gratitude for all they've brought.

Natalie Lakosil, my superhero of an agent, none of this would be possible without you. Signing my debut in crayon over mimosas with you is one of my fondest memories, and I can't wait to see what we accomplish next!

Natalie Hallak—I knew within the first sixty seconds of talking to you that you were my dream editor for this book and for the next stage of my career. It was an instant connection, and your vision, creativity, and attention to detail never cease to blow me away! Thank you, eternally, for giving me a chance!

Heather Shapiro, thank you for bringing this book to the overseas markets and for always being on top of things—I feel so confident in your capable hands!

To every single person who's worked on this book from copy edits to cover design to marketing, my gratitude knows no bounds—you're the ones who bring it all to life!

And thank you to Stacy Sivinski and Lyra Selene for the early blurbs and constant support. For over a decade I was on this writing journey alone, and I never knew what I was missing!

J. Elle, Emily Varga, Sarah Mughal, and Diana Urban—your companionship and advice have been paramount to my sanity, and I'm so lucky to be on this path with you.

Raquel and Sydney, I quite literally couldn't do this without you, hence why this whole novel is dedicated to you both. You two are such bright spots in my life, and I'm honored to stand in your light!

To my husband—I'd never have written a single word without your encouragement. Your unwavering support and love are my constant inspiration. I love you more than words can say.

To Mom and Dad, for teaching me to reach for the stars and for truly believing in me. You both are the heroes of my own personal story.

To my girls, Evelyn and Rosalie, for your unconditional love—you have my whole heart.

Uncle Matt, you've been as invested in my journey as I am and are the first person I tell my news to. This journey wouldn't be half as fun without you!

Mac, my bookish wonder twin and work husband, I love you forever.

To Joel, Noelle, Zenna, Alyssa, Michael, and Kienda—your friendship and support are the sustenance that drives my inspiration.

Oh, and hey, Jeff—I actually put that English degree to

good use, so you can suck it (but really, I love you and am so grateful for your presence in my life!).

Last but definitely not least—to all the ARE readers, librarians, booksellers, BookTokers, and Bookstagrammers, you are the lifeblood of the publishing industry, and my journey as an author would look vastly different without you. I owe you so much and will keep writing books as long as you'll have me!

EXCERPTS FROM THE

TEA AND TOME RECIPE BOOK

Mnimi Soup with
Crusty Cottage Bread and Honey Butter

Mnimi Soup Recipe

Ingredients

1 tablespoon olive oil

1 onion, chopped

3 garlic cloves, minced

2 carrots, diced

2 celery stalks, diced

1 potato, peeled and diced

1 zucchini, diced

1 can of diced tomatoes

4 cups vegetable broth

1 teaspoon dried rosemary

1 teaspoon dried sage

Salt and black pepper, to taste

Directions

1. Heat the olive oil in a large pot over medium heat. Add the onion and garlic and sauté until the onion is translucent.

2. Add the carrots, celery, potato, and zucchini and cook for 5 minutes, stirring occasionally.

3. Add the diced tomatoes, vegetable broth, rosemary, sage, salt, and pepper. Bring to a boil and then reduce heat to low. Cover and simmer for 30 minutes or until the vegetables are tender.

4. Using an immersion blender or a regular blender, purée the soup until smooth.

5. Adjust the seasoning if needed and serve hot with crusty bread.

Crusty Cottage Bread Recipe

Ingredients

3 cups all-purpose flour
1 teaspoon salt
1 teaspoon instant yeast

1 ½ cups warm water
(110–115°F)
Cornmeal, for dusting

Directions

1. In a large mixing bowl, combine the flour, salt, and yeast.

2. Add the warm water and mix until a sticky dough forms.

3. Cover the bowl with plastic wrap or a damp towel and let it rest for 12–18 hours at room temperature. The dough should roughly double in size and develop bubbles on the surface.

4. Preheat oven to 450°F. Place a large Dutch oven or baking dish with a lid in the oven to preheat as well.

5. While the oven is preheating, turn the dough out onto a lightly floured surface and shape it into a ball. Dust the ball generously with flour and let it rest for 30 minutes.

6. After 30 minutes, carefully remove the hot Dutch oven or baking dish from the oven and sprinkle the bottom with cornmeal.

7. Transfer the dough ball to the Dutch oven or baking dish, seam side down. Cover with the lid and return it to the oven.

8. Bake for 30 minutes with the lid on, then remove the lid and continue baking for an additional 15–20 minutes, or until the crust is golden brown and crispy.

9. Carefully remove the bread from the Dutch oven or baking dish and let it cool on a wire rack before slicing and serving. Slather with honey butter.

Sage and Brown Butter Gnocchi

From ancient rituals to modern kitchens, sage has been known to unveil truths long kept in the shadows. As it infuses its essence into dishes, its very presence demands transparency. With each savory bite, it encourages us to speak our minds and face an unvarnished reality.

Ingredients

1 pound (about 4 cups) gnocchi

4 tablespoons unsalted butter

A handful of fresh sage leaves

Salt and black pepper, to taste

Grated Parmesan cheese, for serving (optional)

Directions

1. **Boil the gnocchi:** Bring a large pot of salted water to a boil. Cook the gnocchi according to the package instructions or until they float to the surface, usually about 2–3 minutes. Drain and set aside.

2. **Brown the butter:** While the gnocchi is cooking, melt the butter in a large skillet over medium heat. Allow the butter to bubble and foam. When the foam subsides, add the fresh sage leaves.

3. **Sauté the sage:** Cook the sage leaves in the butter for about 1–2 minutes, or until they become crispy and the butter turns a light brown color. Be careful not to burn the butter; it should have a nutty aroma.

4. **Combine gnocchi and sage butter:** Add the cooked gnocchi to the skillet with the sage butter. Toss to coat the gnocchi evenly with the butter and sage. Season with salt and freshly ground black pepper to taste.

5. **Serve:** Transfer the sage and brown butter gnocchi to serving plates. If desired, sprinkle with grated Parmesan cheese before serving.

Apple Cinnamon Melomakarona Cookies

These cookies bring together the timeless sweetness of apples and the comforting warmth of cinnamon. Together, they tell a tale of fusion, weaving traditions and cultures into every bite. Bathed in honey, sprinkled with walnuts, these treats are more than just dessert; they're a reminder of our shared heritage and the bonds that connect us. Each cookie is a bite-sized story of comfort and celebration, a testament to food's power to unite and create enduring legacies.

Ingredients

For the cookies

1 cup olive oil

¼ cup orange juice

¼ cup brandy or cognac (optional)

½ cup granulated sugar

Zest of 1 orange

Zest of 1 lemon

2 cups all-purpose flour

1 cup semolina flour

1 teaspoon ground cinnamon

½ teaspoon ground cloves

½ teaspoon baking soda

1 teaspoon baking powder

½ cup crushed walnuts

For the syrup

1 cup honey

1 cup water

1 cup granulated sugar

1 cinnamon stick

Zest of 1 orange

Juice of ½ lemon

Directions

1. Preheat oven to 350°F.

2. In a large mixing bowl, combine the olive oil, orange juice, brandy (if using), sugar, and the zest of 1 orange and 1 lemon. Mix until well combined.

3. In a separate bowl, whisk together the all-purpose flour, semolina flour, ground cinnamon, ground cloves, baking soda, and baking powder.

4. Gradually add the dry ingredients to the wet ingredients, mixing until a soft dough forms.

5. Take small portions of the dough and shape them into oval cookies, about 2 inches long. Place them on a baking sheet lined with parchment paper.

6. Use a fork to gently press down on the top of each cookie to create a decorative pattern.

7. Bake in the preheated oven for about 20–25 minutes or until the cookies are golden brown.

8. While the cookies are baking, prepare the syrup. In a saucepan, combine the honey, water, granulated sugar, cinnamon stick, the zest of 1 orange, and the juice of half a lemon. Simmer over low heat for about 10 minutes, then remove the cinnamon stick and set aside.

9. Once the cookies are done baking and while they're still warm, immediately dip them into the warm syrup. Allow them to soak for a few seconds, turning them to ensure they absorb the syrup evenly.

10. Remove the cookies from the syrup and place them on a wire rack to cool.

11. While the cookies are still slightly warm, sprinkle them with crushed walnuts.

12. Let the cookies cool completely and absorb the syrup. They'll become wonderfully moist and flavorful.

Orange Fairy Tea Cakes

In the realm of Tea and Tome, where magic and memories entwine, the orange fairy tea cake emerges as a symbol of rejuvenation and revival. Crafted with care and infused with the magic of zest, the cake becomes a conduit for the restoration of the heart and spirit. Orange fairy tea cakes invite you to embrace the magic of the present and the mysteries of the future.

Ingredients

For the cake

1 cup all-purpose flour

½ cup almond flour

1 ½ teaspoons baking powder

½ teaspoon baking soda

Pinch of salt

1 cup Greek yogurt

1 cup granulated sugar

3 large eggs

½ cup olive oil

Zest of 1 orange

1 teaspoon vanilla extract

For the syrup

½ cup freshly squeezed orange juice

½ cup granulated sugar

Directions

1. Preheat oven to 350°F. Grease and flour a 9-inch round cake pan.

2. In a bowl, whisk together the all-purpose flour, almond flour, baking powder, baking soda, and salt. Set aside.

3. In another bowl, beat the Greek yogurt and granulated sugar until well combined.

4. Add the eggs one at a time, beating well after each addition. Mix in the olive oil, orange zest, and vanilla extract.

5. Gradually add the dry flour mixture to the wet ingredients, stirring until just combined. Be careful not to overmix.

6. Pour the batter into the prepared cake pan and smooth the top.

7. Bake for about 35–40 minutes, or until a toothpick inserted into the center comes out clean.

8. While the cake is baking, prepare the syrup. In a small saucepan, combine the orange juice and sugar. Bring to a simmer over medium heat and cook until the sugar has dissolved and the mixture has slightly thickened. Remove from heat and let it cool.

9. Once the cake is done baking, remove it from the oven and let it cool in the pan for a few minutes.

10. Use a toothpick or skewer to poke several holes all over the top of the cake. Slowly pour the cooled syrup over the cake, allowing it to soak in.

11. Let the cake cool completely in the pan before gently removing it.

12. Slice and serve alongside your favorite tea. Enjoy!

Witch's Wisdom Tea

Green tea contains caffeine, which can help improve alertness and cognitive function. Rosemary has long been believed to stimulate memory and concentration, while peppermint and lemon balm have calming properties that can reduce stress and promote focus. Ginkgo biloba is known for its potential to improve blood flow to the brain, which can enhance cognitive function.

Ingredients

1 teaspoon green tea leaves, or 1 green tea bag

1 teaspoon dried rosemary leaves

1 teaspoon dried peppermint leaves

1 teaspoon dried lemon balm leaves

1 teaspoon dried ginkgo biloba leaves (optional)

2 cups water

Dollop of honey (optional)

Directions

1. In a small saucepan, bring 2 cups of water to a gentle boil.

2. Add the green tea leaves (or green tea bag), dried rosemary, peppermint, lemon balm, and ginkgo biloba leaves (if using) to the boiling water.

3. Reduce the heat to low and let the tea simmer for about 5 minutes. This will allow the herbs to infuse the water and release their beneficial properties.

4. After 5 minutes, remove the saucepan from the heat and let the tea steep for an additional 3–4 minutes.

5. Strain the tea into your favorite teacup or mug.

6. If desired, add a drizzle of honey or a sprinkle of stevia for sweetness.

7. Take a moment to inhale the fragrant aroma of the tea, letting its soothing scent calm your mind.

8. Sip slowly and mindfully, allowing the tea's properties to enhance your focus and mental clarity.

Basil Lemonade Martini

Ingredients

4–6 fresh basil leaves

2 ounces vodka

1 ounce triple sec or orange liqueur

1 ounce fresh lemon juice

1 ounce simple syrup (adjust to taste)

Ice cubes

Lemon slices or basil leaves, for garnish

Directions

1. In a cocktail shaker, muddle the fresh basil leaves gently to release their aromatic oils.

2. Add vodka, triple sec, fresh lemon juice, and simple syrup to the shaker.

3. Fill the shaker with ice cubes.

4. Put the lid on the shaker and shake vigorously for about 15–20 seconds until the mixture is well chilled.

5. Strain the mixture into a martini glass or a chilled cocktail glass.

6. Garnish with a lemon slice or a fresh basil leaf.

7. Serve immediately and enjoy your refreshing basil lemonade martini!

Moonlight Elixir Cocktail

Ingredients

2 ounces vodka

1 ounce blue curaçao liqueur

1 ounce lemon juice

½ ounce simple syrup (or adjust to taste)

A dash of orange bitters

Ice cubes

Lemon twist or orange peel, for garnish

Directions

1. Fill a cocktail shaker with ice cubes.

2. Add the vodka, blue curaçao liqueur, lemon juice, simple syrup, and a dash of orange bitters to the shaker.

3. Shake the mixture well until chilled.

4. Strain the cocktail into a chilled martini glass or coupe glass.

5. Garnish with a lemon twist or a curl of orange peel for a touch of elegance.

6. Enjoy your moonlight elixir cocktail while reveling in the magical atmosphere of the Moonlight Masquerade!

Spells, Strings, and Forgotten Things

A Novel

Breanne Randall

A Book Club Guide

QUESTIONS FOR DISCUSSION

1. The novel explores the bonds of sisterhood through three very different sisters: Calliope, Thalia, and Eurydice. What are the strengths and weaknesses of each sister? Which sisterly bond resonates with you the most? Do you have a similar dynamic with anyone in your life?

2. If you had the ability to do magic but had to sacrifice your memories to do it, would you? What memories would you be willing to sacrifice and why?

3. Discuss the themes of redemption, family, and forgiveness in the novel. Which characters undergo the biggest changes? Who is the most redeemed in your eyes by the novel's end?

4. How do you feel about the town of Gold Springs? Would you ever live in a town like it? Why or why not?

5. Lucien and Calliope start out as enemies but eventually become lovers. What do you think of their

trajectory? Do you think an enemies-to-lovers relationship could ever work in real life?

6. Did any of the plot twists in the book surprise you? Why or why not?

7. What will you remember the most about *Spells, Strings, and Forgotten Things*?

8. Did Calliope make the right choice by sacrificing her memories of Lucien? Do you think they will fall in love again?

ABOUT THE AUTHOR

BREANNE RANDALL is the *New York Times* bestselling author of *The Unfortunate Side Effects of Heartbreak and Magic*. She lives in the sleepy foothills of Northern California with her husband, her two daughters, and a slew of farm animals. When she's not writing, you can find her wandering the property searching for fairy portals or serving elaborate stuffed-animal tea parties.

Don't miss Breanne Randall's
New York Times bestselling
debut novel:

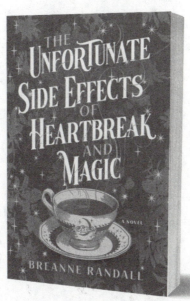

The cost of a young witch's magic is four
heartbreaks in her life. As she faces the last
of her heartbreaks, she has to decide:
Is love more important than magic?

**AVAILABLE
NOW**

alcove
press